PERSEVERANCE:
THE MAKING OF A MUSICIAN

I0590497

STEVEN GREY

ROADSIDE PRESS

Perseverance: The Making of a Musician
Copyright © Steven Grey 2025
ISBN: 979-8-9925009-8-1
Library of Congress Control Number: 2025943518

All rights reserved. No part of this text may be used or reproduced in any manner without written permission from the author or publisher except in the case of brief quotations embodied in critical articles and reviews.

This is a work of fiction. Names, characters, places and incidents either are products of the author's imagination or are used fictitiously. Any resemblances to actual persons, living or dead, or actual events is purely coincidental.

Cover Art:
Igzell Vázquez Mendoza

Editors:
Raye Clemente
Adam Burke

Additional Editing:
James Berg

Perseverance is the debut album by the band Shards of Grey, led by Steven Grey, vocalist and music producer. Bandmate Timmy also provides guitar and contributes additional music. The accompanying lyrics are presented in italics where the author feels they are relevant.

shardsofgrey.com

Roadside Press
Colchester, Illinois

INTRODUCTION

Perseverance, the album, takes listeners through the most traumatic year of my life. Each song encapsulates an event from that year, all presented in order. In this book, each chapter group chronicles the events that inspired those songs.

I've noticed that many music artists are guarded with what their songs are about, and usually only speak to them in vague generalities. I won't be doing that here. Some of my songs are so personal that I took a moment of pause before releasing or performing them. Did I really want to give the world access to these unfiltered traumas, often dressed up in little if any metaphor? I got over it, and I'll have to get over it even more because this book leaves no stone unturned.

This story is about how music is made. Not the technical details, music theory, or even the drama that happens in the studio. It's a story about what it took to finally make me say "fuck it" and pursue that dream from the ground up with no prior experience. Moreover, it's the story of the true events that inspired the songs. These are the things that gave me some real shit to write about.

"Documentarians are supposed to be objective, to avoid having any effect on the story, and yet we have more effect than anyone, because we decide to tell it, and we decide how it ends. Will your story be yet another sad one of yet another man who just wanted to be happy? Or… will your story acknowledge the very nature of stories, and embrace the fact that sharing the sad ones can sometimes make them happy?"—Abed Nadir, *Community*

PERSEVERANCE —
PART 1: THE ECONOMY

JUST A FEW YEARS BEFORE THIS PERIOD IN MY LIFE, I graduated from film school. So naturally, I lived in Hollywood. One night in late January, the snow began to fall. After several mild winters, this season would finally have its revenge on Chicago. Oh, sorry; I didn't live *in* Hollywood, I lived *on* Hollywood—Hollywood Avenue—in Chicago, and as such, very little of what you're about to read will be any measure of glamorous.

Weathermen warned of the worst. Within hours, it snowed more than it had in the last few years combined. I ventured out to stock up on a few days' worth of food. Walking to the corner store and back, I passed snow drifts that towered above my six-foot frame. So much snow fell that they even canceled El train service; yeah, trains, those machines that famously plow through anything in their path. However, there was just so much fucking snow, all reinforced by... more snow. Miles of six-foot-high drifts created an impenetrable wall that brought the daily bustle and traffic of city life to a screeching halt. The roads were impassable, and the city plows wouldn't help us.

Under the guise of saving money, Chicago made the foolish decision not to plow after any snowfall that year. As feet and feet of snow fell, everything shut down. Stores closed, schools closed, and even office jobs gave in. The news reported that this would take millions out of the Chicago economy. Surely the city would relent and deploy the plows, I thought, but they remained unyielding. Cars were abandoned on major thoroughfares as they became encased in the relentless offensive of winter ice. Many people became essentially trapped in their homes. As for me, I was now trapped both literally and figuratively.

There was nothing star-studded about this Hollywood Avenue apartment. No movies were filmed here. The rent was surprisingly cheap. Maybe that was because the place had cockroaches. Perhaps it was because the windows were right across the alley from the train, which roared by every couple of minutes, twenty-four hours a day, drowning all our senses in sound, pausing conversations until the all-consuming rumble subsided. In the midst of this storm, however, the silence was just as oppressive.

We begin a few years into the Great Recession, triggered by the housing market crash, the worst recession since 1929. Creative jobs were almost completely eliminated the very *moment* the tides turned. I remember *the day*: it was that fast. Despite those odds, I had previously landed a job as a Creative Director at a video production company, mostly working on video shoots and graphic design projects. It *sounds* cool, and sometimes it was, but this place was a real hole-in-the-wall. It was not turning a profit. I worked twelve-hour days, six days a week, earning a salary so low I was paid under the table to avoid a paper trail. Even with that, my boss was months behind on paychecks when the company went out of business. I was trapped in every way: financially, creatively, and now even physically.

My increasingly antagonistic domestic partner and I fell behind on our internet bill, and our service could not be restored any sooner than a month and a half out. We were cut off from most of the information and entertainment others had access to. It was just her, me, and a small stack of DVDs. This was just before smartphones were commonplace; they existed, but I was utterly perplexed at how anyone in this economy could afford a month's worth of rent on such a luxury. Suffice to say, neither of us had one of those either, so we genuinely were cut off.

My sort-of long hair was starting to become chin-length as I couldn't justify the expense of a haircut. I still had some decent clothes from that time before, and a few other nice belongings like a decent laptop. If I wore out a piece of clothing, I just owned one less piece of clothing. If anything happened to my laptop, there was no chance I could replace it. I had a decent flip phone from some years before, and it had to last, too.

I was lowering my standards more and more for what type of jobs I applied for. Every day, I hauled my four-year-old laptop down to the

Starbucks on the corner with Wi-Fi access and applied for up to a dozen different job postings, whether it was the scarce creative job or just a position stocking shelves. Today, the snow made the one-block walk a pilgrimage. No surprise: they were closed due to the weather.

The day before, I started applying for a job at a run-of-the-mill department store and found myself actually reading the fine print in the agreement on the website, which astonishingly allowed the company to spy on you as part of the application process. It granted the company the right to contact your professional contacts, friends, and even family members about anything, work-related or not. It didn't just mention phone calls; it explicitly granted them the right to show up in person and interview anyone in your life for any reason, at any time, present or future, regardless of current employment or hiring status. I wouldn't have believed it if I hadn't read it myself.

All that just to work at a failing department store. I took that to mean companies were testing the waters with exactly how much they could get away with. As the year wore on, I'd confirm that theory many times over. However, those issues would be eclipsed by what else was in store for me.

The prospect of creating music was barely a twinkle in my eye at this point, but over the next year, I'd amass plenty of pain to fuel my future muse. I was about to go through so many successive all-time lows that at the end of it, I literally learned how to make music from the ground up just so I could express it all.

PERSEVERANCE —
PART 2: THE GIRL

I LIVED WITH MY GIRLFRIEND, GEMMA. She was definitely interesting; Gemma dressed like a stereotypical stoner but with a dash of feminine flair, so she was a type of woman I had rarely encountered. She called me "dude" way more than she called me by my name. I'd never done any kind of drug and held that as a point of pride, but I never cared what anyone else did. Meanwhile, she was perpetually stoned. She wore almost entirely muted browns and other earth tones. It always came off very '70s to me. In contrast to her, most people considered my presentation darker and more chic. This isn't to say we were an unlikely couple, but it was at least an interesting dynamic.

On account of the storm, her smoking stash had dwindled to nothing. In hindsight, I can see how a steady supply of weed made her much less… combative. Being stuck inside, I was beginning to reflect on things. This woman was one of the most stubborn, fiery, and ignorant people I'd ever been with, or even met. It was clear to me when we got together that this would not last long. There's no better indicator than a conversation we had after we were together for about a month.

Gemma told me, completely seriously and with the gravity of something gravely important, "Steven, we need to talk."

I spent a whole bus ride to her place like 'Oh, fuck: here we go.'

When I got there, she started with, "Look, things between us are great, but they aren't perfect…"

I thought she might continue that thought but she… didn't.

I gave her a confused look "That… doesn't sound like it's actually an issue… What's the problem, exactly?"

"There's no problem. I'm *happy*; it's not that… I just think we could do better."

Now I was more confused. "Okay. How, specifically? Did I do something? Can you give me an example?"

"No, no, you didn't do anything. There's no examples or anything like that. I just think we can do better."

It's easy to read that and think, 'Oh, she's just playing mind games.' No, mind games are *intentional*. They have an *end game*. They imply a certain level of deception. If she was anything, she was sincere to a fault.

I used to call this Disney Princess Syndrome. In my experience, it simply meant that her expectations in a relationship were entirely based on the gender stereotypes often seen in kids' movies. Not having enough real-life relationship experience, that became the bulk of what was informing her perception of relationships. It meant her role in the relationship was entirely passive. It was up to me to woo her, and she didn't have to do anything in return except decide what else I needed to do to hold her attention. If things weren't working for me, I had to suck it up. If things weren't working for her, it was my job and my job alone to fix it.

I used to have my own sheltered version of this. I could call it "Say Anything" Syndrome, based on the movie of the same name where the male lead stands on the lawn of his love interest, holding a boombox over his head, playing a love song for a girl through the window. I used to think a grand overture like that could realistically spur a lasting relationship. However, I'd since gathered enough relationship experience to realize how silly that was. Gemma wasn't *quite* there yet. Ironically, she probably would've liked it if I still believed that.

When we got together, she told me this was her first relationship. Gemma was an attractive woman in her mid-twenties in a big city, so I found that hard to believe. Even further, she was a server at a restaurant and interacted with many people. According to her, getting hit on was part of the job. There were people who she could theoretically call an "ex." Previously, she was at least in a long-distance relationship, but maybe she wasn't counting that. Maybe the others didn't meet the criteria of "serious." Maybe it meant this was the first time she'd exchanged "I love you's." Although, if memory serves, she told me all this before we said those words, so there must have been some other measure for "serious".

Not long after our first "I love you's," her job asked if she wanted to convert from part-time to full-time.

"Oh, great news, Gemm," I said to congratulate her.

"No; I said *no*! I just want to concentrate on our relationship; you loving *me* and me loving *you*," her smitten voice drenched in wistfulness. You could damn near hear the butterflies in her stomach as the smile stretched across her face.

"I appreciate that—I really do—but you should have said yes. Don't let me stop you from advancing your job prospects. Besides, I'm not going away anytime soon, but opportunities like that certainly will."

It's easy to read that and say, "Oh, so she was kind of clingy." Once again, she *wasn't*. She *never was*. Her thoughts and feelings were so nebulous it was hard to say exactly what she was at all.

I was sure we would burn out in those early days, but I was willing to try. After some time, we mostly worked through some of those initial differences, and she was able to temper her expectations, shedding that initial Disney Princess Syndrome. Things leveled off enough for it to become serious and we moved in together. It was the first time either of us lived with a partner.

We were both artists, but she was far more intuitive about it, whereas I was more cerebral. She improvised based on vibes and feelings, whereas everything I did was meticulous, researched, and intentional. Neither way is better. I actually thought it was pretty cool that we were both artists but had wildly different processes.

The methodology she used with her art was the same lens through which she viewed our relationship and life. It was amorphous. It could be anything at any time and didn't have to be consistent or compatible with what it was five minutes ago. She never even seemed aware that her views would change. It was almost like her thoughts were frequently exchanged with those of Gemmas from various parallel dimensions, where the same events had occurred but she had radically different feelings about them.

She was a painter, and I thought she had some interesting ideas. She spent almost our entire relationship working on one painting that she kept second-guessing herself on. She started it almost completely over a half dozen times throughout our relationship, painting over it each time, perhaps providing further evidence to the parallel dimension theory. At a certain point, the paint must have outweighed the canvas.

At first glance, the painting looked like a high-color picture of some flowers, but after a couple of seconds, it became clear that among the flowers was a dead bird shot by an arrow. As intuitive as she was, I doubt she knew what the painting would be when she started it, and I doubt she had any idea why the concept worked so well. Nevertheless, it did. It presented itself to the viewer in two distinct phases and was a great piece of juxtaposition.

One person saw her painting and said: "It's happy..." then paused, noticing the dead bird, "...and sad."

That painting ebbed and flowed along with the status of our relationship. Even the concept of it was emblematic of our pairing in many respects: "It's happy... and sad." It was only roughly blocked out when we got together. I could swear it was the most complete when we were at our best. She neglected it when we had rough patches. She started it over many times with a fresh perspective; for example, wanting to redo the background and painting over the whole thing in the process, as if restarting the painting came with a renewed and completely different view of our relationship.

This snowstorm was one such instance when her perspective had swapped with an inter-dimensional counterpart, and the painting was fresh yet again.

PERSEVERANCE — PART 3: WEATHER THE STORM

THE TYPE OF ART I WAS DOING WAS ALL VIDEO-RELATED, with a dash of illustration and graphic design. My crowning achievement at that time was a short film where illustrated comic book panel images were meticulously lined up with live actors and were used to transition between certain shots and scenes. The idea was to levy both my illustration and film skills. (Back then, I think that might have been the first time that concept was used, though as of writing it's been done a few times.)

This piece had previously landed me in a gig role with a film director's unit that even now remains a household name. I also got to make film shorts with the writer behind what is now considered to be a modern comedy classic. But that was *before*, and with the recession in full swing, 95% of creative jobs were completely wiped out.

Even with those pieces on my reel and other accolades, Gemma wasn't particularly impressed, at least not on that day. She admired my work when we got together, but I had a different Gemma today. I found this out when we were talking about our respective art. We had been together for maybe a year and lived together for a few months. This was the first I heard of it.

"I don't respect what you do as art," she said.

Her sincerity was a quality she held to a fault.

"Wait, really? Why?" I asked, more perplexed than offended, "I've shown you my work. Are you saying you didn't like it? It seemed like you did."

"No, no, it's *good*. I'm not saying you're *bad* at it. I just don't consider it *art*, because it's *digital*, it's not *physical*; you know what I mean? You didn't make it with materials or with your hands."

"So it's not the creative quality of the product, but if it's physical or not? Weren't you a theater major? What I do isn't much different than that; we just add a camera. There's plenty of physical stuff involved."

"Yeah, but in the end, it only exists on a digital screen," she reasoned.

This went on without any budging on her end. It was a hell of a lot of superiority for someone who had spent the last year working on a single painting of a cartoon bird that she couldn't finish. She was occasionally just ignorant as hell like that. Since her feelings on everything were completely nebulous, I probably could've brought it up a month later in a slightly different context, and she'd have felt differently about it.

It was far from the only thing she was stubbornly ignorant about. Being stuck inside without much contact with the outside world had me reflecting again….

Once at a party, she had asked a friend of mine, Tom, "What do you do for a living?"

Tom used to go to film school with me. With the recession, I knew whatever Tom's answer was, it wouldn't have anything to do with film, which was too bad because Tom was an extremely talented cameraman.

Tom explained that he was now in construction and that jobs came project by project.

"What do you do between jobs?" she asked Tom.

"There's a special type of unemployment for construction workers that you can collect between jobs," he explained.

"*What?!* You shouldn't be collecting that. If you want to get paid, get a *real* job."

"I mean… *All* construction workers do it, especially in the off-season. There's no other choice." Tom said it like he genuinely felt he had to justify it.

"If you wanna get paid you should *work*. You're basically a leech!" She stormed away.

"What the hell was that about?" Tom asked me, clearly taken aback, "That was really shitty. That really hurt me."

I'd hesitate to call Tom sensitive, but he was such a chill and friendly guy that I imagine people rarely, if ever, came at him like that.

"Yeah, that *was* shitty," I assured Tom. "I'm really sorry about that. I'm not even going to defend it just because she's my girlfriend. It was *shitty*. Gemm just… gets like that sometimes. I'm sorry about that, man."

Given that this was at a party, maybe she only got like that if she was drinking. She had a beer a day and sometimes one or two more. It would be easy to lose track on my end. Maybe she had a beer or two when she was criticizing my art.

Gemma was a mostly functional alcoholic, but I did not realize the gravity of what this really meant when we started dating. Closer to the beginning of our relationship, before we moved in together, we had a conversation that went something like this:

Her, completely out of the blue, not at all related to anything that was going on at the moment: "Can we go get some beer?"

"What? That's kind of random, why?"

I wasn't much of a drinker. I'd drink socially when with friends, but other than the odd bottle of wine, I never had any alcohol in my apartment. It just wasn't my thing.

"I have to have a beer or two around five or six every day or I'll start to get a headache."

"Oh, so you're an alcoholic," I remarked. Those words remain burned into my brain years later, for whatever reason. I suppose I could be pretty blunt, too, though I said this without judgment.

"What?! No, of course I'm not an alcoholic!"

All she had heard was the negative connotation that she thought was implied.

"I'm not saying it's a bad thing. I haven't seen you go ruining your life about it. But if you get headaches without it, that's a physical dependency. Your body needs it. That's the definition of being an alcoholic, right?"

"Yeah, I guess so," she reluctantly agreed.

"So you're an alcoholic," I said once again without judgment. I was pretty daft then and had all the social awareness of someone visiting Earth while on vacation that didn't know the social faux pas.

She shook her head as she processed the information. She was maybe less socially adept than I was. "Then I guess I'm an alcoholic!"

After that, it would occasionally come up casually, well into our time living together.

"Well, we better get a beer in me," she might say, "since I'm an alcoholic, you know."

A comment that sounds completely like sarcasm on paper, like she was taking a dig at me for calling her that. *But it wasn't.* She was almost *never* sarcastic. "Better get some beer in me," this was especially true with us succumbing to cabin fever with this storm.

Other than those previous incidents, the relationship was pretty chill up until this historic snowstorm in January. Two days had passed, and now the streets were technically drivable, but covered in a permanent three-inch layer of slush. The constant city traffic splashed and moved it around, so it refused to re-freeze. I got us some food and also some beer at her request.

Tonight, the fact of her alcoholism would finally come to its inevitable conclusion. She always had one or two beers, but tonight she had more. There was no particular occasion. She did not announce her intent to get drunk, nor did she communicate her rising level of intoxication along the way. I could've sworn I only counted three beers, so I thought she was a bit buzzed at best. Every can looked the same, so maybe I had no idea how deep she was. At the time, though, I was none the fucking wiser. I had no clue she was even trashed at all.

She flew into a rage that night vaguely prompted by some complaint about my generally calm and collected affect, a quality she definitely did not possess and apparently did not appreciate. After getting increasingly antagonistic, poking and prodding at me with her words, voice raising further and further, she cornered me in the kitchen. I could tell she was trying to get a rise out of me, but I had not taken the bait, which seemed to infuriate her more.

To make some sort of point, she came at me with a machine gun of punches, most of which I blocked, but one got through and hit me right in the eye. She kept punching, yelling about something or another, and I kept trying to block, ducking lower into the corner of the kitchen to make myself a smaller target. She told me before she'd been in her fair share of fights, which implied that she'd resort to violence faster than most other folks. I feigned pain under the hope that her compassion would kick in and she'd stop. If I shrugged it off, I knew she'd come at me harder until she got the reaction she wanted, because she just *kept coming at me*. I was balled up in a corner on the kitchen floor against the entrance to the apartment now, arms up, blocking incoming blows.

"What, you can't take a punch?!" she yelled at me, "*I* can take a punch, why can't *you*? You're a man!"

Welp, feigning pain had not been a good idea. Her anger only grew.

Her statement was soaked with a gendered toxicity that I had avoided most of my life. The measure of a person is hardly reliant on gender, and knowing how to take a punch doesn't make a man—or a woman—any better than the next person. At this point, this was not yet a common topic of politicized discourse, so that type of ignorance more often went unchecked.

"Aren't you going to fight back?!" she yelled as she continued to punch.

"I'm not going to fight you!" I yelled back. "If you *care* about me, then why are you hitting me?"

No, no... Stop the tape. Let's pause for a moment. What I *actually* said was "If you *love* me." Not "if you *care* about me." Maybe this is silly, but it was hard to get that on the page just now, that word "love." To write that someone I loved was attacking me felt too vulnerable, I guess. But... let's go with what's real. I loved her; she loved me. Supposedly.

"If you *love* me, then why are you hitting me?"

Hearing this, she changed tactics from physical to verbal abuse. It was almost as if she at least had to acknowledge, yes, we do love each other. She did not dispute the implication of love, but she offered me no time to savor that.

"Oh my god, this is pathetic," she started.

She launched into a long verbal tirade of insults so generic I couldn't even take them personally. None of them were terribly specific, so I still didn't fully understand *what* was fueling this anger.

I didn't *know* she was drunk, so I still had no explanation for her behavior. This wasn't even an other-dimensional version of her. It felt like some demonic force had suddenly taken over her body. I'd never seen her like this before. I knew she could be fiery and impulsive. I knew she could fly off the handle at little stuff, as she had with my friend Tom and his unemployment. I kinda *knew* what she was mad *about*, but it still didn't explain *why*. Something didn't make sense. I had to figure out what that was first.

Sure, I could've fought back, but that would've made things a million times worse, so I didn't. I didn't feel like I was in any real danger yet, at least if she was content to stick with sloppy punches. As long as I could deflect the majority of these blows, I should be fine, right? She got angry; I could either get angry back and feed the cycle or not do that and let it fizzle out.

The best thing I could do was separate myself from her physically. I made a retreat, but she pursued me. The only place to escape to was the one and only bedroom. I had almost slipped through the doorway when Gemma stumbled into the door behind me, slamming the solid wood door onto my middle and ring finger, with her full weight against it. My ring finger got caught right in the faceplate hole, crushed between that and the latch. That really did hurt this time, and it was on my dominant hand. It wasn't intentional, but it still wouldn't have happened if she hadn't become unhinged.

I did not call the police and didn't want to make a big deal out of it. The prevailing assumption back then was that if a man was the victim of a domestic violence case, it was usually the unwritten policy of the police to arrest only the man. I didn't know if that was really true, but I also didn't want to find out. Even if it *wasn't* true, what good could come of it?

From the solitude of the now locked bedroom, I posted a thread about what happened on Reddit, plucking away a letter at a time with my remaining good hand, via a hastily created anonymous account. I simply said something to the effect of "domestic abuse can happen to dudes too" with a very brief explanation of the events and my injuries. I must have done this because I needed to hear someone else tell me that she was wrong; I wasn't sure I'd hear that from her.

My fingers were swollen and bleeding. After Gemma fell asleep, I snuck out of the room at one point and crudely wrapped them in toilet paper.

In the morning, I awoke with a black eye and two throbbing fingers. Idly checking Reddit, I saw a reference in another thread to what could've been the post I made last night. I checked it, and it had absolutely exploded. I hadn't even thought about how it could've taken on a life of its own. It made it to the front page and had *thousands* of comments. I opened it up and read the top comment.

It said something like, "You don't deserve this. You need to get out of this situation and relationship immediately."

I don't know exactly what I expected to hear, but that sentence reflected a level of reality I hadn't considered at the time. I hadn't thought about what happened in the context of how I understood "abuse." Part of me must have known when I posted that thread; I had even used the word "abuse" in my title. But part of me also felt like a fraud—like this didn't really count—because I was a man, because it was an isolated incident, because I hadn't been injured *enough*, at least intentionally.

I thought that all this could end with an apology, as if an "I'm sorry" could undo everything that had transpired. A thousand Reddit commenters saw what I couldn't. I had some serious compartmentalization going on until that moment, as if *violence* wasn't necessarily *abuse*, somehow. I couldn't face that reality, so I didn't read beyond that first comment. I clicked away, closed my laptop, and never looked at the thread again.

Peeling back the layers of toilet paper wrapped around my fingers, I could see my ring finger had split open and white inner flesh protruded. Gemma's painting sat in its usual spot, painted over for the moment. She was still asleep on the couch. She looked peaceful and delicate again. I resented that. I couldn't reconcile it with what had transpired the previous night.

The sun shone brightly into the apartment, a complete juxtaposition of the current state of our relationship. At least it caused enough snow to melt that I could make it to the hospital. One cab ride later, I was there. I lied to the doctors about how I had gotten my injuries. Honestly, I was even dodgy about it with the cab driver. As a dude, this felt really easy:

"I got into a fight," I said with shame.

That was so unlike me, but the hospital staff didn't know that. The shame was real, the reason for it was not.

They told me that the tips of my fingers were both broken. I had managed to make it through my entire childhood and adolescence without a single broken bone, so this was a somber first. It was not a cool story. If people were going to talk about 'first broken bone' stories, I'd probably just shut the hell up. I hadn't fallen from a tree or taken a spill off my bike doing a jump, or some type of thing kids would do. It was just me, in my twenties, getting my fingers slammed in a door as I tried to escape my girlfriend's rage.

"These bones are too small to set," the doctor told me, "but they'll heal."

As I suspected, I needed stitches on the split finger. The doctor needed to clean the wound first. He got through a small bottle of cleaning solution and just needed a little more.

"It looks like all we have is this large bottle of saline solution, so we'll have to use that."

It looked to be about a gallon. He definitely didn't use the whole amount. I was not as concerned about my injury being slightly cleaner as much as I was about the cost. I knew as soon as they opened up that big-ass bottle of glorified saline solution it would end up on my bill and would probably be three hundred dollars or so.

I was almost on my way out when the doctor stopped me: "Oh, and these stitches don't dissolve, so you'll need to come back in six weeks to get them removed."

Great, another bill we couldn't afford.

When I got home, I was sure this would not be over. I was sure Gemma would defend her actions. Instead, she was *surprised*; of every reaction I thought she might have, that one was dead last on the list.

"Where were you?" she asked. Noticing the splint on my fingers she continued, "What *happened* to you?"

"Are you fucking serious right now?" I asked, clearly annoyed, "You remember last night, don't you?"

"No, dude, I don't. I was *so* drunk. I remember being mad at you, but that's it. I don't remember anything more than that, or even what I was mad about."

Only then did the pieces finally fit: it was basically alcohol-induced psychosis. Any resentment I had for her mostly left me at this point.

"Alright... I guess I better tell you what happened..."

I sat down and told her everything, blow by blow, word by word, only because she needed to know. I recounted the incident in the same tone as a teenager delivering a forced apology. I felt disassociated from it. I hated every moment. Shock and surprise increasingly rolled over her face as I recounted the blows and verbal assaults. Her apologies and regret increased with emotion and intensity at every revelation.

"I am so, *so* sorry, baby… I can't believe I did that to you!" she said.

I felt sort of relieved. It wasn't *her;* it was the booze, I thought. I couldn't really blame *her*, could I? She didn't even remember. She didn't even know why she was mad. I didn't know how the cycle of abuse worked back then. Having told her everything, I wasn't sure what else to say, so I sat there staring ahead, as still as stone.

She kept assuring me: "I *love* you, baby. Please understand how much I love you. I want to *marry* you. I am *so sorry* I did that. *Please, please* forgive me."

That was the first time someone had said those words to me. "I want to marry you." I remember how earnest Gemma was when she said that. She hugged me and covered my face with kisses as I distantly contemplated the previous night's events. She only ever said exactly how she was feeling, so this was not a ploy: she really meant it. She was simply not clever or disingenuous enough to lie about those feelings. A thousand people in the comments of that Reddit thread I didn't read would probably have told me that the sincerity of the apology was not at all important.

"I will *quit* drinking," she said. "I won't let something like this happen again," she assured me.

Given her at-least-a-beer-a-day lifestyle, that promise shocked me. I wondered if she could keep it. At least it told me she was serious.

After a brief pause, she continued: "I won't have any more than a beer a day."

Oh… That's not quite quitting, is it? But still, it was an improvement. I'd hold her to it, at least.

"Unless I'm like... out at the bar or something ...Or at work..."

The next beer she had was that same fucking day. It stared me down like I owed it money. It sat on the table, warping space and time, ominously taunting me. Hand to mouth, all details surrounding it obscured by the sheer, raw gravity of it. Rather than the can tipping to her face, the earth, gravity, and reality itself shifted to move the liquid into her mouth. The can controlled all of it. Gemma's casual chat drifted into the background, muffled as the can itself became the center of my focus. Was this the last one for the day?

Was going down to one beer a day a good enough change in behavior? Even back then, I thought it was a half-measure. Even if she made a full, lasting effort, it was still no excuse. The fact remains that I shouldn't have put up with that.

Until that night, the worst way her temper had manifested was in the form of criticism. I could take criticism all day. You can't get out of film school without your professors completely tearing you and a couple of your projects to shreds. Anything less than that was child's play and I could take it without even a bruised ego. This... this was different, though. This had surpassed words. She was able to stick to just one beer a day. But the previous night's events happened, and she couldn't take that back. I foolishly forgave her. But in a lot of ways, even then, I knew there was no coming back from this.

That was harder to write than I thought it would be. This was my first all-time low that year.

PERSEVERANCE — PART 4: THE PINCH

GEMMA CAME HOME FROM WORK EARLY one afternoon.

"I quit my job," she dropped casually. "I think I can find something better."

"Wait, *what*? At the height of a recession? Why didn't you talk to me first? We can't *both* be unemployed. What about rent?"

"Oh *please*!" She said, rolling her eyes. "People always need servers. I'll have a job again in *two weeks*."

                                                    SMASH CUT:
TEXT OVER BLACK:
                        Two months later.

"What are we going to do about rent?! And what about *food*?!" Gemma asked me, with perhaps the most concern I had ever heard her speak with; well, outside of that... other moment.

Her last interview had taken place in a room of twenty other people, all vying for just *one* position. If it were like that all day, then perhaps hundreds of people were interviewed. Only then did she finally believe the recession was real. She didn't get the job.

There were no "I told you so's." The situation was too real for both of us without any extra squabbling. Gemma didn't know it, but I was on food stamps already. Recalling that conversation she had with my friend Tom, who was in construction, I knew I couldn't tell her. She never thought to ask how I came home with groceries time after time even when she knew damn well I only had a few dollars to my name. Could I tell her now? I didn't see a choice.

"We'll be okay. I have a food stamp card. I've had it for months. It's been the only reason we've had food on the table many times already."

Cue dramatic pause. Was she going to get judgy about this?

"Oh, *good*… Thank god…" She sighed with relief.

"So… you're *not* against us being on food stamps?"

"No, not at all. We need it."

And that was that. Only now, when we were nearly destitute and without any other options for survival could I tell her about it. As soon as we needed it for our next meal, she was no longer critical of getting help.

Now that she knew, though, we could head to the place where food stamp cards are issued and get on a joint account, which would give us a little extra assistance. That felt like the realest shit we had ever done together, sitting in that office, with all the same furnishings they must have given it in the seventies when it was presumably built. Me in my finger splint and Gemma in her earthy style of dress that put her in exactly the same fashion as this old '70s office. I was just glad she could evolve her worldview, maybe.

Our source of income was now exclusively my occasional freelance work and me calling up my old boss and demanding some of the thousands he owed me in back pay. Although he owed many people money, I had continued to work longer than most for the scant *possibility* of a paycheck. My co-workers inversely had all given up and embraced the grind of unemployed life. I figured the *possibility* of a paycheck later was better than no paycheck at all, the way things were going, but even all the occasional work there had long since dried up. My former boss was too hard up himself to come up with any of what he owed me now, so things went from tight to really tight. Now, it was all about freelance.

One such freelance job came from a highly motivated individual with a lot of ideas. He paid me a few bucks up front. He brought me with him as he went into the bank to get approved for a business loan, which he was, so he had the means. He walked out and showed me the cash. In that economy, that he got approved *at all* was impressive.

Stranger still, he lived in the same apartment building that an ex of mine, Elisa, had lived in while we were together. It was a bit surreal visiting that place after I already walked out of it once, thinking full well it would be the last time I ever graced the spacious lobby with its ornate columns. It was a nice building. He clearly had at least some means even before the loan. "Money is not an object," he assured me.

Once there, he showed me a massive tattoo he had just gotten of his business name. It was a long enough name that it was split between the two sides of his torso. It was fresh enough that the skin around it was still red. The tattoo told me he also had dedication.

The product he was looking to make was so, *so* stupid that I won't even say what it was. Imagine the stupidest invention you can. Take a minute, even. His actual idea was a *million* times worse. But it was a paycheck. I worked diligently on an ambitious project for his business. This gig would be our rent for that month.

Yet, a few weeks later, he began saying that money was tight, and he was suddenly hyper-critical rather than permissive about our work. He wanted to scale things back. He became hard to reach. Suddenly, there was no business: it never took off, partners dropped out, and he was on a Greyhound bus back home to another state. He couldn't pay me but said he'd sell his laptop to reimburse me for my work. I was thankful. Then, suddenly he wasn't doing that anymore, and he told me I was selfish for wanting a paycheck to cover my rent.

Days later, he suddenly was in town and had my money. He told me he had stashed it in a garbage bag in a bush outside his apartment, where he was recently evicted for lack of payment. Obviously, this was sketchy, but what choice did I have? I could go there and *probably* find nothing, or I could *not* go there and *definitely* find nothing. There was no money, and I was right that he simply wanted to make me chase my own tail. He probably wasn't even really in town. Here he had me checking in bushes at the same building my ex-girlfriend Elisa used to live in.

I tried to find out what I could about him online. I was able to sleuth enough that I found his blog. What I read here recontextualized everything about the man. In his blog, he came right out and said he was "the worst of the worst drug addicts." What kind of drug? "Every kind," he wrote. All his bluster was fueled by cocaine. All his money went to drugs. He was in college, but now he had dropped out. He was using the business loan and somehow also his college tuition money to bankroll his massive addiction. He really had left town in a blaze of spectacular failure. Days later he deleted every entry on the blog leaving only a blank web page.

With days to go until rent was due, we had no money, and I had no leads on gigs. I got back on Reddit, explained what happened, and begged for some last-minute work. It was tight, but I got it done. I delivered their work and people sent me money, even as some users insisted this must be a scam. Reddit was the Wild West back then. These days, as of writing, you couldn't even ask for a favor like that. Requests for help were eventually segregated to smaller and smaller corners until they didn't exist.

Every month was exactly like this but with some other set of challenges in our way that caused us to barely make rent. In March we had a shortfall yet again, and my best friend Kevin lent us some money to make it up. It had been a while since I had seen him. He moved away a little over a year earlier. At the time, it was probably the biggest favor he'd ever done for me.

I was finally able to find a sales job. My desk was a foldable card table and there was only one other employee. We sold radio ad placements over the phone to small businesses. I was illegally paid way less than minimum wage, so paychecks were issued under the table.

If my former boss who owed me a bunch of money was shady, this guy was even worse. After a couple of weeks, it became clear that the ads we "sold" never ran: not a single one. I never quite got the hang of it, so I hadn't partaken in scamming anyone, thankfully. When I quit, the boss refused to give me my last paycheck.

I managed to claw my way to the final round of interviews for a job that promised to utilize my art skills. I researched the hell out of that company. I prepared an answer for every interview question on the planet. I dressed in a full suit. I was dropping the names of the CEO and other board members. If I got this job, it could solve all our problems. It would be the best job I ever had if I got it. By the time I got to the final round of interviews, I was one of three people. I had a pretty good shot, I hoped.

Gemma finally found a part-time serving job. I kept on with freelance and whatever else I could do, including yelling at my former boss to come through with a few bucks of what he owed me whenever he could. We managed to pay my best friend back and make rent the next month, but we had to fight like hell for every penny and exhaust every resource we had, every single month.

It was under this context—in this and the preceding chapters—that I decided life in Chicago wasn't particularly enjoyable and that I might want to leave. The scam sales job was the final straw. There was no opportunity here anymore. The city I loved had hurt me too much, and I hated it now. I could also stand to get out of my increasingly toxic relationship. I had maintained for years that I'd never leave Chicago; now it was all I wanted. But how? The thing fueling my distaste for Chicago was also what was keeping me here: I was poor.

Like many people who end up in Chicago, living there had become quite the point of pride and engrained itself into my personality through the years. I had never lived in any place for as long of a single stretch as Chicago. That's still true as of writing. It is difficult to define exactly how beaten down I had to become to want to leave behind a core part of my identity, but my toxic relationship and the failing economy finally got to me.

I now realized that seven weeks had gone by since I got those stitches. I could get them removed. I wasn't about to sign up for another bill, though. Perhaps I could rip these stitches out myself. It might hurt, but so would removing myself from my girlfriend and everyone I knew. I was open to it. I was looking for an exit.

There are a lot of nerve endings in your fingertips, though. After cutting the loops with some nail clippers, I used tweezers to pull them out. The first little tug and already my brain was on fire, begging me not to do this to myself. I did it quickly, gritting my teeth. The next few were deeper and more connected to the nerve endings. I had to psych myself up, but I did it. The pain shot up my arm and into my head like white-hot lightning, but I did it. I could take the pain, the stress. Not just the stitches: all of it, everything. This was the worst it could get, I was sure of that. There was nowhere to go but up.

Sometimes life will bring you down so low
You're glad to hit the ground below
Until the bottom drops out

PERSEVERANCE —
PART 5: MR. & MS. FORTUNE

I'VE ALWAYS BELIEVED IN FATE TO SOME DEGREE or another. If we presuppose the existence of a metaphysical force that's in charge of fate—like the Greek deities of old—I know this being doesn't care about justice. I know this version of fate doesn't care about balance. I know because good things can and do happen to bad people. Bad things can and do happen to good people. Sometimes it's the reverse, but definitely not always.

Perhaps fate is completely random and without judgment. But if it isn't, fate must consist of two beings: Fortune and Misfortune, each with opposing goals. First, a theoretical demigod named Fortune: good luck is like coins spilling out of his pockets as he walks along aimlessly. Fortune has long since stopped caring where they fall or who picks them up. If you get any of his lucky coins, you were just in the right place at the right time.

Second, we have Ms. Fortune. She would be an altogether different type of being. When someone's *only* power is to hurt people, they tend to hurt people. They might even grow to like it. Ms. Fortune might be more like a kid sitting over an ant hill with a magnifying glass, focusing the light to kill the ants. The ants didn't do anything, so how does she choose the next ant? She's not looking for a "bad" ant, she's looking for the ant that's there: wrong time, wrong place. Ms. Fortune has killed a lot of ants today, like every day. She wonders what *else* she can do. Aimless slaughter is becoming boring. How much could she hurt an ant and yet still let it live?

Maybe it's all purely, 100% random. Maybe no one is in charge. Maybe we're all just rolling dice. Statistically, if you roll two dice you're most likely to get numbers in the middle. The highs are rare. The lows are rare. But they happen. However statistically unlikely, it is possible to roll a pair of dice and get snake eyes dozens and dozens of times in a row. However unlikely, if it can happen, it eventually will happen.

This would soon become a chapter in my life of trial after tribulation after trial. I'd live a lifetime of misfortunes and then do it again, all in the same year. I don't know if Ms. Fortune was getting deeply experimental, or if I had just rolled new lows, lower and lower, all year long. At a certain point, it becomes so statistically unlikely, that it feels like there must be a creative force of some kind behind it. Either way, this was about to be one nightmare of a year: "the nightmare year." There would be no shortage of struggles to inspire my future songs.

SUNSHINE —
PART 1: IN THE RAIN

MY BEST FRIEND KEVIN HAD SEVERE WANDERLUST and was living across the country. He was the same friend who had recently lent me a few hundred dollars to keep me and Gemma from becoming homeless. That was the last major interaction we had. He helped us when we needed it most.

Now, he'd offered me a room at his place in a small hipster town on the east coast. He had no idea I was looking for a way out. At first, I didn't take the offer seriously, but he kept asking. If I took him up on it, it'd be my *only chance* at an exit. In any other case, this would not be worth considering, but I had absolutely *nothing* here.

There was nothing for me to miss. I was poor, unemployed, and in a toxic relationship. If I didn't leave soon, I'd probably end up leaving under less ideal circumstances. In nine years of living in Chicago, I had never thought about leaving, but for the first time, I was looking for a way out. Then, here comes my best friend Kevin, who I hadn't seen in over a year and I dearly missed, who had recently helped me out in a huge way, asking me if I wanted to move in with him across the country.

I had known him long enough that I was sure we could get along in close quarters. Back in the day, I'd sometimes hang out at his place for days. It was as if Mr. Fortune had intervened to offer me salvation, served up on a platter. All I had to do was agree to his request. Three letters—a one-syllable word—and I could be gone. "Yes." I took him up on the offer. I was going to move.

A sense of optimism began boiling up inside me. It was clear to me that friendships were more stable than relationships. I had known him longer than any relationship I had been in had lasted. I had lived in Chicago for nine years. For a while, I was looking forward to being able to say I had lived here for ten, but I couldn't hold out just for that. I didn't owe that city shit.

For the month leading up to the move, Gemma and I entered a twilight period. All previous sins were forgiven. I knew the end was near, but I wanted to enjoy our relationship in our time left. I had always been a good and thoughtful partner, but now I was in overdrive. I was the sweetest boyfriend alive, now. If the end was inevitable, I'd make these last moments count, and it worked. Our relationship was never better, and she had never appreciated me more. But I was still leaving, and she still wasn't coming with me.

My exit was a certainty, but even as I packed, it did not seem real. Even when Kevin arrived a few days before to visit, it wasn't quite real. He arrived in a rented car, and I could take whatever would fit in it. I had only days left now. This included only about half my clothes and my video camera, so I could hopefully continue doing freelance work in my new home. This camera wasn't mine but was on a semi-permanent loan from my former boss, who once again, owed me *so much fucking money* that taking this camera with me was not a huge ask.

I had a final night out with my friends. Even that night, my departure felt far away. These were people I'd miss, and I was setting myself up to not see them again for years, or maybe ever.

It was only when we woke up on the day of the move that it finally loomed over us. Like the distant lights of a train approaching, it was here, and it could not be stopped. Maybe I should call that place I interviewed at and got to the top three, and see if I was still in the running for the job. I cannot imagine what would be worse: not getting it, or getting it, just as my exit became unavoidable. I suppose *they* would've called *me*, anyway. I suppose I had beaten dozens, maybe even hundreds of folks just to have my hopes dashed in the top three.

When the moment came to walk out of that apartment and out of Gemma's life, I asked Kevin to head down to the car to give us a few minutes.

"Alright, but hurry up because we have a long drive ahead of us," he said.

That was somewhat cold, but maybe he had a point. As soon as my best friend walked out that door, Gemma and I went in for one last hug—one last kiss—in the living room, near the once again painted-over picture of the bird in the grass. We had barely started touching when we both simultaneously burst into tears.

"*I love you.*"

"*I love you.*"

We repeated it back to each other like a skipping record, over and over. I wiped away one tear and it was replaced by three more, so I just stopped trying. Our faces were so wet with our collective tears that we could taste them in our final kiss.

"I'll miss you."

"I'll miss you, too."

You make me feel like
I threw it all away
I love you so much
My soul died that day
I threw it all away
Our love died that day
As we cried
Our love died

As soon as I let go of her, it would be the last we'd ever see each other. This kind of vulnerability was almost beautiful. It could be the perfect ending. Swept up in the emotion of our goodbye, I thought about canceling the whole move. But I knew I couldn't. There was no hope for me in this town, in this economy. I could stay and we could grow more bitter to one another. We would surely die a slow death over the next few months. Our relationship had run its course, and this was the only way to end it with any dignity.

I was mad at the weather for being so sunny that day in April. It was the first nice day spring offered, even if it was still a little cold. I thought it might rain like a dramatic moment on TV. This moment had played out in my head a hundred times leading up to the move, and it was definitely supposed to rain in this scene. Nature declined to provide us with a poetic final kiss in the rain. Instead, our faces were wet only with our tears, and we cried a river in those final moments.

Why is the sun shining?
Nature is defying
But we still kiss in the rain
Of the tears that our eyes drain

SUNSHINE —
PART 2: THE CONSTANT

In our final moment
I now regret this
You, my Constant
Inspiration I will miss you…

IF I DON'T WRITE THIS HERE, NO ONE WILL LIKELY EVER figure out the connection, so here it goes:

In the TV show LOST, there was an aspect of sudden and unexpected time travel that occurred to some characters. In what I and many others regard as possibly one of the best episodes of any television show to grace the small screen, a character named Desmond was subject to this uncontrollable time travel in an episode called "The Constant."

Desmond didn't *physically* travel in time in this episode. Instead, his consciousness from the present day and the past swapped places. If Desmond "traveled" back to 1996, he found himself in his 1996 body in the place he was at that moment in time, but with full access to his future memories. Back in the present (2004 in the episode), he was confused and panicking, not understanding where he was, who he was with, or why he was there. He thought it was 1996; he did not yet have his future memories.

With each time travel event in the episode, Desmond experienced increasing side effects: Nosebleeds, fainting, and even catatonic episodes lasting over an hour. If he continued to experience those symptoms, the time travel side effects would kill him, a fate met by another character in the episode. To fight against these side effects, he needed to find a "constant."

A constant must be a thing that anchors Desmond at both those points in this life: something that remained a "constant." It is something, often an object, that they could hold onto and focus on that would keep their minds from being short-circuited by the time travel. The challenge was that he must have direct access to the constant. Desmond's constant was not an object, but a lost love who he had been separated from for years. Her name was Penny; she was Desmond's constant.

Desmond had just broken up with Penny in 1996, a decision he regretted deeply. Under that context in 1996, he had to convince her to make contact with him eight years later in 2004, at a specific time on Christmas Eve, which happened to be the date he came from in the future. This phone call would be the thing that saved him from insanity and death, stopping his conscience from being displaced in time. A desperate phone call affirming his love for her on Christmas Eve 2004—their first contact in years—saved his life.

I know you're not here for LOST spoilers, so here's the point: Gemma was my "constant." Now I was missing that part of me that kept me grounded, sane, and alive. I wasn't sure if it was worth leaving, and much like Desmond, that regret loomed over me at every moment. I hoped it was worth leaving. I wasn't sure if it was worth staying, either. I was a little more sure of that. One thing was certain: The cost of my departure was high.

Leaving to a better place

As my friend and I drove away, I continued to cry silent tears. Focused on the drive, he never saw that. He carried on a fairly casual conversation. The gravity of my situation was clearly lost on him. But still, he was offering me the best chance I had, the *only* chance.

My girlfriend and I—or, ex, now—exchanged a few more goodbye texts, but we rarely talked after that. She lost *me*, but I lost *everything*. Her, the city I once swore I'd never leave, every friend I'd ever met except one, and my family. I cried every night for months. I could just lay down for the night and decide to cry. And so I would, every night.

The departure was my choice, but it was one I made only to avoid a worse fate. My pride kept me from moving back home like almost everyone else I knew had already done. This felt like my second all-time low of the year. However, this time I was sure the night was darkest before the dawn. I'd build a better life with my best friend, Kevin. Starting over with him could balance out my loss. This was the worst it would get. This was the worst it *could* get. There was nowhere to go but up.

Heading to the coast,
where my heart is the most.
Gotta make something outta me,
maybe one day you'll see it.

SUNSHINE —
PART 3: A NEW HOME

ON OUR WAY TO MY SOON-TO-BE NEW HOME CITY, we stopped to spend the night with some friends of Kevin's. I had never met them before, but they were nice—they were a couple. The lady half of them was a redhead with a rockabilly vibe.

"You know," I told Kevin, "I know we are on our way to your place now, but I just realized that until we get there, I am, technically speaking, homeless."

He reassured me: "No dude, you live with me now. You have a home. You just haven't gotten there yet."

That was a nice thought. I guess I wasn't homeless.

Heading to the coast
Where my heart is the most

When we finally arrived at my new home, a fair bit more south than Chicago, I realized I'd managed to fully skip spring. The trees all had leaves, and it was actually warm out. I could see the mountains from our backyard. Coming from the flat Midwest, the sight of mountains was majestic. The change of scenery rejuvenated me. It gave me a boost every time I saw it.

Living with my best friend wasn't so bad. We knew each other well enough that it was chill and we didn't get on each other's nerves. Kevin lived there with his girlfriend, Claire. He also had a dog.

"It's legally a malamute, but actually 100% wolf. These are very hard animals to take care of. They need a lot of attention and socialization. My dog is a wild animal, plain and simple."

He wasn't complaining about it; perhaps he hoped I'd be impressed at the undertaking.

"Oh, so you must be putting a lot of work into training him."

"Well, I *should* be. But I've been really, *really* busy lately."

"You're making him sound a bit… dangerous. It sounds like you really ought to be putting more time in."

"I know, I *know*. I really should be. But he *does* listen to me, mostly, and I am the *only one* he will listen to. He gets out sometimes, but he always comes back. He once was away for *two full* days. Sometimes I wonder how many people's cats he hunts when he's out there."

This was starting to sound like it wasn't an impressive undertaking as Kevin framed it, but a problem of neglect that he needed to address.

"Dude, that's not cool. That's horrible. Those are people's pets. Can you stop him from getting out?"

"I have tried. I have tried *everything*. He digs holes under the fence. I'm trying to install some electric wire to stop him. It won't hurt him, just provide a shock."

The dog lived almost entirely outside tied to a dog run. Kevin brought him inside only once, that I saw. The dog had no spatial awareness indoors: He looked stressed, and he paced and circled nervously, heavily panting, his tail knocking over everything in its path as it wagged.

"While he's in here, try to keep an eye on him if you can. I'm not sure I can trust him with the cats. He's not very well housebroken."

The dog actively avoided anyone other than Kevin and They had two Siamese cats. The cats were mostly his girlfriend's, and the dog was mostly Kevin's.

I met some new friends through Kevin. One of them was a musician and rapper. He described his music as "socially conscious hip-hop." His critiques of society echoed the types of criticism you might hear in old-school punk songs, which made sense considering he had told me he started off in punk bands before transitioning to hip-hop.

Another friend I met had a stage name of "The Creep." He and The Rapper were great friends and seemed to come as a pair. The Creep wasn't actually creepy: he was pretty down to earth. He was, however, an eccentric performance entertainer, hence the stage name. He'd often do a hybrid dare-devil circus-side-show act, sometimes as an opening act for The Rapper. In one performance, The Creep held a cinder block directly on his head as The Rapper broke it with a metal baseball bat. Henceforth, I will refer to them as The Rapper and The Creep.

One of the first things we did when I got there was a hike-in camping trip. Even the ride there was breathtaking. Sometimes we would pull over and enjoy the view. You could see layers and layers of hundreds of tree-topped mountains for miles and miles, filling the entire horizon. Compared to where I was from, this was probably the most nature I had ever seen.

On our way hiking in, I dropped my well-worn hoodie on the trail and didn't realize it until the sun started setting. As poor as I was, even a thirty-dollar loss felt devastating and could take weeks to recover. I was determined to retrieve it the moment I realized it was gone, but Kevin was sure that hiking alone in the dark would be dangerous, so he insisted on going in my place. He was gone for about an hour and miraculously returned with my hoodie.

Back at my new home, I stumbled upon a national-level news report saying that of all the cities in the country devastated by the recession, this, my new home town, was absolutely the worst in the entire country: the unemployment rate here was over 20%. This new town was very much a hipster town with lots of hippie culture. Some people told me the hippie culture was driving the unemployment rate and that most unemployment here was intentional, so I should be okay looking for a job.

I had a four-year-old flip phone, and my old boss who owed me a ton of money put me on his plan and was paying the bill to ding away at his massive debt to me. Occasionally, he couldn't pay it and the service would go out. This was one of those times. I called him through a Google voice number on my computer and left a scathing voicemail since I was trying to find a job and needed to be able to get callbacks. It always happened at the worst times. When I called, his service was always still on, somehow.

I managed to land a job doing sales. I didn't want to do sales again, but the economy was in historical levels of shambles. The job paid minimum wage, but they expressed it as a weekly salary, so the number sounded impressive to me. However, it wasn't *really* minimum wage, because you only got *one* day off a week, not *two*. Yet, it was still the best deal I'd gotten since the recession started. I theoretically made more at the production studio in Chicago that went under, but of course, that wasn't accounting for missed and late paychecks.

In previous positions, I had consistently been making sometimes as little as pennies per hour, because I was getting paid "salary" or "commission." It was like this ever since I graduated college, right into the recession. The almost-minimum wage would still be the most I had ever made.

These types of sales jobs are usually scams, to some degree. If the sales-person is honest, which I was, the customer is not usually the person getting scammed, but rather the employee. If you were new at this job, you put any sales you got under the boss's name. That seemed sketchy, but I was unsure what the scam there was. I was still getting my almost-minimum wage, so I didn't worry about it much.

Kevin, who was unemployed, started attending EMT classes, as did I. We did this at no cost by volunteering for the county's rescue squad, who were commonly tasked with things like searching for lost hikers. Free was the only way this could happen. The opportunity was part of what convinced me to move here. EMTs made basically no money, but at that time, the thirteen dollars an hour they averaged seemed absolutely baller to me. It was the best career opportunity I could get.

Kevin was supported financially by his girlfriend Claire, who was an exotic dancer. She hated the profession and wanted to do literally anything else, but without that, they'd have no income. Kevin reasoned that since he was going to EMT school, he couldn't also hold down a job, so she just needed to stick it out for about eighteen months while he finished up his training.

This was suspect considering I was working full-time and managing the same EMT class he was, but to be fair, I did have virtually no free time: every spare moment I had was spent studying for the class, going over the textbook and re-listening to the lectures which I had recorded. I was determined to pass this class with flying colors.

Kevin also put on a nice birthday thing for me and all his friends attended, who were quickly becoming my friends as well. We all had a good time.

"My friends are your friends," he said.

That was good; I was unlikely to make friends any other way, at least anytime soon.

SUNSHINE —
PART 4: SING

ONCE WHILE KEVIN WAS OUT FOR THE NIGHT, his girlfriend Claire invited me to a karaoke gig. I could sing pretty well, but not many people knew that. If they did, all they really knew was that I was making that *claim*; they might not have seen it since the opportunity rarely arises. However, I was comfortable enough now around my best friend that I partly hoped he could tag along and finally see me in action, but it ended up just me and Claire. She sang too and was pretty solid.

Arriving back at the house later, Kevin had gotten home.

"You should have seen me, man, it was fun," I said.

"Can you sing?" he asked.

"Yeah, I've told you before. You know that. You just haven't seen it yet."

"Yeah," Claire chimed in, "Steve can definitely sing."

"You know, I can sing pretty well too," he said confidently. "I listen to Tool all the time and I'm pretty good at that Maynard Keenan style. I could totally be in a band if I wanted to. Maybe I should."

I absolutely didn't believe him, by the way. Obviously, merely *listening* to a band won't make someone good at singing. It's easy to get carried away in the emotion of the performance and mistake that feeling for being good, as if, somehow, passion translates directly into learned pitch and tone. It's hard to tell if you are good until other people *tell you* you're good, unprompted. It took me years to become just *okay*. It would be years more until I was confident I was *good*. There are way more people who think they can sing than people who genuinely can, so skepticism is natural. Maybe I shouldn't fault him for not believing me, either. No one will tell you if you are bad, but they *might* tell you if you are good. Likewise, I did not voice my skepticism about Kevin's claim but merely responded in kind.

"I'd love that too, I love singing," I replied, but not earnestly or with elation because it seemed out of my grasp. "I'm not sure how I'd even get started, though. Or how I'd find the time. Or what I'd even write about. Breakups, maybe, but it's been done a million times. The way it ended with Gemm was kind of different, though, maybe there's something there. That's like, *one* song worth of material, though."

SUNSHINE —
PART 5: FORTUNE MAKES A PREDICTION

KEVIN AND I TRIED KAYAKING IN THE LOCAL RIVER one afternoon. In some rapids, Kevin overestimated his abilities and spilled out of his kayak. Soaking now, he got back in the kayak.

"Are you *trying* to fall out of that thing?" I asked.

"That's the best way I saw to go! Leave me alone!"

He often feigned anger for humor's sake.

"Well, now you're all wet. I'm trying to avoid that."

Farther up, we were challenged again by the rapids.

"There are different levels of rapids," he told me, as we maneuvered around rocks and fallen trees, "These ones get up to three in some parts."

"How high do the levels go?"

"The hardest you could realistically survive is level five."

"So, what's level six? Is there one?"

"I believe that means a route that no one has yet survived. Someday I'd like to be the first person to survive a level six rapids."

"Wouldn't it become a level five at that point?"

"Probably not. It would still be pretty fuckin' hard, *right?*"

He always had to be the most interesting person in the room, but that was fine. He was always like that. He took risks for no reason. I much preferred to respect the river first and see where my abilities were rather than challenge it blindly.

Kevin often wanted to be the first person to do this or that dangerous thing. Then he'd learn the basics over a couple of weeks and proceed as if he were an expert. Getting to whatever goal he wanted immediately was the only way he knew how to get there. But even with that, he rarely saw things through.

We met in film school and he dropped out about halfway through. I had hounded him to come back, and he wanted to regardless of my encouragement. The school's policy stated that based on his situation, he couldn't be re-admitted. Yet, somehow, he convinced them to let him back in. Then, he blew it again the *very next semester* and failed out for the final time. The way I was disappointed in him when this happened, you'd have thought I raised him from birth.

The river offered more challenges ahead. There were spots where there was only a narrow safe path through, and you had to cross quickly to get to the safe part, but Kevin would refuse to play it safe. Kevin fell out of his kayak yet again and yelled for me to help him; first to save the kayak, so it didn't float away, then with saving *him*. I had to get over there fast and fell out myself as he flailed in the water. It didn't matter how smart my moves were if he ignored all common sense. His recklessness made our adventure needlessly difficult. We were still having fun, mostly.

When we decided we'd had enough, we ended up in an open field some-where. Suddenly, a blanket of rain swept over the river, advancing toward us like a moving sheet of water. It was so heavy that we were somehow wetter from the rain than from falling into the river. Lightning quickly followed. We traced the tree line to avoid being a tempting target for

Mother Nature. Dragging kayaks behind us, we made it to a road to find ourselves behind a fence topped with barbed wire, keeping the road just out of reach. A chain and lock blocked our way. We'd have to backtrack and find a different path to the road, still in the pouring rain, with lightning threatening, but the sun still shining from the other direction.

Upon inspection, Kevin found the lock on the fence wasn't even latched to the other end of its chain: it was pure theater. We walked out easily and put the chain back. Maybe Kevin did make life more difficult just by being there, but it was a story. He figured out the lock thing, at least. If there was an opportunity or a shortcut to get something done, he found it. We got picked up by The Rapper, as planned.

That night, we ordered Chinese food. After all the energy we expended, it felt like we earned it. It probably tasted better than it really was.

"What did your fortune say?" I asked. "Mine's lame. It says, 'The early bird gets the worm, but the second mouse gets the cheese.' I haven't heard it that way before, I guess, but it's more advice than a fortune."

"Hmm, mine's good," Kevin replied. "It says: 'Good fortune will come to you in six months.'"

"Oh, that's interesting. You should keep it and see if it comes true."

"Actually…" He paused for a moment. "You can have it. I give this fortune to you, and all the future luck that comes with it."

"Alright. I'll keep this. Let's see what happens six months from now."

I'm a sucker for sentiment. I wrote the date, six months from that day, on the fortune and kept it in a place where I often saw it. Perhaps Ms.

Fortune would take a backseat to Fortune that day. Perhaps one of his lucky coins would find its way to me. Given the circumstances of my exit from Chicago, a little good luck would be welcome.

Gotta make something out of me
Maybe one day you'll see it

MYSTERIA —
PART 1: THE FESTIVAL

KEVIN WANTED ME TO GO TO THIS CRAZY-SOUNDING FESTIVAL and offered to get me a ticket for my birthday. The concept of this festival was whatever its participants wanted it to be. There were no attractions other than what folks set up themselves. No currency was allowed to be exchanged on the premises, nor could you barter. Anything given was to be given without expectation of anything in return.

The only currency
Is generosity

We intended not just to attend, but to contribute to the events and installations. Although it was too late for me to champion anything significant, I was able to provide execution on one concept: Bacon. It's the only food we brought, and almost the only food we ate. If you walked up to our camp and wanted bacon, you got bacon. The Rapper would perform. Kevin wanted to build a geodesic dome to house his performance. I'd record the event with my professional camera.

The geodesic dome involved a lot of cutting and bending of pipes to specific lengths. I did 90% of the work, as Kevin lost interest and I, for some reason, became determined to help. Claire created a "butterfly tent." This was a screened-in tent where you could hang out surrounded by actual butterflies. Kevin left a day early to set up the dome, and I left the next day in the same car with Claire, which was a nice opportunity to get to know each other a bit better.

When we arrived at the festival gates, Kevin met us to help load in. He suddenly remembered that there was some insane hazing ritual to get into the festival if you had never been before. Claire confirmed. He wouldn't tell me what it was but stressed that it was bad. I wondered aloud if it was worth the price of entry. When the moment came, I was hit twice on the butt with a flyswatter and that was it. That was the ritual. The real haze was hyping up what the haze was.

Upon entry, a greeter told us "Welcome home," which really warmed me up to the place. Once I was in, fire was everywhere: Gas-powered lanterns, bonfires, and people doing tricks and acrobatics with flaming torches. Sculptures and installations stretched as far as the eye could see.

The first night, our entire group wandered about and found a docile, snake-like dragon, sleeping peacefully with its massive mouth left agape. Its mouth was easily twelve feet tall and twenty feet wide. This slumbering dragon was easily an eighth of a mile long, its long body weaving over the hilly topography of Mysteria's landscape. Without hesitation, we wondered into its mouth and deep within its innards. It was so long we wondered where the end was as we traveled through. The dragon must have preferred meals of soft plushy things, as its innards were filled with all sorts of random fun things like inflated balls and stuffed animals. We had a bit of fun throwing some random soft things at each other, weaving and ducking out of the way behind some of the larger items lying about inside.

Throughout other parts of Mysteria, another dragon roamed. Unlike the sleeping dragon, this one was fully mobile, lumbering slowly through the festival, making the rounds every so often. Not as soft and fluffy, this one was made of metal. Partiers rode on its back barring music. It breathed fire out of its mouth as it roamed.

Of course, these were not real dragons, but creative art installations. The dragon's mouth we entered was a long tunnel made of parachute material. The metal dragon was a small school bus with a plethora of creative additions. It really did breathe fire, though, and the head would bob up and down slowly as the bus drove along. It was truely a mechanical marvel.

The next day, to my surprise, the same redhead who I met while on my way to my new city with Kevin also arrived. The community vibe had rubbed off on me, so I gave her a warm welcome. She came alone but knew some of the other people there. With her, the festival's cast of characters was now complete. Overall, the notable folks in my circle at the camp were myself, The Redhead, the Rapper, The Creep, Kevin, Claire, and The Artist (who we haven't met yet, but will soon). A festival like this warranted cool names, so we'll go with it.

MYSTERIA —
PART 2: THE PREMONITION

ON MY SECOND DAY AT CAMP, I MULLED OVER SOMETHING I'd been considering doing for a few weeks that was pretty out of character for me. Many people at the camp knew I'd never done any type of drug in my life. I'd been 90 percent sure of my decision, up until today, but now I figured I'd do it: tonight, I'd do DMT provided by The Rapper. Everyone knew this was happening and seemed invested in my experience as a newcomer.

After researching the substance, I learned that small amounts occur naturally in the human body. As I understood it, the substance is at least partly responsible for causing dreams. My justification for not doing drugs up until this point was to not alter my consciousness with foreign substances, so DMT got a pass on two fronts: First, it was not a foreign substance. Second, any time I'd ever dreamed I'd technically already done it.

My dreams were sometimes an enriching experience that could give me insight or inspiration, so I was looking forward to seeing what else I could discover in the inner space of my mind. I thought that perhaps on DMT, I could close my eyes and go on an internal journey that was far more intentional than the random nature of dreams. I didn't realize it right then, but many people seemed to think that for a first-time drug experience, DMT was a trial-by-fire.

The Rapper, The Creep, and I wandered the outskirts of our makeshift town. We found a secluded spot in the woods where the noise of the festival faded. Trees surrounded us on all sides and obscured the sky. Ferns covered the forest floor.

The method of delivery for this drug was smoke. The Rapper didn't have any fancy pipes, just some stuff cobbled together from otherwise ordinary items. None of us had any idea what we were doing. The Rapper went first, haphazardly sucking in the smoke with his makeshift contraption. Within seconds, a huge smile came across his face, and his eyes were wide with excitement. He was drawn in by the forest.

"The rhododendrons..." He kept repeating.

"What does that mean?" I asked.

"It's this species of flower. They're everywhere among the ferns," he explained.

I remember The Creep taking his turn and looking around at all the sights, eyes darting, trying to take in as much as he could with a smile wide across his face.

I'd asked to go last, and now I was up. I'd had the odd cigarette in the past, but never anything habitual; that was my only reference point for this. The smoke from the DMT burned in a way I wasn't prepared for as it traveled into my lungs.

All my surroundings slowed down like a cassette in an old-school tape player running down the last of its batteries. The distant sounds of the festival, the ambient sounds of the wind, and the wildlife of the forest all faded away into a striking silence. I took in the forest for a moment, as my friends had. It breathed and moved, not as many organisms but as a single unified organism. My surroundings smeared as I turned my head. Kaleidoscopic vision trails lagged behind the ferns as my eyes moved.

"Alright," I announced, "I'm going to try to go inside, so please try to be quiet for me while I'm there." In retrospect, I'm not sure they had any idea what I meant by that.

I closed my eyes and covered my face, blocking out any light to eliminate outside interference.

At first, I saw just geometric fractal shapes. Then images pushed through as if persons and objects were pressing against a curtain. There were thin layers of yellow light creating an alternating striping effect with the darkness, giving a sense of 3D space as things or persons pushed against the veil. Within that metaphor, the curtain was a clingy thin silk that hid few details except colors.

I briefly saw a mother holding a baby, and then a fellow with shoulder-length hair resembling classical imagery of Jesus. Then, a figure of some sort of supernatural authority manifested before me. He towered over me with a top hat and beard, and the shape and image of his face weren't entirely discernable. His mouth moved as if to talk, but he remained as silent as a desert mirage. Whatever his message was, it would remain unknown. Who was the man in the top hat?

It felt like I was watching a play: Nothing was literal, just representations and actors conveying whatever lesson I was supposed to receive. Just like a movie based on real events, I hoped it could offer useful lessons.

I'm looking for the question to an answer

I opened my eyes again. My vision seemed artificially stereoscopic. Everything appeared in alternating layers, similar to when I was "inside." The ferns all had a subtle technicolor sheen.

I went back inside. Perhaps I could control the environment I ended up in. I imagined a desert and placed myself in the landscape. I saw dunes, and then a black hole or passageway. I entered. My environment moved as I stayed still. I do not recall what happened next. I wrote down my experience some days after it occurred, and the entry I've revisited to recount this event here stops abruptly in the middle of a sentence just saying, "But after this."

And although my friends are near
Technically I'm far away from here

The experience had a lingering effect that lasted for another few days. I was buzzing with a new energy of some kind. It didn't seem strange at the time, but in retrospect, I have to wonder what biological mechanics DMT could have triggered to bring on such a strong sensation.

MYSTERIA —
PART 3: BURN

BACK AT CAMP, THE REDHEAD WAS HAVING AN EMOTIONAL CRISIS. "I've got demons I'm trying to work through," she said, staying intentionally vague on the details.

I didn't prod any further. Perhaps I could still help, though. I grabbed two blank pieces of paper out of my notebook, along with a pencil, both of which I always had on me. I asked to borrow a lighter from someone for a while.

"Go into the woods and find a place where you can be alone," thinking of the same spot where my other friends and I had just been, I continued, "I know a spot. Take this pencil and paper and write down all your problems, all your demons, and everything you don't like about yourself. Let those things exit you and become transferred onto the paper."

Every word I said came out on autopilot, a purely intuitive moment. The suggestion alone had her worked up. Tears began to well up in her eyes. Her lips trembled. The idea of committing her demons into tangible words on paper seemed to be intimidating.

"And then," I said, handing her the lighter, "you're going to burn it."

She looked relieved, but also a bit confused.

I continued: "Burning the paper represents you letting these things go. As the pages burn away, let yourself be released from those things."

With that, she relaxed even more. I showed her most of the way to the spot I was at earlier. However, this was one of those things she had to do alone. I watched her disappear into the forest and headed back to camp.

She was gone for over three hours. I began to worry. But she re-emerged from the forest, no longer burdened. Her eyes were red and her face was still wet with tears, but a slight smile of relief was affixed to her face, and she glowed with joy just underneath the surface.

"It was really, really hard to let go and put that flame to the paper, but I did it. I did it."

She sighed in relief. It felt like I was some sort of sage. It was a rare moment for me to be able to come up with an impromptu therapy on the spot. With her journey completed, however, there was no need for that role anymore. From then on, we were inseparable: as friends and equals.

Demons undesired
Can be burned with fire

MYSTERIA —
PART 4: MANIC PIXIE DREAM GIRL TYPE STUFF, BASICALLY

MY ENTIRE LIFE, I TOLD MYSELF I WOULDN'T PUT foreign substances in my body: my justification for being drug-free. DMT was not strictly foreign, so the rule was still unbroken. But, it got me thinking: Even something as benign as a chicken sandwich was *technically* foreign, so maybe that's not the best measure for such a rule.

Long story short, someone had offered me Psilocybin mushrooms, otherwise known as 'shrooms, and I was thinking of doing those now, too. Hoping to have a companion on this journey, I asked the Redhead if she'd like to do them with me. She wasn't sure she would join me, because she'd done a bunch over the last few months, which apparently meant that they might not work on her. She did, however, offer to guide me as I did them.

I told *one* other person that I was merely thinking about it. Everyone I knew at the camp had heard about this within *two hours*. People turned to others and whispered whenever I approached, but I managed to over-hear some of it.

"Did you hear? Steve might do 'shrooms!" one camper whispered to another.

"I heard that," I said it like a parent overhearing the schemes of their child.

"Well, are you going to do it?"

"I'm thinking about it. Who told?"

"I think I heard it from Judy," I hadn't told Judy—one of the less notable folks at our camp at the festival—who I haven't mentioned until now. "But everyone's been talking about it."

Kevin thought it was interesting: "A lot of people become more aware and enlightened because of experience with psychedelics. You kind of got there without them. It's interesting that you got there first on your own. It's like you waited till you were really ready."

When the time came, The Redhead had changed her mind: she was down. Now, *she* played the sage. She told me the 'shrooms were supposed to taste bad, but instead, it tasted like nothing.

"In about thirty minutes," she said, "you'll feel like something is about to happen. Then, it'll suddenly kick in."

We found ourselves at one of the nearby music camps, dancing to a DJ's set. The sun was setting so nearby fire lamps became our main source of light. My half hour was up, but I still wasn't getting anything. *Maybe* I felt like something was about to happen? I supposed so, but it could have been a placebo effect, I reasoned. If this was what it felt like, it hardly felt like anything.

In another ten minutes though, the feeling hit me with a sudden intensity, like a sixth sense alerting me not to danger, but to something profound. It was as if I suddenly realized some brilliant life-changing idea. But there was no idea, just the certainty that something would happen, and *soon*. The feeling was unmistakable after all.

I instantly became enamored with everything surrounding me. We wandered deeper into the woods, to the outskirts of the festival. I became annoyingly happy. I was amazed by the leaves on the trees, thinking it would be fun to eat them. The Redhead had to talk me out of it. We found a quieter place where the music had faded and laser lights darted through trees, re-enforcing the magical feeling.

The Redhead held my hand. In the state I was in, it made me smile. We stayed like that for so long that it began to feel like we were always attached. We wandered all over the festival for hours and hours. Parts of the festival were as dense as a busy city street and other parts were secluded and tucked away in the woods.

Mysteria was putting on a massive fire effigy that night. It stood as a wooden sculpture, three stories tall. It resembled the peak of a castle, and on the very top was a wooden statue of a person with their arms stretched into the sky. Massive sparklers shot out of the top. It was a little slow to start burning, but after not too long the flames licked the sky. The fire was so large that you could feel the heat hundreds of feet away.

People ran around it while hollering. The Redhead's hand was still permanently attached to mine while we ran, too. I recall a moment as we were running when she looked back at me, hair flowing as we ran, her backlit by the massive fire, with a contagious smile that instantly spread to me.

The only thing I recall beyond that is that we ended up in a drum circle. I hadn't ever seen anything like that; I thought we could only observe. I was surprised we were invited in. The beats evolved slowly and organically. I had barely touched a drum before that moment, but I found that playing along came intuitively. At the end of the night, we fell asleep in the butterfly tent.

I wish I remembered more from that night that I could recount here. All I can say is that in an instant, The Redhead and I suddenly felt like lifelong friends. It was purely innocent and childlike. We had no intentions: we knew we were both attracted to each other in a broad sense, but romance wasn't the point of this. It was about a genuine, human connection. I was well aware that she had a boyfriend back home. The hand-holding, she assured me, did not cross any lines. We enjoyed each other's company as if we were children, uncomplicated by the prospect of potential coupling. I didn't expect that level of closeness as we explored the festival, but I welcomed it earnestly.

MYSTERIA —
PART 5: THE ARTIST. THE SAGE

THE NEXT DAY I WENT AROUND THE CAMP and asked everyone individually "If you could give someone one piece of life advice, what would it be?" I thought it might be interesting to see what wisdom various folks might impart.

In hindsight, I only recall one answer, coming from someone who I will call The Artist. I expected he'd have a good answer. Through my brief interactions with him, he seemed to be a bit of a sage, but until now we hadn't talked at length. He had an ordinary name, but it wasn't his real name; at some point, he had adopted another one. He was well-read and had a degree in math, of all things. He talked "southern" but without the drawl. In his home of Louisville, Kentucky, he was a respected and regionally noteworthy tattoo artist. Of all the people in our camp, he was easily the most interesting.

He had an impressive, well-kempt beard and long hair. He looked mature, though not old, and he dressed in the style of the 1930s. I often saw him wearing a top hat. That presentation was familiar to me for one unlikely reason: the combination of the beard and the top hat looked *a lot* like the manifestation I saw towering over me during my DMT experience. Who *was* the man in the top hat in my vision, anyway?

While I was very certain that The Artist was in fact *not* literally the metaphysical being I saw during my DMT experience, I had to wonder if the resemblance indicated that The Artist might have some significance for me in some way. I couldn't know how this potential might realize itself. Does this mean we'd become great friends? Louisville was hours and hours away. Therefore, becoming friends long-term wasn't particularly likely. I might never see him again after this event. For now, the only way I knew of to take advantage of his potential significance was to pay special attention to his answer to my question:

"If you could give someone one piece of life advice, what would it be?"

I put his answer directly into the song that would be eventually written about this event:

I asked advice, he thought a while
Said treat everything as worthwhile

Unlike my DMT experience, this time I heard the words: "Treat everything as worthwhile." I interpreted his advice to mean that you shouldn't dismiss people, ideas, activities, or anything else outright. If something isn't, say, overtly dangerous, give it a try. Have an open mind. Give stuff a chance. Although The Artist was almost certainly not who I saw in my vision, it was still good advice, and I took it to heart.

MYSTERIA —
PART 6: CLAIRVOYANCE

LATER I WONDERED—PROBABLY NOT TOO SERIOUSLY—if my recent experiences may have offered me some sort of clairvoyance. Laying down with my eyes closed, relying only on my ears, I tried to describe a person who passed through our camp. All I had to go on was a voice and the words he spoke. After he left, I gave some folks at the camp my description of what I thought the person might have looked like and how he dressed.

After a pause for consideration, The Artist told me, "That's... about right, actually," with an upward inflection that indicated he may have been a little impressed.

I'm not sure how earnestly I believed I was being clairvoyant, in any genuinely supernatural sense. I just remembered that, at least according to The Artist, I was essentially correct. It wasn't proof of anything, but it was a fun experiment.

I did have a working theory, though. There's a certain amount you can glean from a person from reading the words they say. For example, a large vocabulary might indicate a certain level of education. There's a certain amount more to be gleaned from hearing how they say it. Accents, tone, emotion, inflection informs the bulk of context. Had I seen the guy, there would have been more still to be gleaned from mannerisms, how someone presents themselves, what they do, and how they act. All these things present a certain amount of information about a person—a certain amount of context clues—that a person intuitive enough can pick up on, no substances required. It's something I'd always been good at.

However, expressing this theory seems impossible. There's just so much information and cultural context that could be considered at any given time, that to try to define the process would be pointless. Obviously, information can be gleaned from how a person presents themselves, but what precisely can be ascertained and from what mannerisms could fill a library. It would take longer to meaningfully explain it than it would to learn it if you were able.

Years before, I told a friend that the new roommate they were considering, who I had only met for a few minutes, would be trouble for them. I couldn't explain why—it was fifty different tiny things, meaningless on their own—a flip of the hair, a look they gave, the jacket they wore, and much more, that all pointed to this conclusion. My friend wanted to know what I thought would happen. I didn't know. So, they took on the roommate. Less than two months later, the new roommate disappeared and left everybody to cover their share of the rent. I found out when I got an exasperated call starting with, "You were *right*." Sometimes it took longer for things like this to come to fruition.

It's not always bad. Sometimes you can tell when someone is good, conflicted, or secretly hurting. From a logical standpoint, it seems dumb to judge people this way, so I never took these intuitions as proof of anything until evidence surfaced to confirm them. It's not supernatural; if I can't prove the suspicion, it's probably wrong. If I got anything negative, it was just a cue to be extra vigilant with that person.

When I first met my best friend, Kevin, I got a bad feeling about him initially. The red flag I thought might confirm this was his claim to be "really good at manipulating people." Because of that, I kept my distance for like a month. The month turned into a year, then two. I didn't really see him manipulate anyone, so I figured he was fine. Maybe he was saying that he *could*, not that he *would*.

Overall, he was just kind of edgy, which could occasionally be annoying, but so far hadn't gone beyond that. He dressed that way, too: tattoos, piercings, long hair, etc. We had known each other for years now and were best friends for nearly all of it. We were the type of dudes that could hug sometimes, the type of dudes that could say platonic "I love you's." Kevin had proven himself to be a good friend to me. Therefore, my intuition must have been wrong.

It was the only time my "clairvoyance" had faulted me. The only other time it seemed to fail—with a different person, place, and time—it just turned out that the bad stuff was simply delayed by a couple of years. However, Kevin and I had known each other for *seven* years now. If he was going to wrong me in some overt way, I figured it would've happened by now.

At the end of the festival, I helped Claire let the butterflies free from the butterfly tent. Watching them fly away was a majestic sight and a beautiful way to end the festival.

Yesterday we built this town
In three days we tear it down

DARKHORSE —
PART 1: A NEW FRIEND

SINCE MOVING AWAY FROM CHICAGO, I made an interesting new friend. Although it was new, this friendship was actually years in the making.

Let's go back in time. It's the mid-2000s. I had cultivated a sort-of chic look that happened to be in vogue, which was good because I'd have done it anyway. This was before beards and general scruffiness had taken over masculine fashion. I regularly bleached my hair platinum blonde. People of all ages were devouring Harry Potter books as they came out. Most phones were flip phones. People composed text messages on them using a keyboard of just nine buttons.

The social media site of choice was not Facebook, but MySpace. They didn't make you use your real name. Music would play on your profile. Unlike Facebook, it didn't feel like it had to be real-life friends, too. If someone seemed cool or interesting, you added them. Maybe you talked, but probably you didn't.

That's who this friend was. They had previously added me on MySpace, and as everyone transitioned over to Facebook, only one person who I had never met made it over to my Facebook friends. Her name was Bella. We communicated sparsely over the years, until the nightmare year, not long after I moved in with Kevin.

We got to talking, and talking turned into confiding. Over the next few weeks, we became mini-therapists for each other, trauma-bonding over chats. After a few weeks of chatting, we upped the ante to texting. After another few weeks, we're video chatting almost daily. We both looked forward to this nightly ritual.

She had shortish blond hair and a sort of timid tone to her voice. She dressed in a fairly cutesy look, with lots of feminine colors, as if she had stopped updating her style in high school. There was a shyness about her, even as she made clear and overt efforts to better become my friend. She worked in a lab at a research-focused job that utilized a chemical science degree of some kind. Altogether, if you were to compare her to Gemma, she couldn't be any more different.

She lived hundreds of miles away in the city of Louisville, Kentucky, coincidentally the same place some of my new friends from Mysteria lived. She and I became close, but given the distance, it was purely platonic.

My heart is a darkhorse
Could love be on its course?

DARKHORSE —
PART 2: CRASH

It was less than twenty-four hours since I left Mysteria and rejoined society. Like a sugar crash, the joy of life was suddenly sucked away as I realized I had to get back to my normal responsibilities. However, I felt changed by the experience.

I woke up early that morning. I had to get to the grocery store to buy some lunch supplies before I got myself to work. I told me housemates I'd be right back. I should still have enough time to whip up my usual salad and get to my job. I regretted that I probably couldn't tell my coworkers much of what went on, because I really wanted to. Even if it wasn't Mysteria, life was good, and I was feeling good.

As I drove back home from the store, a guy in a large truck almost missed his turn. From a lane over, he tried to cut me off at the end of a turn lane that he could've entered hundreds of feet before. An asshole move, but whatever. Just then, the light changed yellow, and I had to slam on the brakes since the truck significantly reduced my available stopping distance.

I had enough room to stop before. Even with the truck trying to squeeze in, I still should be okay, I figured. Or rather, I *would* have enough room to stop if the car wasn't still full of camping supplies from the Mysteria trip, adding a good amount of extra mass to the vehicle. I was breaking, but I also started to see it wasn't enough. I slammed on the brakes harder and held. The tires screeched for a long time as my perception of time slowed.

Our cars made contact, but in the moment it didn't seem too bad. Maybe the bumper would get messed up. The momentum caused my head to bob forward, but I wouldn't have called it whiplash. I was experiencing time in slow motion now. Even as the car should've stopped moving, it slowly crumpled into the truck in front of me and the hood folded up. It seemed to take ages but probably only lasted two seconds.

I was completely fine; so were the other drivers and their respective cars—except for mine… and—*oh shit*—this was *not* my car. Poor people can't afford cars, and I was one of those. I had my license but had never owned a car. This was my best friend Kevin's car. Fuck.

Outside of the car, I assessed the situation. I found out the guy who cut me off had also hit the car in front of *him*, which was also a large truck that similarly took almost no damage. Officers arrived at the scene. They interviewed me and the two others involved.

The driver in front of the guy who cut me off described him as "a bat out of hell." He looked at the hood of my car and said "That should pound right out."

The officers cited the fellow who cut me off as the person at fault for the accident. The car still ran, at least. I pulled into a nearby parking lot and made the hard call to Kevin.

I just got to the point—ripped the Band-Aid off—"I got into a car accident."

"What happened?" he asked.

"Someone cut me off and I slammed on my brakes, but I still ended up hitting him."

"Okay, how's the car?" he asks. He's surprisingly cool about this.

"From what I can tell, it just looks like the hood is bent."

"Oh, that might not be a big deal. How fast were you going?"

"Well, I was going maybe thirty-five, but I had slammed on the brakes, so I don't know how fast I was going when I hit him, maybe fifteen?"

I was painfully unaware of the physics of what happened: they didn't teach me that in art school. Even though I was actively breaking, the slowing speed of the car at the moment of the impact wasn't as relevant as the momentum I was still carrying from the weight of the car and my initial speed of thirty-five.

I was relieved by Kevin's calm tone. I could hear Claire in the background, who at this point I counted among my friends. She was worried, asking what happened.

"Somebody hit Steve," Kevin said nonchalantly.

"Well, like I said, although I think the accident was the other guy's fault... technically I hit *him*," I reiterated.

Claire was suddenly on the phone now.

"*Steven, are you okay?!*" she asked, anxiously.

Given the frank, informational, and even-toned conversation I just had with Kevin, her tone surprised me. She was really concerned.

"Yeah, I should be fine. Just a minor fender-bender. It's okay. You don't have to worry."

"Okay, good." Her tone stayed concerned. "Just let either of us know if you need *anything*, okay? Where are you? Can we come get you? Do you need to go to the hospital?"

"I'm in the grocery store parking lot. I don't have to go to the hospital. It really is okay. You can definitely come get me, though."

I called my work, let them know what happened, and told them I didn't know if or when I'd be in. My boss also asked if I was okay. I told him I figured I was fine.

I let our local friends know about the accident throughout the day. They all asked if I was okay. That was a phrase I got used to hearing. I could downplay the severity of the accident all I wanted, but everyone asked if I was okay. I'd never been in a situation like this before, so the compassion people showed me was an alien concept. I told Bella about it too and she also showed her support and compassion.

"I wish I could give you a hug," she said.

"That would be nice, actually," I said.

Back at home, I started to file a claim with Kevin's insurance company. All the various follow-ups took so long that I didn't even make it to work that day. The insurance on Kevin's car was just liability, so that wouldn't help us. We had to hope the insurance of the person who *caused* the accident would cover this.

The evidence was on our side: We had a police report faulting the other driver, and another driver involved who was also providing a statement—the same fellow who had described the at-fault driver as "a bat out of hell." If the insurance company were able to pay for repairs then we would be all set. We just had to wait a few days to hear the determination.

All of that as the result of wanting to make a salad.

DARKHORSE —
PART 3: WAKING NIGHTMARE

The next day, I returned to work. My exit from Mysteria to reality was further sobered by yesterday's events. I came crashing back into everyday life—literally.

My new job was a hardcore sales job. I had quit my first sales job in Chicago a few years prior and sailed right into a creative job. I told myself then I'd never return to cold sales, but here I was. The recession laughed at the dreams and goals of the poorest millions.

I had finally put together the scam my new boss had going on. That morning on a district-wide conference call, the higher-ups praised my boss for "getting in the field every day and closing so many sales," showing us new guys how it's done. We all knew he hadn't gone into the field in weeks, much less every day. Even if he was in the field the one day I was at Mysteria, the numbers did not add up. So where was all this coming from?

Then I remembered: He had new guys put *his* name on their sales. I didn't know the full details, but I suspect that if he made the sale, he got an additional commission as a salesman on top of the cut he got as the boss. Although he still ultimately had to pay us, it must have shaken out in his favor by some margin. After all, our pay was actually *capped* at minimum wage. If we made less, he treated us as being in debt to him, even if he didn't literally expect the money back. If we made more, perhaps he could pocket the difference.

We sold cable packages to unsuspecting shoppers in big stores. If you walked past us, you were going to hear our pitch. The job was only scammy internally. As a potential customer, we were just annoying.

I approached the next potential customer. I lifted my hand and intended to speak, but I just... didn't? Then I noticed that the person had a deformity of the face. It was weird that I didn't notice that when I first saw him. No matter, though. Again, I went to say hello and roll into my pitch, but I still couldn't get the words out. He was getting closer now, and I suddenly noticed his arm was deformed too. It was overlong with angles and bends that most people don't have. I looked back at his face again and it had no symmetry to it. All of his features were out of place. I had one last chance to talk to him before he passed me, but the only thing that came out was a slight stutter, just the very beginning of a consonant. He lumbered away strangely.

I could get in trouble, because I was expected to pitch everyone. At the very least, I had to pitch the next person. Several more people were approaching, so I had my shot and was determined to make up for my fumble. I once again opened my mouth, but no words could exit. My thoughts were as clear as day, but my ability to verbally express them was simply gone. Aware of this now, I tried even harder to speak, but the words still would not come, as if I had somehow forgotten how to talk. I looked at another group of approaching customers and found once again that I was looking at strange abstractions of people. It was as if Picasso-esque portraits had come to life.

The world was quiet now. Slow, serene, cozy. The chatter and sounds of this echoey superstore were gone, replaced by a faint high-pitched ring.

Seeing someone that looked like the first man was not a common sight. Now, I had seen half a dozen folks like this within twenty seconds. This was no longer a coincidence. I looked back at my co-worker. The man who looked quite typical just minutes ago was now nightmare fuel. Shelves, boxes, and other items around me looked normal, still. It was clear now that there was nothing amiss with anyone. Something had gone awry with my perception of other humans. This was reinforced by the fact that I suddenly couldn't speak.

Strange sounds entered my ears, like a language I had never heard before.

My coworker morphed back into the form of his usual self. A slowness in time and an eerie muffledness faded gently back into normal life. The strange sounds were my coworker speaking to me. The speech made sense now; I understood again.

"Hey. *Hey!* Are you okay? You're not looking too good."

"I… I think,"—at least I could speak now—"I think something's wrong."

For lunch that day, I enjoyed what might be the most expensive salad ever.

That night I hit up a community cookout and talked to a doctor fellow I'd met previously through Kevin. He said it sounded to him like a concussion and that it would heal on its own in several months. He explained it more technically, but my takeaway was I had bruised my brain. I guess the car crash *had* given me whiplash.

It was interesting which part of my brain temporarily broke. Humans are hardwired to recognize other humans and find them familiar. That's why we see faces in clouds and grains of wood. It's why people see Jesus in toast. There was an internationally circulated news story about precisely that around this time. I had temporarily lost that. I saw how strange people really looked. Eyes are weird if you think about it. A nose is weird. A mouth is terrifying, even: puffed-up skin—some sort of fat wet snake in there—bones sticking out. For a moment, I saw these things as foreign rather than familiar.

DARKHORSE —
PART 4: SEVEN YEAR ITCH

AFTER A FEW DAYS, WE FINALLY GOT WORD from the insurance agencies: They declined to cover even one goddamn penny. As it turns out, the state we lived in was what the insurance company called a "1% state." If they could find even 1% fault with a party involved in the accident, the insurance company didn't have to cover that person. They'd just raise the rate and call it a day. You weren't technically costing them any more money, but they were happy to charge you more. 1% is a profoundly low bar: a 1% fault could be argued in most accidents.

"What about the police report?" I asked. "That's a legal document—the *only* legal document in this case—and it supports that your driver was at fault."

"A police report is just one of the tools we use to determine fault in an accident," the lady informed me.

"Wait, who decides who is at fault? Wouldn't that be the police who were present at the scene to investigate?"

"No, we as the insurance company decide who is at fault."

"Hold on, are you seriously telling me that everyone is legally required to carry insurance, but you can just decide on your own not to cover anyone if you don't want to? What are people paying you for, then?"

"We follow the law, and the law is that the insurance company gets to decide."

"What about the third person involved in the accident? Did you talk to him? Because he'd certainly support the account I've given you."

"Actually, the version of events he gave supports our case that you were at least 1% at fault."

"That can't be. I talked to him. What did he say?"

I didn't expect much from this question, but to my surprise, the agent gave me that person's version of the events word for word. What she reiterated was not only *not* what happened, it was not even what that same man had described to me only minutes after everything had gone down. He had changed his story—at least if the insurance company could be believed.

I had no recourse at this point, and just like that, I now personally owed Kevin an undetermined amount of money, depending on how much the repairs ended up being. Being poor, an unforeseen expense of even a few hundred dollars would set me back months. Only some weeks prior, I had worried about the cost of a lost *hoodie*. There's no way this wouldn't cost more. Hopefully, it was just the bent hood.

"One thing we can do for you," the insurance rep said, "is pay for a doctor's visit, and I'd encourage you to do that."

"How does that work? I don't have insurance."

"That's not a problem. We mail you a check that should cover the visit, so long as you send us the bill first."

Throughout this ordeal, my main motivation was to do right by Kevin. He was the only real friend I had in this town and my best friend of seven years. Anyone else I knew was through him. I wanted to fix this. I wanted him not to be upset with me, and I didn't want anything owed between us.

The writing was on the wall: This could easily go downhill in a variety of ways. I mentioned at the outset that this would be a story of a succession of all-time lows. This was the third one. It was July: my nightmare year was only about half over.

Seven long years
Into the void
Good memories
Being destroyed
They say with friends like these
Who needs enemies?

When a romantic relationship ends there are a lot of ways to talk about it. There are lots of outlets for that type of expression. Countless songs have been written about lost love. It's acceptable to talk about and to grieve. You expect to be sad. When you lose a best friend, lots of folks don't get it. It can take months to even realize you *should* be sad. There are no outlets, not many songs, no resources. I don't even know if we have the proper mechanics in our language to talk about it. When I say "lost love," you know exactly what I mean. When I say "lost friend" you might think I know someone who needs directions to get somewhere. What's the phrase? Nothing comes to mind.

When you lose a romantic relationship, you feel denial, then bargaining, then sadness, then sometimes anger, and hopefully—eventually—acceptance. You can move through these phases quickly. When you lose a friend, you move through these phases much slower. With nonexclusive arrangements like friendships, they could theoretically come back into your life at any time, right? This possibility can drag the denial phase out for a damn long time.

Maybe I was just spiraling. Maybe I wasn't about to lose my best friend. For me, the title "best friend" was the highest honor I could give a person. A car crash wouldn't change that if our roles were reversed. With everything this year was throwing at me, I did not need to lose my best friend, another pillar in my life, just to gain more emotional strength. I had already lost my love and my city, and access to everyone else I had ever known up to this point. I couldn't build any more character by surviving this misfortune. I had already maxed out my potential growth for strength.

At least I'm invincible now.

I could take anything life could throw at me, now, I thought, and this would be tested because life was about to throw a lot more. Ms. Fortune was only getting started.

A CANCER UPON THIS EARTH — PART 1: THE BLOWUP

KEVIN RETURNED HOME AND ANNOUNCED he had just gotten back from the mechanic. The hood had bent up but the car otherwise ran, so hopefully he had good news. It seemed reasonable to hope for a best-case scenario. Claire was home already.

"I think I had a concussion the other day," I mentioned. "I was at work, and suddenly it looked like everyone was deformed and I couldn't speak."

"Steve, you really should go to the doctor," Claire said.

"I talked to our doctor friend… if that counts."

"The other driver's insurance might pay for it," she advised.

"They did mention they'd cover that. Maybe I'll do that."

"It's not even worth it to fix the car," Kevin started, ignoring our conversation.

"Why wouldn't it be? It still drives. What all is wrong with it?" I asked.

He listed off a bunch of parts and issues. I knew next to nothing about cars at this point in my life, so didn't even know what most of these parts were. As an adult, I had only ever lived in Chicago where many agree a car isn't a necessity. I was too poor to have gotten my own car when I was a teen. I had only gotten my license on the theory of "Why not?"

When I was sixteen, I received a birthday card from my family with a key inside.

I was utterly confused: "Why is there a key in here?"

They let me sit there for like three minutes wondering and asking aloud why an old car key was in my birthday card.

"Did this get in here by accident? Is this yours? Or maybe yours? Who do we know with this brand of car?"

After they finally realized that I was too clueless to get it, they explained it to me: I was supposed to assume I had received a car for my sixteenth birthday, the joke being there was no car.

"Oh, we're way too poor to afford another car. I obviously am not getting a car, so that didn't even occur to me. Besides, I'm still on my learner's permit."

Car ownership would be out of my grasp for my whole life, I thought. There was an upfront cost, upkeep, gas, insurance, and so on. The only other hard, unskippable bill I'd ever had was rent, and so far I had struggled to make that nearly every month of my adult life. A car was not in the cards.

Back in the present, Kevin was listing off car parts: "...and the radiator is all bent and fucked up."

"Well, how much is that?"

"Too much to be worth it. He didn't even tell me."

"How about the hood?"

"That was the cheapest part. It's everything else that's the problem. The whole car is *totaled*. It would cost more to repair it than what it is worth."

"How much is the car worth? I fully intend on paying you for the value of the car if it can't be fixed."

"I don't know exactly… It was a gift from my grandpa. Even though it's twenty years old, it only had seventy thousand miles on it."

This tracked—it looked like how cars look when they sit in a hot driveway for years and years and only got used for trips to the grocery store once a week—but I got it. Fewer miles meant you could expect the car might last longer, despite its age.

"Okay, well we can look up the value. And whatever it is, I'll owe you that and pay you back as quick as I can."

For all the bad news, my friend was being pretty cool about all this so far. Yes, he was frustrated, but who wouldn't be? So was I, after all. Suddenly, Kevin just cleared the coffee table, swiping everything onto the floor. His action did not match his emotional state from a moment before, as if it was a calculated move rather than an emotional response.

"*What are we gonna do?!*" he yelled.

The way he said it felt like he was a student actor. He had raised his voice, but there was no emotion on his face. For a moment, I wondered if this was a terrible joke.

His girlfriend Claire was engaging with him now: "Kevin! Please stop!"

He found the remote on the TV stand and threw it on the ground. The batteries flew out and rolled across the floor. I no longer wondered: this was a genuine reaction.

"Stop throwing things!" Claire yelled.

Never mind me just some minor brain damage
You're the real victim here how do you manage

My role in this interaction had just changed. Kevin was showing an increasing level of violence. I put my hand in my pocket and readied it on my phone. I was no longer engaging him but monitoring the situation.

"We are so completely *fucked!* How are you going to get to your club to dance?!" he yelled.

He was pacing now, moving quickly between different rooms and areas in the house, finding new things to throw.

"We have another car! I'll use that!" his girlfriend reasoned back. The level of panic in her voice rose even further and tears began to stream down her face.

She followed him around frantically picking up the items he was throwing around the house. And, *oh yeah*, you read that right, reader: There were indeed *two cars*. I had previously driven the other car and it seemed perfectly fine.

"That old fucking thing can't make it that far! Remember when it overheated? We're totally screwed!" he screamed back, pulling plates, pots, and pans out of the dish rack and throwing them to the floor with a dramatic crash. He broke a drinking glass and a dinner plate in the process.

Claire was full-on sobbing now. He moved quickly, pacing between the living room and the kitchen. I wasn't engaging with him, but she was, and it seemed that was enough that she got all his wrath. My hand was still on my phone. I told myself that the exact moment he decided to hit her, I'd call 911 immediately. It seemed inevitable as the anger poured out of him.

"I'll go to the other club in town and dance there!" she cried back, following him.

Kevin was probably afraid that his girlfriend wouldn't be able to get to the strip club a town over, causing the household to lose most of its revenue stream. He wasn't working, she was.

"How am I supposed to get to school on the nights you dance?!" he yelled, continuing his rampage by pulling out a drawer in the kitchen. It fell to the floor and some of the silverware bounced out.

"We'll figure it out! I can go on different nights!" she reasoned back through tears.

I realize in retrospect that the second car made his whole reaction seem infantile, but for whatever reason that's how it went down. I'd also put together that they must have a joint bank account because Kevin spent money on dumb shit all the time, like those kayaks. Maybe he was afraid of losing that cash flow, I don't know. What I *do* know is that the other car had just made it over a hundred miles to the festival and back and didn't have any problems. It was reasonable to think it should be fine. But if he was concerned enough to ransack the house about it, maybe that was a bit of a miracle.

Never seen you so upset and bitter
One hand on my phone I really thought you might hit her

To absolutely no credit, Kevin did not hit his girlfriend Claire that day. He only used his violence on inanimate objects. I had never seen him like that before, and It might have been the lowest I'd seen him go. His actions were probably meant to intimidate Claire and me, but I was too busy making sure it didn't go any further than that if I was supposed to get the message.

Kevin stormed off. I helped Claire get the kitchen drawer he pulled out back in place and on its tracks. I helped her clean up the broken glass. She grabbed a broom. I cautioned that you're supposed to clean up broken glass with a wet cloth so that the shards of glass don't stick in the broom and come out later. We wiped it all up while Kevin fumed in another room. This was without a doubt the most vulnerable moment that Claire and I shared.

A CANCER UPON THIS EARTH —
PART 2: TRYING TO FIX THIS

I ENDED UP GOING TO THE HOSPITAL TO SEE A DOCTOR in an official capacity. I didn't learn anything more than what the doctor friend had told me when I talked to him at the cookout. They didn't even do any tests. I got the bill sent out to the insurance company.

I found out that there was a store that you could go to and look at the Blue Book of car values, so I went there to figure out how much I owed Kevin. With the car and some accrued rent from my time job searching, it looked like I owed my friend around seventeen hundred dollars. Depending on your income level, this number is either devastating or inconsequential. But for me, this would take a lot of work.

Taking a page from my own book, I was back on Reddit, asking folks in the local city group if anyone would be willing to lend our household a car. I didn't know anyone locally well enough that I felt I could ask for such a favor, or who seemed like they could go without a vehicle.

As of writing, the mere thought of asking strangers on a message board if they'd be willing to lend me a car seems *utterly insane*. Maybe that serves as an indicator of how desperate I was at that moment. Internet panhandling was my absolute, *last* fucking resort. The thought of doing it only occurred when I had literally nowhere else to turn. Unlike last time, I didn't have any professional services to bank on, because I didn't need to get paid, I just needed to borrow a car.

I wrote a gut-spilling overlong post and amazingly one guy was willing to help. His name was Phillip, and he was absolutely saintly. He had a car but could take the bus if needed. We worked something out where we could use his car most days unless he needed it otherwise. He wasn't even worried about gas. It was everything we needed at that moment. To be able to come to Kevin with a development like this was a game-changer.

I had a pretty low overhead at this point, at least. I calculated how long it would take me to pay back Kevin. If I stayed on a shoestring budget and gave my friend like 80-90% of my money, I could get this out of the way and we'd be back to the good times in like two months.

That was the worst case. The *best* case would be to hit up my old boss; he still owed me a *ton* of back pay that would cover this in one lump sum, with extra to spare. It was almost as if it was a *good* thing he owed me money. Not only did I have a plan, but I also had a backup plan. I was good. Things were going to work out.

I gave my old boss from Chicago a call.

"Oh hey, Steve. How's life in your new town? I've been wondering how you are because that's what thoughtful people like myself do. I can probably send you the remainder of the money I owe you if that's what you're calling about. I guess we could do a money order. Does that work?"

"I'm good, thank you," I replied, "and that's perfect, actually. I really need that money right now because I was just in a car accident."

"Oh, holy shit. *Are you okay?* I am singularly concerned with your well-being in this situation, as any decent person should be."

"Yes, thank you for asking. It's very thoughtful of you to say that, and unsurprising given your character as a human being. I'm overall fine. I just need to pay for repairs on the car I was driving. It was actually my roommates."

"I'm just glad you're okay. Let me get you all taken care of today! I'll let you know once I have the transfer information. I'll start working on that now."

The above phone conversation is, of course, a *complete* fantasy, beyond a Lord of the Rings level of mysticism, leveraging a suspension of disbelief too great for most audiences to accept even in fantasy fiction.

In actuality, I had to leave a message, and my old boss never returned the call, as usual. I called my old boss about needing money all the time. Sometimes he came through, and sometimes he wasn't good for it. Since I left Chicago, though, I hadn't heard back from him once. Our only form of communication since then was my phone going out and me leaving angry voicemails from Google Voice on my laptop about how my service was going out at the worst time.

There was only one good move now, and that was to sue the guy who caused the accident. I could pay back my friend with my own money and then sue the guy to recoup my losses. The idea of suing someone was purely a theoretical concept to me. I looked up how to do it. All the information I needed was on the police report. I found out that you didn't need a lawyer, there was a filing fee of a hundred and fifty dollars, and the losses you claimed had to be greater than a thousand dollars, which they were.

All I needed was Kevin's co-operation. I just needed him to attest that I was paying him back or had paid him back; otherwise, I'd have no argument. After all, it wasn't my car, but Kevin's car. Without his cooperation he'd get both my money from paying him back and the money from the small claims suit, I figured. I went to the courthouse. I got a few copies of the police report. I got the form I needed to file a civil case.

I was now balancing on a thin tightrope. Everything needed to go perfectly from here on out. But all I needed was my best friend at my side. It didn't seem like much to ask. If our roles were reversed, I'd have done the same for him. I was sure he knew that and would return it in kind.

A CANCER UPON THIS EARTH — PART 3: A WARNING

I NEVER WANTED TO LEAVE CHICAGO: NOT REALLY. I MEAN, I hated that city now because of how it treated me, but still, not *really*. The only reason I left was because of a perfect storm of misfortunes that had soured me on my life there, and my best friend Kevin's well-timed exit offer. At that point, I hadn't seen him in over a year, so I missed him.

Not everyone was a big fan of Kevin, and I got that. He'd burned a lot of bridges in his past. If you were only familiar with the dramatic headlines of his history, sure, it'd be reasonable to say: "Hey Steven, don't move in with that guy. "However, I was working from a more day-to-day view of him when I accepted the offer. I saw a lot more than just those dramatic moments that made the gossip.

The last time I saw him in the flesh before I moved in with him, he was full of regret and trying to make amends with people. That implied he was through hurting people. The last major interaction I had with him otherwise was when he helped me and Gemma avoid homelessness when we were short on rent that one month. He saved me then, and he kind of did again by offering me a new start in a new town.

I have another friend, Alex, who always reminds me that he warned me against moving in with Kevin back when it was still just an offer. For credit where credit is due, "best friend" is not an exclusive title in my world. I usually have like two or three best friends most of the time. Even so, the title is not given lightly. It's worth mentioning that Alex is my best friend, too. In the world of Steve, Alex is a key player. He has gravitas. When he shows up, a theme song plays. He may not be a key character in the story of this year of my life, but this should be considered a big-name cameo that either needs to for sure be in the movie trailer or kept tightly under wraps as a nice surprise for audiences.

Since I don't explicitly recall the conversation where Alex warned me not to move in with Kevin, I'll have to embellish the details somewhat with my best guess as to how it might have gone. It happened about a month before I moved. The following may or may not be historically accurate:

The floor cracks around me, and devilish hands rise from the fissures. I am suddenly surrounded by undead creatures with hellish features. All hope is lost, it seems, as the shadows of these unholy monsters descend upon me. The ceiling crumbles in my Chicago apartment. Ominous clouds are seen through the newfound hole.

The clouds part! A ray of sunlight pours through and shines brightly on the exposed floor of my apartment. Its brilliance is so blinding that it appears like a stripe of white disrupting reality. Disembodied angels sing sustained notes, harkening to the arrival of the savior: *Alex*.

He rides down on the sunbeam, covered in shining platinum armor that reflects the sunlight brilliantly, so brilliantly that Alex tosses me a pair of dope-ass sunglasses. I put them on; I look fly as hell.

His armor barely contains his muscular physique. It is said that Dwayne "The Rock" Johnson comes to Alex for workout tips and only gets roles because Alex turns them down first. Alex sits atop a white horse. He is so jacked that the horse is also jacked by proxy; it has legs as wide and as strong as tree trunks. The horse is wearing roller skates because, obviously, that makes this even more awesome. Alex holds a big-ass sword in one hand, and the horse skates around as Alex rides, in a spectacular feat of agility.

The horse is doing flips and shit. He's got his roller skaties. Enemies fall with the flick of Alex's wrist as he wields his big-ass sword atop the majestic horse, skating around at impressive speeds, with moves more agile than a horse *not* wearing roller skates would be capable of. The heads of hellspawns fly as Alex uses minimal effort to dispose of each foe. I am safe yet again!

Alex comes to a smooth stop before me, the horse's roller skates barely even scratching the wood floor. He removes his gleaming helmet, beard flowing majestically in the wind, and the music stops suddenly as the camera closes in on his face. There's a dramatic pause before he speaks. This is the big cameo the audience has been waiting for. His mouth begins to open in dramatic slow motion! What wisdom will Alex impart?

"Sup?" Alex asks.

"Nothing much," I answered. "You?"

"Same. Same. Just thought I'd see what's going on with you."

"Oh, well actually I do have news, come to think of it."

"Yeah?"

"I'm gonna move in with Kevin, across the country. I'm just sick of Chicago right now and the job market sucks here."

"Seems like a terrible idea."

"What, why?"

"C'mon, you know what he's like."

I paused. What does that even mean? …Oh. Right. *That*. I almost forgot about all that.

"I know what you are talking about and I know that was some fucked up shit Kevin did, but that was years ago and he has shown a lot of remorse for those actions."

"Even if he has, still. You know what he's capable of."

"I'm certain I've earned a level of loyalty from him that would make me immune to that kind of backlash. Besides, with this job market, it's either this or move back home, and I will do literally anything before I move back to that shitty town."

"You do what you gotta do, homeskillet. But when shit goes south, don't say I didn't warn you."

Alex then departs upon his horse, up the ray of sunlight and back into the clouds from whence he came. The clouds dissipate into a sunny day. I hear birds chirping outside. The world is safe again.

"Hey!" I shout to the heavens through the hole in the ceiling, "Were you gonna fix this fucking roof or something, please?"

Through the hole in the ceiling, I hear Alex reply, shouting as if he were a regular dude on the sidewalk outside and just so happened to hear me: "Oh shit, my bad."

The rubble floats up and returns to the ceiling as if it had never been broken.

That's *probably* how it went, anyway. As I said, I don't quite remember. If it didn't go down like that, then maybe we were chatting on a messenger service of some kind.

It tracked that he'd have warned me, though, and based on how Alex tells it, there was probably at least a horse.

A CANCER UPON THIS EARTH —
PART 4: WE NEED TO TALK ABOUT KEVIN

FOR CONTEXT, WE NEED TO TALK ABOUT KEVIN. I must give a full history lesson on my best friend.

Whether I knew it consciously at the time or not, I had a *pretty good idea* of some of the ways the car crash situation could go wrong. I knew what Kevin could be like when he was mad at someone, and it wasn't pretty. There were things I saw my friend do that I had reasoned away, or assumed he had grown past, regretted, and learned from. This context is going to make me sound like an idiot, too, like the writing was everywhere, all over every wall.

There were definitely signs, but years could go by with nothing but good times. Some years, he was living elsewhere on account of his wanderlust, and we were nothing but conversations that started and ended with "I miss you, dude." The last thing Kevin did for me before I moved in with him was to save me and Gemma from homelessness. He'd been shitty to *others*, but he had a ton of good credit built up with *me*.

As far as the accident, I didn't think I was the party that had wronged my friend, so I thought he'd have no reason to be mad at me, specifically. But, there's a pattern of behavior. Without this context—this history— what happens next in the nightmare year might seem, to be frank, too goddamn insane.

All these accounts will take us back to Chicago, some years before the nightmare year.

Three years before the nightmare year.

One such sign happened on the morning that I was set to shoot 80% of the footage for my senior film project. It was the most important project in all of film school, and I couldn't graduate without it. It took a month of planning. I managed to pull together the A-team of camera people at my school, including Tom (the fellow that Gemma would later berate for collecting unemployment). At this point, Kevin had already dropped out. I wanted his help because including my close friends on projects makes them kind of special to me. I also thought he might want to keep his chops up while he was out of school. He agreed, and he wanted to help. It was a pretty early shoot, but he made it clear he was down to help.

My whole crew met up with me near the school. Everyone was there—a couple of camera people, a few other crew folks, and my actors—everyone except my best friend Kevin. We had about twenty-five minutes to catch a suburban electric train to our shoot location in Indiana. I gave Kevin a call:

"Hey man, where are you at?"

"Shit. I'm sorry, my alarm on my phone didn't go off."

"Well, we still have some time. If you can get out the door in the next few minutes you might make it."

"Okay," I heard him shuffling through some things. "You know what, I can't find my train card either. And I'm pretty low on funds. You said we had to get on another train too, is that right? How much is *that*?"

"I'm paying for all of that. If you can come up with the two dollars and twenty-five cents to get here I'll pay you back for that too. This is a skeleton crew; I really need you."

"I actually can't find my *entire wallet* right now, dude. This is a *big problem* for me."

"Well, now it's a big problem for me too. This is a skeleton crew. Everyone has a specific job."

"What will you do if I can't find my wallet?"

"I don't know what I'll do. I really needed everybody on this."

We had to leave without him, though we did find a way to manage.

A week or two later, Kevin admitted he never lost his wallet: He just didn't want to wake up that early. He even admitted that he sat there on the phone shuffling stuff around pretending to look for it. I let him know that this was extremely shitty of him. Kevin agreed and readily admitted he was a piece of shit for that and needed to work on it. He had essentially apologized, even if the words "I'm sorry" didn't quite arrive, so I let it go.

That wasn't the first sign, though, or even close to the worst. Let's go back in time even further...

WAR I: PATRICK

Five years before the nightmare year.

Kevin used to throw fairly legendary parties at his apartment. It was college, after all, and these were our classic college years. At this point, I hadn't yet graduated and Kevin hadn't yet dropped out.

Even as I write this now, it's not hard to look back on these gatherings with nostalgia. It felt cool to be Kevin's friend. He was so outgoing that I could make friends just by hanging out with him. I met him at the perfect time because my last college friend group started hanging out less and less, for no particular reason.

Kevin so effortlessly brought people together that being his close friend immediately put me at the epicenter of one of the two main social circles at our film school. It wasn't long before I realized I was spending the majority of my social time with Kevin. Nearly everyone in our major attended the weekly parties he threw, and those quickly became the highlight of every one of my weeks. Everyone knew Kevin and I were a staple duo at our school. I even met and dated a girl named Elisa for over a year because she wanted someone to accompany her to one of Kevin's parties, and she decided to hand-pick me as her date. For a good long while, Kevin was awesome.

After about six months of seeing Kevin pretty regularly, I came to feel like he was a best friend to me. I told him this, and he reciprocated the sentiment. I already had a well-established ethic that anyone I deemed a best friend would get nearly unconditional loyalty from me. At this point in my life, best friendships had always outlasted any of the romantic relationships I'd been in, so best friendships felt like the pinnacle of chosen relationships. I told him that too, and he pledged the very same loyalty to me.

Kevin frequently took needless attention-grabbing risks. The first such risk I was witness to was Kevin jumping out of his fourth-floor window onto the rooftop across the alley. He got a handful of other guys to do it too. He tried to get me to follow, but I declined. I didn't doubt I could do it, but the risk of falling four floors definitely far outweighed the reward of... being on a roof? If I were to do it, I would've preferred to be wearing clothing that was a little more conducive to my mobility. So I gave him my answer:

"I'm not wearing my jumping pants."

It became an inside joke between us.

"Can you come out tonight?" or "How do you feel about going in on a pizza?"

If the answer was no, there was a chance I'd come back with: "I'm not wearing my jumping pants."

Another inside joke we had revolved around Kevin's attachment to his astrological sign. "I'm [like this or that] because I'm a Cancer," he often said.

"Ah, yes," I'd reply, "You are a Cancer upon this earth!"

"I am indeed a Cancer upon this earth," he often replied.

Kevin had a roommate, Patrick, who recalls that he might have been among those who jumped across the roof. Patrick also went to the same school as us, as a different major. He was a mainstay at the parties. It probably helped that he lived there. I became good friends with him as well.

Patrick was a big stoner and was usually the chillest guy in the room. If he wasn't in the room, I was usually the chillest guy in the room. For Patrick that counted for a lot, because I had a reputation for being unflappable, and yet he did it better. He was very intellectual, but more pragmatic and less high-minded than Kevin and I, whereas I was probably somewhere between the two.

Kevin and Patrick had another friend named Valerie. She also went to school with us and had a kind of valley-girl vibe. She was rather bubbly and always had an infectious smile on her face. She was generally well-liked and seemed to put a lot of guys under a spell just by being around.

Patrick had a no-fucks-given attitude, so he was initially unaffected by the spell Valerie otherwise projected. However, over several weeks and several parties, Patrick and Valerie grew more attracted to each other. If Patrick—the most unflappable guy in school—was even somewhat fazed around Valerie, perhaps that was the best validation she could receive. They were an unlikely couple, but it got serious when, apparently, she just decided that she lived with Patrick now, and that was that. No discussion, no questions.

Valerie was also a self-described sex addict. When she first said that, I wasn't sure how seriously to take it. When she and Patrick were dating, she mentioned that she hadn't gone without sex for more than a week since the age of sixteen. That gave him pause when he remembered she had recently been out of town for *two* weeks. To the best of my recollection, she confessed to me that going two weeks without sex was incredibly difficult, but that she managed to be faithful while she was away.

One fateful day, Kevin told me that the dynamic in the apartment suddenly broke down over the weekend.

"Something happened between me and Patrick," he started. "We are not friends anymore. He did something that seriously hurt me to my very core, and I *need you* on my side with this."

It sounded serious, but it was hard to imagine Patrick fucking anyone over. Kevin said he went out and got himself a nightstand one morning.

Kevin returned to the apartment with it and decided he might like help carrying it up the stairs, so he called Patrick.

"Hey man, can you help me carry something up the stairs? I'm just outside."

"I probably shouldn't," Patrick said, "I'm pretty sick right now and should probably take it easy."

So Kevin hauled it up four flights of stairs. It was a lot of work and he was exhausted when he got up to the apartment. When he finally got through the door, the first thing he saw was Patrick sitting on the couch smoking weed. I can safely assume this was a pretty common sight in that household because Patrick was marijuana incarnate.

As Kevin recounted the story to me, he ended it on that note: "...and he was just sitting there... smoking weed."

There was a pause. There must be more, I thought. But he's wasn't saying more words.

"Wait," I asked, "so do you think he was lying about being sick?"

"No, it's not that. It was the *way* he was sitting there. Just the *fact* that he was smoking and not, like, in bed resting. If he could smoke weed, he could've helped me carry something."

"Dude, it's Patrick. His default state is smoking marijuana. There is no additional information you can glean from that. Also, I'm pretty sure smoking weed is a lot less strenuous than carrying a nightstand up four goddamn flights of fucking stairs."

"I need you to understand just *how much* that hurt me," he said, over-emphasizing his words and gesturing broadly to try and sell me on his sadness. In return, I was clear with him that I was dead sure he was overreacting.

According to Patrick, things progressed slightly differently from his vantage point. He was unaware that the above situation was the breaking point for Kevin. He was probably similarly unaware that Kevin was going around our school and trying to sell this as the reason that everyone should hate Patrick now.

Patrick recalled getting more stingy about chores and household expenses and saying to Kevin: "Maybe you shouldn't use my dishes if they are just going to sit dirty in your room for days."

Maybe that was a bit harsh, but the place it came from was fair enough.

Within a few days, Patrick and Valerie broke up and she started sleeping on the couch. According to Patrick's version of events, she had cheated on him with some other random guy and he broke up with her. (I recall her admitting to the cheating as well.) Perhaps the sex addiction was legit.

Kevin, meanwhile, took advantage of her sex addiction: he ended up more or less together with Valerie within a couple of days, and she started staying in his room. In Kevin's version of the events, he claimed to have seduced her into cheating on Patrick, as part of Kevin's evolving revenge scheme against Patrick. Looking at both sides, Patrick's version makes way more sense.

Depressed, Patrick found himself sleeping most of the day. He was, of course, working on moving out as well. He was able to secure a new place within a couple of weeks. He even got a form from the landlord to release him from the lease. He just needed his former roommates to sign it, which was a small ask since they probably wanted him out just as much as he wanted to be out.

As the events of this situation made their way around the school, Kevin was somehow shocked to find that he got very little sympathy and that everyone had sided with Patrick. The parties stopped. Would anyone even come? I still hung out with him, but what I thought about what he did to Patrick was no secret: I told Kevin all the time he had majorly fucked up. He was ever stubborn though: Kevin maintained that Patrick had earned any revenge he got because this was the most betrayal Kevin had ever felt. All that for not helping him move a piece of furniture.

Over the next few weeks, Kevin's behavior escalated. Yeah, the Valerie thing wasn't *enough* revenge for him. He casually asked me one day if I'd be down to help—*uuuh*—physically assault Patrick. I politely declined. He said he was trying to get a group of guys together to wear masks and jump Patrick when he was out around town. He'd even figured out where Patrick had moved to.

Kevin claimed he already had one guy on board, someone I knew to be quite mild-mannered: our friend Tom. The same Tom that my *future* girlfriend Gemma (at this point in time) would later offend at a party because he collected unemployment. Chill as all-fuck Tom… apparently was down for masked assault. I couldn't imagine Tom agreeing to do something like this; it was completely against his character. In retrospect, Kevin was probably totally lying. It was just a sales tactic: If one person was on board, others were more likely to agree. The plan to assault Patrick luckily never came to fruition.

Meanwhile, Kevin was officially with Valerie now. During this whole time, he also had a "girlfriend" who lived in Europe whom he kept stringing along. Every once and a while he got a call from her and disappeared for forty minutes or so. It was kind of an open secret, but by the time I found out, blowing the whistle on that didn't seem like it was worth sabotaging our friendship over. (I definitely told him that was shitty, though.)

Patrick later confirmed that Kevin started sending him harassing texts and voicemails, one starting with: "You should hear what Valerie says about you now." This fell on deaf ears as Patrick had absolutely no respect for Kevin's *or* Valerie's opinion of him at this point, and he didn't read further than that.

Kevin began threatening people who talked about it, but most folks were undeterred.

"If he didn't want people hearing the truth, then he shouldn't have done those things," one mutual friend said.

Kevin tried to get me to stop being friends with some of these people out of loyalty to him. It was a tough sell, though, since I agreed with everyone else that Kevin had absolutely fucked up in every way with Patrick, and eventually, Kevin gave up on it.

Kevin and Valerie abandoned the apartment they shared with Patrick after they failed to find another roommate to share the space. Without a third roommate, the rent was far too expensive. They hadn't signed or returned the document that would remove Patrick from the lease, either by malice or laziness (but probably malice). Years later, the landlord came after them for unpaid rent. Somehow, Patrick was the one that got stuck with the bill, totaling well into the thousands. It may have simply been a case of him being the only one to bite, or the other two being harder to find.

Back then, I reasoned that I could be friends with both Kevin and Patrick. I had no intention of helping Kevin with any of his Patrick-related revenge plans, and I actively talked him down from escalating things further. Strangely, this cemented our friendship further. I felt Kevin had potential as a force of good in the world, and just needed some coaxing to do the right thing sometimes.

I took it upon myself to be the angel on his shoulder. Perhaps the stuff with Patrick would've turned out worse if I wasn't there. I felt that encouraging my friend's better nature was a noble cause, and in hindsight, that's why I stuck around. Kevin took notice as other friends dropped off like flies, which probably cemented our friendship on his end as well. At least once, I agreed to hang out with him simply to check on the Patrick situation and de-escalate it if needed.

It was important to me to show loyalty to friends; it just seemed intrinsically good, so I never thought about needing to justify it. Loyalty to friends meant that I wouldn't help Kevin take any revenge on my friend Patrick. It also meant that I wouldn't stop being friends with Kevin. It also meant that if Kevin ever got any nefarious plot against Patrick off the ground, I might have to warn Patrick about it. Kevin, however, seemed to lose interest in his revenge plots against Patrick after a few months.

WAR II: VALERIE

Four and a half years before the nightmare year.

Very soon after the incident with Patrick, Kevin and Valerie found a cheaper apartment and moved in together, but their relationship did not last much longer. They broke up, and she moved on with another partner. Kevin did the same with a woman named Kat, and Valerie quickly moved in with her new boyfriend. Once again, Kevin had trouble finding a new roommate.

Kevin's reputation at school was in ruins and his grades started to slip. He had to work more hours at his line cooking job to keep up with the extra rent, and couldn't afford to miss work to go to school. I reminded him that our school made it easy to create a class load that only required you to attend two days a week. Most students did just that.

"Why don't you just change your availability at work? It's just two days. It's not a big ask," I suggested.

"I'm not sure that's something you can do," he reasoned back.

Weirdly, he seemed unfamiliar with the concept of availability at a job.

"I mean, of course it is. Besides, if you don't fix this soon, you'll fail out for not hitting the attendance requirements."

And that was exactly what happened. I didn't see him for months, and as a result, my social life became much emptier.

Then, sometime the following year, without warning, I ran into him in the hallway at school. He told me he'd convinced the staff to re-admit him, even though their policy dictated that he was ineligible to re-enroll. I told him we should hang out, but he acted mopey and dismissive. I'd never seen him more depressed, but I was just happy he was back.

For whatever-the-fuck reason, Kevin immediately made the exact same mistake, missed a bunch of classes, and failed out *again*. Perhaps his reputation was still tarnished, and other students made that clear. Maybe that explained his mood.

He never filled Valerie's old room, and at some point, he became unemployed. With no other choice, he planned to move back home, hundreds of miles away. This happened right at the beginning of the big recession that would eventually flip my life upside down. He was one of the first people I knew who bailed on the city. He certainly wouldn't be the last.

I'd only seen him twice in nine months at the point of his exit. I was sure I'd never see him again. I agreed to help him pack up and load the truck in part because it was my final opportunity to see him before he left. When I arrived, I found I was the only one there to help. Usually, he had no trouble gathering up people, so I was surprised.

"Is it going to be just you and me?" I asked.

"Honestly, I think you might be the only real friend I have left in this town. So yeah. You're the only one I asked, and you're the only one I figured would show up anyway."

"What about Valerie and her boyfriend? Aren't you still friends with them?" I asked.

Kevin explained that they were not friends anymore because he resented Valerie, not for leaving the relationship, but because she left the *apartment*. Apparently, his resentment had snowballed into yet another revenge scheme.

Recycling his revenge plot on Patrick, he told me he was moving mid-lease without even telling the landlord. Valerie was still on the lease, and he'd stick her with the bill just like they had done to Patrick. I warned her about this, but the damage was already done. Valerie ended up on the hook for the back rent pretty quickly. It would be another few years before the previous apartment caught up with Patrick.

So that was that: Kevin moved away. The mere concept of visiting someone who lived states away seemed impossibly expensive back then. He might as well have moved to another planet. I was convinced the chapter of my life that included Kevin was over.

War III: Lola

Three years before the nightmare year.

I had an on-and-off girlfriend named Lola. We got together a few separate times trying to see if we could make things work. At that time, we were together. She and Kevin were also acquainted as we all went to school together.

As a sort of surprise, Lola invited me over one day and said there was "someone" at her house that I'd want to see. I arrived, and there was my best friend Kevin. Lola had a ridiculously large living room (or "front room" in Chicago vernacular) with a bunk bed for the occasional guest and Kevin slept on that. Three other roommates lived there as well.

Kevin wanted to move back to Chicago. He just needed a place to stay while he figured out a job and an apartment. He aggressively searched for both and found himself all over the city for many hours on any given day. He took and made so many calls that he had an extra battery and battery charger for his cell phone. By all accounts, he was *on it*.

I met him downtown one rainy day for lunch. On the cab ride back, he randomly asked me:

"Would you be mad if I slept with your ex from college? I have not slept with your ex, to be clear: just asking, for now."

The ex he was talking about was Elisa. I was with her near the end of college and had more or less met her at one of his parties. Although there's no way she would have gone for Kevin, that wasn't really the point. We were together for about a year and a half, things grew stale, and I found myself back with Lola again.

"Dude… no," I replied. "Don't sleep with friends' exes. Standard bro code. It never goes well."

"I don't believe in that kind of stuff. Just let people do what they do, and don't make a big deal out of it. If you slept with one of my exes I'd be okay with it, you know."

I was speaking from experience because I had previously been on both sides of the "bro code" situation, and each time strained the hell out of another very important friendship. I considered it a lesson learned. I told the story to Kevin, and how it reinforced my reasoning.

"Alright, alright. I get it," he said, "I don't agree with that type of stuff, but I have a lot of respect for you, so out of respect I won't try anything." And to his credit, he didn't.

The thing is, though, Kevin had already done something similar with Lola without my blessing...

About a year prior.

It happened at a Halloween party Lola threw, before we were together this time, but after we were together the last time. She was single. I was with Elisa. Lola was anxious about whether anyone would show up to her party. Kevin was among those in attendance. Lola was happy to have such a good turnout because she'd never thrown a party before.

At the party, I noticed Kevin and Lola dancing. I asked them both to please not make it weird between us three by getting romantic in whatever capacity, and they both vaguely agreed not to get entangled. I wasn't sure if I had the right to police other people's romantic relationships, but it felt like I could ask them as friends, since I wouldn't do that to either of them. It felt weirder still to ask since I was with Elisa romantically at the time and she was there with me at the party.

Elisa, as usual, hated *every moment* she had to hang out with my friends and dragged me home early. Back at the party, the rest happened later without my knowledge. It was a sexual fling that only lasted a single weekend. In my view it was basically a proximity thing: it happened just because they were there.

Lola called me a few days after the fact, upset about something, but really dodgy about the details. I asked her what exactly was wrong, and she got defensive at the very question, so I still had no idea. Then it didn't come up for a while.

Lola came clean about the fling something like nine months later. She really wanted my forgiveness. I forgave her as the friend she was. Maybe I was okay with it because I was still with Elisa both at the time it happened and when I found out. Given that, I'd cemented the idea in my head that Lola was just a friend, and she could do what she wanted.

Lola explained that she was sure the fling between her and Kevin was the start of a relationship. She was a real heart-on-her-sleeve type. She'd probably tell you she was more naïve back then. To Kevin, it was always just a fling. None of that was communicated up front, so Lola got her feelings hurt. Then, some months after that, Kevin moved away as described prior.

Kevin didn't live in Chicago anymore when I found out, and I didn't know if I'd ever see him again, so it wasn't a grudge worth holding. However, I figured I'd have to clear the air with Kevin, just so there'd be no bad blood there. When I mentioned this Lola asked me not to tell him I knew, so I didn't. I let it be.

In hindsight, there's many ways this could've played out that would've damaged my friendship with Kevin, but by whatever chance, it played out in the one way that didn't. As for Lola, I was basically never going to hold this against her. Intentional or not, Lola basically got played.

Back to three years before the nightmare year.

When Lola and I got together again, that was already water under the bridge. Even now, at this pertinent moment with Kevin in the cab, after he asked me if I'd have a problem with him attempting to sleep with my ex Elisa, I didn't bring it up. Lola had always been a friend first and I was keeping my promise to my friend not to tell him. It was also difficult to put much weight onto the question because I was confident Elisa wouldn't be into that, anyway.

Later, I asked Lola what she thought about all this. Last I heard, she was not happy with him at all. Hadn't she still been mad at Kevin for how he handled their brief fling?

"Well I was," she admitted to me, "but it's been long enough that I just didn't want to be upset about it anymore. Besides, I have you now."

"Yeah, but isn't offering him a place to stay a little much?"

"No, I don't think so, because I know how much you missed your best friend, and I just wanted to help him move back so you guys could be friends again. Also, this is *very* temporary. I'm not even giving him a key."

"Oh, I see. I guess I didn't fully put that together. I'm glad he's back though, so thank you."

Okay, readers. We're taking bets. What happens next in this one? The chapter has "war" in the title after all. It's twenty to one in favor of my best friend trying to put moves on Lola again, or her trying to get with him, right? What else could it even *be*? Should I do a page break for suspense; make you turn that page to find out? Or maybe I could talk about something else while people make their bets? Yeah, let's do that.

Kevin arrived back from another long day of apartment and job searching.

"I think I have a lead on a job. I interviewed at two places today. I feel good about one of them for sure. Maybe both of them."

"Well I hope you can make this work, I'd love to have you back around."

"I'd love to be back around. I missed the heck out of you, dude."

Kevin suddenly realized he couldn't find his spare battery and battery charger for his proto-smartphone. He looked all through his bags, everything: no sign of it. The next day, he went out again looking for work, but also retraced his steps to see if he left his stuff anywhere. He came back that evening defeated about it.

"I couldn't find my battery. I can barely get through the day on my main battery. It cost me like seventy-five bucks and I can't afford to replace it right now."

One of Lola's roommates, Sean, arrived home. Sean made some small talk with us, then got a phone call and went into his room.

Kevin leaned over to me, sure to keep his voice down: "Hey man, did you notice he had the same phone as me? You don't think he'd have taken my battery pack, do you?"

"Why would he just steal something from someone staying in his apartment, though?" I reasoned. "It's too risky."

"I don't know, but he has the same phone: That's motive. He could've gone through my stuff at any point while I was out: That's opportunity."

"I don't think just having the same phone counts as motive, dude."

That's right, reader. You've all lost your bets, this is 100% about fucking phone batteries now. No infidelity occurred. The war was with Sean. Lola was just a casualty.

I had seen my friend do shitty things before, just never directly to me. Lola could get caught up in the moment, but above all else, she was faithful as a partner, maybe even to a fault. That's not where this is going.

Over the next few days, Kevin grew increasingly suspicious of Lola's roommate Sean. He was convinced that since Sean had the same phone he must have taken his battery. Sean denied taking it. While Sean was gone, Kevin very stupidly, and against my advice, went through all of Sean's things in his room. He found nothing.

Sean noticed his stuff had been moved around and confronted Kevin: "Did you go through my stuff? I told you I didn't take your charger!"

Kevin denied it. But Sean knew. Kevin even admitted he made it obvious someone had gone through Sean's stuff. He *wanted* him to know. As Kevin grew increasingly frustrated that he couldn't find his spare battery pack, he also became increasingly bold with Sean.

Without warning, Kevin went through Sean's stuff *again*. This time, he stole a digital camera, reasoning that it probably had a similar value to his battery pack and he could pawn it to recoup his losses. By the time Lola and I found out, it was already pawned. At this point, there was no chance of tempering anyone's mood. Kevin once again took things too far.

For Sean, the damage was done. He moved out in a huff of anger one afternoon without warning, rightly furious that someone in the apartment felt they had the right to steal his things. Lola constantly apologized all the while. Lola and her remaining roommates were, of course, less than happy with Kevin. The situation put another timer on his ability to stay there.

Kevin still tried to lay down roots in Chicago, but couldn't get it done. Utterly defeated, and disappointed in himself that he couldn't pull it off, he retreated once again to his parent's place. Left in his wake were Lola and two other roommates who suddenly had to make up a deficit in rent. It took them two whole months to get someone in that room. Everyone struggled significantly to make up the deficit. I saw it every time I was over. Extra shifts, borrowing money for rent. Kevin regretted how things played out, but his remorse did not extend to Sean. He was convinced Sean was the culprit, and that justice had ultimately been served.

My best friend was gone *again*, and I thought I'd never see him *again*, so I didn't think it was worth my energy to have any strong negative feelings about this. The quick succession of my best friend returning, the escalation with Sean, Sean leaving in a huff, and my best friend in turn leaving again all gave me a sort of emotional whiplash. In the sudden absence of the constant drama, things were abruptly quiet. I didn't talk to him much for a good few months after that.

Lola and I ended up together for another few months and lost our steam again for unrelated reasons. We once again reverted to friends and each moved on. Lola ended up moving to Hawaii about six months before the nightmare year. We stayed in touch all the while.

The pattern I saw then, was that Kevin would go nuclear on people who he perceived wronged him in some way, to a level I've never seen before or since. What I didn't realize then is that all the people he went nuclear on were also his *roommates*. I was completely unaware I'd inserted myself into such a dangerous category in the nightmare year.

So that's that one. If Kevin ended up getting with Lola, like, *while her and I were dating*, there's no way we'd still be friends. There's no way I'd have moved in with him in my nightmare year. But, nope. All this bullshit over a *phone battery*.

I was not the wronged party here, so I still thought I was above my best friend's wrath. The unhinged things he did to Patrick, Valerie, Sean/Lola, and others were things he wouldn't do to me because of the loyalty I was sure we had for each other.

I was above it.

I was sure of that.

At the time.

Peacetime

A year and a half before the nightmare year.

About a year after the previous incident, Kevin rang me up one evening. Most likely we hadn't talked in at least a few weeks at that point.

"Are you free tonight?"

"I guess so, but… you don't live here, so… why would you ask?"

"I do now. Surprise, dude!"

Kevin was back in Chicago trying to make a comeback, yet again. He did not want to make the same mistake as before, so this time he had a place, some savings, and only had to look for work. I had been single for a few months. I worked at a sales job making pennies on the hour sometimes. Kevin kept trying to get back together with his ex, Kat. He somehow convinced Kat's sister—of all people—to let him have an empty room in her apartment and split the rent.

Kevin wanted to have a night out with friends. To the best of my recollection, it was a bridge too far for Kat and she did not attend. Her sister was there, though, and so was I. Another mutual friend from school, Dan, was there too. Dan was pretty good friends with Patrick as well, though Patrick was not in attendance tonight… for obvious reasons.

Kevin had one too many drinks and got in a mood. He *begged* me, literally on his hands and knees, to give him Patrick's phone number so he could call him up and tell him that he missed him. This went on for a while but I continued to refuse out of respect for Patrick. He did manage to get the number from Dan, though, and belligerently called Patrick.

Patrick later recounted the conversation (which I witnessed Kevin's side of):

Kevin opened with, "I have a confession, I want to be friends again. I *really* missed you dude."

I could hear the regret in his voice. In the middle of the bar with music blaring, he gestured and moped dramatically on his knees while on the call. I thought this was sincere, even if it was a bit showy. I figured he'd just had one drink too many. But it was good to see him showing remorse for at least one of his revenge crusades. Maybe he was turning a new leaf.

"Well," Patrick responded, "I haven't missed you… at all," and hung up, presumably like a boss.

In hindsight, perhaps Kevin felt making up with Patrick would vindicate his own self-worth, somehow. After all, his revenge crusade against Patrick was the thing that snowballed into his downfall and initial exit from Chicago. But, he never *apologized* for his actions. He only expressed *regret* that they weren't friends. I am of the mind that forgiveness, by definition, cannot be offered unless the party that has wronged you expresses an apology. Forgiveness, here, means allowing trust to be rebuilt and proceeding **as if you haven't** been wronged. Forgiveness without an apology is naivety. Regret is not an apology. Regret indicates a person has issues with the *consequences* of their actions, not the actions themselves. This doesn't mean you can't let go. You don't have to hold on to anger to be smart enough not to let people into your life who aren't even sorry they hurt you.

I got along with Kat's sister pretty well that night. She was an interesting, artsy-oddball type: bohemian chic, but without really trying. There was something about the way she walked. There was something about her mischievous Cheshire cat smile. I thought I should try my shot with her, so I got to know her over the course of the night to see if I could seal the deal somehow.

She had a box of random trinkets in her room. I asked what all these little doodads were.

"If I see something on the street that looks interesting, I pick it up, clean it up at home, and put it in this box."

I looked through everything in it. There was an impressive collection of weird rings and odd little pieces of metal that had caught her eye.

Holding up a particularly interesting ring, I exclaimed, "Wow, you just... found this outside?"

I went through a bunch of the stuff in there and she'd tell me the story of how she found it, what she thought the thing was, or where it might have come from. She had somehow collected more than one pair of eyeglass frames in various states of disrepair.

"I can't remember a single time I've ever seen a pair of eyeglasses just laying around on the ground, and here you have like three pairs. That's kind of impressive."

"I guess I have an eye for it!"

I'm not sure if the pun was intended.

Kevin, who was more sober now, had caught on to my interest. While his ex's sister—his roommate—was out of the room he point-blank asked me:

"Steve, are you going to sleep with my roommate?" He asked, phrasing it as if she had no agency in this equation. His tone sounded like he was disappointed in me.

"Dude, I don't know. I'm just hanging out. I'm not trying to sleep with anyone."

This was a lie. I was definitely, absolutely trying to sleep with his roommate.

Kevin always claimed to be a bit of a ladies' man. I never personally saw any evidence of that, but I didn't have any reason to doubt it, either. The tables had seemingly turned that night as I, for once, tried to seal the deal in one night with his roommate.

I had never "sealed the deal" with anyone in one night before. That wasn't my style. I don't think I'd ever even tried. But, here we were. I didn't even have to broach the subject. The way the night proceeded, I could've sworn it was her idea. She invited me to sleep in her room and kissed me the moment we sat on the bed.

SLOW DISOLVE TO:

INT. BEDROOM - MORNING

I had to get to work the next day, so I had to split at like 6 AM to get back to my place for a change of clothes. I said goodbye and she sleepily said goodbye back.

Over the next few days, I didn't hear from her. I didn't leave my info, but obviously, she could get that from Kevin. Maybe I messed things up. I wasn't sure how. Worse still, I'd see her again if I were to hang out with my best friend Kevin. Would it be awkward? Probably, yes.

It must have taken almost a week, but I got a call from a number I didn't have saved. I almost didn't pick it up. It was her, and she wanted to see me again.

I hung out there for a long weekend and we continued to gel. We made things official early on. She was a painter, which I thought was really cool. She in turn seemed impressed by my film work. She was working on a new painting that was still pretty rough. She had just started it and had only recently begun with the background colors.

"What is it going to be?" I asked my new partner.

"I'm thinking…" she paused as if she hadn't been sure what it would be until I asked her about it, "…a dead bird… in the grass."

Sound familiar? That, reader, is how I met Gemma. Yup; that was her—the sister of Kevin's ex, Kat. She started on the painting that ebbed and flowed with our relationship almost exactly when we got together.

Describing how we got together, she told people: "We had a one-night stand and when I woke up the next day he was gone."

That surprised me the first time I heard it. I had said goodbye, hadn't I? I even told her I just had to go to work. She was just too tired to remember. That was the only one-night stand of my life, and it instantly turned into a year-and-a-half relationship.

Within days of that, I accepted the job at the small production studio, which would eventually go under with the boss owing me thousands of dollars. That's when these events finally connect back to the beginning of the nightmare year. But we're not there just yet. Rather, this is really where *this* war story finally begins.

War IV: Kat (Kind of) & For Some Fucking Reason, Valerie Again

After Kevin settled in for a few weeks, he said he had to take a quick three-day trip back home.

Gemma and I found it odd the trip was so short. Excluding travel time, he'd be home for little more than a single day.

"That's a really short trip. Is it even worth it to go down there?" I asked him.

"Yeah, it is. I just want to see a couple of people," he said, weirdly dodgy on the details.

He left for three days just as he'd said. After he returned, his phone started blowing up. He was getting a text message from an unrecognized number literally every five seconds.

Every text said the exact same thing: "Never come near Valerie again. Leave us alone."

With the way phones worked then, Kevin couldn't block the number. With the texts coming in every few seconds, his phone was also rendered useless; he couldn't do anything without being kicked into the next full-screen text notification. He could receive calls but couldn't be quick enough to make them. It was also a plan where these texts were starting to cost him money. If I talked to him on the phone I could hear the buzz every five seconds like clockwork.

His exact explanation escapes me, but Kevin said that while he was back home, he found out that someone showed up at Valerie's new house in the Chicago suburbs where she lived with her now-fiancé and was harassing her in person.

It couldn't have been Kevin, obviously, as he was hundreds of miles away, back home. He had a solid alibi. Or *did he*? A trip home is just what he *told* us. His reasoning for it was vague. He was evasive when pressed for details. He acted weird about it. Smaller details began to make more sense, in this context.

When he left, he told us, "I will be 100% off-grid. Service is kind of spotty out there. You will *not* be able to get a hold of me for *any* reason."

"Well if service is just spotty, you should be able to at least get texts, right? Even if they take longer?" I asked.

"No. I'm actually going to turn off my phone as soon as I get in the car."

I pressed a little further. It just seemed like an odd thing to do, but he stayed elusive on the details. Whenever I asked about it, he maintained a firm and rehearsed slow tone. Before he left, I thought it was just odd and nothing more. Now that he was back, with the context of Valarie having been harassed, this really raised some questions for me and Gemma. Could Kevin have turned off his phone so he couldn't be traced to Valerie's place?

"So, like… just to be sure: You didn't go and stalk Valerie, did you?" I asked, lacking any tact as usual.

"It was *not* me," he claimed, "I wasn't even in the *state*."

How did *they* get his new number? He didn't know. Why and how would he even know Valerie had been stalked? I forget his explanation, but he had one. It was not out of his character to at least *want* to do something like that. If he did, however, it would be an escalation of behavior.

Valerie's fiancé was a bit of a hacker type and most certainly was responsible for the automated text messages. It seemed like a lot of trouble to go to if they weren't absolutely sure Kevin was the one harassing them.

Kevin's phone would buzz every five seconds, without fail, for days. He finally had to relent and get a new number.

Gemma and I could only speculate. I couldn't say for sure it *wasn't* him... or that it *was*. In my mind, the question of Kevin's involvement remains open to this day. There were a lot of coincidences that cannot be ignored. Usually, when everything points to a singular explanation, that explanation tends to be the answer. By that logic, Kevin *had* harassed them, but I hadn't seen anything that could outright prove it. If he did do it, Kevin clearly left a lack of proof by design.

Once again, Kevin failed to lay down roots in Chicago. He was unable to find a job. After about two months, he moved back home after running out of money. He ended up in a few other places after that. I wouldn't see him again until he came to pick me up to move in with him in that hipster town.

Now that I was dating Kat's sister, Gemma, I got to know Kat better too. Kat was also Kevin's ex, and he was still my best friend. He wanted to patch things up with her so badly that he asked me to see how she felt about him.

Kat was guarded about what happened between her and Kevin, but it was clear that irreparable damage was done, and the fault lay with Kevin. She did not want me going back to Kevin with any information on her, and I respected that as a matter of personal privacy. She was also my girlfriend's sister after all, and I wasn't about to mess with her already small family. I have a small family too, so I knew better than to mess with that.

For context, when Kat and Kevin got together, Kevin was still roommates with Valerie. Although Kat didn't want to get into specifics about how she and Kevin parted ways, she told me one thing that stuck with me: Kevin told her to get used to the fact that he may frequently cuddle with Valerie. The ironic part is that I don't believe Kevin ever had that agreement with Valerie. I think he just thought he could get away with that, with Kat *and* Valerie. It was a position that required *incredible* hubris.

The fact that he straight up told her that to her face, and was just so casual about small infidelities, was the straw that broke the camel's back for Kat. Imagine having to be okay with your partner "cuddling" with their ex, who they still lived with. There was more to it, Kat said—lots more—but I never got details.

MONTAGE:

EXT. CHICAGO - DAY

```
Fall leaves give way to winter snow. Snow
gives way to spring rain, summer flowers,
then back to fall leaves, winter again,
and then early spring.
```

MONTAGE:

```
Gemma and I move in together. The company
I work for folds. Lola moves to Hawaii.
Gemma and I have our drama. My best friend
Kevin remotely saves us from being home-
less. Kevin picks me up to move in with
him. We drive there, see the mountains, I
meet the dog, go to the festival, and I
get into an accident with Kevin's car…
```

Back to the nightmare year.

So there's your context. Kevin had a history of behavior. He took advantage of Valerie to try to get back at Patrick and intentionally stuck him with a five figure bill for back rent. He tried to rope some folks into a plan to assault him and only backed down after I repeatedly talked him down—all over not helping to move a nightstand. He pulled the same rent stunt with Valerie, that time not even informing the landlord he was moving just to maximize the bill she got stuck with. He stole some stuff from Lola's roommate Sean on a long-shot suspicion over a phone battery, leaving the remaining roommates to scramble to cover extra rent for the next two months. He tried grooming Kat into being okay with what she considered to be borderline infidelity. He maybe/probably stalked Valerie at her new place with her fiancé. I *knew* all this when he offered me the room, when he picked me up, and when I moved in, so now you know it too.

Those are the scandalous headlines that would make someone like Alex tell me moving in with Kevin was a bad idea (while riding a horse, no less). At the beginning of these flashbacks, I said this context would make me look like an idiot. Kevin tried to burn people's lives down before. More than once, even. That's the context.

I thought Kevin wouldn't ever do anything like that to *me*, in part because he had occasionally helped me in certain ways—in part because he'd shown remorse about the Patrick situation—in part because he kept telling me a list of big favors or sacrifices that he'd theoretically make for me. In hindsight, one of the biggest favors I'd asked of him was to help me with my senior project, where he abandoned me by lying about losing his wallet.

When I moved in with Kevin, I was working under two assumptions:

1. I had earned Kevin's ultimate respect and loyalty over seven years of best friendship: after all, that's how *I* felt about *him*.
2. Since the accident wasn't strictly my fault, he shouldn't feel like I had *personally* wronged him.

On both accounts, I was very wrong.

I was doing everything in my power to make him whole again. I had even secured a car we could use freely and indefinitely. He should be whole even while I was working behind the scenes to make him *more* whole. So, yeah, sure, things were bad, but they should turn out okay, right?

It was only July, maybe only a week had passed since the crash. The nightmare year was far from over. I had *no fucking clue* what I was in for.

A CANCER UPON THIS EARTH —
PART 5: WAR V ME

BACK IN THE PRESENT—THE NIGHTMARE YEAR—I was fresh off my friend Kevin blowing up and trashing the house. It was beginning to occur to me that among the chorus of people asking me if I was okay after the accident, only one voice was missing: Kevin's. He was the only one who never asked me if I was okay. The idea that he truly did not care started to become real. Could he just be stressed out by the situation? It was reasonable to believe that once he had a car again, everything would be fine. Why wouldn't it be?

"Okay, I've been coming up with a plan to make things right," I explained. "Even though the accident wasn't strictly my *fault*, I was driving, so I think it's my *responsibility* to make it up to you."

"It is, and I've been meaning to talk to you about that," Kevin responded.

"Well, same here, and I have a plan."

"Fine, let's hear it."

"The first thing is, I have secured a car that we can borrow pretty freely."

This was big news. We essentially had a car again. I was sure this would impress him.

"Great. Can we get it Thursday?"

Or not.

"Yes, I already brought that day up."

"Good. I will need it every Tuesday and Thursday. What else?"

"I want to sue the guy that caused the accident so we can recoup the losses for the car. I got the paperwork, and I already have his information. There's a fee to file, but I think it will be worth it." This is the part where I needed his help for everything to work. "I just need you as a witness to say I'm paying you back. I figure I pay you back as soon as I can, and then we sue the guy so that I can recoup my losses, or pay you back the remainder of what I owe."

"Okay, well what about the paying me back part?"

"I thought about that. I don't really spend a lot of money other than food. I'm willing to give you like 90% of my money until I can get you fully paid back."

"That's not good enough."

"90% isn't good enough?"

"No, it's not. Talk to your boss: tell him you want paper checks. When you get paid, you will sign your entire paycheck over to me directly. I'll cash it, and that's it. It's all mine. If you want food, use your food stamps. As far as you suing anybody or whatever, you can do whatever you need to do, but you can do it on your own. I'm not helping you, and you'll have to come up with the fee some other way than your paychecks."

This rendered that whole plan useless: without his help, I couldn't even pursue it.

"Well, I guess I could—"

Cutting me off, he continued: "Also, you can no longer share food with us. Get your own food, and don't touch ours. I won't touch yours either. You can't use our plates, silverware, cups, or anything. If you want that, get your own. At some point, I'll take that desk I'm letting you use out of your room. I guess I'll let you keep using the mattress." He stopped to think a second, "And one more thing. I expect you to do the dishes every night, without fail. When I come out of my room in the morning, I don't ever want to see a dirty dish in the sink. If I do, you are out of this house. If you want to continue to live here, you do not have a choice in any of this."

As objectively crazy as Kevin's demands were, he was right: I had absolutely no choice, and he *knew* he had me cornered. Given the gravity and insanity of this conversation, every nuance and syllable Kevin spoke sticks with me to this day. The words echoed in my head for years.

One of this book's editors left me this note on Kevin's above speech: "This seems objectively insane, and I feel like most readers would want you to unpack it."

Who needs therapy when you have editors? I do not know how to unpack this. I was immediately aware that this was a toxic situation that I'd have to remove myself from. I just knew I had no options other than to comply or be homeless, and I was confident I could fulfill my debt over two months or so. I figured I should just plow through it. He *knew* I was a thousand miles away from anyone not also attached to him. With the distance, the list of those I could ask for help from was quickly reduced to zero. He *knew* he could make any demand he wanted, and I'd have no choice but to go along with it if I wanted to sleep with a roof over my head.

My job was increasing the hours required a day, and school plus study was demanding. If I was going to move out, I'd need time that I simply didn't have to look for places. On the other hand, I also thought I could probably weather through this until I paid my friend back. I figured once he was whole again, we would be 100% fine.

From then on, Kevin abruptly shuttered me from the social life he previously included me in, the only social life I had.

"Hey man, we are going to hang out with [The Rapper], do you want to come with us?" was replaced with "We're going out, I don't know when we'll be back."

That was eventually replaced with unannounced exits. I would often walk out of my room to find myself alone with only the two cats and the dog tied up out back as company.

I didn't realize I wasn't Kevin's friend anymore until that started happening regularly. Mutual friends assumed if they invited Kevin someplace that he'd include me. It took both me and mutual friends time to realize I was being shut out and isolated. After all, he still had people over at the house sometimes, and I'd hang out with him and those folks, so for a few short hours things felt deceptively normal.

I was working fifty-four hours and had six hours of school a week. School required at least twelve hours of study a week. The class crammed a year's worth of material into three months. I was completely isolated from the outside world now. I worked, studied, and slept most days, or worked, schooled, and slept the others. I even had to spend my lunches studying because we had to get an 85% or greater on every test. Anything less was considered a failing grade.

I came home one night and noticed my laptop was no longer connecting to the internet.

"Hey, Kevin, did you happen to change the Wi-Fi password?"

"Yes."

"Okay, what's the new password?"

"You can't have it."

He was intentionally drawing out this conversation at this point.

"Okay. Why not?"

"Because you're not paying for it."

"Bro, I am literally giving you all my money. I *am* paying you."

"Not for the internet you're not."

I saw what he was doing right then. I gave him all my money, but it was for whatever he wanted it to be for. I had no say in what I was paying him for. I was just paying him. I didn't even try to argue. He just needed some kind of 'gotcha' logic to justify his behavior. The next day, the main power outlet in my room stopped working. I informed my friend, thinking it went bad.

"No, I cut the power in your room because you aren't paying for it."

It was the same logic as the internet: I was paying him, but he didn't want to count it towards that yet specifically so he could justify cutting off some of my basic needs. Our mutual friends agreed that his behavior was aberrant, but there wasn't anything I or anyone else could say to convince Kevin otherwise.

This was long enough ago that you could still occasionally find unsecured Wi-Fi networks. Luckily, someone down the street had a Wi-Fi network I could get on if I lined my laptop up with the window. Another power outlet in my room still worked, and I kept that information to myself. I appreciated these two things because they enabled the *only* thing I had to look forward to: talking to my new internet-found friend Bella for a few minutes each night.

A CANCER UPON THIS EARTH —
PART 6: OTHER CANCERS

USING THAT SHODDY INTERNET CONNECTION from the neighbor's house, I'd chat with Bella, my solitary escape from my increasingly bleak reality. I introduced her to my favorite song. This song also offered a form of escape. It was a sweet, soft song you could fall into every time it played. I'd get lost in it for the full four minutes and often would go back and instantly play it again, sometimes three or four times.

As much as all my favorite music meant to me, this song eclipsed everything else combined. If I could only take one song to a desert island, that was the song. Bella began asking me to sing it to her every night over our video chats. The song meant so much to me, that as it began to mean something to Bella, we became closer. This ritual became a welcome replacement for my bedtime crying sessions.

Bella wasn't having an easy time of life either. She had just exited a revolving door of polyamorous relationships. She was always the third wheel. She knew that her needs weren't being met.

"You clearly want to be in a monogamous relationship, it sounds like."

"Yeah. If only you lived closer," she mused.

She verged on panic attacks describing the abuse that one such ex, Samuel, put her through.

"We were in a submissive/dominant relationship, but there were things he did that I wasn't consenting to. He once carved his name into my abdomen. He got about three letters in before he finally listened to my pleas to stop. Now I have to live with that reminder of his abuse for the rest of my life."

That last line really stuck with me. There was a laundry list of other stuff, but that was probably the worst. Just the same, I kept her updated on my increasingly toxic home life, including a brand new development:

"The latest thing Kevin has pulled on me is, my professional camera disappeared today," I shared, "and he has been avoiding me since, so he probably already pawned it off."

Our conversation that night was interrupted by a crash and a bang from the other side of my room's door. I could hear Kevin lamenting:

"No, no, NO!" He ran somewhere with heavy footsteps. "FUCK! NO!" he continued. This was followed by a minute or two of frantic running and doors slamming.

His girlfriend Claire was in on it too, now. "Oh my god! What happened?!"

Kevin went to the backyard and shouted, "*No! No! No!*" over and over.

It didn't sound like lamenting anymore. It sounded like he was mad.

I put it together through what little context I had that whatever was going on, at least it didn't sound like he was finally abusing his girlfriend for real this time. The yelling wasn't at *each other*, it was just yelling.

"We need to go NOW!" Claire yelled. Their remaining car screeched dramatically out of the driveway, taking off at full speed. It was quiet for about an hour. Bella and I tried to put together what happened, but we just couldn't be sure.

When they returned, Claire was sobbing and sobbing.

"I'm sorry. I'm sorry," Kevin kept repeating. Probably the only time I had ever heard him say those words, in retrospect.

Every few minutes Kevin got frustrated and randomly yelled "FUCK!"

I went to bed with that mystery.

A CANCER UPON THIS EARTH — PART 7: THE DOG

Several days passed, and I finally ran into Kevin in the living room.

"Did you take my professional camera?" I asked directly.

"I did. I have it."

"I need that back. That does not belong to me, for one. It belongs to my old boss who owes me money. Eventually, I'll need to get that back to him."

"I have it somewhere not in the house. It's safe. You'll get it when you pay me back, I promise."

"Well, for two, I can and have used that camera to make money. That has often been my livelihood. If you want me to pay you back, I'd think you'd want me to have that."

"You can't have made *that* much money with it."

Like with the karaoke thing, he just *couldn't believe* I'd done anything the least bit impressive.

"That thing was the only reason we made rent half the time. You know for a fact I've done lots of freelance work. I have a film degree. You really think I wasn't out there making money with that camera?"

"I don't know, it just… seems like it would be hard to do."

"You *know* I've made money with that thing. I've made more money with that camera than what the camera is worth by itself."

"*Really*. Huh."

The only explanation I can think of to justify that response is that he was a bit envious. If I hadn't been getting gigs, then he could have felt better about failing out of school and not having any footholds in that world.

He trailed off on that. "Listen, there's something else I need to tell you about, too. It's something I feel very sensitive about, and I don't want to talk about it, but you should at least know."

"Okay. Go ahead."

"You might have noticed that you haven't seen one of the cats in a few days."

Both the cats looked identical. I'd seen at least *one* of them a few times, which could've been *either* of them, so I hadn't noticed.

He looked down, perhaps in shame, "And the reason for that is, is because one of the cats got outside in the backyard somehow. The dog saw him and attacked him. It was bad. We rushed the cat to the animal hospital, but it was too late. He died on the way there."

"Damn. That really sucks. I'm sorry to hear that. What are you going to do about the dog?"

"We don't know. I really don't want to give him up, but we might have to."

Out of respect for the loss, I did not dish out the otherwise obvious "I told you so." Obviously, the chickens had finally come home to roost on Kevin having never trained or housebroken the dog, who he previously bragged was "a wild animal."

That explained the commotion the other night: The yelling was at the dog, the hurried footsteps were my roommates leaving for the animal hospital. I guess the dog *really was* wild, as my friend had claimed, but he didn't *have* to be. Kevin failed that dog in every way.

The next day, Claire saw the dog in the backyard through the window and sorrowfully said, "I just don't think we can keep the dog. I can't look at him the same way anymore."

"It's my fault," Kevin regrettably replied after a heavy pause, "I came in the back door that day. I must have not closed it all the way. It's my fault the cat got out. It's my fault."

In retrospect, he may have been hoping for pity by saying that. An uncomfortable silence held the room. It certainly wasn't my place to say anything. I did not at all feel bad for Kevin for leaving the door open if that's what he wanted. Instead, I felt bad for the cat who died. I felt bad for the dog, who frequently went weeks outside with no human interaction, except for Kevin putting him in the kennel for the night or throwing some food in his bowl.

This situation stays burned into my brain as a prime example of pet neglect and its consequences. When Kevin bragged before that his dog must be responsible for many cat deaths in the neighborhood, he probably hadn't even considered that one of those cats might end up being his own.

A week or so later, Kevin told me they gave the dog to a lady who lived on a huge fenced-in farm. It sounds cliché, but I didn't have any reason to doubt it. He said he visited the dog once or twice and that he had plenty more room to run around outdoors and even seemed more well-behaved indoors. Kevin was happy to admit the dog was doing much better there. Perhaps the dog really did just need a more engaged owner and more space to run around in.

A CANCER UPON THIS EARTH —
PART 8: WAR V, CONTINUED

RECENTLY, KEVIN FREQUENTLY HAD A NEW FRIEND OVER. He'd usually stay the night, sleeping on the couch. He was a German immigrant with a common German name like "Wolfgang." That might not have been it, but I'm committed, now. When he was over, I'd hang out with both of them. In those moments, it felt like me and my best friend were cool. It seemed like we were just going through some stuff that would pass.

After Wolfgang had been over four or five times, Kevin asked me for my copy of the house key so he could give it to Wolfgang temporarily. He'd be spending the night more frequently. I began to realize that this dodgy request was made like so many others: while we were alone. When he demanded that I literally sign over and hand-deliver my full paper paychecks to him, his girlfriend was not in the room, much less anyone else. Was she complicit in all this? Or was he counting on me not talking to her about what was going on? He always mentioned that she was aware of everything he was telling me, but in hindsight I saw no evidence of that.

Either he was playing both of us or they were both playing me. I knew for a fact he was playing her at least a little. Kevin was still pretending he couldn't possibly hold down a full-time job while taking EMT classes (never mind that I was doing exactly that), justifying his access to all Claire's money. Yet, Claire was so much warmer than Kevin, and she never referenced any of this stuff. It's entirely possible she didn't know.

So, I gave him the key. I felt like I didn't have a choice because it was more his place than mine, sort of. Maybe I was dumb to think that. But what was I supposed to do? Refuse? Get kicked out? Literally sleep on the street, having no real friends or family for a thousand miles? My friend forced me to choose between being moneyless or homeless, and I chose the former. He assured me he'd simply let me in when I came home for the night.

A few days later, he asked me if I'd be willing to give him a game system and games I had, and he would count it towards my debt to him. I wasn't much of a gamer and was too poor to buy games now anyway. If he wanted to play my old games so much that it knocked off a good chunk of my debt, then it was worth it. We worked out a fair value for the system. I asked him how much he was thinking for the games. The trade-in value would be so low that I thought about keeping some of them, but he seemed to be more interested in a trade of sorts.

"I don't know, man. Maybe like twenty bucks a piece? ...Yeah, twenty bucks."

"Hmm, that's actually pretty generous, so I guess we have a deal."

All totaled, this counted for a couple hundred bucks of what I owed him. I apologize for making you read about haggling prices on video games, but it was a good sign, right? He was at least trying to work with me.

A CANCER UPON THIS EARTH — PART 9: GUNS ARE A PART OF WAR

I CAME HOME ONE NIGHT AND THE DOOR WAS LOCKED, which was unusual. I knocked: no answer. I called Kevin: no answer. I sat on a chair on a porch with my laptop to pass the time. I called him again and finally got through.

"Hey, where are you guys at? I've been sitting on the porch for about an hour. You told me this wouldn't happen when I gave you my key."

"Listen, this wasn't intentional. We were only planning to be out for a bit. We'll head home soon and let you in. This isn't me being a dick, we just took longer than I thought."

I never heard him say he was sorry for anything other than the situation with the dog and cat, but at least his tone was apologetic. Even so, It took another hour for them to get home.

A week later it happened again: a knock and no answer. I didn't give my roommate the benefit of the doubt, that time. I didn't even call him. I checked the front windows. All locked. I walked around back where I knew a ladder sat in the backyard. I brought it around to the side of the house and propped it up to the easiest-to-access window. The house was on an incline, so I was using the full length of the ladder to reach this window.

I climbed the ladder, hoping the neighbors weren't looking on and thinking I was a burglar. This window was, fortunately, unlocked. I pushed it open. I hoisted myself up even further to close the remaining gap. I spilled through the window and into the house. I knocked over a TV tray below the window upon my graceful entrance. On the TV tray was a deconstructed AR-15 rifle, and all the parts fell to the floor.

I caught a glance at how the pieces were arranged before I knocked everything over, so I quickly put everything back into place while it was still fresh in my mind. I closed the window, hurried out the back door, retrieved the now-fallen ladder, and put it back in its place. I headed back inside, locking the door again. Everything was now as it was.

I don't necessarily have a problem with gun ownership, but it was concerning that Kevin had any. He had a clear history of anger issues. I knew there was a good chance he'd left it out as an intimidation tactic. The AR-15 rifle he had is well known today as the weapon of choice for mass shooters. It's often considered the closest legal alternative to an assault rifle.

He also had a military-issue handgun that he kept at his bedside. I don't know how accurate that assessment is, but he told me previously that the thing that made it a military-issue handgun was the absence of a safety mechanism, which also made it more dangerous to handle.

There's certainly an argument to be made that no one needs guns like these, but my friend's case was different. Most people agree that it's a good thing that felons aren't allowed to have guns. Kevin wasn't a felon, but he'd *done things* that would qualify him as a felon. The only difference between Kevin and a felon is that he hadn't been caught.

Seven years before the nightmare year.

When we first met in film school in Chicago, Kevin told not just me, but an entire class of people this story while the professor was out of the room.

When he was nineteen—a few years before this moment in film school—a few years before I met him—he said he got involved with a guy who ran drugs for a living. They'd stuff a trunk with packaged cocaine and transport it where it needed to go. His companion would try his best to drive according to the law, but for whatever reason, after doing a dozen or so of these trips, police lights lit up behind the car.

Kevin's companion looked over at him while pulling over and said, "Okay, listen. You're only nineteen. You've got your whole life ahead of you. I'm going to take the fall for this. I want you to figure out what you're passionate about. Go to college and become that. Don't say a word. Let me do the talking."

They arrested his companion and let Kevin go. Kevin said he never saw the guy again. He knew the guy was convicted, but he wasn't sure for how many years. For all Kevin knew, he said, he was probably still in prison at that moment.

He bookended the story by saying: "So that's why I'm here in film school. This is what I decided to do with my life."

It seemed to imply fate brought him there. It seemed to imply he was turning his life around after a sobering close call with the law. The entire class took the story with just a "Huh, wow," so I didn't think much of it at the time.

At this time in the nightmare year, I heard this story probably seven years prior, and the events would've happened ten years prior. It's ironic, I suppose, that his companion's sacrifice would ultimately end in Kevin failing out of school—twice.

A CANCER UPON THIS EARTH —
PART 10: OH YEAH, THERE'S MORE

ONE DAY, I CAUGHT KEVIN'S SIDE OF A CONVERSATION on the phone with some other friend.

"Yeah, I have this guy living here and I don't know what to do about him."

I keep a pretty low profile I guess, but he should have known I was home. There was a chance he *wanted* me to hear this conversation. However, there's a popular saying: "Never attribute to malice what can be explained by stupidity." That rule might or might not have always apply to Kevin, but it's certainly possible he didn't know I was home.

He continued, "Yeah, he doesn't pay bills, he doesn't pay rent. He's a squatter."

Except for me *literally signing over my entire paycheck to him every week under the threat of homelessness,* so that was a lie. It was also completely hypocritical: Every cent *he* had came from either me or his girlfriend Claire. By his own account, he hadn't had a job for close to a year, providing the dubious reason that he was in school. Never mind that I was in the same class and holding down a full-time job with overtime.

"Yeah, I was talking to the landlord the other day," he continued, "And she was like, 'Well, if he doesn't pay rent, then I don't want him there either.'"

Well fuck. I certainly wish I were there to set the record straight with the landlord. The money I was paying him certainly counted for rent: I included that and other bills in the total I owed him. (Those amounts were much less than the car, mind you.)

"Yeah, man, I agree. It sucks."

He was already spinning a bunch of lies about me, twisting current events heavily to fit a skewed narrative, and now he was farming pity out of this too.

The next day, when I got home, there was an unfamiliar car in the drive-way. It looked a lot like Wolfgang's car, so I *almost* thought it was his. It was a similar make, model, and color. Like Wolfgang's car, the back was covered in bumper stickers, from the bumper to the rear window. It almost flew under my radar. However, upon further inspection, I realized that all the bumper stickers were different. It was a different car.

I was shoveling over every cent I made from my job to my roommate so that he could replace his car. Was this that? Had he finally bought a car? I had given him enough money that he could have. This was fantastic news. A huge weight off my shoulders, even. Maybe this meant my Kevin and I were squared up now. Maybe he'd stop holding a grudge. Maybe we could go back to the way things were.

I don't think I saw him for another day or so, but I was eager to put all this drama behind us, so it was the first thing I asked him about.

"So, it looks like you might have gotten a new car?" An upward inflection in my voice signaled that this was the most optimistic interaction we had in weeks. "I saw a car parked in the driveway outside the other day. It was similar to Wolfgang's but definitely a different car."

"I didn't buy a new car. I don't know what you are talking about, actually."

"This is a pretty small neighborhood. Who else would park right in the driveway?"

"Dude, I have absolutely no idea what you are talking about," Changing subjects, Kevin continued, "and hey, listen, I have something else I wanted to ask you about."

"Yeah?"

"My laptop has been acting up. Eventually, I'll need to get a new one. But at the moment it's not very reliable."

"Do you know what's wrong with it?"

He listed off several vague issues. None sounded like major problems, or even like they were issues with the computer itself. I asked him if he tried a few things that might help. He fired back some reasons those things didn't or couldn't work. Some of the reasons he gave didn't even make sense. It was a little suspect, but I had no reason to assume ulterior motives... until...

"So anyway," he continued, "I was wondering if I could use your laptop during the day while you're at work."

This motherfucker was about to get a hard no from me. He managed to get my camera by stealing it when I was out of the house. He sort of strong-armed my game system away from me, but I didn't play it much so the bar was pretty low there. He essentially took my key under duress. But this was asking a literal ton.

"I actually take my laptop to work with me," I explained, "I don't leave it here. It goes everywhere with me."

"Well, don't you think I need it more than you at this point?" Kevin replied.

"No, I don't. You have a mostly working laptop. If I let you borrow mine then I have no laptop and you basically have two. So, no."

"Well, really it works maybe 20% of the time... or less, really," he said, backpedaling.

"And how do I know you aren't going to swipe it like you did that camera?"

"I still have the camera. You'll get it back. And this isn't like that. I'd only use it during the day."

"Listen, I need this laptop. If my phone goes out, as it often does, it's the only way I can communicate with anyone. I couldn't lend you this laptop even if you gave me collateral. I wouldn't lend this laptop to my own mother. The answer is no."

"You'd think if you wanted to keep living here, you'd be nice enough to lend me your laptop."

"If you're going to kick me out for not lending you my laptop, then I'm *definitely* going to need my laptop, so the answer is still no."

It was good to be putting my foot down on something. Maybe it would make him back off a bit. Or maybe he'd get more aggressive. It was tough to say.

I needed to find a way out of this house soon. Kevin was delving deeper into his paranoia. He had a theory that my boss was splitting my checks so I could pay Kevin less than 100% of what I was making. That hadn't even occurred to me. It didn't seem like something a business would entertain. I wasn't trying to drag my personal life into work, after all, but there were signs.

One night after work, my boss either caught on, or I just didn't have the energy to hide it.

"How are you doing at home, Steve?" he asked.

"Honestly? *Rough.* I might have mentioned that offhand. But yeah. It's rough."

"Well, what's going on? How is it rough?"

I gave him the cliff notes version. The crash. Kevin taking all my money. Getting locked out. The stolen camera. Having no local resources or support structure to do anything about it. He maintained eye contact, kept a firm posture, and was businesslike.

Even so, this company was only a step up from a pyramid scheme. This manager was twenty-one years old and in charge of a rag-tag office of sub-minimum wage employees. I already caught on to a scheme he had going where he was half-scamming the company and half-scamming the employees. Needless to say, I was trying to keep this guy at arm's length.

Finishing my explanation, he paused for only a moment and said, "Well, how would you like to stay with me? I have a couch you could sleep on."

The offer surprised the hell out of me. He had a wife and two young kids. Given this only just came up, he obviously had not run this by his family first. I thought about it for a few seconds.

"Wow, I appreciate the offer. But, to be honest, I think if I had to live with my boss in his house, that's just too much power for one person to have over me."

"I get it," he replied.

I imagined what could very well turn into another Kevin situation, except this time the person was *also* my boss. It'd be even easier to mess with my paychecks then.

And I was absolutely right. A week or so prior, a coworker told me to pass on to my boss that he'd miss the afternoon meeting at the last minute.

When I told my boss, his response was: "Wooow, well, *he's* fired."

That co-worker was wrong to skip the meeting, but firing him was over-kill. Imagine if I crossed some small line at work and lost this job. Would I suddenly be without a job *and* a home? If I no longer worked for him, his motivation to let me continue living in his house would drop to profoundly low levels. It could be a tightrope even more dangerous than the one I was on now. If I got out of my current place, at least I'd still have a job. But if I lived with my boss, my home and work life would depend on each other. I'd never really have a break. And that's pretty much what I told him.

"I get it," he responded. "That makes sense."

"I do appreciate the offer. I'll figure it out. I'll figure it out. I'm going to have to."

A CANCER UPON THIS EARTH — PART 11: EXIT

I GOT HOME EXHAUSTED. It was one of those 8 AM to midnight kind of days. I wasn't ready to spend an hour being my best friend's servant with the dishes. I'd try to make quick work of it. Maybe he took it easy on me tonight. I walked into the kitchen and found no less than every dish in the house stacked up in the sink and on every counter. How many people ate dinner here tonight? Half a dozen pots and pans alone were piled three feet high out of the sink. In one day, he managed to cook an entire feast.

I was more certain than ever that he was fucking with me. Perhaps he had piled clean dishes in the sink. Nope: All dirty. Really dirty. Okay, there must be tons of leftovers in the fridge, at least. I checked it. Totally bare. This was not a one-hour job. I could've spent three hours cleaning all this up, so I said fuck it and went to sleep. If he wanted to kick me out over one missed night, then so be it.

When I woke up the next morning, he confronted me first thing, like he woke up early just to call me out.

"I noticed the dishes didn't get done last night. Why is that?" he asked flatly.

"Yeah. Sorry, I had a really, really long day yesterday. I got home at like midnight and just needed to pass out."

"That sounds like a personal problem."

I didn't know then that was some quippy bullshit some power-tripping manager would say to an employee who was eight minutes late because his car wouldn't start. I just took it at face value.

"I mean, yeah, it absolutely is, but you asked, so that's what happened."

I was sick of this shit. I went to work. I had another long day.

That night, I came home really late again. There was Kevin. He was lying comfortably on the couch, facing the door, which told me he was waiting just for me.

"I need to talk to you."

Nobody wants to hear that. I let him continue without interjection.

"I do not care what you do, or where you go, or what happens to all your stuff. But I want you out of this house, and I want you out *tonight*."

All these years later I remember that verbatim.

Kevin knew a few things full well: I had no place to go. I had friends here, sure, but they were all *his* friends too. He knew that with such short notice, I'd have no place to keep my things. They'd end up in the yard, and he'd pawn them all off, or destroy them. He had been taking every cent of my paychecks. He knew I'd have to sleep on the street. He knew I couldn't afford a hotel, motel, or even a hostel. He knew I'd have little more than the clothes on my back. He knew I'd have no way to get back home. I couldn't buy a plane ticket, a car rental, or even a bus ticket.

He knew he got me, and knew he got me good. I kind of saw this coming. At some point it was inevitable, and today it was more inevitable than it was at any time before.

CUT TO BLACK

TEXT OVER BLACK:
                    Earlier that day...

INT. BIG BOX ELECTRONIC STORE – DAY
STEVEN is at work. He looks nervous.

> **STEVEN (VOICEOVER)**
> I know I didn't do
> those mother fuckin'
> dishes last night. I
> know my asshole former
> friend is going to
> come at me about it. I
> know what he is capa-
> ble of. I should be
> prepared.

MONTAGE
STEVEN is making calls. He's searching the
INTERNET. He's putting his hand to his
chin and making a face like he's thinking
really hard about stuff. He is—perhaps pre-
tentiously so—shoe-horning movie script
formatting into an already self-indulgent
memoir that, like, four people are going
to read. Hi Tim! Thanks for maybe reading
this! Do you read much these days? I know
you used to. You're right: you made the
cut. You're in the book. Probably much
earlier than you thought you'd come up. We
haven't talked too much recently at this
point in the nightmare year and for valid
reasons. We'll get there. Tune up that
guitar, buddy.

That day I knew exactly what I had to do and I was getting things done.
Kevin was absolutely going to pull some shit. I didn't know what, but
three things were sure in the world: Death, taxes, and me not sleeping

in that house one more goddamn night. With recent events shining a new light on my now-former friend, I'd developed a more unbiased view of him. I knew one thing he didn't know: he didn't know much. I was definitely smarter than this guy. Another thing he didn't know is that when I get put in a corner, I am capable of doing a great many miracles. (Unless miracles involve last night's dishes.)

Today was payday so I'd get a check tonight. The timing on this was perfect, which was part of my justification to nope out on dishes last night. I called a storage place and reserved a unit. It was a lot cheaper than I feared. I wouldn't lose any of my few belongings. I called Phil, who was lending us his car, and made sure he was cool with me having it for the night and maybe a lot longer. That was easy. Next, I needed a place to stay. This would be harder.

I fired up a website on my laptop, which I might not even have had if Kevin had his way, and hopped on a website I heard of in the mid-2000s for people who needed to "couch surf." These were temporary short-term places to stay that people offered up free of charge. It was intended for travelers, not to stave off homelessness, but it'd have to work. I found a good listing. It was also the *only* listing, so this *had* to come through. It was open for the next week. I called the guy; he explained that he promised the space to someone else that same day.

There was no plan other than that. I couldn't afford a hotel. AirBnB didn't exist yet. Even if it did, I also couldn't afford that. Other friends were too connected to the person I was escaping from, or couldn't offer their space, or I didn't know them well enough to feel like I could ask.

As a last resort, I called a homeless shelter. Sure, I was poor, but I'd probably be the fanciest looking guy there.

They told me the deal: "We close our doors at 4 PM every day and then you have to be in for the entire night. We fill up every night. I'd start lining up at two if I were you, and the last time you still might have a shot is three."

That's not going to work, I work until five. What the hell is that shit anyway? So here's this shelter available to the community if you need it, but you effectively cannot use it until you've hit *absolute* rock bottom and become homeless *and* unemployed. I was still determined to leave that night, even if it meant homelessness.

After work, I dropped by the fire station where I volunteered for the local Rescue Squad. I told them that I was bowing out and why. I asked them not to tell Kevin, because he was why I was leaving. I tried to call Bella just to vent. Suddenly my phone was no longer in service. Always at the worst times.

Next was to hit up a Walmart to cash my check and pick up some things. I stood in line waiting to cash my check, knowing that once I cashed it—once I was no longer signing it over to my former best friend—that was my point of no return. I'd have no choice but to go through with everything. I'd need every penny to have a chance to survive this.

Ironically, with the value of the camera and the agreed-upon amount for the game system stuff, I now owed my former friend under two hundred dollars. He wouldn't get that tonight. If I wasn't leaving tonight, the check I'd give him would fulfill my debt to him entirely. He clearly wasn't keeping track of the totals, but I definitely was. However, I was reasonably sure he wouldn't accept the debt as paid even if I gave it to him. He'd never even made a reference to how much I'd paid him. To him, perhaps signing over my paychecks was never about paying him *back*. I was just paying him. How else could he justify the dubious claim that I wasn't giving him anything for rent and bills? Since I felt I had no choice, perhaps I had been fooling myself into thinking this was all for something.

I bought two bottles of Five Hour Energy. It was about to be a long night. I bought a car adapter that lets you plug in any three-prong power cord just like a home outlet. I might be living out of this borrowed car for a bit. It beat the street. I bought a ten-dollar Tracfone since my old boss hadn't paid the cell phone bill again.

As I walked out of the Walmart a homeless fellow caught my eye. In this hippie mountain town, the homeless folks I saw were not the same as the homeless folks in Chicago. In most big cities, many chronically homeless folks suffer homelessness as a symptom of mental illness or as a result of drug addiction. As such, you can often recognize that many big-city homeless folks do not always have their full mental faculties.

This fellow outside Walmart was a completely different case. He was not hanging out and passively asking for change. He moved quickly and with purpose. He clearly had all his wits about him. The reason you could clock him as homeless was his appearance otherwise: he had messy unwashed hair and a big bushy beard. His face was dirty and he wore dirty overalls with no shirt underneath. He looked like a chimney sweep in one of those old-timey movies at the end of a long shift. He carried a large patched-cloth messenger bag that was stuffed full. He was on the move. I got the impression he seemed resourceful. Perhaps he hopped train cars from town to town much like my grandfather did in the Great Depression. Here I was in the second-greatest depression.

I had to pick up my pace to catch up to him. My question for him was more of an impulse question—I didn't have time to think about it. I quickly humbled myself to get the words out.

"Excuse me, sir?"

He turned around. There was no going back now. I humbled myself even further.

"Yes?" he asked.

"Listen," I thought about how best to phrase it, "I'm going to be in your position soon."

I couldn't bring myself to say I was about to be homeless. I didn't want to give that power by putting it into words. He knew exactly what I meant.

I continued: "And I'm just wondering if you have any advice as to how I can make that work."

"Alright, listen," he started, "There's three things you need to know: Never stay in the same spot for more than a few days, try to stay hidden, and never tell anyone what you got."

I thanked him, and he was off as quickly as he came.

That last one stuck with me. "Never tell anyone what you got." It sounded like something that you only learn from experience. If I mentioned off-hand that I had a laptop or a phone, that could make me a target for theft. Perhaps this applied most when dealing with other homeless folks who are down and out and might find a phone or laptop extra tempting.

In the car, I activated my Tracfone and tried to call my old boss to yell at him for not paying the bill. I expected to have to leave a voicemail as usual. This time, I got a disconnect notice. This is bad. Maybe hard times came for him, too. My much-needed free phone might be done for.

I called Bella and recounted my day. I told her I had a place to store my stuff, and a car to get it all out of there, but I still didn't know where I was staying long-term. That felt less important than getting out now. Right now. Tonight. Bella freaked out about me having to sleep in the car, but from where I was standing, I was lucky to even have that. It was late enough now that there was no avoiding it.

I might as well get this over with. Might as well head back home. Kevin's house. Or whatever I should call it. I opened that door with the silence of the vacuum of space. I hoped my former friend was out for the night. Maybe he could just come home and find my room empty, and me gone. But yeah, no. He was right there on the couch, staring at the door, waiting *just* for me.

"I do not care what you do, or where you go, or what happens to all your stuff. But I want you out of this house, and I want you out *tonight*," he sat casually, feet up on the couch, as he coldly delivered the news. He'd probably rehearsed that line in his head all day.

"All this over dishes?" They were still piled high; nearly every damn dish in the house.

"Yes," he nodded slightly, "All this over dishes."

"Okay, well, actually, I was planning to leave tonight anyway. So yeah. I hope we can still be friends, but yeah, I'm out."

That was a lie. I did *not* hope we could still be friends. Fuck this guy forever. But I knew I could take a page out of his book: he thought he was this great master manipulator. If I played remorseful, I could make my exit without him literally at my throat, so I pretended to be sad about it.

"Where are you going to put all your stuff?"

I had a place for all my stuff and I knew he wasn't counting on that.

"I have the car tonight and a place to store my shit."

"Do you have a place to stay?"

"Nope, and I'll sleep in the car if I have to."

I wasn't sleeping on the street like he surely had hoped. I joyed in denying him my suffering.

Fueled by the power of two Five Hour Energys, I began packing. Kevin insisted on staying up to supervise. He claimed that the bins I was using to pack my stuff in were his. I recounted how he should remember that I had them when he helped me move here. I recounted how my mom brought them over to my old place when I first planned this move. He still insisted. I still resisted. They went in the car and that was that. Every time I walked away from the car to grab more stuff I closed and locked it: every time.

Kevin made no attempt to help, and I wouldn't have accepted any from him. At one point he commented this was the fastest he'd ever seen me move. I even packed up the fortune from that fortune cookie he gave me the evening after our kayaking adventure: "You will receive good fortune in six months," it said. The six months hadn't passed yet, and so far my luck had only gotten worse, but that didn't mean it couldn't get better later. He insisted on supervising my exit even as he complained about how tired he was. As determined as I was, it still took me until 4 AM to get fully packed.

Finally, I was ready to get the fuck out of there forever.

"Listen, man, thanks for staying up with me while I packed," *fuck you, actually*. "I'm really sorry things had to go down for us like this," *I look forward to never seeing you again*. "Maybe I don't agree with this overall, but I get it," *there's nothing to get. You are absolutely the asshole*. "I know you're not happy with me right now, and that's understandable, but I genuinely hope that in time, we can still be friends." *I will literally never forgive you*. "Before I go, let's bring it in for one last hug."

Can you hug someone sarcastically? This was that. The real surprise was that he actually went for it. He sighed with annoyance, but he hugged back. I'd successfully defused the situation.

I hope he had fun doing those dishes.

A CANCER UPON THIS EARTH —
PART 12: A CALM IN THE STORM

THE NIGHT BEFORE I MOVED IN WITH KEVIN was the night I mentioned I was technically homeless. My best friend assured me I wasn't *actually* homeless because I lived with him. We just hadn't gotten there yet. Now I really *was* homeless, and that was also because of him.

I was fresh into my third all-time low that year. I drove around looking for a place to park the car and get some sleep. If I fell asleep right away, I could still get three hours of sleep in. There were several empty lots, but I feared I'd stick out too much there. The police might spot me. Kevin might spot me.

I ended up opting for a Denny's parking lot on the far side of the building. They were open twenty-four hours, so I figured I wouldn't be out of place there. There were other cars, so I'd blend in. I hung a shirt up using the sun visor in my side window to somewhat hide that I was in there. Overall, this was a mistake, too many people were around. Every car door slam and voice jolted me wide awake. I probably slept for thirty minutes all combined.

I got to the self-storage place the minute they opened and unloaded my stuff. I kept a suitcase of clothes in the car. I had to go straight to work from there. A new calm washed over me. I felt different now that I was out of that house. I'd sleep in the car again that night and fucking love it.

That day during work, I got a text from the couch-surfing guy. That also meant my service was back on, just in time. His spare room had opened back up. Obviously, I jumped on that. He knew about the situation between me and my former friend, at least in broad strokes.

He warned me: "Do not bring any of that drama here."

"I definitely won't."

That night, I got a call from Bella. Our feelings for each other were overflowing by this point. We'd done everything but outright say we were deeply infatuated with each other.

"You should come live with me," she said

"Oh, um, hello to you too," I replied.

"It's crazy. I know. But if we could do it, right now, would you?"

"Absolutely. It honestly might be the only way we can be together. We just have to skip steps one through four and move in together. Let's do it."

"I knew you'd say yes! I took Friday off. I traded cars with my dad. This car can make the trip. I'll come get you on Friday. Maybe now you can sing me our song in person."

Now it was official. In a few more days I could say goodbye to this stupid fucking town forever.

However, there was still one hanging thread between me and Kevin: We were both in the same EMT class. We were going to see each other there. Hopefully, my fake friendship overture from the night I left still held. It was also clear some part of him hated me now. I could skip it: I couldn't finish the whole course anyway. But I wasn't about to give my former friend that power. I went to the class, prepared to be on guard: there was a real chance Kevin would pull some shit. Like he did with Patrick, like he did with Valerie, Lola and her roommate, and ultimately me. The tension built as I walked into that building, through those halls, and into that classroom.

When I rounded the corner into the doorway of the classroom, he...

wasn't even there. The professor warned us that by the end of the class, we could expect only 40% of those present on the first day to remain. Indeed, the class got a little thinner every week. My former friend just contributed to that statistic. Unfortunately, I'd contribute to that as well, despite having something like a 96% average in the class.

I suddenly recalled a conversation from a few weeks prior in which Kevin was on some bullshit about taking the next level EMT class while still in the first one.

"It's going to be *so* much work," I recall him boasting.

The whole idea seemed unnecessary and needlessly risky. I recalled some convoluted logic he served me where he said he could take *another* version of the basic class *and* the intermediate class at the same time, for a grand total of three classes. Just like when we were kayaking, he preferred dangerous and risky shortcuts. High risk, without much more reward. Just like jumping out of a fourth-floor window across an alley just to be on a roof.

"You heard the teacher: the class is *really hard*, so I figure this is a safe-guard in case I fail," I recalled him saying.

"You'd be spreading yourself pretty thin that way. Wait, *are you* failing the class?"

"No, no... I'm not... I'm not. I just... want the extra chance."

"Yeah, but if this class is your *only* chance, then you *have to* pass it. Isn't it better to stay in a situation where you are forced to succeed? Where you can focus your efforts?"

I got the high marks I did in that class because I studied day in and day out. As far as I could tell, Kevin wasn't doing that. In hindsight, I wonder if he was really passing the class at all.

During each class break, I wandered around, trying to force an interaction he might find awkward. I wasn't trying to start anything. I knew just being in the same room would make him uncomfortable and show him I wasn't afraid. I couldn't find him at all. Could he really not face me? Or did he just drop out? Maybe both. Maybe he dropped out *because* he couldn't face me. Or maybe he failed out—twice? He had a history of that, I guess.

At my temporary abode that evening, I wrote a post on Facebook, visible only to Kevin and other folks in this town. It said I was heading back to Chicago. Of course, I was *really* moving to Louisville with Bella, but I didn't want him to know that. I was telling local friends I was heading back to Chicago, too, just to throw Kevin off track in case word got back to him. Not long after posting it, my phone buzzed. It was my former friend.

"There's something seriously wrong with you, you know that?"

He's brave through texts, at least. He wasn't supporting his statement in any way, so it was clear he was just trying to get under my skin.

I replied: "Even if you hate me I still intend on paying you back the rest of what I owe you."

That was genuine. I fully intended to get him that last one hundred and eighty bucks, even if not soon, or in person.

"You haven't paid me any money at all," he replied.

I knew how he thought and I knew what this was. He was trying to create a false narrative where I still owed him the full amount. Now that he claimed I hadn't paid him at all, I knew I couldn't finish paying him back anymore. If I gave him any money now, this could be construed as me implicitly agreeing that I owed him whatever he claimed, and I wasn't about to set myself up to pay him double. I didn't owe much at this point, but now he wouldn't even get that.

He also tacked on: "Those games aren't worth that much, btw."

I took this to mean he was going back on the deal we worked out to milk even more money out of me. I reminded him what I had paid him already and what we had agreed upon for the games just so that was on record, too.

Perhaps realizing he'd been cornered, he ignored all that and moved on:

"You won't be happy if we see each other again. And you will see me again."

Obviously, I saw this as the veiled threat it was. I wasn't about to give him any satisfaction from that, so I played dumb.

"Actually, I'd love to see you one more time before I leave. I'll have some free time on Saturday if you want to meet up."

He did not reply. I'd be way out of town by Saturday, which was entirely the point.

I didn't hear from him about Saturday, but I did end up seeing him again.

I had one more EMT class before my move. During the first break, I wandered around, trying to force an interaction Kevin might find awkward. I wasn't trying to start anything—just being in the same room would make him uncomfortable and show him I wasn't afraid. I couldn't find him. Could he really not face me? Or did he just drop out? Maybe both. Maybe he dropped out *because* he couldn't face me. Or maybe he failed out—twice? He had a history of that, I guess.

Later, however, the class Kevin must have been in had a break, and students filed by my classroom through the window in the door to the hallway. I caught a glimpse of him through it: he looked in—right at my usual seat—which he probably expected to find empty. I gave him a nonchalant nod and a wave. He made eye contact for a second and sheepishly looked away. Perhaps I sensed some guilt, but that was probably wishful thinking.

A CANCER UPON THIS EARTH —
PART 13: PROFESSIONAL PIECE OF SHIT

You're a professional piece of shit
You deserve everything that you get
You are delusional and ego mad
That's why you lost every friend you had

THE SONG "A CANCER UPON THIS EARTH" IS—to put it mildly—an angry song. When I wrote it, in the year following these events, I was so inspired by my newfound hatred for my former friend Kevin that Tim and I completed the entire song in a few hours, recording and all. I wrote twice as many lyrics as what made it into the song, all written in a single sitting.

I only felt angry about this situation in retrospect: when I wrote the song. In the thick of the events—day to day—I was just trying to survive. I was still working through losing my best friend. Maybe that was the denial phase of grief. By no means was I pining to reconnect with him, but I was still sad to lose what we had. If anger only happened a year after that, it tracks that losing my best friend had me going through the stages of grief very slowly.

Why did Kevin artificially prolong his EMT schooling, forcing his girl-friend to keep doing an exotic dancing job that she hated and personally felt was demeaning? Why did he force me to sign over my paychecks under threat of homelessness, rather than just *let me pay him back*? The answer: because he *could*. He exploited us professionally. He did what he did because it *made him money*. It's how he made a living—his only source of income the entire time I was there. He was a piece of shit—a professional piece of shit.

It took me years to realize that what he put me through was textbook abuse. It was hard to identify because I thought of abuse as something that typically happened between romantic partners, or between parents and children, and tends to be physical. I never heard about friend abuse or roommate abuse—at least in the context of abuse as I understood it. That Kevin was an asshole was obvious. That he was abusive took more time to put together.

Everything was there: Intimidation through violence against objects and implied threats. It wasn't for another couple of years that I learned implied threats were even illegal. I thought people could just dress their words up the right way for a threat to be received but still operate in the realm of legality.

That's not the end of the abuse either: He capitalized on the ability to isolate me from friends and family by trying to cut off some of my available communication methods. This went double as he was perfectly aware that my phone would sometimes go out. I was lucky, and he failed by virtue of a neighbor's open Wi-Fi network.

Last but not least, he was controlling my money. That's financial abuse. Yeah, I owed him money, which is the only reason I put up with it to begin with, but he was taking every cent I had under the threat of home-lessness. I wanted to do things the right way, and he still needed complete control over me in the process.

He was doing it to his girlfriend Claire, too. She badly wanted to stop doing an exotic dancing job that she felt was sexually demeaning. Kevin's excuses to not even attempt to look for work always appeared to me like they were well-timed to draw out his access to her money. He didn't care if she had to demean herself night after night because he got paid by proxy. If he didn't even care what *she* was going through, he *definitely* didn't care what *I* was going through. When he tried to intimidate me by trashing the house, he'd done the same thing to her by default. If he was being abusive to her, then he definitely was to me: after all, he didn't just have *access* to my money, but took it through coercion.

Writing these things out here is a weird hybrid of regression and catharsis.

The catharsis outweighs the regression, at least. Thinking about this as of writing, I took a test that says it can determine the danger level of a domestic abuse situation. It is intended to be used by professional psychologists. My results stated that the accuracy of its rating was over 75% and that my danger level was a seven out of ten. It was a bit sobering. It made me glad that I played the situation smart rather than aggressively.

Even after getting every cent I earned while I lived in that town, he still never bought himself a car, as best as I can tell. The car that appeared randomly in the driveway remained a mystery, but if I had to guess, his ownership of it was short-lived, or it was a genuine case of someone parking in the driveway mistakenly.

Much later, I heard he got Claire to give him *her* car, increasing his total cash haul to two incomes (neither of which were his own), a professional camera, a game system and games, and a new-to-him car. It sounds like a prize haul from Wheel of Fortune. Technically, he got his car: Instead, Claire was the one who lost a car in the long run. He and Claire broke up some time later, but he still kept the car. We were literally his income: he was a true professional.

Kevin had a pattern: After a bout of war-waging, he'd try to drum up pity to justify his shitty actions. When that didn't work, he'd move on to a short-lived white knight phase. In a white knight phase, he'd try to do something positive, but there was always a self-interested spin on it.

He once wanted to start going around offering random acts of kindness to people, but he also wanted it to be a *movement* with a name, with marketing. He wanted people to *join* and *follow* him. He wanted to be the face of it. He described wanting media attention: *praise*. He told me stories where he'd strong-armed people into accepting help who'd initially refused several times over. Funny how he couldn't even *help people* without being a piece of shit about it.

Once again, it might kind of make me look stupid that I didn't recognize all this sooner. However, you're only reading the highlights of his misdeeds. He did me some solids in many years previous. Meanwhile, our fallout crescendoed over only a few short weeks. We had many perfectly enjoyable interactions until we—you know—*didn't*.

A CANCER UPON THIS EARTH —
PART 14: A FUCKED UP DOCUMENTARY

I heard later that Kevin failed out of EMT school but still publicly claimed to be an EMT. For a bit, I thought maybe he was saying that because he'd eventually finish school on his own time. Later, it occurred to me that perhaps he couldn't admit he'd failed at something. He'd been open about his failures before, though: very open, even. Now, I realize it was none of those things. He probably just liked the praise.

Imagine: "What do you do for a living?"

"I'm an EMT."

"Oh wow, that's so selfless!" or "Damn, so you're like an everyday hero!" or "Wow, that's a really hard job!"

Each reaction is a little dopamine hit. Maybe it's the validation he loved. Even when doing terrible things, he spent a lot of energy trying to convince people he was justified, that the depths of the pain he'd endured, by, for example, *(checks notes)* not getting help to *move a fucking nightstand*, caused him such torment that he was completely justified in trying to burn Patrick's life to the ground. Even when I was trying to talk him down from various nonsense, he probably liked the sudden concern and focus on him it generated.

Not long before the time of writing, I started to understand where Kevin's behavior and mindset came from. I recently (as of writing) had a friend who dealt with a person with narcissistic personality disorder, who confided with me about that person's behavior. Many of those behaviors reminded me of my former friend Kevin, including going scorched-earth at any perceived slight.

My interest in their situation and in psychology prompted me to research the disorder. I found narcissistic personality disorder painted a *perfect picture* of my former friend. Narcissists assume they are naturally good at everything. That tracked with how he thought he could take shortcuts to becoming an expert at something, be it kayaking or EMT school. It tracked with his constantly throwing parties and doing dangerous stuff to get people's attention, like jumping out of fourth floor windows. It tracked with how he thought he could manipulate people to achieve his goals instead of putting the work in; there are fewer examples of that because he was bad at it, but he sure loved talking about how good he thought he was at manipulation.

There were also far more obvious symptoms of Kevin's narcissism. In retrospect, the most poignant and obvious example happened when we were in film school. So—yeah, yeah—let's cut to another flashback... (Given I had a whole chapter about an episode of Lost, you can't say I haven't set the precedent.) I used to think of this as a funny story about a friend with a huge ego. However, after discovering he was a narcissist, these events can be viewed in an entirely new context.

Six years before the nightmare year.

"Okay, dude. I know what I want to do for my documentary project. Hear me out on this. Have an open mind. Are you ready for it?" Kevin asked, dramatically.

"Yeah, sure. What's your idea?" I responded.

"I'm going to do... a documentary on..." He paused for dramatic effect. Whatever he came up with, he must have been sure it was profound, "... *myself.*"

There was another pause, but this time, it wasn't dramatic. I was trying to figure out if that was really his idea. Maybe he was kidding or maybe there was more to it, but he wasn't saying more words.

"…My dude," I responded, "that is the most egotistical bullshit I have ever heard of, and I promise on the grave of—I don't know anyone good who's died, okay—but I promise to *never, ever* stop making fun of you for this."

We were pretty tight back then: ribbing was allowed. But also… *really?*

"*No*, dude," he said disappointedly, "you don't *get it*. I have a lot of fucked up thoughts in my head. You have *no idea* the kind of constant chaos that goes on in there."

I have no idea what Kevin's internal thoughts looked like, but this was a claim he often made. The instructor shot my friend's idea down. A week later, he came at me with another idea.

"Okay, here is my new documentary pitch: Similar idea, but I found someone *else* I can do the documentary about. Someone *even more* fucked up in the head than *I* am."

"Oh, okay. I suppose that could work."

"Dude, I cannot *begin* to *describe* how *fucked up* this guy is. He's so *screwed up* and has such *chaos* in his head that he wants to remain anonymous."

I already agreed it could work, and here he was still trying to sell it. He continued:

"I'll have to get a headless actor to 'play' him on camera, and I'll have to do the voice-over myself. I might do the acting myself, too, actually."

Cut to a week later and he had an update:

"My idea got shot down again. I'll have to think of something else. And, to be honest with you, that other fucked up guy I found? …That was still just me."

It goes without saying that the concept of doing a documentary on your-self aligns perfectly with the ego-mad mind of a narcissist. I've found I had to dig pretty deep to find information on what the internal thoughts of a narcissist look like. What information I have found confirms con-sistent "internal chaos" and a constant need for validation. His advertise-ment of this chaos was also soaked in a "please feel bad for me" angle, or perhaps "be impressed by my level of dysfunction."

Contextualizing that, when I was in college, the culture around mental health was completely backwards. It was common for people to infor-mally compete to be the most fucked up person they knew. I knew dozens of people who flaunted conditions and personality disorders as proudly as olympic medals. Kevin was simply playing that game. He always wanted to be the most interesting person in the room, and back then that also meant being the most fucked up person in the room. That may provide some context to this next part as well…

The documentary Kevin ended up making was maybe worse. He literally just interviewed all our friends and would poke and prod them emo-tionally until he got them to cry on camera. The documentary wasn't even *about* anything. It had no central themes that he could define. The concept behind it remained vague even into its final stages.

He came to class and bragged: "I got Tom to cry on camera. Here's the footage."

He played it for the whole class while we worked in the background. The exact same thing happened with over half a dozen other people: Interview, crying, "Here's the footage."

He talked me into doing an interview as well. When I was the only one who didn't cry on camera, he told me he wanted to do it again to try to get me to "open up more." He wasn't hurting anyone, really. People con-sented to these interviews. The whole thing could be spun as an exercise in emotional vulnerability, so this flew under my radar back then, too. It was fucked up only later, after finally taking his claim that he was great at manipulating people seriously.

Okay, back to our regularly scheduled nightmare year.

In psychology, narcissists are defined in part as people whose entire self-worth depends on receiving a constant flow of validation. They might wake up and immediately get on social media, or start contacting people to fulfill this need. A full-on narcissist is singularly devoted to getting the validation fulfillment they need. This could mean anything from getting praise to getting a rise out of someone emotionally. They are incapable of operating in any other regard.

I've heard some professionals say that as a full-fledged personality disorder, a narcissist cannot take medication or go to therapy and expect to be able to work toward complete change. At best it can be treated and managed, but some psychologists say that a narcissist might instead use therapy to learn how to further their own agendas and get better at manipulating others.

I never felt my friend outright manipulated me. I wasn't a minion of his, defending him every step of the way, or doing his various biddings. Few people did, actually. I never thought he was much of a master manipulator, but he definitely knew how to capitalize on an opportunity that fell into his lap. I was absolutely vulnerable in that town, thousands of miles away from anyone I knew, and relying on him while I was getting back on my feet. He got to me less through manipulation and more when he had *leverage*. However, perhaps that documentary about people crying proved he *was* good at manipulating some folks.

Before, I thought Kevin used flawed logic to justify his shitty actions. For example: "I can say Steve's not paying me *rent* because I've decided this money is for the *car*, so it's at least technically true." But knowing he's a narcissist changes this completely: It means he *absolutely believes* his own bullshit. It means despite him being the only person in the house who wasn't employed, he really sat there living off of two other people's money, *genuinely* thinking I was the lazy bum coasting on a free ride.

Narcissists also tend to put people through loyalty tests. He tried to pit me against several friends who didn't take his side in his wars against Patrick and Valerie, both of whom he also tried to pit me against. I must have technically failed every one of those loyalty tests. I wasn't interested in taking sides and telling people to fuck off forever. My version of loyalty was being friends with Kevin even though he'd done some terrible things.

However, as it turns out, if someone is capable of doing something terrible to someone else, they're absolutely capable of doing it to you, too.

I learned that the hard way.

EPILOGUE: YUP, IT'S DEFINITELY, FINALLY OVER NOW, LIKE FOR REAL

I WAS SURE THE SAGA WITH KEVIN WAS OVER. He thought I was heading back to Chicago: at least if he saw my fake Facebook post. I'd be out of this town forever in just one more day. I lost a lot of battles, but ultimately I'd won the war.

Clearly, I'd soon be living happily ever after with Bella, who was willing to upend her entire life just to help me, just to be with me. Kevin tried his damnedest to destroy me, but now I was mere hours from being delivered from it all. It was a hell of a half-year or so I'd just been through, but I could see the soothing light at the end of the tunnel. It was a good day to be alive.

I'd move to Louisville with Bella. I had friends there from the festival, even. I'd have more friends there on day one than I *ever* had in this shitty hipster town. Bella and I would start a loving relationship, one that on all accounts was shaping up to be the opposite of the turbulent relationships we each just got out of.

Bella was sweet, thoughtful, and caring. Gemma was none of that. I was a romantic at heart with no desire to dabble in polyamory, much less psychological or physical abuse, as her exes had, especially since I just escaped an abusive situation myself. We were *exactly* what the other needed *exactly* when we needed it. We'd *both* get our happy endings. It was *finally* over—end the book, slap-an-epilogue-starting-here, *over*, my life will be all roses starting *now*—over.

However, it was still only the end of August. From the car crash until now was only *six weeks*. Haven't I been calling this the nightmare *year* all this time? Eight months is a bit shy of a full year, isn't it? Little did Past Steven know, Ms. Fortune still had a third of a year to get creative, with or without Kevin. Past Steven did not yet know this was a *full year* of nightmares.

Let me *have this*, Future Steven: You can stop writing now. I don't want to hear *any bullshit* about ominous foreshadowing at the very moment I'm finally escaping this nightmare-eight-months. Pay no mind to the distant thunder.

Yet, this book has a *suspicious* number of pages left in it. Maybe it's just the longest epilogue ever? Shit, we've still got unresolved questions here. What was the significance of the man in the top hat in my DMT vision? Also, we're only five songs worth of events down. Maybe it's more of an EP than an album? Maybe this is like one of those online recipes where the author has to include their entire life fucking story before telling you how to make a goddamn salad? (Hold the car wreck, please.)

If I could've bottled the optimism Past Steven had at this point in the year, I'd have cured depression. But it would turn out to be a drink that spoils fast.

Anyway. On to the salad recipe.

THE GREATEST ACT —
PART 1: COMING UP ROSES

IT WAS FRIDAY. BELLA WOULD BE HERE TO PICK ME up soon. I coordinated with Phillip to drop off his car for good and thanked him again in our final goodbye. I left a thank you note for the fellow I had been staying with along with his key. I had to quit my job real quick. Being in sales, the only way to do it was on the day of. If I'd given them any notice, they'd let me go on the spot. I didn't have two weeks' notice on this latest life upheaval, anyway, and I needed every penny. Now I just had to wait for Bella.

An unfamiliar number rang on my phone. The area code was from Chicago. I almost didn't pick up. A stern and authoritative voice greeted me.

"You were in the hospital recently, right? You know you still owe us money, don't you? When *exactly* were you planning on *paying* that?"

"Yeah, I suppose so. But hold on, you're calling from Chicago? I haven't lived there in months."

"This would've been in January. Does that ring a bell?"

Right. Not the car accident, but the broken fingers with Gemma. It seemed like a lifetime ago. Gemma and I were ancient history now, especially with Bella less than an hour away.

"How much is it?" I asked. The world stopped as my question hung in the hair.

"Forty…

Forty fucking *thousand* dollars?

"...Five..."

Forty-five goddamn thousand?!

"...Dollars."

Forty-five dollars. The gravity of it was instantly lost. The world resumed motion.

"Yeah, I can't pay that right now, but I guess that's not that much, so... hopefully soon."

It must have been more, originally. I later learned that hospitals typically reduce the cost after the fact for low-income folks. Then they likely sold the debt to a debt collector for less than even that, where it finally turned into forty-five dollars.

When Bella was close, I waited on the balcony leading up to the apartment. I saw her car pull into the lot. She got out. We'd done enough video chatting that there was no mistaking each other. She looked up at me on the balcony, made brief eye contact, then looked back down and ran up the stairs in record time. She came at me full speed and held onto me for dear life.

"I came to save you," she said.

To this day, the mere act of her picking me up and getting me out of that town, away from my former friend, was the greatest act of kindness anyone has ever done for me.

When no one was there
You were there
Scooped me up from the middle of nowhere

This is an awful lot of detail for an epilogue. I thought this nightmare was supposed to be over?

We got to my storage unit and started packing the car. I slid an end table into the back seat.

"Hey, you're scratching my new car!" she exclaimed.

"I don't think I did. I was at least an inch or two clear."

We examined that area on the interior door. I had no idea why I was indulging this. I definitely did not scratch the car.

"Yeah, this is totally fine," I confirmed.

"Are you sure?" She took a closer look: it was not scratched. "Oh, okay. Just please be careful. I just got this thing."

We were less than an hour into this and I'd started to wonder if this hyper-criticalness would be a theme in this relationship. It was a sign, but it wasn't proof of anything, so it could be nothing.

I also understood wanting a new-to-you car to remain nice. It wouldn't be fair to dismiss her concerns outright. She was already doing more for me than anyone ever had. This *one little thing* was not about to affect the big picture.

Godammit. Is that supposed to be foreshadowing? In an epilogue? I should be on the other side of this bullshit.

THE GREATEST ACT —
PART 2: AM I DOING BETTER NOW,
AT LEAST

AFTER A LOG DRIVE TO LOUISVILLE, BELLA AND I settled right into our relationship. As promised, she still requested that I sing to her some nights. It was a catharsis for both of us that our coupling became a reality when just one week before it seemed impossible. We both felt that our partnership was ordained by fate. There were so many moving parts to everything that brought me to where I was at that moment, and to her. Perhaps fate was finally working *for* me rather than against me. Maybe Ms. Fortune was taking a backseat to Fortune right now.

I met many of her friends. She even got to meet some of my (admittedly new) friends. Some of the people in my camp from Mysteria were from Louisville, furthering the idea that a measure of fate was involved in my new location. The most noteworthy of these friends was The Artist, the old-world looking tattoo artist who resembled the being I saw in my DMT experience. This included Judy, who was only mentioned briefly until now.

The Artist invited Bella and me to a cookout. As we arrived, he was warm and welcoming with a revolver openly holstered to his side. It was a bit of culture shock from Chicago, where the average citizen isn't packing. But this was Kentucky: nothing about that was out of place here. Bella wasn't fazed, so I took this to be fairly typical.

Judy was another redheaded lady who was a completely different flavor than The Redhead, who I spent most of my time with at the festival. Judy was a lot more tomboyish. She always wore a baseball cap, kind of dressed like a trucker, and had a masculine energy despite her petite frame. You could say the presentation of it was all very Kentucky. She was friends with Kevin's girlfriend Claire, which usually meant she was currently—or at least used to be—an exotic dancer. When I asked her what she did for a living, that's almost what she said—minus the "exotic" part:

"I'm a dancer."

I found that a bit surprising without any other context. It was just as if someone said they painted for a living. Like, painting pictures? Or painting houses? It could mean a lot of things.

"What kind of dancing do you do?" I wasn't even sure if I should ask. I almost didn't.

"Oh, all kinds." She then rattled off a long list of styles she could do, on which exotic dancing was extremely low on the list. "I just like dancing. It doesn't really matter what kind."

I supposed that if a woman wanted to dance professionally, exotic dancing—for better or worse—was by far the most available and highest-paying job. But still, she took other dancing gigs. It was basically a freelance thing.

Not long after being in the room with these folks, I gave them the disclaimer:

"I have something I have to tell everybody. Some of you might remember Kevin who I lived with and was at Mysteria. We had a huge falling out. He tried to kick me out suddenly in an attempt to make me homeless. He forced me out of all my money in an attempt to assure that fact, and he stole some important stuff from me. All this was in retaliation for me getting into a car wreck with his car that wasn't even my fault. If it wasn't for Bella here, I'd probably still be in the thick of that situation—she kind of saved my life. All that is just to say, Kevin doesn't know I live here now, and I don't want him to know where I am, so please do not tell him that you saw me."

"Shoot man, I'm sorry that happened to ya," The Artist said. "For what it's worth, I didn't really know the guy very well."

"Yeah, that's pretty fucked up," Judy said. "Are you doing better now, at least?"

"Oh definitely," I said. "I'm just glad to have some folks here I can be friends with. I've had to completely start my life over in a new location two different times this year. I really appreciate that this time around I might be able to start out with some friends."

"Absolutely, man," The Artist replied. "My door is always open. You don't even have to knock. I have so many friends in and out of here all the time. One more definitely ain't gonna hurt."

After a nice and pleasant evening of hanging out, Bella and I headed home. It was a twenty-minute drive. I barely even got through the door when my phone buzzed a few times.

It was my former friend, Kevin: "How dare you go to Louisville and hang out with my friends," the text read. "You have no right to hang out with those people…" The rant continued for another few texts, each a paragraph long.

I was there for *two days* and already my cover was completely blown, even after *explicitly asking* for discretion. I knew who betrayed me: it was Judy. She was the only person that made sense. She knew Kevin's girlfriend. She even left earlier and therefore had more time to spill the beans. Meanwhile, The Artist was still probably entertaining some of the other guests at this very moment. Judy must have told Claire, and then she must have told Kevin.

She couldn't even wait *one hour* before selling me out to my abuser. It made no sense. Had I offended her in some way? Was it a careless slip of the tongue? Was the gossip just too juicy for her? Was it malicious?

But most of all, why did she do it the *exact fucking moment* she walked out the door? I can't think it was malicious. I have to imagine it was just gossip—why would she sell me out for *no reason?*

"Hey, did your boyfriend really do these things?" she might have asked.

Her response would've depended entirely on whether she was in the loop on what Kevin did to me; a question that remains open to this day.

That could have quickly turned into "Hey Kevin, I guess Steve lives in Louisville now."

The jig was up. I like to think Judy didn't intentionally betray my trust, but the possibility remained. I was sure enough that I could trust The Artist, but everyone else was apparently suspect. We couldn't have my friends over. Even someone I trust might accidentally slip and give up some info that could make it back to my former friend.

Bella and I were great, even if she was a little particular when we packed my stuff into her car. Sorry if that was a misdirect. She wasn't contributing to my misfortune. It turned out to be Kevin who I wasn't really free from, yet. I thought I was, I really did. It lasted two days, maybe fifty-six hours. That's it: not even a *single fucking weekend.* I *very nearly* had a completely fresh start. But nope.

My best move was to go full no-contact with Kevin. I didn't reply to his message. I'm not sure I even read past the first sentence. I couldn't give up the "free" phone plan from my old boss, so I couldn't change my number. This was before phones had readily available blocking features, so it might not be the last time I heard from him, either.

THE GREATEST ACT —
PART 3: THE NIGHTMARE IS OVER, RIGHT

I GOT MY LAST CHECK FROM MY JOB IN THE HIPSTER town mailed to me. It ended up being ninety-five dollars when it should have been a *hundred* and ninety-five dollars. It was the one last shady move my boss from the hipster town could pull on me. I'm sure he pocketed the rest.

Shit—speaking of checks—I was supposed to get a reimbursement check from the car insurance company for that doctor's visit. They sent it to my old address, *Kevin's address*, so that was gone. I guess I paid him back in full after all because I'm *damn* sure he found that check and forged my signature to sign it over to himself. In fact, with that, he'd owe *me* money.

I didn't even do an address forwarding with the post office. I couldn't verify with enough certainty that a notification with my new address would or would not be sent to the old address where Kevin lived, or maybe the forwarding label might make it onto an envelope, but still might be sent mistakenly to the old address—you never know. It was too risky—it wasn't worth the three hundred bucks from the insurance company.

I tried to get back into some type of EMT training program in Louisville, but there was no volunteer program or other way to get in without paying thousands of dollars. My new career choice was now dead in the water.

All considered, though, everything was awesome. Louisville was awesome. Within a week I was getting interviews. It was *way* easier than it was in that east coast hipster town and exponentially easier than in Chicago.

I had one interview for a graphic design company, where they straight up told me at the end: "Listen, I think you would be a great fit for the company, and I'd love to hire you, but the owner's nephew is also applying for this position and I get the feeling they're just going to give it to him, no questions asked."

So it wasn't *completely* better here… but still *better*.

A few more applications later, I was back to doing cold sales. I told myself I'd never do this again and now I was on round three of breaking that promise. This time it was door-to-door at residences. It was pure commission which meant I could be making pennies on the hour, but it was something I could do while continuing to search for another job.

Bella and I had a conversation on one of our first dates that steered to Lola.

"I have an ex—we're still friends—who recently moved to Hawaii," I remarked.

"Oh, nice!" she exclaimed. "So when are we going to Hawaii?"

Her response surprised me, and not because it was a trip I'd never be able to afford in a million years. Gemma was intensely jealous of Lola, partly because she was an ex, which I found quite annoying. I had no intention of stepping out on my relationship with Gemma, but she tried to tell me I shouldn't be friends with Lola anymore. To keep the peace, I only talked to Lola if Gemma was not around. We rarely saw each other. If we did, it was in group settings. No infidelity occurred, physical or emotional. I was really glad Bella had no such insecurities.

Bella had other stuff going on, but I considered it minor. Her entire apartment was stuffed full of supply bins and binders. She still had every school supply and every hard copy of every assignment she'd ever done, from high school through college—everything from colored pencils to printed book reports. She never used or referenced these—she just wanted them. She was basically a hoarder but with an OCD spin on it: There was *a lot* of stuff, but everything was meticulously organized.

There was barely any room for me to store anything of mine. Luckily, I didn't have much.

Her OCD hoarding didn't just extend to keeping old things. She was constantly acquiring new things, too. Every day after work, she took me somewhere with some newly released knick-knack she wanted. It was barely September and she already had a long list of hard-to-find collectible ornaments that she absolutely needed for her Christmas tree that year. There was some new thing she needed literally *every single day*. I wondered what portion of her income was going into all these different collectibles. It must have been significant.

On the plus side, the ornament hunts reminded me that at least I wouldn't be alone for the holidays this year.

She was quite particular about every detail of her life. Everything had to be just right. This extended into... *other*... areas, too. Without getting into too much detail, this made intimacy a chore. I don't like to kiss and tell, but I guess I have to explain for this to make any sense: She hated being in control, even if just slightly, in *any way*. Her role had to be 100% passive or she'd just shut down: it couldn't even be *equal*. That sounds like it'd be kinky, but she was so particular and rigid that it sucked the fun out of the act.

As for the emotional side of the relationship, we started strong.

She kept repeating: "Can we say it yet?"

"Can we say *what* exactly?" I asked the first time she inquired.

"You know... *it*. How we feel about each other."

Oh. Oooh. She meant, could we say "I love you. "Obviously, I wasn't going to say it until it was true, but I was confident we would get there.

"Can we say it yet?" I heard this every day.

It felt fantastic to care about someone and have them care in return.

"Soon," I replied. "It'll happen: we'll get there."

THE GREATEST ACT —
PART 4: HERE'S A PRETTY WEIRD
SUBCULTURE

BELLA WAS IN AN ODD SORT OF SUBCULTURE that revolved around submissive and dominant scenarios. This is often billed as sexual but it isn't always, necessarily. I knew she ran in this circle, but now that we were together, I was essentially in it just by being her partner.

If you were a member of the goth subculture or adjacent subcultures in the 2000s, you might have heard this stuff talked about. This wasn't an extension of that: it functioned as its own separate subculture, with its own traditions and slang. Only a few people in this group presented themselves as vaguely alternative, and most folks didn't look that way at all. In this subculture, the submissive and dominant stuff was the core focus, not on the periphery of it.

Bella's abusive ex, Samuel, had set himself up as a leader in the scene by renting out a clubhouse space where people could act out these scenarios. She was not fond of Samael being at the center of everything, but the problem was that all her friends hung out there. She could either put up with his presence or remove herself from all her friends. So, she decided to put up with his presence. Samuel actually came off as really friendly—obviously, he wasn't always—but you wouldn't know just by being in the room with him.

Under the surface, though, it was clear that Samuel was trying to start up a sort-of diet cult. It was his club. There was a culture of secrecy around the clubhouse and its location. Bella even cautioned me about mentioning it to anyone outside the group. There was a big table where Samuel had a place for himself set up at the head of it. He'd ostracized people before, Bella told me, which essentially cut them off from an entire social circle. Aside from the clubhouse, he had a hold on many outside social activities too, most of which he planned.

I never saw any risqué stuff going on at the clubhouse. Certainly, it must have occurred at some point now and again. But whenever I was there—a decent number of times—people were just hanging out and talking. At one of these secret gatherings, I struck up a conversation with a fellow who was originally from Cleveland.

"I haven't been to Cleveland." I told him. "It feels like I only know about it from that TV show that took place there. Outside of that, I've actually heard it's kind of a shitty town. What's it really like?"

"Yeah, I know the show—everyone there does," he replied. "Honestly? It's not a great city. I did end up *here*, after all. It's kind of weird that Cleavland somehow has a good reputation."

As we talked, Bella sat on my lap. The gesture felt like it was for show, but I still took it in a good way—like she was trying to show everybody that she belonged to somebody, now. I actually hate that phrasing—it's as if she'd deny her own autonomy—but I bet that's how she'd have put it. In some ways, the *whole group* felt like people who wanted to treat their significant others like pets and people who *actually liked* being treated like pets.

I observed a lot of interesting psychology in this group. Anyone who considered themselves dominant appeared to be compensating for something in one way or another. It seemed to me that they liked the idea of having a secret life. The dominant folks mostly worked low-wage, high-pressure jobs. I think they liked the idea of walking around and believing that once they clocked out they could go someplace where they could feel like they were in power. Ordinary by day, superhero by night. They'd constantly make self-affirming statements like "I'm not afraid of anything!" They had to project their supposed dominance at every opportunity.

Meanwhile, many folks styling themselves as submissive had more control in other areas, whether they liked it or not. Bella worked in a lab with chemicals all day; one tiny mistake could mean disaster. She had to maintain control and keep order at work. At home, it was the opposite. She wanted me to make all the calls. Perhaps these folks wanted to experience the opposite of their daily reality. Or maybe it was a self-esteem thing: maybe she subconsciously felt like she deserved to be treated as lesser.

Wanting to be treated like pets? That was not an exaggeration: That was occasionally literal for Bella. She sometimes liked to pretend she was a puppy. There wasn't anything sexual about that, either, it was more of a psychological release. There were even formal playgroups she had previously attended where people did this. I'm not even going to sit here and make fun of it, as easy as that would be.

Maybe groups like this in other cities were different. I don't know. But here, that's what it was like. There was just some psychology going on there, is all, and probably a lot of it.

THE GREATEST ACT —
PART 5: THE KENTUCKY COUNTRYSIDE

MY NEW JOB WAS SELLING SECURITY SYSTEMS door to door. People hate door-to-door sales folks, so it might be no surprise that the whole office performed poorly. The company saw the bulk of the sales folks as just door-knockers. Someone more seasoned like the manager would close the sale. The managers were the ones that *really* needed to perform. As such, we had a new manager every couple of weeks, as they cycled through people that couldn't hit their sales goals. This job was just a temporary stopover for me while I looked for something more consistent, so I wasn't super concerned with the details.

We found ourselves all over the state, in rural areas and on country back-roads, often with lush green fields as far as the eye could see. The clouds in Kentucky were different. In Chicago, the sky was often either clear or totally overcast. In Kentucky, I often saw picturesque clouds right out of a landscape painting. The sky was more blue than in any place I'd been. I often stopped in my tracks to take it all in.

The main cast of characters at this job were Lenny, Michael, and Trent. They were all just a few years out of high school at best. Meanwhile, I'd been out of *college* for a few years. With jobs from my trade wiped out, this was a huge step back, but it still beat moving "back home," which 95% of people from my college had already done.

Trent spent his childhood years in Chicago, so immediately we had Chicago in common. Michael, I think, grew up in Louisville, but had little if any accent. Meanwhile, Lenny was country as fuck. I can practically hear him reading this and saying "Hell yeah I am!"

We all hung out on occasion. Lenny once hooked me up with a one-day gig where we both de-shelled walnuts for an afternoon. We made twenty bucks for our efforts. As we sat there tossing walnuts into a bucket, he quizzed me to see if I was pronouncing Louisville the right way.

"Say 'Louisville,'" he said. Actually, I think he managed to communicate the request without saying the city's name.

"I know it's not pronounced *Louis*-ville. It's more like, *Louie*-ville."

"Nope, still wrong. Listen to me. 'Looa-vull'. You gotta have that southern draaag on it."

"Looa-vull."

"There it is, now you got it!"

The next day I was going house to house with Lenny at the door-to-door sales job. There'd often be long stretches between houses in these rural areas. We walked up to a house in the middle of nowhere. It was big and square, two stories tall. There was an older truck in the driveway.

Lenny egged me on, "Hey, you should pitch these guys."

We were basically taking turns and I was up, so it didn't seem like an odd request. For some reason, though, he was jazzed about it. I could see these people were farmers. They were outside working as we walked up the dirt driveway, so we didn't even need to knock.

I rolled into my pitch, but with every point I made the guy came back with "We're not interested in stuff like that" or "We don't need anything like that."

"Stuff like that" stuck out to me as a peculiar phrasing: it seemed to imply something beyond just disinterest in security specifically. As I took in my surroundings, it began to dawn on me: These people were *Amish*, maybe Mennonites. The truck in the driveway threw me off. I now noticed candles in every window, the style of dress could fit, and the farming equipment was pretty old school. Needless to say, they were not about to go for a security system. "We're not interested in *stuff like that*"—as in... *technology*.

After we walked away I verbalized my suspicions, "I think those guys might actually be Amish."

Lenny responded, "Yeah, I know, that was *hilarious*!"

"Wait, so you knew they were Amish? Why did you want me to pitch them?"

"It's *funny*, dude, come on!"

"I don't think so, it seems kind of disrespectful."

Meanwhile, Trent was more-so the kind and sensitive type. He always wanted to help. Michael struck me as somewhere in the middle. He knew how to have fun but not at anyone's expense. We all became fast friends, even if Lenny was a piece of shit sometimes.

THE GREATEST ACT RESS — PART 6: CAN WE SAY IT YET

BELLA AND I FINALLY SAID "IT." The words came out by accident. We were moving faster than I would've preferred, but considering we were living together starting the same day we met in person, I guessed this was par for the course.

I offhandedly said something like "I love you too much to let that happen to you."

I don't recall the context. I realized what I said the moment I said it and froze. I wondered if she caught the slip or not. It seemed like she didn't, but I couldn't be sure.

I stopped her and said, "Look, I think I accidentally said 'I love you' a minute ago, so I think we can say that now."

We kissed.

"I love you, too," she said, with expertly crafted puppy-dog eyes.

Can we say it yet?
Or is it too late?
Can we say it yet?
Had me believing in fate

I'd been in town maybe a month now, and my hard work was paying off: Within the span of a day or two, I suddenly had three job offers. None of them were particularly fancy—the recession had completely wiped out jobs in my trade—most jobs, even. I also had some sales racked up at the door-to-door job, so I was expecting to get a payout soon.

The job I accepted was at a copy and office supply store chain. I accepted this job over the other two because it was the only one of the three offering full-time employment. I was looking forward to having fancy things like "time off" and "health benefits." After graduating into the gig market of the recession, I literally never had either of those things. Maybe I could finally do fancy shit like... going to the dentist. It felt like I was finally coming up in the world. I'd had jobs, but having real benefits finally made it feel like a *career*.

The owner ran two different stores. They explained how it worked on my first day:

"We will split your time between the two stores..."

I didn't expect that, but that could be fine.

"...You'll get full-time hours, but really it's kind of like having two part-time jobs..."

Weird way to put it, but fine.

"...So you won't have anything like... paid time off... or health benefits... but... it *is full-time*!"

The upward inflection on the phrase "full-time" clearly indicated I should be excited even just to get forty hours.

I was so ecstatic I could barely contain myself. But somehow... I did.

Thanks for waiting to tell me until my first day. It appeared I was in *yet another* job that operated within a questionable area of legality. At this point, I hadn't had a *single* recession job that wasn't taking advantage of employees in some overt way, legally or illegally. The tradition continues. This had now happened in Chicago, on the east coast, and in Louisville, so I could be sure it was a national trend. This was a step up though: The only thing I was getting screwed on was benefits: it was the first time in a while I was making more than minimum wage.

I was just happy to have something stable… I guess. At my door-to-door sales job, I didn't even technically quit. I needed all the money I could get, so I asked if I could still come in on my days off; they said yes. So that was still on the table if needed.

WEAPON —
PART 1: THE FATED DAY ARRIVES

BELLA AND I WERE IN THE CAR ON THE WAY to work. She'd drop me off at my job before heading to hers. After moving in together, she instantly latched on to nearly my entire music collection. If we were in the car, I'd always have something playing.

Today marked six months to the day that Kevin gifted me a fortune from a fortune cookie that predicted its bearer would receive good luck in exactly six months.

"Today is the day," I told Bella. "My good luck day that I told you about."

"Do you think something good will happen?"

"Yeah, maybe. Even with everything that happened with me and Kevin, the gift of luck could theoretically be unaffected."

"Yeah! Anything could happen if you're open-minded."

"I've had to start my life over twice this year. I think I'm due for some good luck."

"Well, now you're here with me. No more starting over. …What song is this? This is really good."

I told her. "It's interesting that you like this, it's fairly niche stuff. If I ever get to making music, there's a good chance it might sound a little like this."

"Maybe that could be the luck. Maybe you'll meet someone who can help you with music."

"Yeah, I'm not sure how I'd get started otherwise."

"Alright, here we are. I love you! I can't wait to hear about your day, later. I hope something good happens!"

I got out of the car but turned back to say goodbye.

"I love you too. You'll definitely hear about it."

Some people believe that if you want something bad enough, it will find its way to you. I'd never tested that concept more than I did that day. I spent the day vigilant for whatever luck might offer me. Every person and place in my proximity was a potential opportunity.

Maybe I'd get some good news. Maybe I'd meet a potential musical companion. Maybe I'd simply find a twenty-dollar bill on the ground, kind of like those lucky coins spilling out of Fortune's pockets. If I found money, maybe I could buy a lottery ticket just to test how far my luck could go. But it didn't have to be money, I'd take any kind of good luck.

As evening approached, though… nothing happened. The sky grew dark as the certainty set in. Bella picked me up after work as usual. I contemplated my day to the rhythm of the windshield wipers on the rainy car ride home. The day wasn't over, but it was unlikely anything would happen just hanging out at home.

"You're being quiet," Bella remarked after a minute.

"Oh. Yeah. Sorry. Just thinking."

"Well, talk to me. How did today go? Anything lucky happen?"

"Honestly… no. I was almost bummed about it for a minute too."

"Aww, I'm sorry, hun."

We pulled into the lot of her—our?—apartment building and kept talking after we parked.

"Well, the thing is, I realized I already *got* my good luck. I'm living it *right now*. I moved away from Chicago to get a fresh start. It didn't happen the way I thought it would, but I got it. I made it out of that crazy situation with Kevin. I'm here now, with you. I finally got a decent job. What else could I even ask for?"

"I was afraid it'd be forever before we could be together. But here we are. It's fate."

She looked at me with those same puppy dog eyes she used when she first said 'I love you.' I smiled and reached out to hold her hand.

"Even Kevin hasn't harassed me since the weekend I got here. Sure, my luck didn't come dramatically and suddenly on the day predicted, but I still got it."

Bella turned off the car. The windshield wipers sat affixed halfway across the windshield.

"Ooh, I love when that happens."

Bella lived a meticulously ordered life. She seemed to love these small moments of acceptable disorder, as long as they fell within some very well-defined lines. Luckily, living with her so far seemed to be a shake-up that also fell within these well-defined lines of acceptable disorder. Sure, I'd impeded on her meticulously organized living space, but we managed to find harmony within that. I'd be homeless otherwise. However, living with Bella was not just the only way my life *could* work, but it was also the way I *wanted* it to work. I was lucky to be able to fit in her life.

That must be the lesson here: Fortune had *already* paid back my karmic debt. I just had to realize it. The real luck was the friends we made along the way. *That's* the epilogue. The protagonist prevailed. I saved the damsel. Well, I did a little, but she saved me even more. We'd live happily ever after. This was a well-earned good ending after a couple of hard months.

Fade to black—credits roll.

Honestly, though… that doesn't feel like I'd earned it yet. And more importantly, we're still right in the middle of a book about a "nightmare year" that still has a good few months left in it...

WEAPON —
PART 2: I DEFINITELY DID, THOUGH

IT SEEMED MY LUCK WAS IMPROVING. The only points of conflict that came up were a couple of small things that happened between me and Bella—*small* things—nothing that meant anything more.

She scooped me up from work one afternoon and said: "You forgot to clean out the bathroom sink this morning after you shaved."

"Really? That's weird. I remember cleaning it up, but maybe I didn't, I guess."

When we got home, she made a beeline to the sink and pointed to about half a dozen stray facial hairs that lay in it.

"Oh. I can see I missed a bit, but I *did* clean up after myself. I can get the rest."

"No... you *didn't*. At all." I still remember the slow and deliberate sheer indignation of how she said the words.

There was a pause as I processed her stubbornness. She held her gaze. I looked at her, gauging if she was serious. It seemed like she was.

"If you want me to clean up *better* next time, that's fine. You can ask me to do a better job; I'll do better. But I don't appreciate you telling me I didn't clean up at all when I definitely did."

I knew it was some kind of red flag, but it was a small one, I thought. The fact that it was such an inconsequential thing made it *weirder*, but there was no need to let it put a dent in my happiness—in *our* happiness. Maybe it was just her OCD thing.

It often felt like I needed to walk on eggshells with Bella. The smallest mistake could be a major slight to her. I reached to grab my water bottle one evening and accidentally knocked over one of her rapidly accumulating knick-knacks. It was still in the box.

"Oops," I casually exclaimed, figuring it was fine.

"Heeeeey... You did that on purpose," Bella pouted.

"That was an accident; I was just reaching for my water bottle."

"That *wasn't* an accident..." she said indignantly, looking away.

"C'mon... of course it was. I'm sorry I knocked it over. And it's completely fine, see?"

In hindsight, a reaction like that probably came from a place of abuse. I could imagine someone abusive—maybe Samuel—knocking over something important to her, breaking it, and feigning like it was an accident, but with an obvious undertone of mockery. That certainly could flavor situations of genuine accidents in the future.

Given that, maybe she earned a break.

WEAPON —
PART 3: I STILL CAN'T BELIEVE THIS ACTUALLY HAPPENED

AT THE NEW JOB, I WAS NOW ON MY FOURTH DAY. The business buzzword employers were looking for people to embody was "self-starter." It meant knowing what you had to do and doing it without being told. So that's what I did. I wanted to impress these people. Whether or not a copy and shipping store was the place to go all out didn't matter. It was still the most stable job I'd secured since graduating from college during the recession.

Business was slow at the second location: only three people came in the whole day.

The last customer was a local business owner.

"I just need five copies of this document," she said.

The manager told her about the various paper weights and finishes and asked which one she wanted. She went with something on the lower end, but not the cheapest one.

"Okay," the manager lady said, "would you be okay with picking those up tomorrow?"

"Oh, I guess that's fine," she replied.

"Well, I could at least get those started, if you like," I said to the customer.

My manager lady interjected: "Oh, that's okay."

"Oh, I don't mind at all," I said, doing that "self-starter" thing.

"You really don't have to," my manager lady said.

The business owner seemed pleased, "Oh wow, he's eager; I like that. I wish I could hire eager people. He can come work for me if he wants! I don't mind waiting a bit."

The business owner and I made small talk about her work as I took some paper from the cubby labeled with the type she chose. I started a test print before letting the rest go through: standard procedure.

"We can finish this up later," the manager said to me. Turning to the customer, she asked again, "Do you mind picking up these copies tomorrow?"

The customer agreed and left. The first copy finished seconds later.

"Okay, you did good," my manager told me, "but it looks like you used the wrong type of paper. Now we have to throw these away."

She explained their paper cubby labeling system; each paper type was labeled on the shelf *above it* rather than the shelf it was *on*.

The next day, I trained at the same location with another guy, although he wasn't a manager. He must have been twenty-three or so. He was a really chill dude. Management insisted that new folks are taught everything, down to exactly how to staple a document together, even dictating the precise location and angle of the staple. My co-worker spent the day showing me the ropes of various other small tasks that also generally required no explanation.

About three minutes before the end of my shift, he got a phone call from the manager I worked with yesterday.

"Hello? ...Yeah, he's here... Yeah, everything went fine... He did good... Oh, okay...."

Now at the end of my shift, I leaned in and said quietly: "I'm going to head out, is that cool?"

"Wait a second, don't go… Okay, do you want to talk to him? …What happened? …And it has to be *me*? …Alright, fine, I'll see you Monday." He hung up the phone, looking a bit frustrated. Turning to me, he said, "That was the manager. I'm really sorry to have to tell you this, and I have no idea why *I* have to be the one to do it, but she said you're fired."

"Really? Why?"

"She said she told you not to do something and you did it anyway. Something like, you made some copies when she said not to."

"What? Really? She told me I didn't *have to*, not that I *shouldn't*."

"I don't know, man. I'm just the messenger."

I walked outside and sat on a cement divider in the parking lot. I had about half an hour before Bella picked me up. Ah, shit—how was I going to break this to her? I knew how particular she was. This might be the most trivial firing in history, but this would be a problem for her, and therefore for me—for *us*.

I should've gotten a card from that business owner the day before. She literally told me she'd love to hire me. Ironic that the same eagerness that had her wanting to hire me was the same quality that caused my dismissal. Maybe *that* is what the man in the top hat told me during my DMT vision. Perhaps his unheard words were: "Don't make that fucking copy."

I went into problem-solving mode. It was that exact same feeling as when I needed to get out of the house with Kevin by the end of the day: All the potentialities connected all at once, and suddenly I knew my best move.

I called the big-box electronics store. They offered me a position just last week. Rather than a formal offer, they just asked me to come in on a certain day, which, having accepted the other job, I didn't do.

Careful with my words, I told them: "Hello, I was supposed to be at a new hire orientation last week, but I missed it. Would I be able to get in on the next one?"

I held my breath, waiting for an answer. I'd probably lost my shot, but it was worth a try.

"Oh yeah, no problem! What's your name?"

That was that: I was in. But I couldn't just replace a full-time job with a part-time job.

I called up the third place that offered me a job. It was a shipping company, and I'd work on the warehouse side. They offered me a job via an automated message, but I didn't respond since I didn't intend to accept. I called them up and simply pressed "1" to accept the position. That was that: I replaced one job with two.

I started at both of those places in two weeks. What about before that? Easy: I'd go back to the door-to-door job. I'd literally be back to work on Monday.

I still had to break it to Bella, though. As finicky as she was, I knew this would be a big deal to her, so I felt like I had to show her I felt really bad about it, too. So I treated it like I had some earth-shatteringly bad news.

That turned out to be a mistake. I shouldn't have felt bad about this: the whole thing resulted from micro-management so timid that I had no idea the manager's polite suggestions were actually direct orders. I've heard of folks making errors in the range of ten and even forty thousand dollars without a big deal being made. I shouldn't have felt bad about getting axed over a twenty-five-cent mistake.

I went on to explain the details of what happened to Bella. She took it well once I explained that I already had two other jobs lined up. However, the stakes were still extremely high. I had to get my life back on track. I *needed* things to go well.

And guess fucking what? That twenty-five-cent mistake was about to cost me a lot more. Fortune cookies be damned, my luck hadn't changed at all. I hadn't hit rock bottom; this was just another pit stop on my way down.

WEAPON —
PART 4: IT'S ACTUALLY NOT OKAY, THOUGH.

BACK AT THE DOOR-TO-DOOR SALES JOB, I once again inquired about my paycheck. Lenny helped me out. He was only a jerk sometimes: today he was cool.

"You can check it on the computer," he explained. "I'll show you. You *approved* it, right?"

"Wait, what?" I replied.

"Dude, nobody told you how to approve your pay?"

"No, and why in the absolute *fuck* is that even a thing? Is anyone out there denying their pay?"

"I dunno man. It's weird, I guess, but I'll show you how to do it."

I supposed I'd actually get paid now, but it meant I'd need to wait yet another week or so.

Back at home, I explained this to Bella. This time I was just annoyed, I didn't make it a big deal.

"Do you think it's a scam?" she asked skeptically.

"No, plenty of other people work there, and they've gotten paid," I assured her. "I'm sure they wouldn't be there otherwise. I'm sorry this is taking longer; it's a surprise to me too."

"That's *supposed to be* my rent money for the last couple weeks."

"Yeah, I know. You'll get it as soon as I have it."

Actually, I *didn't* know. We hadn't worked all that out yet. I guess this was her way of telling me. But it was fair enough. It might be tough to eat, but I kept that to myself.

"I don't think this money is ever coming," she said in a defeated tone.

"It'll come. I'm sure of that. Worst case, I've got those two other jobs lined up. We'll be good."

"You know, my ex, Samuel, is a big powerful lawyer for the government. I can't even *tell you* what he does because it's so top secret."

"Okay…" I said quizzically, wondering how this was in any way related to the subject at hand.

It almost sounded suspicious. Like, perhaps he was figuring out legal loopholes in which the government could operate? The dude might be a real-life supervillain, for all I knew. How many other ways was this guy sketchy as hell?

"He told me that when he was in law school, the professor once asked the class to raise their hand if they ever were fired before… and *no one* raised their hand," Bella explained.

"Okay, but who would just raise their hand and admit that?" I asked. "The only thing that measures is how many people were willing to admit to it in front of an entire class."

The exchange probably implied she had sought Samuel's advice on how to feel about this matter, but I didn't raise that concern.

I was beginning to see the major difference between me and Bella. I was poor, she wasn't. She had never struggled before. Her reckless spending habits were proof of that. She must have thought this would be a temporary hiccup for me and not an uphill battle. All considered, I was doing excellently. I was still working my way up despite my circumstances. Lawyers? Law school? That sure as hell wasn't anything that existed in my world. She must have seen my struggles and not had any concept of what they really looked like.

Her behavior started to change, too.

"Listen, I'm going to hang out with Samuel tonight," Bella told me one night.

"Wait, what? How is that a good idea?"

"Look, you *aren't going to stop me*. I love you, and this *isn't* a cheating thing. I *wouldn't do that*."

"I'm not over here trying to control you; I'm not worried about cheating. You described some really horrific abuse he put you through. He tried to *carve his name into you*, for god's sake. My concern is with your *safety*. I hoped that was obvious."

"*No*," she said, looking at me with those puppy-dog-eyes again, which did absolutely nothing to curb my concern, "it's okay. That's *over* with."

It was becoming clear her puppy-dog-eyes look was a rehearsed response, designed to disarm. I've even heard people call it a manipulation tactic, but back then I had no idea.

"Just because it's over, doesn't mean you should be friends with him again."

She made direct eye contact with me, speaking slowly and reassuringly. "It's okay. It's *really okay*... I promise: it's *okay*."

Who was she trying to convince? She had anticipated I'd be *jealous*. She didn't even consider that I might just be *concerned*. That might explain why the only response she could muster was to repeat "it's okay" over and over.

After they hung out, she assured me everything was okay, that he hadn't tried anything, and that they just talked. I didn't see any evidence to cause me to doubt her version of events. She became further confident they could be friends again despite his former abuse.

At the same time, my former friend Kevin had sent me a barrage of texts explaining that he sold my camera on eBay. I was surprised he'd only just got around to that. So now he's back, too. Unbeknownst to him, he said, the battery latch was broken. This probably happened because I typically don't feel the need to explain the condition and quirks of stolen goods to the person stealing them. I'll try to be more considerate next time.

He needed to refund the buyer a hundred dollars, and now I owed *him* that money, he said. I straight up scoffed at that one. I wasn't about to pay *him* for something he stole from *me*. I also didn't care how much he managed to *sell* the camera for, I counted it in my debt to him according to its actual *value*. You don't get to haggle the price of stolen goods.

Imagine, a mugger holds you up and steals your bag with your laptop.

Your natural response might *not actually be*: "Okay, but don't forget the charger, and I suppose I'll have to give you the password, too."

I left that bullshit on read, as usual.

WEAPON —
PART 5: NO ADDRESS

MEANWHILE, BELLA AND I WERE IN THE PROCESS OF unraveling even further. Something about the copy store job and her paranoia about the money from the sales job had her spooked.

When we started this experiment of a relationship, we had a standing agreement: If it didn't work out, I'd need one last favor, namely for her to drive me back home to my mom's place where we would part ways amicably. It was a few hundred miles, but with an early start, the whole round-trip could be done in a day.

"I'm giving you two weeks to move out," she told me one day.

I guessed that was us breaking up, but that's not what sticks out in my memory. I was far more concerned with having a roof over my head.

I told all the guys at the sales job, "I have only two weeks to find a new place, guys. If you know of *anyone* who needs a roommate, or if you hear of *anything*, please let me know, like immediately."

Trent piped up, "My best friend and I are about to move in together in just a couple of days. There's three rooms in the house, maybe you could stay in the third one. I'll talk to him."

"Bro, it's a literal *miracle* on this timing," I responded. "Please talk to him. I have no idea what I will do otherwise."

Honestly, I didn't have a plan this time. I didn't come up with some crazy big-brain last-minute scheme to barely pull off like I had when leaving Kevin's place, or when replacing my one job with two (technically three). I'd used up all my gas on the last miracle. I was burnt out. Usually, people get burned out on something like work and need a break or a vacation. I was burnt out on *life*. There was no vacation from that.

Meanwhile, Bella had absolutely no interest in being in the same room as me. She'd leave me stranded in public places for anywhere from four to six hours after work and would only pick me up in time for me to go to sleep. This happened nearly daily. It was the same shit as me hanging out on the porch waiting for Kevin to come home and let me in, the *exact same shit* she told me was terrible. There I was stuck in a Wendy's over forty-five minutes after it was closed waiting for her to pick me up. I was just thankful the employees were understanding.

She went back and forth on whether I should sleep on the couch or not. She had already done me enough favors, so I left it up to her. It was the bed the first night and the couch after that.

I made the absolute, most terrible mistake of telling her I managed to find a lead on a place to live. Nothing finalized: just a *lead*.

"*Yes*. Okay, you're going to move in there."

"This is not a sure thing. My guy hasn't gotten back to me yet."

"This is *going* to work. You're moving in there."

By the next day, this had turned into: "You're going to move out *this* weekend. So you better get things in order with that place you found."

That reduced my timeline from two weeks to just four days. Back at work, I talked to Trent again.

"Shoot, I didn't get a chance to talk to my friend yet, I'm sorry," he explained. "Don't worry, buddy. I am *going* to make this work out for you. I won't let you be homeless. I'll convince him."

"Okay, thank you," I responded. "At this point, I think I'm counting on this. I don't know what else to do."

It *was* just like the shit with Kevin: Here I was uncertain if I'd have a roof over my head in a few days, *again*. As it stood, Bella and I were set to last about six weeks. I did not hold the same contempt for her that I did for Kevin, at this point. She had still done me perhaps the greatest favor that anyone ever had.

Everything was happening pretty fast now. Ms. Fortune was going for comedic overkill. It was just into October and I had been through so much shit that I stopped building character in August. I had already reached the human limits of emotional endurance. I was so numb to it now: numb to everything. There was no reason I had to be *this* strong. I couldn't imagine the situation that could be bad enough that I'd need this kind of preparation.

That paycheck was coming up and so was my now-shortened deadline to move out of Bella's place. I was beginning to think about my survival: I could either give Bella that money or use it for my basic needs. Without it, I'd only have a couple of bucks to my name.

I had two new jobs and no way to get to them. I had to take the bus to do a drug test to qualify for one of the jobs and learned that the public transportation system in Louisville was *abysmal* for a city of its population and size. The bus ride was a four-hour round trip. That was not going to work once I started those jobs.

Talking to Bella, I said "Listen, I know I owe you for rent... and the money I'm getting from the sales job is pretty much *exactly* what I owe you. But, if you want me out of your place *this quick*, I'll need that money to buy a car. If you still want to take a road trip to get me back home, then I'll give you that money for rent instead."

"I can't," Bella replied flatly, "I made plans this weekend. That's part of why I need you out."

"We had that standing agreement, remember? What about next weekend?"

"Can't. Made plans then, too."

My situation was so parlous that it barely registered at the time that whatever the fuck those plans were, they were apparently worth more to her than hundreds and hundreds of dollars.

"Alright. Then I guess I'll need that money for the car."

The standing agreement… I put so much trust in her with that. If our relationship broke down, I'd need *one last favor*. I trusted that even if she totally lost interest, she'd agree to get me to a place where I'd at least have a roof over my head. I had nothing to enforce this request. No backup plan. No other choice. It was completely dependent on her willingness to be decent. Without that, I'd be homeless for the second time that year. I guess that was too much to ask.

"Okay, I'll just hold on to your stuff until I get paid back." She perhaps said this smugly, but I was too focused on the possibility of homelessness to pick up on it.

It became my fourth all-time low. Several times, "Something in the Way" by Nirvana came up on my iPod. "Underneath the bridge." "Living off of grass." I wondered if that would soon be my reality. I wondered if you could really live off of grass. Because I might fucking have to.

WEAPON —
PART 6: RAGER

BACK AT WORK, TRENT FINALLY GOT back to me.

"My friend said yes, you can move in! I didn't even have to convince him: he just said yes."

So that was that. I had a place and the move-in date happened to line up with when I needed to be out.

Bella dropped me off at my new place that Friday night. I could only bring a few sets of clothing and my laptop. I left Chicago with half of my belongings and now I was starting over *again* with 10% of just that: I had very close to nothing. The house was on an odd stretch of road with three houses next to each other, and a mile of absolutely nothing on either side. It wasn't much of a neighborhood.

There were a ton of cars in the driveway, and maybe a dozen people in the front yard. I did not expect this. Bella was unphased and just eager to get rid of me. It seemed like I was in for some lonely times. That first night, though? It was anything but. My two new roommates were just six months out of high school. So, they had... different priorities. The house was packed wall to wall with a bunch of my roommates' teenage friends, all of whom were, of course, drinking.

I was by far the oldest person there being a few years out of college. It was almost a gross feeling, but I didn't have anywhere to go without a car. I wandered around the house, weaving my way through the tightly packed crowd every step of the way. I was half curious about how packed the place was, and half wondering what the house looked like because this was my first time in it. I found the basement. It was also packed wall to wall with drunk teenagers. I roamed around and made sure things didn't go totally off the rails.

A couple of kids pulled up in cars that must have been worth eighty thousand dollars. Who is buying their high school kids shit like this? This was not how it was where I grew up. The mere concept was perplexing. That type of money was unfathomable to me. I knew that much money could exist, and that some people might have that much of it, but I was only familiar with it as a dense theoretical concept: like quantum mechanics and superpositions, I could probably watch a documentary about that much money and understand it for the next few days until the details began to fade.

I caught some high school kids doing coke off the toilet lid in the bathroom.

"Hey! Don't do that shit in this house."

I didn't know if they even knew I lived there given I'd only moved in an hour ealier, but they quickly complied with an "Oh shit."

After midnight, I had enough. My room was miraculously empty, even as the house was otherwise packed. I went into my room and fell asleep on the floor in a borrowed sleeping bag, courtesy of Trent. The sound of three hundred teenagers raging became white noise. I don't know how I got to sleep, but I did. The next morning, I woke up and a few stragglers were still there. The floor had a new layer of cups and beer cans.

All our art school parties were, frankly, just not like this. Yeah, we'd drink, and yeah it would get a little rowdy, but not like this. We weren't naturally extroverts. We bounced ideas, projects, and theories off of each other. What happened last night was sensory overload. My roommates agreed that it was out of control and that they wouldn't do that again. Thank god. It wasn't the party that was weird for me. It was that it was all basically kids. At least my roommates had graduated. I don't think that was the case for all their friends at the party.

That day, my coworker Michael was kind enough to help me out with the gift of a futon frame and a bunch of extra blankets. No mattress: he didn't have it. We carried it in kicking unseen empty beer cans all the way to my new room. That became my bed: A futon frame with a nest of blankets on it, just thick enough to be sort of mattress-y.

Without a car, something as simple as getting food became a strategic process. I asked Michael to swing through a drive-through. I only had about forty bucks to last me until I started getting paychecks again, so it was the dollar menu for me. Michael offered to pay. I couldn't afford to decline. Most people politely refuse such charity. I couldn't afford to have my pride and eat, too.

So there I was. In a new place with nothing more than my laptop, phone, and a week's worth of clothes. All my other possessions, all my old art books, all my film school projects, my entire professional portfolio, all held hostage. I preferred it when it was just stuff like a camera and game system: not my entire body of work.

Things were pretty bleak now, but at least I had those jobs lined up. It could theoretically be smooth sailing ahead.

Actually… I probably should've stopped telling myself that.

WEAPON —
PART 7: THE NURSE WHO LOVED ME

I SPENT THE NEXT FEW DAYS GOING BACK AND forth with Bella trying to figure out where the relationship went wrong. What was the final straw? According to her, it wasn't the job thing or the delayed check she was worried about; I might have understood that even if I disagreed. Instead, she claimed I said something rude to a friend of hers. I asked her who it was. She told me.

"I don't remember saying anything rude to him. What did I say?"

"I don't remember exactly. But it was rude, and that's a dealbreaker."

It was that fellow I had talked to at the clubhouse gathering a few weeks ago about being from Cleveland. My question about the quality of Cleveland could *possibly* be construed as rude. I managed to find the guy on social media. I wanted to make things right with him.

"I heard I might have said something that may have offended you at that party. I'm not entirely sure what that could've been, but if that's the case, I wanted to reach out and apologize as that was not my intent."

"No, we're all good, man. You didn't say anything that I took offense to at all."

If I had any illusions of patching things up with Bella and continuing the relationship from separate residences it must not have lasted long because I don't remember feeling that way. But I wasn't out here trying to make enemies, so I still wanted to make sure I was good with this guy.

I came back to Bella with this, and she was completely unmoved: "It doesn't matter if he wasn't offended. It was still rude."

So on paper, she was ending things because I said something rude, like *five weeks ago*, that she *didn't even remember*, to someone who was *not offended* by it. I was sure now this was completely made up. I wasn't going to get the truth out of her. As combative as Gemma was, I'd still have preferred her bluntness to Bella's mind games.

I wondered if her abusive ex Samuel was spinning up tall tales of me offending people. Maybe he was taking back what he thought was his property. Bella would probably be *into* that. I've heard many times that someone being abused by a romantic partner will have to leave them seven times before they fully exit the situation. Maybe this was that. Sometimes other attempts at relationships are sprinkled throughout.

She held two competing ideals in our relationship: her OCD tendencies and her insistence on being essentially controlled. She'd only ever lived alone as an adult. If her OCD told her nothing could be out of place, and everything had to be exactly a certain way, she couldn't also let someone completely take the wheel in the relationship or household. She wasn't even willing to move boxes and containers she hadn't touched in years to give me a place for my things. Where she needed me to be was a place she didn't want me to go. It's not even that *we* were incompatible. What she needed was incompatible with *itself*. We were doomed from the start.

Part of me suspected that as part of her supposed submissive nature, she would claim control over small things, and then secretly expect me not to respect that boundary. This was a subtle observation I noticed where "submissive" types would sometimes try to subtly push their partner's buttons to provoke the desired reaction. If Gemma couldn't get that out of me, then Bella sure as hell wasn't going to either. Fuck me for not trampling all over Bella's boundaries, I guess. I wasn't about to become an uncaring emotionally abusive partner on the off chance she was *into that shit*.

I was extremely grateful that Bella removed me from an abusive situation. Our relationship ending didn't change that. On the other hand, I was extremely resentful that after empathizing with my Kevin situation, she turned around and almost immediately put me in an identical situation: unsure where I'd be living at any given moment. Stranded outside, locked out of the house. Holding my possessions hostage: worse than Kevin, she had my life's fucking work. That is: hours of raw footage from film school, hard drives with video editing files, and notebooks and drawing pads you could stack two feet high. It was *exactly the same shit I just* escaped from. The fact that she could do that, with *full awareness* of what I just went through, made her misdeeds even worse than my former friend's.

This time, it didn't feel like abuse: it felt like she was just being vindictive. While still grateful for the huge favor she did for me, if she really empathized with my situation with Kevin, I didn't see how she could turn around and do the *exact same shit*. The greatest act of kindness ever done for me was just an act.

Justifying the breakup, she told me one day, "I'm not selfless anymore." It felt to me like a line that was fed to her. I wondered again if her abusive ex Samuel was in her ear, trying to flip her life all around just for fun. She had been over there at least once a week, and now that I didn't live with her, I had no idea how frequent those visits became. She seemed to be saying the kindness that helped birth our relationship was now gone. Interesting that she saw fit not just to *cut me off* from that kindness—which is well within her right—but to apparently *nuke that entire part of her personality*.

I didn't see the difference between what Kevin did and what she did—it *had* to be intentional. It *had* to be done specifically to hurt in the worst possible way. Kevin was like the "wild" dog that he couldn't raise: Everything he did wasn't much more than a crime of opportunity. He couldn't change—I'd tried. Destruction was in his nature—but *this?* What Bella did was done with malicious intent. She gathered *intelligence* through my trust and used *every bit* of it against me. My nightmare year was over for a bit, but she brought it all crashing down. Now it was back in full force.

I was deceived by a friend with a knife
Your care received I owe you my life
I was relieved as you tended the wound
a love conceived when I assumed I was doomed

you soon became my most trusted nurse
but you betray me and then hurt me worse
you grip the blade and slowly push it in
breaking the skin of the same wound again

Your love is a weapon

PLEASE DIE & EVERYTHING — PART 1: AND FIRST PLACE GOES TO

I MADE IT OFFICIAL: I HATED BELLA. I SHOULD PREFACE this: I think it's a sign of immaturity if someone hates every ex they have. The hate is usually misplaced love, longing, entitlement, or whatever. Hate is easier to deal with and live with. This was different, and to be fair, I did miss her a bit. But moreover, she did *a lot* of damage to me: the relationship being over was the least of my troubles.

What made this worse was that she insisted we be friends. I was uninterested in maintaining a friendship on any deeper level, but I didn't cut her out, either. After all, she still had 90% of my belongings, including almost every art project I'd ever created.

"I need you not to hate me," she told me one day.

Like many of her post-break-up statements, this once again came out of nowhere. She must have been sitting at home and internalizing this stuff, and then coming to me with her various half-baked conclusions.

"Why would I hate you?" I asked. "You did me the biggest favor anyone ever has."

"I just need to hear you say it. I need you not to hate me."

"Okay, fine. I don't hate you."

This was a lie.

I knew it *right then* when I said it. I just didn't need any more conflict in my life. Maybe she *did* understand what she did to me: She knew hate was on the table. I always thought she never realized how I felt. But maybe she knew.

You
Need me not to hate you, but I do
Said I didn't, I lied to you
Faith and hope eradicated
Play the sub, emotional sadist

Sometimes I wonder what would've happened if I said "Yes." I think I know: it would've triggered her self-worth issues. It would've given her something she had to prove to me. Her previous partners kept putting her down, not giving her the time of day, and treating her as a poly-amorous third wheel; not much more than a plaything. Every previous relationship she told me about had clear signs of that. She needed to prove her worth to people who clearly didn't want or respect her. Once she had that worth and respect from me, there was no more need for the relationship: it was mission accomplished.

All that wasn't even the worst of the emotional fallout. The worst thing about the breakup was that my favorite song—the one she once had me sing to her nightly—was ruined. It could no longer disarm me; instead, it just made me angry, reminding me of all the bullshit she put me through. She managed to take away my most treasured escape: that was the one thing that made me *truly* resent her. I could've had that song as an emo-tional escape for life, and she took that from me.

The only sort-of silver lining to the whole thing is that she managed to take the title of "Person to Damage Me Most" in the nightmare year. How is that a silver lining, you may ask? I'm just glad Kevin didn't get that title because he'd probably have secretly liked that.

PLEASE DIE & EVERYTHING — PART 2: MY FIRST CAR

I WAS VERY CLOSE TO STARTING TWO NEW JOBS and still needed a car. I didn't have my money from the sales job yet, but I was trying to time it so that I could get my car the second it was in hand.

One of the first cars I saw was a station wagon. If I could help it, I did not want a station wagon. I hoped my first car could be at least vaguely cool. Lenny checked it out with me and acted like he knew about cars, but when pressed it seemed like he didn't know much more than I did.

The second car I saw seemed promising. I asked a long list of questions that I came up with to ensure I wasn't getting a lemon. I was nearly ready to test drive it when the guy gave me a *slight* disclaimer.

"The car just has one, *small* problem," he told me. "Probably not a big deal at all."

"Okay, that's probably fine," I agreed, but asked: "What is it?"

"You could probably get it fixed for cheap. The small problem is that it won't go in reverse."

"Uuuum, I don't know if that's a small problem..."

"No, it *totally* is, it's probably just a gear or something that needs to be replaced."

"I have to park my car in a driveway. How is that going to work? How do parking lots work?"

I knew nothing about cars, but I still knew this was a major issue, probably worth junking the car over. If you know more about cars than I did, you probably just yelled at this book like you yell at a horror movie protagonist not to go into that room.

There was a new guy at the sales job who had a car he could sell me. Everyone there regarded him as a bit of a putz, so I'll call him The Putz. I didn't see why he was so disliked and had previously defended him. He agreed to my budget and just said to swing by and talk to his dad.

Lenny and I arrived to find the car had no bumpers on either end, half of the insides were torn out, including several seats, and it had no radio, just a hole in the dash. I offered him a lesser amount due to the condition.

"Yeah, there's no way I'd go that low," The Putz's dad said, "I'm gonna sell this car for [number way higher than even the blue book value]."

"Uhh, [The Putz] said he'd let this go for a lot less. But that was before I saw that it didn't have any bumpers, or radio, or all the seats. I mean, I'd be willing to test drive it at least…"

"Do you have insurance?"

"As I understand it, you need a car to have insurance. I'm trying to buy a car precisely because I don't have one."

"Well, I'm not selling it for any less. It's *my* car, it's not [The Putz]'s car to sell. And I can't let you drive it without insurance, so you can't test drive it either."

I guess the apple doesn't fall far from the tree because Putz Sr. was absolutely wrong. Standard car insurance insures cars, not drivers. I knew that pretty well from the accident back in July. Lenny and I left perplexed at how foolish this whole situation was. When I told The Putz what happened later, he was utterly defeated. He never told us it wasn't actually his car. He was just so sure he could sell it, though. I had been skeptical at first, but his status as The Putz was now thoroughly confirmed.

Another few cars were bought out from under me before I could snatch them up. With only hours to go, I ended up calling the station wagon guy back. It had been over a week, but miraculously this was the one car that stayed on the market for longer than a few days. The same reason it was still available was the same reason I didn't want it at first: *Nobody* wants a station wagon. But I could no longer be picky.

He was selling it for just a smidge over what I had. I told him my budget.

"Would you take that much for it?"

I prepared to hold my breath. Let the awkward silence ride until he folded into a 'Yeah, what the heck, sure.'

Instead, he damn near cut me off with a "*Yup.*"

That night I finally got my paycheck. It was about sixty bucks short of what I expected. Not a huge amount, but I was supposed to buy a car in another forty minutes, so I needed to make up that gap fast. Michael was kind enough to lend me the difference I needed. He had to be one of the more selfless folks I encountered this whole year.

I picked up the car with the help of Lenny, and then I finally had a car: my first one. I had Michael paid back a few days later. I never needed one in Chicago and never could afford one as a kid. I felt pretty good about it. Just in time to make it to the first days of my two new jobs.

PLEASE DIE & EVERYTHING —
PART 3: MY LIFE S WORK

SOMETIME AFTER GETTING MY CAR, I WAS HANGING out with my new room-mates and recounting my bad luck these last few months, perhaps the first time they heard the full story. I got to the part where Bella had all my stuff, including every film and art project I had ever made, going back over ten years.

As I verbalized it, I realized that her having all the files in my video portfolio could potentially render my *entire* college degree useless. A video reel is a hard requirement as it demonstrates your competency in all aspects of video production. Some of the final edits were streamable online, but not everything, and no matter how you slice it, I was losing the original footage *and* editing files for hundreds of hours of footage, all years in the making. I was losing a full bookshelf worth of drawings, writing, and other creative notes.

Even if I never worked in the video sector again, the amount of blood, sweat, tears, and years I put into those projects eclipsed anything else I'd done by an exponential margin. The value of that isn't a month and a half of rent but rather the grand total cost of my *entire college education*. Regardless of Bella's intentions, the effect would be magnitudes greater than anything Kevin had even *considered* doing to me, even when his intentions shifted into pure malice. I was the first in my family to go to and finish college. That's still true as of writing. Was my *entire body of work* about to be reduced to a piece of paper saying "Congrats, you did it"?

The gravity of it now dawned on me.

Sort of inspired, I ended with, "You know what? I'm going to go get my shit back: *tonight*."

I waited until about 7 PM, figuring that Bella probably went shopping after work like she always did. I had a short speech rehearsed in my head. I didn't want to be pushy about it. Just knock and say my piece: the rest was up to her. This might not be the most effective method to get my stuff back, but it was *going* to work because it *had* to work.

I knocked on her door. I was alone. I didn't know who would answer, really. For all I knew, her abusive ex Samuel would be there. I had not announced my intention to come over specifically so that she couldn't assemble a team of misguided white knights to stop me from getting my stuff, or worse, maybe try to rough me up. It wouldn't have been her idea, probably, but I am sure their dominant alpha bullshit would've taken over. I couldn't be sure what she or her friends were capable of. Inversely, for her benefit, I also felt it was important I was alone. I didn't want to show up with a bunch of my new friends—even if they were just there to help carry stuff—and have that taken as an intimidation tactic.

Based on what she told me, she went through a pattern in every relationship: The relationship, then a breakup period in which the ex was considered a complete monster, and then suddenly she was friends with the ex again. It always happened over the course of about a month. Samuel was, of course, genuinely an abusive monster. I had seen the scar she told me he inflicted, after all.

However, she had tried to spin other exes as terrible people too for far more nebulous or subjective reasons. Perhaps her relationship pattern— from a partner to a monster to a friend—was so dogmatic that it held even when a previous partner was *actually* a monster. The context here is that I was pretty sure she'd spin me up as the next monster of the week in her world, no matter how diplomatic I played this. If that was the price to pay for getting back my life's work, then fine. I'd be the new monster, now. Rawr.

Each second after that knock felt like an eternity. I didn't know if she'd even answer the door after seeing me through the peephole. However, only seconds later she cracked open the door and peered out.

I gave her my rehearsed speech: "Look, I know I owe you some money, but you are hanging onto ten full years of every art project I've ever done, including my entire college portfolio, every client project I've ever done, and every personal project I've ever created or written, which amounts to my full life's work. I don't think that's fair collateral for a couple weeks worth of rent, so I want that stuff back."

"I just got home. How did you know I just got home?" she said sheepishly.

There it is. She was immediately setting a precedent to spin me up as some sort of stalker. Even so, this too could be a trauma response learned from previous experience.

"I remember that every night after work you go shopping. All I did was wait until you might be done."

I kept my distance as much as the porch would allow. I go by vampire rules: I don't come in unless invited. If someone asks me to leave, I do so immediately. (Sometimes, this backfires on someone who doesn't really want me to leave but is just playing mind games.) Surprisingly, Bella came out on the porch with me, which brought my guard down a little. She did not invite me in, so we both stood on the porch.

"How are you going to get this stuff home?" she asked.

"My car." I gestured to it.

"You bought a car?!" she said, jaw nearly on the floor.

"I mean, I told you I'd get one. ...What? You didn't believe me?"

"I don't know..."

"Yeah, I bought it as soon as I got my money from the sales job. The money you never believed was coming."

"Oh…"

This was the kind of I-told-you-so that, if you could capture its energy, would provide the earth with *unlimited power*. It is perhaps one of my greatest moments of one-upmanship.

With no resistance, she started gathering some of my things. Once I got the hard drives, original footage for my film projects, all my drawing notebooks, and all my writing notebooks, I was relieved. And that was all I explicitly asked for, but she kept bringing more until I had everything.

I'd spent all my adult life working on this stuff, so in a very literal way, I was getting my life back. It was the first time in a while I had the means to advocate for myself and got exactly what I was advocating for. So far, it was my most important victory all year.

PLEASE DIE & EVERYTHING — PART 4: FUCKIN LENNY

ON THE OFF DAYS FROM MY MAIN TWO JOBS, I still did the sales job whenever I could. We all hung out outside of work to various degrees as well. Something must have happened to Lenny's car at some point because I remember giving him rides occasionally. He did the same for me when I didn't have a car, so he'd earned it.

This dude begged me—literally *begged* me—to take him all the way across town so he could see his girlfriend for like twenty minutes. It was only because of this prolonged, pitiful begging that I finally relented and took him. As we began the drive, I must provide the context that it did not appear that Lenny had anything on his person.

We were driving.

"Thank you, thank you," he said.

"Yeah it's cool, I guess. Just try not to take forever because I have to work tomorrow, you know."

"Yeah man, I get it."

I let the silence ride. Dusk began to fade into night. The last bit of light was leaving the sky. We were on a long stretch of a lonely two-lane road. There weren't too many cars out that night. The only investment I'd made into my new-to-me car was a fifteen-dollar tape adapter, but I got it from my new job at the electronic store, so it was like five bucks after my discount. I had music playing—I always did. If I had a friend in the car, I'd keep it low enough not to inhibit conversation.

"I love this song," Lenny said.

It was a song he had introduced me to. It was maybe the only musical thing we had in common.

"Yeah, I know. Me too," I replied.

It was a damn good song.

Silence again, except for the music. As we cruised through that serene little slice of Kentucky—stars starting to shine in the night sky, as the trees became clouds of black that whizzed by on the ground—the peaceful silence was broken by an unmistakable sound.

Krrchhhk!

That was the sound of a can being opened. I looked over at Lenny, who I could've earlier sworn didn't look like he had an entire unopened aluminum can just in his fucking pocket, and this mother fucker is hunched over with puckered lips about to take a sip of a PBR, which, hailing from Chicago, I was sure was responsible for 70% of all beer sales.

"Dude, what the absolute fuck do you think you are doing!?" I yelled, breaking the silence.

"Dude, what? It's just a beer!"

"You can't have an open container in a car!"

"I'm not even driving!"

"It doesn't matter, that's still illegal! Did you seriously not know that!?"

"No, dude. Sorry. Here, I'll chug it."

"No, don't chug it, get rid of it!"

"Well, I'm not going to waste it!" he said, immediately before shotgunning the beer in about nine seconds.

"Fine, whatever, just throw it out the window."

He did so.

"...Thank you!" I said, clearly frustrated.

I sighed—let the stress out—got back to driving. Hopefully, it would just be a chill drive again. I thought about how maybe it could be theoretically possible that this dude could've been sheltered enough—in just the right way—that he might have missed that it's illegal to have an open beer in a moving car. He was still fairly young. I believe he was nineteen—maybe twenty—which reminds me that I'm not sure how he readily had access to beer at that age. But either way, that was done. At least he knew *now*. Nothing bad happened. I'll let it go, I guess. The silence breathed again. I was back to focusing on the road and the peaceful Kentucky night sky.

Krrchhhk!

I look over, and this *motherfucker* has *another* beer in hand.

"*Are you absolutely goddamn serious right now?!*"

"*You said to get rid of the beer! I'm getting rid of the beer!*"

He began to chug.

PLEASE DIE & EVERYTHING — PART 5: SONG RETROSPECTIVE

I FEEL IT'S MY DUTY TO CLARIFY THE NATURE OF THIS SONG. While I certainly had, uh, *zero desire* to have anything to do with Bella, both in the moment and at the time of writing of writing the song (a year or two after the events), this song is not literal. Although I don't feel like I generally owe any explanation regarding my feelings for her (and yet here I am *writing a fucking book* about it), I do feel I have a social responsibility to clarify the place the song comes from.

The song is meant purely tongue-in-cheek. Its sentiment is not a serious one. I don't have any genuine ill will towards Bella. She got me out of a horrible situation. We both knew there was a chance the relationship might not work. In a way, the song is supposed to be a parody of how I was *supposed to* feel. In the title, "Please Die & Everything," the "and everything" should subtly indicate how flippant this remark is. That's why when the title phrase occurs in the song, it's followed by a tongue-in-cheek "thank you." It should come off as dark humor.

Please die and everything
Thank you

I genuinely don't hold any ill will towards her. She had a lot of complex issues going on that she probably couldn't help. I think these issues heavily contributed to how she handled things. I strongly suspected she had OCD and was objectively a hoarder, although her OCD ensured it was an extremely organized version of hoarding. She likely had some serious self-worth issues that her ex, Samuel, was probably manipulating. As such, any attempt I made to build her up might have caused her to subconsciously pull away.

But wait, didn't I say I hated her earlier? Well, yes. I'm not sure that lasted long. Even so, I don't think that hate and having ill will have to go hand in hand. She was the worst, and I hated her, but I felt bad for her, too. I genuinely hope she figures her shit out. If she cut her knickknack budget by 35%, she could probably afford some much-needed therapy.

All her various issues were fundamentally incompatible with maintaining a serious cohabiting relationship. If it didn't end how it did, we'd have self-destructed sooner rather than later.

She insisted we remain friends, even though the friendship was terrible and came from an insincere place.

"I'm friends with all my exes," she told me, "so we should be friends, too."

It was the sole justification for our post-breakup "friendship." She popped up exclusively to make snide comments that were never going to faze me, but *oh boy did she try*. Just like when Gemma got drunk, Bella was now trying her damnedest to see if she could get under my skin. As soon as I got all my stuff back from her, it seemed she was desperately searching for some other form of leverage over me, even if it was just her trying to irk me.

In one such instance, she tried to undercut me for having to work two (technically three) jobs.

"Most people only need to have *one* job," she said snidely.

I didn't dignify that with a response and simply continued on with the previous topic. It further cemented the main cultural difference between us: economic class.

We were at the height of the recession, and "success" was declared by economists and government officials even if the monthly job loss numbers had managed to *merely tick down*. That is, each month millions *more* were out of work, but this month a *few less* jobs were lost than last month, so they'd mark that up as a victory. Working two or more jobs was a reality for millions of people who managed to remain employed, so *under*-employment, not just *un*employment became rampant.

Suffice to say, it wasn't just happening to me. The recession had laid out nearly everyone I knew. I was doing better than most of my peers by simply being employed at all and not having to live with a parent.

Under a continuing stream of passive-aggressiveness, I ended the friend-ship with Bella. Neither of us made any attempt to reach out after that. She didn't even try to get that rent money—not that I had any to spare.

SHIPWRECKED —
PART 1: TOO MANY JOBS AND NOT
ENOUGH MONEY

WITH THREE MAJOR VILLAINS OF THE NIGHTMARE year down (Kevin, Bella, and to some degree Gemma), it's time to meet the fourth: Crippling loneliness.

I was filled with a sense of longing and I wasn't sure who or what it was for. Did I miss Bella? Maybe in a way. Maybe I missed my friend Lola who had moved to Hawaii. Yeah, I did. Maybe I missed Gemma. That relationship was far more substantial than the one with Bella, lasted a lot longer, and was more solidified emotionally. Yeah, I definitely missed Gemma. I wished I didn't, but I did. All the bad memories with her started to dull with time.

I hadn't seen The Artist and his group since that initial gathering where Judy sold me out to my former friend Kevin. In small part because I resented what happened that night and in greater part because I never got a chance to settle in after a whiplash of transitions. I was too busy working three jobs, anyway.

It is hard to express how profoundly lonely this period of time truly was. I was working two—technically three—jobs. I saw my friends from the sales job less and less as my days were filled morning to night working my two main jobs. I had such a shallow support network in Louisville that when my new shipping job asked me to write down an emergency contact, I genuinely had no idea who to put down. That's how alone I was. The very question nearly made me spiral into a crisis. If I ended up in the hospital, who would even come see me?

Every day, I'd wake up anywhere between 4 and 8 AM for the shipping company job, packing boxes in a truck all day by myself. It was so dull, I'd think of a song and see if I could recite it to myself to keep my mind busy.

We had to do a full security check daily, and everyone had to leave their phones in their cars. The security check was unpaid but mandatory. I saw news stories about other companies settling class action lawsuits for unpaid wages because of exactly that scenario. There was a union here, but it was a complete farce and not a true union. It was purely an extension of the top brass of the company, designed to trick you into believing someone there had your back. They did not.

On my first day of training, the manager was extremely clear: *"Do not throw packages."*

Then, it was the shift lead's job to show me the ropes from a more beat-by-beat perspective. The nano-second the manager was out of view, my shift lead started throwing packages.

"Wait: didn't he just say…?"

"There's no way to keep up without throwing packages," he explained, "just *don't get caught*."

After the first day, my interaction with anyone there was minimal. If this place was run like the other shortlist of major shipping companies, it's safe to say that every package you have ever received has seen some flight time. The whole job was like playing a game of Tetris, but every piece was a different size than all the others. It could be both frantic and dull, even at the same time. On any given day, I could be at this job anywhere from six to eleven hours.

I could've sworn the legal minimum was two fifteen-minute breaks, but this place got away with two ten-minute breaks a day—not a *second* more—and sometimes a half-hour lunch. Compliments of the "union," I'm sure. The break room was so far out of the way that these ten-minute breaks were more like five, and lunch was barely long enough to eat. My two-jobs schedule did not allow time for pre-making a lunch, so every day I ate some bullshit from the vending machine. Easier and cheaper.

Once done there, I'd drive straight to my second job, find a spot in the parking lot, check if anyone was around, and then swap into my work shirt for the big box electronic store. I had superficial interactions with customers there, giving me a cruel teaser of the genuine human interaction I wasn't getting elsewhere. I worked there until 10 or 11 PM.

Before bed, I might swing by a fast food joint to get two items off the dollar menu, complete with a free water. It was all I could afford and all I had time for. Some nights I was lucky to get four hours of sleep. The next day, I'd repeat it all over again.

The heat broke at the house, and we had to wait to get it fixed. The house became empty as my roommates retreated to their respective parents' houses. I was alone at home, now, too. I bought a cheap space heater and secluded myself in my nearly bare room. It took a few months to get internet service, so I was even cut off from a major communication method with friends back in Chicago or my hometown. Each day I got up and scurried to each job where I'd be isolated in a slightly different way.

I rarely had a full day off, because I nearly always worked at least one of these jobs. If I didn't, it was back to the door-to-door sales job, because I was on the razor's edge of barely scraping by. I had friends there, but I spent most of my time wandering neighborhoods alone ringing doorbells, with most people not being home or pretending not to be. Every neighborhood was another ghost town.

I was so poor I couldn't even justify the cost of insurance on my car. It was months before I could even afford to transfer the plates. I turned off the road if I saw a police car because I couldn't afford a ticket for those things, either.

At my shipping job, I'd sometimes see a package coming from the town I grew up in—a little over an hour from Chicago—and I'd become nostalgic for the place I moved halfway across the country to avoid going back to. Missing that shithole town was the clearest sign that I had hit rock bottom. Yup: it was my fifth all-time low. Things had been bad, but this was worse.

Some nights after work, I'd drive to a nearby Starbucks and get on their Wi-Fi with my laptop. One night, it was so late that Starbucks was closed. I drove to my door-to-door sales job and snuck on the internet from the parking lot. The lights were on. The manager sat on the other side of the full-length windows, just chilling on the couch in the lounge, watching TV as I hung back in my car. The manager this week was from a town two hours away. She must have been staying overnight in the office to avoid the cost of a hotel. It was hard times for everyone; both her and me, I guess.

SHIPWRECKED —
PART 2: ACTION SCENE IN A VEHICLE
MOVING AT HIGH SPEED

I LEARNED A COOL NEW TRICK AROUND THIS TIME. I could put on head-phones, cue up some good songs, close my eyes, and completely lose myself in the music. I became the music. Every song would give me chills. Or I might go on a drive just to listen to music and sing along as loud as I wanted, getting lost in my own emotions. It was my only escape from my bleak reality. Sometimes the song I sang to Bella would come on, and I'd try earnestly to let it take me away like it used to, but its healing power was still stripped away by the wound she caused me. I skipped it every time.

There were a couple of nautical-themed songs I was really digging. Being out at sea always seemed to be used as a metaphor for turmoil and loneliness. Now, *that* I could get. Maybe I could write a song like that, I thought.

Sometimes I'd work at the door-to-door sales job just to have some social interaction, even if I really needed a day off. Today was one such day. Maybe I'd earn a few extra bucks.

Michael had requested more responsibilities because his girlfriend was six months pregnant, and he wanted to step up, so today he drove the van carting us around. This meant the troop I was with was all buddies and no bosses, which made it all the more chill.

On the way out to our location for the day, I often put on my headphones, closed my eyes, and drifted off into the music for a little. Once we got there, I stuffed my headphones in the pocket behind the passenger seat in the van. Didn't make a single penny that day. Not uncommon.

Heading back at the end of the day, it was music time again. I fished in the seat pocket for my headphones: they weren't there. I checked the other seat. I turned around and checked the other rear seats. No sign of them.

"Has anyone seen my headphones? I put them behind the seat here, but now they're gone."

Everyone said they hadn't seen them. Were they stolen? And if so, by who? But more importantly: *why?* I sat there in silence, idly searching other crevices of the minivan. Nothing.

That was my only pair of headphones. I couldn't afford to replace them. I sat there thinking about how long it would be until the next time I got paid. Could I afford to replace them then? No, I had rent coming up. That always took at least one full paycheck. Even so, we'd be talking about going several weeks without my only escape, my only constant in my lonely world. I sat there absorbing that reality, defeated, for a few minutes. A few weeks without being able to zone out into my music would feel like an eternity in a void. I wasn't sure I could even make it.

"Hey, Steven," Lenny piped up, "I know where your headphones are."

"Oh, awesome, where are they?"

"I hid them in the van. Just look."

Now, this motherfucker had me half tearing the van apart as we cruised sixty-five miles per hour down a lonely split highway.

"Just tell me where they are. I already looked everywhere," I said, clearly annoyed.

"I've got them here."

He lifted up a paper bag I hadn't checked, because why would my headphones be in a paper bag?

"Finally, thank you," I said, annoyed, reaching for the bag.

He pulled his hand away, starting a game of keep-away where I was supposed to try to grasp for my headphones, supposedly in this paper bag. Instead, I grabbed his other wrist and used the leverage to better reach the bag in his other hand.

"What, you think you can fight me?"

"I don't want to fight you, I just want my headphones," I said, raising my voice.

"You got another thing coming if you think you can take me. I wrestled in high school, you know."

I couldn't be sure if that would actually be a benefit in a real-world situation.

What happened next is a scene too crazy for most fiction, but here I was, living it. This motherfucker used every free inch of his side of the van and took a wrestling stance, low to the ground with hands out. Only a few feet were between us. He charged me, caught me center mass, and attempted to get me on the floor. I don't know if this is considered a good move in wrestling, but in my mind, it was pretty stupid: As soon as he hit me center mass with his shoulder, this move begged for a headlock, which I put him in instantly. I held him in that headlock and he began to struggle for freedom.

"Just give me my headphones, and I'll let you go. I'm not trying to fight, I just want my headphones."

"I'm just messing around dude, don't take it so serious!" he said.

"Well, I'm not just going to let you attack me."

It seemed that was that. I let him go. I reached for the bag. He snatched it before I could reach it, and started playing keep away again.

"Motherfucker, just give me my goddamn headphones back," I said, reaching for them again.

"I'll throw them out the window!" He rolled down the window and mimed like he was about to do it, hand well outside the bounds of the vehicle.

"Dude, I can't afford to replace those right now, if you throw those out the window, you're replacing them *today*!"

All this in a minivan traveling at sixty-five miles an hour down a state highway.

Michael, who was driving, chimed in finally: "Lenny, will you quit fucking around and just give Steve his headphones?"

All through the commotion, he had not even slowed down, probably thinking that this certainly must be the end of it. He rolled up the window using the driver's controls.

"Fine, fine," Lenny relented, "I'll give you your headphones."

He reached out, offering my headphones like an olive branch. I reached for them, like a peace treaty handshake. The war was finally over. The frontline soldiers would soon erupt in celebration. We're going home, boys.

"Psych!" Lenny exclaimed, withdrawing the headphones yet again.

Cancel the victory parades. Before I knew it, Lenny had squared up his wrestling pose yet again. Perhaps this was an ego thing, perhaps he did not want to be bested or be the one to relent. So here he was, coming at me with the same dumbass move he tried just moments ago. Just the same as before, I caught him in a headlock. Is this considered standard in wrestling? Do people simply lunge at you and expect to get into a headlock and that's just part of the deal? Once again, he tried to get me on the floor. Once again, I resisted.

I wasn't all that strong at the time (if at all, honestly), but I'd always been pretty nimble and had an innate understanding of how best to use my own leverage. So, Lenny continued failing to pin me, and I continued to hold him in a headlock. He took potshots at my stomach. I was utilizing my full core to keep him in this hold, so my abs were fully flexed, and his punches barely fazed me.

"You're going to have to try better than that," I said through gritted teeth.

"Dude, let me go!"

I did not let go.

"I'm not letting you go until I'm sure you'll stop fucking with my shit."

"Just let me go!"

He wasn't explicitly agreeing to leave me or my headphones alone, so I wasn't letting go.

"Say you'll give me my headphones back, and you've got a deal."

We went back and forth like this for a long, *long* time. Maybe he finally had enough. I was genuinely getting bored. I loosened up a bit. I could let him think he had broken the hold; maybe we would be good after that. He wriggled around and got out of the lock. He reached for the headphones frantically, in such a way that it was pretty obvious he did not intend on giving them back at that moment.

He turned and went for the window again. As he turned, I got him in another headlock almost immediately. This time we were both upright and I had him in the headlock from behind. He flailed his arms and tried to escape, but I had him at the optimal angle, so he couldn't reach me.

"Stop trying to fuck with my stuff. Just stop. Tell me you're going to stop."

Once again, he couldn't tell me the words. I figured I'd wait him out again, but this time I wasn't going to give him any benefits of any doubts. I held him there for a significant amount of time, occasionally repeating my request. He continued refusing to say the words.

After what could've easily been ten solid minutes stuck flailing in a headlock, he finally started to run out of steam. I again repeated my request.

"Okay, okay," he finally relented.

I had learned my lesson, so I was not satisfied. "Say you'll stop trying to steal my headphones."

"I won't, okay?"

"Say the words. Say the full words."

"Why? I told you I won't do it!" he reasoned.

"I'll let go when you say the words."

"Fine, fine," he relented, "I will let you have your headphones back."

"Permanently. Not for just a second, not for just a minute. Say it again."

"I will let you have your headphones back for good, okay?"

"Okay, now say that you'll stop trying to fight me."

"Dammit, fine. I will stop trying to fight you."

"I don't like doing this. I'm not out here trying to fight people. I'm not into all that macho bullshit. I don't want you to ever do some bullshit like this ever again. You can do that stuff with your other friends, but not with me. *Do you understand?*"

"Fine, I get it, dude. I'll stop fucking with you."

This wasn't the first time he had come at me with one of these moves, so consequently it was not the first day I had put him in a headlock. This shit was not my M.O. and I hated it, even if I was handling it.

I continued, "Alright, good. I'm going to let you go. Can you calm down?"

"Yes, I'll calm down. I'm sorry. Please let me go."

"Okay. I'm going to let you go. ...But first, I need you to say 'uncle.'"

I forget exactly where I first heard that saying. My best guess is that I pulled it straight out of a Looney Tunes cartoon I probably hadn't seen since I was ten years old.

"What does that even mean? Why do you want me to say that?"

Huh, I thought that was a universal cultural touchstone. Maybe not. Now that he had posed the question though...

"Yeah, I don't know what it means to be honest with you. But the only thing you have to concern yourself with in the present moment is saying 'Uncle.'"

"Why? Just let me go!"

"Just say it."

That continued for another minute or so.

"Fine! Uncle! Uncle."

I let him go and grabbed my headphones. He spun around and fell backward dramatically, obviously on purpose. There was no reason to do that. No force had acted upon him. I hadn't pushed him. He landed against the door, quickly looked over at the door handle, then placed his hand on it, trying and failing to feign like he landed there naturally. As he did, he opened the door, a move which I could see was very intentional, but one he hoped would look like an accident. He then pretended to fall halfway out of the moving vehicle, with his hand still on the door handle for support, being sure to keep his center mass inside the vehicle for balance.

I felt such disdain for him in that moment. I could feel my opinion of him drop instantly from "kind of a jerk" to "legitimately pitiful." The feeling was palatable, and I remember it clearly to this day; it felt a little like pity but without the concern. What he was doing was so, *so* stupid and engineered for attention that any concern was forgone.

The noise of the wind filled the vehicle. We were still going at least sixty. Lenny reached his hand out to me to help him back into the van. The 'help me' look on his face was just so rehearsed, and his ploy was so very transparent. I almost suggested acting lessons right there on the spot.

Fine. If that's the consolation prize Lenny wanted, he could have it. I reached out my hand. He grabbed it. I pulled him in.

Finally, Michael pulled over. He turned around like a parent on a road trip that had to get the kids to behave.

"Lenny, I swear to god if you don't cut this shit out, I'm going to come back there and beat your ass a second time," he yelled. "Now *close the fucking door!*"

One miscalculation and he could've fallen out of the vehicle. He probably would've died. It would've been difficult to explain the story without sounding like I straight-up murdered the guy. But luckily, he didn't fall. He didn't die. But he *could* have, and all over some incredibly misguided attempt to make himself seem like a victim instead of an aggressor.

That was the last time Lenny tried some dumb shit with me. We were still friends. He started to be less of a piece of shit, at least to me.

Fuckin' Lenny, though. I swear to god.

SHIPWRECKED —
PART 3: THE HOLIDAYS WHEN YOU HAVE NO ONE

THANKSGIVING WAS COMING UP. With no family or long-time friends for hundreds of miles, I knew I'd spend the day alone. There's another area where being poor and isolated gets weird: everything is closed on Thanksgiving. I never had time to shop, so I didn't have a big stash of food in the house. I had to plan ahead if I wanted to eat that day.

The day before, I hit up a grocery store after work. It was nearly midnight and they closed in another few minutes. I bought some milk, cereal, and a couple packs of ramen noodles. I wasn't sure we had the pots to cook them, but if not, I could always eat more cereal.

The mere prospect of this was depressing. If I had still been in Chicago, my hometown would be one trip away. This year I had nowhere, nothing, no one. Yeah, I had friends, but they all had their own family gatherings. I didn't. My roommate Trent said I could play his video game system whenever I wanted to. I rented a game from a kiosk just to have something to do. Otherwise, I'd just sit there, spinning my wheels and thinking too hard about my situation.

After a few hours of video games, Trent came through and got me the hook up on some food. I arrived at his house after dinner, skipping any awkwardness, and just hung out and got a plate. I hoped I looked young enough not to be out of place with all of his nineteen-year-old friends that also showed up, but it was this or cereal. Trent had previously clocked me a good few years younger than I was, so maybe I was good.

I was so lonely during the holiday that I kept thinking about my ex, Gemma. Things felt unresolved between us, now. The fact that she had punched me in the eye (among other injuries)—and that our relationship was various levels of terrible—didn't even register anymore. I needed

something familiar, something that made me feel less displaced—
something to anchor me to less turbulent times—a "constant," if you
will. Something to keep me from losing my fucking mind like my boy
Desmond almost did in that titular episode of LOST.

I escape for a minute or two
but the tide brings me back to you

Over the next few days, I thought a lot about calling her. Could we pick
up where we left off? Would she welcome me back as earnestly as Penny
did with Desmond? Maybe not right away. Would we just catch up, or
reconnect on a deeper level? I hadn't solidified any expectations, I just
knew I wanted to call her. Whatever I hoped for needed to start with a
call, anyway. We'd have to work up to anything more. After a few days,
I decided I'd call her. I spent a few more days gathering the nerve to
actually do it.

One evening when I only worked my morning job, I decided that if I
didn't bite the bullet now, it wouldn't happen. I just had to push through
my reservations and do it. My nerves should go away as soon as I passed
the point of no return. So I called Gemma. I sat down, preparing for
what could be a lengthy conversation.

The first miracle is that she picked up.

I provided a standard greeting: "Hey, how's it going, I thought I'd just
call to catch up."

"Heeey you, it's good to hear from you," she replied.

The second miracle: she was apparently open to talking. Hearing this
really disarmed me and gave me some hope. She wasn't just open, she
wanted to talk.

"What's been up with you?" I asked.

"Oh man... so much! Hey, listen... Can I call you back in a few minutes?"

"Oh, yeah, sure. I'll be around."

That was fine, I guess. It took me days to dial her number, so what's another few minutes?

A few minutes became twenty. Then an hour, then two, then four. I held on to the hope that she was calling me back, but it was getting late. I turned the ringer on my phone up in case she called. I fell asleep staring at my phone.

I could call *her*, you might think, but it doesn't work like that. You can't want it too much, or it turns people off. More obviously, it's not like I could just send twenty gut-spilling texts to her either: that would be even worse.

One night became two. She was not calling me back. I resigned myself to this fact. Over those next two days, I made my peace with it. She was just trying to be polite while still blowing me off. It wasn't what I wanted, but I knew I couldn't just convince her to want it.

What's it matter?
You're not there
What's the matter?
You don't even care

On the third night, I finally came to a very earned closure. Gemma wasn't calling me back. It was a stupid idea anyway. Maybe I didn't *need* to talk to her. Maybe this was a *lesson*. Maybe I was *better off* this way. Perhaps that door was better off closed. My phone rang. It was her. I picked it up *immediately*.

"Oh hey, what's up?" I asked.

"Oh, I'm just calling you back. I'm sorry it took so long…"

I didn't ask if she was still single, but she didn't mention any romantic entanglements. Although, I suppose I didn't get into that either. It was pleasant, and it filled me up right when I needed it.

However, we didn't keep that up, so it didn't help me to feel any better in the long term. If I needed someone else to be happy, I wouldn't really be happy anyway. I know *for sure* that's not how that works. How would that work, anyway? There were much fewer—if any—jobs in Chicago, from my experience. At least here I was only *under*-employed. If I went back to Chicago, we'd be right back where we started.

SHIPWRECKED —
PART 4: DOG PERSON

ONE DAY, I CAME HOME AND TO MY SURPRISE, there was a cute-ass little puppy in the house. It might have been a basset hound. I was not a dog person back then. I was well known for ignoring dogs, but for some reason, they'd take a deep interest in me in response.

That was not the case with this puppy. My days were just work, sleep, work, sleep. It had been weeks since any of my basic psychological needs were met for any longer than five minutes. I had no time or energy for a social life. I didn't have the mental bandwidth to wonder about intellectual things anymore. I still couldn't know what the man in the top hat in my DMT vision at the festival told me as his lips silently moved, or even who he was. I couldn't care about high-minded stuff like that when I was barely feeding myself, barely keeping a roof over my head, and didn't even have a shell of a social life.

I had little to look forward to, so even though I wasn't much of a dog person, I loved that puppy *immediately*. And that puppy loved me back because he loved attention. My roommates made an error in getting a dog at all, though. They were never home. I worked three jobs, so neither was I. I'd try to spend time with the dog whenever I could, but most days that wasn't much. I often had 6 AM to midnight days. I'd let him outside when I was home so that he could do his business and I could have a change of scenery, but it wasn't enough.

After a couple of weeks of it being crystal clear that my roommates did not have time for a dog, I finally convinced them that even all combined we did not have the time to raise a dog. They agreed they needed to rehome him.

Although the stakes were lower as this was not an aggressive breed, I managed to prevent another long-time neglect situation like Kevin put his dog through. This wasn't a case of reckless neglect, just a case of a couple of kids fresh out of high school underestimating the amount of time you have to put into properly raising a dog. Unlike Kevin, at least, they didn't view the dog as a trophy. They knew this wasn't working. They knew the dog deserved better.

My roommates soon found the dog a good family home where he'd get a lot more attention from adults and kids alike. I didn't miss the dog so much as I was just relieved he got a better home. He deserved it.

STILL ALIVE —
PART 1: I REALLY NEED TO
START DRINKING

CHRISTMAS WAS ON THE HORIZON. I took it for granted that I'd be alone again. I was lucky to get six hours of sleep most nights. My whole existence was consumed by three menial jobs. I'd often go weeks and weeks without a day off. After a couple of months, it started to really wear on me. This was no way for anyone to live. And yet, in theory, this was an improvement from my time in Chicago, because I'd found regular employment.

In my heart of hearts, I knew I'd always be poor. I saw no way out of it. I had to work twelve to sixteen hours most every day just to get enough to pay for rent, food, and a few odd bills. If I wanted to get out of this, how would I even do that? I couldn't afford to take time off for interviews, or even realistically have a free moment to take calls to *schedule* interviews, especially with my phone locked up, by order of the shipping company, during most all business hours. I was stuck in this.

I needed something to help deal with the never-ending flow of monotony. What did other people do to deal with this type of stress? I didn't even have to think about it: the answer was obvious: People drank. If I wanted to tolerate my existence, I'd have to drink too.

I'd only ever drank socially, other than an odd glass of wine here and there. I never did it to *cope* with anything, that would be new. That's what made the prognosis (ironically) sobering. This was yet again, a new low. This must be my sixth all-time low of the year, then.

I felt sort of wrong as I pulled into the liquor store parking lot, recognizing that simply turning the wheel of my car was the first tangible action I'd taken toward this potentially destructive action. I contemplated the lowliness of my position as I browsed the shelves. I was in Kentucky, so

I guessed I might as well go for bourbon. It also meant I could get drunk for cheaper. I felt dubious as I checked out: I felt like the cashier knew. Or maybe he was used to it. Maybe depressed people filed through here daily and he grew accustomed to the air of sadness. He seemed pretty down himself, actually.

On the drive home, I asked myself: Was I really about to go down this path? Was there something else I could do? If there was, could I afford it? I needed something now, though, and I had already pulled the trigger on this, so it was *going* to happen.

I got home. I drank enough to get buzzed. I supposed I felt a little better.

Actually... I didn't. It just made me care less that my life sucked.

I kept the bottle on the windowsill near my bed, so it would always be there. If I was feeling down, I could look up and know that option was there.

"Well, at least there's that," I sometimes thought to myself, looking at the bottle on my window sill. Even just the option was comforting.

That bottle felt like a person, somehow. It permeated a presence. It greeted me when I got home. It demanded attention.

"Is tonight the night you just give up and say 'fuck it'?" it would ask me.

"Ehh... No. I'm just tired. If I get to sleep now, I'll at least get a solid five hours. Maybe tomorrow."

"Alright, dude. Well, you know where to find me."

It was something I could always turn to ...but I didn't turn to it. I never drank alone other than that one night. I had always been pretty good with self-control, I guess.

Or maybe I was just too busy working three dead-end jobs.

Too busy to even drink.

STILL ALIVE —
PART 2: THE PROFESSOR

LET'S REWIND FOR A CHAPTER, BACK TO ART school again.

I graduated as a film student but started college as an animation major. Sometimes I still think about an animation professor I had. I grew up fairly sheltered, so it blew my mind when my eighteen-year-old self walked into that classroom for the first time and a British professor was teaching us how to draw. I had only seen British people on TV before that. He wasn't posh-British, he wasn't all prim and proper British, he was punk-rock British: mohawk, studded belt, wallet chains everywhere, the whole bit. Let's call him "The Professor".

He was kind of animated, which was perfect for a professor of animation. He got us up and moving to think about how people moved so that we could be more informed in our processes. He took time out of his day to meet one on one with students. He had everyone's respect because of this natural air of "cool" he possessed. If you disappointed him it felt devastating because it felt so good when he was proud of you.

His classes helped me develop a lot of my earlier work, stories, and characters. I kept developing those over the years and used them in other projects even after becoming a film major, so he was a key figure in my artistic development.

I was not the only person that felt this way about The Professor. He was by far the most popular animation teacher at our school. He was that 'cool' teacher, not that you *had* to respect, but that you *wanted* to respect. His classes were the highlight of every student's day.

I found out later that this man had demons. It was the type of thing you only hear in hushed whispers, as dark secrets you dare not repeat. To me, these were not just rumors. I heard firsthand accounts from people who

I knew extremely well and trusted implicitly.

The way these demons manifested was at least morally dubious and at worst abhorrent. There is no excusing what he did. Yet the positive influence he had on his students was simply undeniable. I could see that his whole air of cool, the way he encouraged people, and even these manifested demons must have spoken to a deep lack of self-worth that The Professor was very good at keeping hidden: his positive traits served to help him justify the worth he wasn't sure he had.

I can say with absolute certainty that The Professor deeply regretted how these demons manifested. I'm sure he had a moment of self-reflection in which he realized the harm he caused. I know that for sure because shortly after I graduated college, he made the one decision he couldn't take back: He ended his own life.

The funeral was private, but the school held a memorial service for him. It was the first time I returned to the school after graduating, and the circumstances couldn't be any worse. Even the train ride there was daunting. I wondered if maybe I didn't go, maybe somehow it wouldn't be real. But I went.

I arrived and one of my other former professors from the film department greeted me at the door. Let's call him Mr. Blue. (Shit, this is the second autobiography by a student he's made it into.)

"Hey, man! Nice to see you! How are you doing?"

"Under the circumstances, honestly, I'm not doing too well." I wore it on my sleeve. I was glad he was excited to see me, but damn… I didn't want to be here, not for *this*.

"Yeah. Of course. That's understandable," Mr. Blue said, his tone changing to match mine.

Everyone I'd ever met while an animation major was there. The whole animation student body must have been in attendance. Every chair was filled. More people stood in the back. There must have been over three thousand people there. I've been to sold-out concerts with fewer people in attendance. They even had to turn people away after the room got too full. Safety concerns and fire codes and all that.

I remember pretty vividly the last time I saw the man. After I switched majors, our interactions were mostly reduced to friendly "hellos" in the hallways. When I wrote this song, I thought I hadn't even said hello to The Professor the last time I saw him.

One day I passed you by
I was busy, didn't even say hi

Reviewing my previous writing on the incident, it turns out I at least did that. This is what I wrote after coming home from the memorial service all those years ago:

> It was a particularly good hello, I remember thinking, and it was just last semester, so no more than two months before he died. I thought maybe I should stop him, tell him I was graduating, tell him I was still using ideas I developed in his classes, and that one such piece in that regard was considered the best of my work by many. He probably hadn't seen any of those projects. But, no, I was busy, I thought. Maybe he was too, so I did not say anything beyond "hello." I told myself, and I *actually* thought this in the moment:
>
> *"There will be a next time."*

You made me who I am
Altering my life's plan
You were an inspiration to us all
Yet these words did not arrive

What does this have to do with the nightmare year, you might ask? At the very least, I revisit this situation in my mind every year when I'm reminded of its anniversary. It was about that time. How does it tie into the nightmare year *specifically*, though?

Well... there *is* a parallel...

STILL ALIVE —
PART 3: TRENT

TRENT ACCIDENTALLY PROJECTED A LOOK LOTS OF OTHER dudes spend way too much time trying to cultivate. He had naturally blonde hair that he kept short. He often wore jeans and a simple white shirt. He usually paired it with a simple chain necklace. He essentially looked like an early-career Eminem. But I never heard him talk about Eminem, ever, even if people were talking about rap music. Plus, most guys who tried to make themselves into carbon copies of Eminem manufactured a "hard" personality. Trent was anything but that.

I frequently saw Trent passionately intervene on people's behalf when folks were trying to justify doing something even slightly shitty to someone else. He always swayed people too. Trent was always smiling. Trent was always building people up. He was always encouraging people. He was always advocating to help others. He made sure you felt included. There was no better evidence of this than when he helped me get a room at his place when Bella was quickly pushing me out the door. He prevented me from being homeless for the second time that year.

He enjoyed a busy social life. He was well-liked and had lots of friends. He had lots of attention from ladies. If he stopped taking calls or texts, would still always have people calling him up to try to get him to come out, or to talk.

When we were alone, he once admitted something to me in a whispered tone:

"You see this smile?" he said, putting on his signature grin just for show, "I'm known for this smile. But if I'm not on my meds, I'm not like this. I'm a completely different person. Just filled with dread."

He was on some heavy medication for anxiety, depression, and other mental conditions. I didn't know what was what with those pills, but one of them was hardcore enough that it had street value. If he was low on money he sometimes sold a few pills.

"Dude, don't you need those? Are you going to be okay?" I asked.

"Yeah, I do need them, but I need the money too. I'll be okay. Don't worry about me."

Something might break, and he'd need to replace it or get it fixed: never anything scandalous. He never did hard drugs or anything, which should go without saying, but just in case.

Trent started growing distant. Not just with me, but with everybody. His helping spirit didn't change though. I once came home and found a jacket hanging from my bedroom door knob. I knew it must be from him. What really gave it away was a melted candy cane in one of the pockets. It had re-hardened and was a permanent part of the jacket now. I chuckled to myself when I noticed. It was something that would only happen to Trent. I still hadn't gotten myself a jacket for winter, so it came at the right time. (I wouldn't have needed one in that shitty hipster town.) Louisville winters were mild, but you definitely need a jacket for a few months.

Trent moved back in with his parents. I couldn't get him to come out anymore and I really tried. Other people tried, too. He was having a rough time, I heard, so that was the best place for him. He was completely off his meds. That scared me. I knew how crucial they were. I tried to reach out a few times and if I got a reply it didn't come from him directly but from a friend of the family passing on his message and condition as if he were in the hospital or overseas in a war.

Then one day, I got a call that he *actually was* in the hospital... in critical condition... gunshot wound to the head. Somehow, he was hanging on.

This is what I was told:

Trent was at a friend's house with two other friends.

One of the friends, who lived there, said, "Hey, do you guys want to see my dad's gun?"

Trent and the other friend said yes.

As they curiously inspected the gun, Trent took it and said, "Hey guys, watch this!"

He then put the gun to his head and pulled the trigger.

I thought about this for a long time. It sounds... *stupid*, right? As if Trent had no conceptualization of actions and consequences. Did he know the gun was loaded? If he didn't, it would still be *stupid*, but it could've been a bad joke. Did he try to make a bad joke and pay dearly for it? He was alive but in critical condition. Maybe we'd get an answer to that question.

Damn... imagine his two friends who had to see that: Blood spattered—calling 911—trying to stop the bleeding. They must have been more invested in his recovery than anyone outside of his family. I can imagine the PTSD nightmares. They were probably never the same.

Trent survived the gunshot wound to the head for the next *twenty-two god-damn hours*, in critical condition the whole way. Some said he was fighting for his life that whole time. That he wanted to live. But those twenty-two hours ended in his death.

I continued to reflect on this. I remembered the last words Trent said to me: they were immortalized, complete with the grammar of a nineteen-year-old, on Facebook:

"steve your one of the wisest and good lookin men i

know, im glad i had the opportunity to meet someone
like you"

Once I realized those could've been his final words to me, I dug deeper.
He left messages like this for everyone not long before his death. Each
one was a personalized memory or compliment. There were hundreds,
like he was saying goodbye to everyone. The more I thought about it,
the more it made sense. He *was* saying goodbye. It *wasn't* a stupid joke. It
wasn't a senseless accident, as some people thought. It was an *opportunity*.
He saw an opportunity to take his own life, and he took it while it was
available.

Becoming withdrawn and saying his goodbyes was him making peace
with his forthcoming death. Those are classic signs of someone planning
suicide. He probably planned it a different way. Or maybe he was looking
for a way and happened to find it that fateful day. Maybe it was the one
moment that presented itself as an opportunity for a quick death. The
fact that he lived for another twenty-two hours? I didn't even know that
it was possible to survive that for *any* amount of time before this. There's
no way he anticipated that. There's no way he wanted that.

A few people certainly know the details surrounding the death of The
Professor. But Trent? I wonder to this day if I'm the only one that put
everything together. It wasn't my place to topple the legacy Trent had
with his family. To them, I was just a guy who was his roommate for a
few months. They probably didn't even know my name. They've probably since forgotten that I even existed. Who would I be to come in and
fuck that up?

Despite the way I talk about it in the song, I think I did get to tell Trent
what a life-saving favor he did for me by getting me a place to stay so
quickly. But I don't recall any specific conversation about it other than
off-hand comments. My regret is only that I didn't really make a point to
drive that home. Did Trent *really* understand how crucial that was? Did
he *really* get how he may as well have saved my life?

Unlike my professor, Trent didn't have any demons that came out in any negative way. Any damage he did must have been to himself.

When Trent died, he had a nephew on the way. He never got to meet him.

They named him Trent.

I kept the jacket he gave me, of course. I wore it for years after that. I wore it with pride, as a gift from the guy who basically saved my life. I remembered the good times with Trent when I wore it. I remembered the selfless favor he did for me. I always will.

I recall a different time
I made a friend and I was on my last dime
You've got so much to give
My darkest hour, you gave me a place to live

You say the meds cancel out the dread
But your next pill was a bullet to the head
I wouldn't be here without you
This went unsaid

STILL ALIVE —
PART 4: SONG RETROSPECTIVE & THE HIDDEN SIDE OF SUICIDE

I should have told you that
when you were still alive

THE FIRST VERSE OF THIS SONG IS ABOUT THE PROFESSOR. The second verse is about Trent. My intention was for the title of the song to be misleading. "Still Alive": It could be about survival. Getting through tough times. That's exactly what I was doing, anyway. The first time that chorus hits, the reveal of the true context of the title should be a twist, or at least a gut punch, just like it was when I experienced it.

Trent was instrumental to my survival in the nightmare year, and it was tragic that nothing could be instrumental to his. If I had to write about suicide, I knew I also had to talk about The Professor, even if that happened years prior. That was the first time in my life that someone I cared about or had an impact on me committed suicide.

I think there's something to be said for Trent helping me out in much the same way Bella did—hooking me up with a place to live when I desperately needed it—except when *he* did it, it really *was* selfless. He did it for me, not also-kind-of-for-him, and without any expectations in return.

The bridge in this song is a general observation I've had about folks I've met who have taken their own lives: It is a great injustice that the same pain someone harbors inside might also be the motivating factor for helping others. Other people I've known—not just those mentioned in this book—who ultimately ended their own lives were extraordinarily selfless: that cannot be a coincidence. There has to be a connection.

If someone feels like they can't live with themselves, it makes sense they might justify their existence by making the world around them a better place in any way they can. For some folks, making the world a better place, for whatever reason, *isn't enough* to feel complete. The Professor *must* have known he positively influenced *thousands* of students. Trent *must* have known he was a highly sought-after friend. There's a caution here: Look out for people who are always giving, always selfless. Make sure they have what they need, too; you know, like, inside.

Cuz the cruel irony is the suicide inside
fueled the bright light and pride
you were trying to be
now you're gone and I regret I never said
what you meant to me
so I sing this song

I lost my love when I moved cities—I lost my best friend—I became isolated from all my other friends and family due to distance; most of my interactions with people were superficial interactions at one of my jobs. I was betrayed; twice. I was nearly homeless; twice. I had no time to relax at the end of most given days. Work, sleep, work, sleep, repeat. I knew full well I was speeding towards rock bottom.

I had plenty of stuff that could've theoretically motivated me to end it all... but I didn't. I never thought about *ending it all*. To me, that means having suicidal thoughts isn't as simple as someone going through the worst time of their life and deciding that death might be better. If that's how it worked, the nightmare year is when I'd have felt that way. But I didn't feel that way.

Some people must just be pre-dispositioned to feel that way, be that by some chemical imbalance, a neuron that misfires, or whatever else it might be. Even if it's just that their threshold cope is lower, they'll hit that wall sooner than someone else might. Are we supposed to just accept that this is the way things are? I can't accept that. Even if it is baked into the core of human DNA, it's something we need to correct.

I used to believe there must be some calculated combination of words that might make someone realize what the solution to all their problems was. That if you fix the problem, you fix the feelings. If only you could've talked to them, maybe you could've prevented this.

I don't think that's how it works anymore. It's about getting on the right medications, learning effective coping mechanisms, learning to recognize when you're spiraling, and how to break out of the cycle bit by bit. It's not any singular piece of advice you can give or be given. That means no one can be singularly held responsible for anyone with mental health issues, outside of encouraging them to get the resources they need to help *themselves*. The solution might be as simple as taking mental health as seriously as physical health.

The suicide help hotline in America is 988 if you need it.

STILL ALIVE —
PART 5: THE DECEMBER OF MY DECEMBER

IT WAS WELL INTO DECEMBER NOW. The Christmas spirit had not found me. There was nothing to look forward to. I needed to fortify my emotional shell in anticipation. I prepared for another holiday at home alone—just me and my futon frame and a pile of blankets—a Christmas dinner of ramen or cereal. Gifts *for* no one. Gifts *from* no one. No trees or lights in this house. I couldn't afford such things, much less have time to mess with them.

In some ways, I was used to being poor on Christmas. Having small, humbling Christmases as a kid was how I realized we were poor in the first place.

One time my mom sat me and my brother down as kids and said: "Look, we don't have a lot of money this year, so I can only afford to buy you guys one present each."

We got it. Even to my eight-year-old mind, I knew that was some real shit. When school was back in session, every other kid excitedly rattled off a long list of stuff they got. The sheer number of gifts and the expense of them all surprised me. Was every other kid in my school rich? They didn't look rich. It wasn't a rich town or anything. Maybe I didn't know what rich looked like. Or maybe that wasn't rich—maybe that was normal. Most other kids lived in houses. We had a two bedroom apartment divided between the three of us. Either way, my takeaway was that the gap between what we had and what everyone else had was significant.

So, I knew from an early age we were different. I knew we were poor. Poorer than everyone else, at least. It tracked with my mom working two to three jobs to support us as kids. Shit… There's no better sign of the recession and shrinking economy right there… twenty years prior, perhaps my three jobs would have supported three people rather than just me, even if just barely.

I took it for granted: I was not going home for Christmas, obviously, and I wouldn't really have one here, either. I had no long-time friends or family in this town, especially with Trent gone. I had no time for social outings or hobbies. Very little kept me going around this time; the number of things got smaller and smaller until it narrowed itself down to a short list of seriously inconsequential stuff, like a song or a TV show.

I got really into a rare type of smart, heartwarming, dark, and self-aware character-driven sitcom called *Community*. I had no one in my life right now. No romantic partnerships, and I wasn't even really able to see friends, either. I was so alone that it felt like the characters on the show were my only real friends. It was the best half hour of my entire week, every week. I'd rewatch each week's episode nightly; a ghostly version of real human interaction.

A line in their Christmas episode that year really hit home for me: "This December *is* the December *of* our December."

December is sometimes used as a metaphor for the darkest period in a given time. The *literal* month of December coincided with the characters' *metaphorical* year-long December.

Read it again: "This December *is* the December *of* our December."

That line floored me because that was true for me, too: This December was the darkest part of my darkest year, punctuated by an impending Christmas of solitude.

As if Ms. Fortune was hyper-fixated on taking every last fucking thing I had away from me, even that show was put on indefinite hiatus after that episode. Now, even my *pretend* friends were gone. Fate was taking away more and more. Even the small losses started counting for a lot.

STILL ALIVE —
PART 6: CHECK OUT THIS SHITTY DUCK

My former friend and current piece of shit Kevin wasn't done with his bullshit yet, turns out. He texted me out of the blue with a big reveal he thought was designed to rock my world: He had some years ago slept with Lola. Obviously, this didn't mean much; I had known this for years and made peace with it long ago. He didn't know I knew, and I didn't tell him at Lola's request— as I outlined earlier. It was kind of funny how he only just suddenly remembered himself, though. Once again, I scoffed and didn't respond.

Only minutes later, I got a notification that someone posted on a Facebook page for one of my creative outings. Not my profile, but a page. The timing could be a coincidence, but I figured I'd better check.

No such luck; it was him alright. In what might be his lowest, shittiest fucking moment, he posted a half-naked picture of Lola on my public Facebook page. That might be a criminal offense these days, but I don't think it was then. It included some half-assed taunting message.

I thought I had blocked this motherfucker the moment I left that hipster town, had I not? It turns out that doesn't apply to pages. You can't even block someone from a page until they've already posted on it, I found out. So, you have no choice but to wait for the inevitability of your stalker to decide that today is the day. So there it was: A picture of Lola half-naked on my public Facebook page. Luckily, I caught and removed it within maybe five minutes. Perhaps no one even saw it.

I was more concerned about how Lola felt about this than any feeble attempt it had on me. Still, though… Now he was dragging other people into this in a dumb attempt to try and hurt me. It didn't matter if he failed to hurt me so long as he hurt someone I was close to. I called my friend Lola straight away and explained what he'd done.

"...So I guess keep an eye out for him trying to post that picture everywhere," I cautioned.

"You know what? I'm not going to let him make me feel bad about that," she responded, "I'm beautiful."

"Well... maybe that's the best attitude for this. Did you seriously let him take that picture, though?"

"No. I remember that picture being taken by another ex. I guess maybe I sent it to Kevin, but if I did, I don't remember that. For all I know, he might have taken it straight off of my computer," she said with a bit of a laugh.

Her statement had the tone of really taking this in stride. I was glad Lola didn't let that affect her. She had evolved in Hawaii. If this happened before that, I was sure her reaction would be different, and she'd be devastated. Luckily she wasn't, but not for lack of Kevin trying.

There was a clear misogyny in sexually exploiting a woman as a tool for revenge. I didn't take him as a misogynist while we were friends. He probably didn't hold that type of bigotry in his personal philosophy, but if he was willing to stoop that low when he felt like it would get his point across, then Kevin was just a regular misogynist anyway. You know what they say: If it looks like a duck and quacks like a duck...

This was a new low, even for him. He viewed Lola like a conquest; that much was obvious, as if he had stolen my property in the short time they were together. The alternative theory would be that this was about which of us she viewed as superior. If that were the case, it would've meant something to him that she and I were involved both before and after that incident, and that would mean that she must have liked me better. It's not like she ever went back to him. However, I don't think he was simply defining his worth through what she thought of either of us. It was even less than that; he just thought he stole what he defined, consciously or not, as property.

In the taunting message on his Facebook post, he said he had "used her"—his words. So I'm supposed to feel bad about *myself* because *he* was a piece of shit? Why? No. I'll feel bad about myself when *I'm* a piece of shit, not when he is.

REMAKE MYSELF — PART 1: THE THING THAT FINALLY BROKE ME

IT WAS THE WEEK BEFORE CHRISTMAS. The electronic store had me off on Christmas and the day after, but working on Christmas Eve. The shipping company was going back and forth on if they needed the seasonal people at all that week. Eventually, they landed on us having the whole week off. It could be a problem for making rent and bills, but I'd deal with that later, I guessed.

The electronics store held a pre-Christmas meeting where the manager told us: "We get that it's busy here around Christmas, but it's not our goal to take you away from your families. So please, let us know what we can do to make sure you can spend time with your loved ones."

That gave me an idea: If I asked the electronic store for Christmas Eve off, maybe I could swing a quick three-day trip back home. I don't mean my adopted city of Chicago, but *home* home, a little ways outside the city. I would pass through Chicago on the way and could stop there, too.

This whole nightmare year kicked off because my hometown was the last place I wanted to go back to. The town was a dump, but lots of people lived there who I wanted to see, like my family and Tim. When I left Chicago I hated it, too, but that was before life took me down a few pegs.

I thought about it for a few days and kept coming back to all the people in both places that I missed. Lots of folks left Chicago as the recession hit full swing even before I did, but Patrick and Dan still lived there. They had beef (for reasons we need not get into), but I wondered if I could convince them to patch things up. Presumably, Gemma still lived in the same apartment we shared, but I wasn't sure if that was even a realistic ask. I'd probably never see her again; best to get used to that. A little familiarity could do my soul some good, though, whatever it ended up looking like.

The irony wasn't lost on me: I'd gone to so much trouble to avoid moving back home, but now the idea of visiting seemed cozy. Yeah, I *wanted* to visit home. I was already giving these jobs sixteen hours most days. It wasn't much to ask for one extra day to visit home for Christmas.

I talked to the manager at the electronics store. He made good on his word and gave me Christmas Eve off, no questions asked. I was already off at the shipping job, so I was good. I didn't even know if my car would make it that far, but I at least wanted to try.

After nearly a year of misfortunes, I wasn't going to let happiness in without a full-body search. However, I *finally* felt just secure enough to get my hopes up. I might as well let the manager at my shipping job know, though, just for good measure.

"It looks like I might actually have a chance to go home for Christmas next week."

"Oh, what? No, no, no, no. We're definitely going to need you next week. Didn't we tell you?"

"Uhh, the last I heard, you landed on not needing *any* of the seasonal people that week. I guess I only need two days off to make it home for Christmas, though. Can that be arranged?"

"No, I don't think so. I can look into it, but I doubt it. Plan on coming in for now and we'll see."

He walked away. I had to get to work. I'd never worked anywhere with this level of blatant disregard for employees. Don't get me wrong—other places definitely didn't care—but they'd at least put up the *facade* of giving a shit.

I have never been more defeated than I was at that moment. Not because I wanted this *so much*, but because at any other point in my life, I'd have *taken it for granted.* I don't even care about Christmas. It's just… I used to have dreams. Yet, my life had become so constrained by this mundane job that going home for Christmas was now the *singular thing* that kept me going day by day, hour by hour: the *only thing* I had to look forward to. And even *that* was asking too much? Something 95% of people do without a second thought? Like when I was a child, this year's Christmas was once again a stark reminder of what everyone else had that I didn't.

This is a feeling I won't miss
I can't believe it's led to this

I couldn't believe this was getting to me as much as it was. It hit me like a ton of bricks every second. My shift wore on for what felt like days. I finally realized how far I'd fallen. I couldn't *believe* this was the reality I had resigned to.

I'd worked with people with clout in Hollywood. Sure, I was low on the hierarchy in those gigs, but I was progressing towards a dream. I was barely a cog in someone else's machine, now. Now the only thing I could dare to dream of was… spending time with friends and family for Christmas? Yet, within a year, I was reduced to arranging shit in a truck and hoping against hope that I could just… *visit home.*

It wasn't just that though. I mentioned earlier that this period was defined by loneliness. Seeing friends and family would have been the most genuine human interaction I'd have had in almost two months. Ever since Trent withdrew from his life, right before he died, the amount of human interaction I'd had outside of the transactional conversations I'd have at my jobs could be counted in mere *minutes.* How long would it be *now*?

My life had become so constrained by these mundane jobs that going home for Christmas was now an *aspiration.* Ms. Fortune had taken away everything I had. Everything. Then she served up the scraps and gristle of my former life and offered them up as a *reward.* She took away so much that I was willing to *fight* for a miniscule fraction of what I once had. I was so starved, I actually *wanted* it. I would have been *happy* with that fraction. And then she took *that* away, too.

I'm finally down so low
That the smallest loss is the final blow
(from End to Fear)

Barring an intervention by fate, I wasn't going home for Christmas. I'd already appealed to one of the highest authorities in my life: *middle management at the shipping company warehouse.* There was only *one* authority higher...

As I stewed in the back of a shipping truck, letting boxes fall at my feet out of pure spite, I decided I'd make one last-ditch attempt. A phone call to the *only* authority outranking my warehouse overlords: *fate itself.* Of course, since the unpaid security checks prevented me from bringing my phone in, this call had to be dialed not with a phone, but with a metaphorical literary device from a future book that was not yet even a twinkle in my eye. Somehow I was still on hold for over an hour.

"Hello, Fate headquarters? Could I please speak to Fortune?"

"Fortune isn't here. This is *Ms.* Fortune, how can I help you?"

Ah, fuck.

"Uh, yeah, I wanted to make a request, and follow up on some old ones as well," I started.

"Ugh, *fine.* What?"

You should imagine Ms. Fortune depicted by Aubrey Plaza, by the way.

"Yeah, I've lived in like three states so far this year. Do you have any updates on my request to no longer being under constant threat of homelessness?"

"No."

"No update? Then how about—"

"No, I mean, the request was denied."

"Oh. How about being able to work less than seventy hours a week just to live paycheck to paycheck?"

"Oof, that one is up to Economy. He doesn't talk to poor people. Beneath him, he always says. But he did leave a note for you! I can read it verbatim, if you like."

"Okay, great. What does it say?"

"Fuck you," she explained.

"Oh c'mon! Just read it."

"That's what it *says*, Steven, *okay?*"

"That tracks, I guess. Could I get some semblance of a social life? Not sure how I'd—"

"That one is also a no."

"Can I at least get something better than a pile of blankets to sleep on?"

"Nope."

"Fine. Could you at least bring my favorite TV show back? Seems like a small ask."

"Hmm. I can look into that within the next... six months? ...Say, would you like to go home for Christmas? That's coming up."

"That's actually the other thing I called about. Can you make that happen? Everyone else I know gets to."

"Oh, haha, no, I can't approve that. I was just asking if you *wanted* to. I'm kind of *busy*, okay?!"

Click.

It was official: This was a new all-time low. The seventh one this year, and again—by definition—the worst so far, as it compounded with Trent's death and everything else. Every bit of happiness had been ripped from me: From relationships, to friendships to a friend's *life*, to family, to my home—*twice*—to basic human interaction, all the way down to simple things like a TV show that helped keep me going. Everything was working against me. I needed a change, but I didn't even have time to make the change, because I needed to work every waking minute of most every day just to afford to survive.

And I was absolutely fucking sick of it.

REMAKE MYSELF —
PART 2: DARKHORSE

I should remake myself
If just for mental health

THROWING AROUND BOXES ALONE IN A TRUCK *finally* gave me and opportunity I didn't have during all the chaos leading up to this: time to reflect. This new low had me wondering what I really wanted out of life. It wasn't throwing other people's packages. I kept coming back to my desire to make music. I didn't know anything about making music. I knew how to sing: I guess that counted. That's what I really wanted to do anyway. There's something about singing: it always felt good to sing and I wanted better excuses to do it. Not just the odd karaoke night singing other people's songs.

Changing my reality started with the smallest of actions: before work, I ripped out a blank piece of paper from my notebook of ideas. I hadn't added to it in a while. The unpaid security checks limited what I could bring into the shipping job, but I was pretty sure they'd let through a pencil and a piece of paper. I slapped it down in the basket along with my car keys and sent it through the x-ray machine. They didn't say anything about it, so I was good.

That day, in the back of a dingy shipping container, at the loneliest point of my entire fucking life, I was determined to walk out of work with the lyrics to a full song. I wrote a line or two between stacking boxes. At least I had plenty of shit to write about. I started with losing my best friend Kevin. I had a healthy resentment for him, but I also felt the sadness of losing a good friend. As of writing, that sadness has been totally fucking obliterated for years, but back then the sadness of it was the most present.

I had a melody in mind, and I wrote the lyrics to that. I knew I wanted the song to be a ballad of sorts called "Darkhorse". My idea of using the term "Darkhorse"—meaning a person not expected to succeed who ends up doing so anyway—was a pretty plain allusion to my emotional state—defeated, but with the knowledge that I'd make it through to the other side. Not that I was anywhere close to doing that, right then.

From Darkhorse:
My heart is a darkhorse
Could love be on its course?

When I wrote that, I didn't know exactly what it meant. I felt so beaten down after the falling out with my former friend that I was emotionally void and numb to everything. I figured it meant that the feeling of love had a strength that I didn't have the emotional bandwidth to feel, at least until I got to the other side. In the course of writing this, it occurs to me that perhaps subconsciously, the "love" that might be "on course" was potentially for Bella. We were history when I wrote it, but things were still building up during the time that the song is about.

Remake Myself, as a song, is sorta meta. Among other things, it's a song about writing a song. It was the last song written for the album: after I realized I didn't have a song about the moment I decided to turn this shit all around. It came together quickly compared to most of the other songs. Tim and I knew we had something special with this one. It caused us to revisit the entire album and re-form other songs in a similar style.

At least these dark times
Can make for good rhymes
This is some dark shit
Unless I flip it

REMAKE MYSELF —
PART 3: A WILD TIM APPEARS

THERE WAS A PAIR OF PROFESSIONAL-GRADE HEADPHONES on display at the electronics store I could buy to help me with making music. They sat on an endcap product display, backlit like an ancient relic of worship in a museum. That was one barrier to entry for making music.

That headphone display motivated me every day: If I was a little extra frugal, they could be mine. It was a working display, so sometimes I'd plug my iPod into it and listen to whatever song I was obsessed with recently. Music sounded fantastic on them. I'd push back the two in-stock boxes to keep them out of view and lessen the chance of others purchasing them. When one of the boxes disappeared one day, my motivation increased tenfold.

I finally bought them after saving up for about a month. I revisited some of my favorite albums with a clarity that I had never heard before, and it was fantastic. I retired the trusty pair of headphones I'd almost lost to Lenny being an idiot.

Another barrier was a microphone. My mom asked me what I wanted for Christmas telling me she could mail it to me. I asked for a gift card to the electronic store. That way I could get a mic at a discount rather than have her pay full price. Minimally, all I really needed to make music besides a mic and some headphones was my computer. I was still working sixteen hours most days. How would I get this music made? I had no fucking idea.

One day my phone rang from an unknown number. The area code was from back home. It had to be someone I knew.

"Hey, it's Tim. I got a new number."

Ah yes, Timmy: My friend back home who would eventually become my musical collaborator after this nightmare year finally ends. He hadn't had a phone for a bit. He was poor too, after all. I only had a phone because my former boss was still paying the bill. We caught up.

"You make music, right? I'm thinking about getting into that soon, myself," I asked him.

"I mostly play guitar and bass. I have a bunch of songs written, but no way to record them," Timmy responded.

"Well, that's funny, I'm going to have a way of recording soon, but I don't know anything about music theory."

It hadn't occurred to either of us that we could help each other. As poor as we were, the few hundred miles between us were insurmountable. We may as well have lived on different planets. Either way, I was slowly assembling the pieces I needed to make my dream a reality, even if I wasn't sure what that would look like.

REMAKE MYSELF —
PART 4: BAD AT THIS

IF I CONTINUED TO GIVE THE SHIPPING COMPANY all my time, all I'd get in return is depression and impoverishment. It did not align with my dreams, goals, or even general interests. At least at the electronics store, I worked with technology that always fascinated me. Hell, I was way overqualified to sell digital cameras considering I had a film degree. Furthermore, their discount helped me get started with what I needed to make music.

Throwing boxes wasn't worth the sacrifice of my happiness. No... I was *going* to go home for Christmas. The trade-off wasn't worth the price. I kept following up at the shipping job. Eventually, they relented, justifying that since I was a seasonal employee, I could technically say whatever day I wanted was my last day of the season.

On my last day, the manager at the shipping company put me on the hardest truck they had. It easily had twenty times the volume of my usual truck. I grabbed one box and put it on the stack, and by the time I turned back, two more waited for me. Even throwing shit like crazy, there was no way I could keep up. I started grabbing two at a time, but eventually, I still found myself wading in boxes up to my knees. I had no idea how the other guys even got this done.

The manager came by to check on me more than usual. He looked on, stone-faced, as I scrambled at a breakneck pace to keep up with the even faster speed of the boxes. I knew what he was doing: they figured I'd either drown in boxes and they could justify not hiring me on, or if by some miracle I could pull it off, maybe they'd give me a shot. The only problem was: I was bad at this.

I became completely boxed in by boxes, literally entombed in the truck. They finally sent in the guy usually on this truck to help bail me out. He was civil, but only barely hid his seething resentment. Not that he had to: I was well aware of how incapable I was. The shipping company got what they wanted: an excuse not to hire me.

This meant that I'd have to hope for a full-time gig at the electronics store or I was instantly fucked on paying rent and bills. If I could make just the electronic store work, I might be okay. It was at least a step in the right direction. For the math to work, though, I'd have to be brought on full-time, because I was barely making it as-is. Even with that, I'd actually be making less than I was now, so I'd be worse off.

On the other hand, I was kinda glad to be bad at this. Throwing boxes was not what I wanted to do with my life. If I was bad at it, it was not an option. If it wasn't an option, I'd have no choice but to seek out bigger and better things. If this job managed to sink my aspirations so low that going home for Christmas was the only thing that kept me going, then fuck this place. Fuck bills. It's about time I take my life back. At *any* cost.

REMAKE MYSELF —
PART 5: SQUIRRELS ARE
AGENTS OF CHAOS

ON THE WAY HOME ONE DAY, MY CAR DID AN odd thing: It died as I took a turn. The engine powered down and suddenly I was coasting as if I were in neutral. I pulled over with my remaining momentum, fearing the worst: that this car was fucking done. That it only lasted like two months, and this was it. I wasn't going home for Christmas after all. Shit, I couldn't even make it to my jobs if this thing died. The buses *might* allow me to make it to *either* job, but they wouldn't work if I needed to be at *both* on the same day. I went to start the car, expecting no response… but somehow, it started.

I called my friend Michael who offered to take a look right then. He came with his seven-month-pregnant girlfriend in tow. He was perplexed as there was no obvious problem under the hood. He followed me home to make sure I got all the way there. After a couple of turns, he started honking at me like crazy. I pulled over. He got out and told me my car was spraying gas. Once we got back to the house (figuring I could make that short distance), I could see a neat little trail of liquid down the road and up the driveway. Michael identified a section of the gas line under the car that looked like it was chewed on by an animal, complete with little chunks taken out of the sides of the line.

I'd made all that effort now to get home for Christmas just to have my hopes dashed by a fucking squirrel. The mere concept of this happening seemed bizarre, although, apparently it's not unheard of. Are squirrels getting any nutritional value out of a gas line? Gas aside, the plastic tubing (or rubber, or whatever it is) probably isn't particularly high in squirrel-related nutritional content.

What did I ever do to squirrels? Do squirrels understand English? Did I say something considered rude in squirrel culture? No. Their only language is destruction. They are agents of chaos. It would be my luck this year that I could buy the only fully functioning car in Louisville in this price range, and then it tanks on me the moment I own it, because of squirrels. Maybe Ms. Fortune herself was a squirrel. Maybe that explains the callus and vindictive nature of these small furry instruments of destruction.

It's one thing if your luck is bad all the time, but Ms. Fortune was on some bullshit where it seemed like she might finally give me a break, only to dash my hopes right after letting myself believe I finally got a break. That shit is extra. And to use squirrels as the instrument to my anguish? Ms. Fortune was just toying with me now, mocking my efforts to have even the most basic comforts.

I imagined going to a mechanic and getting a quote on replacing the gas line. This couldn't be a simple procedure. There's definitely no way it would be cheap. Even if it was only two-hundred bucks to fix, that's more than I could afford. Even if I could afford it, would it be done in time for Christmas? Probably not. I'd also lose a bunch of money from missed work. Maybe I'd even get *let go* for missing work.

I was spiraling aloud about how much this would cost and how long this would take when Michael stopped me:

"Dude, we can probably fix this for a couple of bucks. Let's go to the auto store real quick."

He had me buy some rubber hose a certain size larger than my gas line and some hose clamps around that size.

"See? Look at this," he told me once we were back under the car, "the fuel line is still intact. It just has a few chunks taken out of the sides. All we have to do is cut this hose we bought down the length of it, put it over your fuel line, and use the clamps at strategic points to keep the gas from leaking." And he was right: it worked.

As we took turns with the various tasks, his seven-month-pregnant girlfriend ended up applying the hose and clamps. We ran the car and checked for leaks. If we found one, we put another clamp there. Now I was good.

Thanks, Michael, for that, and for that futon frame. It was something, something I didn't have otherwise. And thank you for temporarily spotting me the cash shortfall I needed to even get this car in the first place.

I was all set to go home for Christmas. I was visiting home after all, through sheer stubbornness, determination, the assistance of Michael, his extremely pregnant girlfriend, a rubber hose, a couple of clamps, and no fucking help at all from squirrels.

REMAKE MYSELF —
PART 6: TWENTY FEET AWAY

I SPENT HALF OF CHRISTMAS EVE IN THE CAR. Just me, a suitcase, and a playlist. I was getting close to Chicago now. It was a place I hadn't been outside of for more than a few days at a time for almost ten years before leaving. The city had shaped me, for better or worse. I hated the city when I left. Now, though, I was so beaten down that even something I previously hated seemed downright cozy.

I got wistful as the skyline came into view. It really hit me when I saw the train speeding by alongside the highway. I cried tears of joy. It felt like home. No one in Chicago has ever been even *half* as happy to see the Red Line train, I'm sure of that.

Patrick (the first guy Kevin tried to fuck over back in the day) didn't have much of any place to go on Christmas because he was the only one in his family living anywhere near Chicago, so I offered to take him home with me for Christmas. There was no sense in letting him go through the same lonely version of the holiday that I tried so hard to avoid. It wasn't exactly clear if he held the same depressing outlook on this that I did, but I could tell it wasn't all roses, and he didn't resist my offer.

By coincidence, Patrick's new place was less than two blocks from where I lived when I left Chicago, where I cohabited with Gemma. My GPS route took me right past our former apartment. The lights were on. I was so homesick I almost wondered if I could just… ring the buzzer and see what was up.

I did not do that. I did, however, park my car and walk around the neighborhood: The Starbucks where I spent hours a day job searching when we didn't have internet; my favorite hole-in-wall burger place with the same cook and owner that probably ran the place for thirty years;the little Mexican grocery store that kept us from having to cart ourselves all the way to the bigger chain grocery store. All were closed for Christmas Eve, making the block feel abandoned; almost as if everyone else had left it when I did.

My old El stop (the 'train stop', if you aren't from Chicago) showed little activity. The nearest El stop was the landmark by which you'd define your location in the city. Even the 7/11 where Gemma and I used to splurge on ice cream occasionally; all these things instilled a sense of nostalgia and comfort that I have never felt before or since. When I lived with Gemma, that was "our" 7/11. It had no other association to me other than going there when she and I could justify the occasional treat. It was happy then, which made it sad now. It was dark, given the sun sets so early at that time of year. 7/11 was the only business open, the only storefront lighting up the block, drawing me to it like a moth to a flame.

I knew this street well but felt like a foreigner as I walked down it. It felt like I'd been gone for
A lifetime's worth of struggles, yet it hadn't even been one year. This place represented a time when things were at least stable, even if they weren't good. A big part of me wanted it back. But I knew I couldn't have it.

I stopped about twenty feet short of the 7/11 on my way back to my car and checked the time on my phone. For all I knew, Gemma was in that store right now. Even though she still presumably lived a block away, I figured the chances were small, even if she went there every day and took ten minutes, the chances she'd be there at this *exact moment* were still less than one percent.

Part of me wished I'd run into Gemma, though. Our relationship was terrible, but in the context of the last year, it seemed cozy again. What would I even say if I saw her? It felt like we never caught up on the phone at all; once again, I no longer had any idea if she was open to talking or if I was even emotionally ready to talk. Could I face the person I left?

The streetlight near the 7/11 provided the main source of light on the block. Everything else was shrouded in night. I watched as the door was opened by an unknown hand from within. The light from the store spilled out onto the street, illuminating it further, as if to focus on a representation of the place—or person—I had lost when I decided to leave.

As the door opened, an unfamiliar woman walked out. I noticed an obvious beauty underneath a casually alternative exterior. She had that "accidentally cool" sort of vibe. I had a brief flash where I wondered what my life would be like if we somehow got together. She was way out of my league, though. I was sure I couldn't be so lucky, especially not this year.

I snapped out of my internal introspection once I realized that the woman I was looking at *was her*: my ex, Gemma. Almost like after the car accident, when I couldn't recognize people as people, I wasn't able to connect the face I was seeing to hers. It had been too long since I saw it, I suppose. But it was her. It was genuinely… *actually her* standing in front of me, twenty feet away, as if fate intervened at that very moment to finally deliver me from my loneliness. Fortune had not been my friend this year. Did this mean that had just changed?

On TV, this would be portrayed as a Christmas Eve miracle. Just like Desmond in that classic episode of LOST that reminded me of my departure from this city and from Gemma, there I was, making contact with my "constant" in the midst of a personal trauma. Like Desmond, I pined to reconnect with a lost love I regretted leaving. Just like with Desmond, it even happened on Christmas Eve.

If this were a TV show, she'd gasp and run toward me, eyes filled with tears, much like when we parted. These tears, however, would be of joy rather than sadness. As if we were to rewind time (taking a cue from Lost yet again) those tears would flow back up our faces. I'd be coming back instead of leaving. We would embrace for the *first* time in months instead of the *last*. We'd realize what we lost—vow to make it work—make it even better than it was, to never separate again. I paid a heavy price, and this was the reward for my penance after a long road of self-discovery. I'd wipe a tear from her eye as a smile grew across her face, accompanied by a subtle nervous laugh she might have in such a moment.

That *would* happen, on the *TV show*. But this was real life.

We locked eyes.

I should say something… I froze.

She broke the gaze, turned, and walked away.

REMAKE MYSELF —
PART 7: CHRISTMAS

IT FELT LIKE MY SOUL HAD SUDDENLY LEFT ME. This was a mistake. Clearly, from an emotional standpoint, I was not yet in a better state of mind, I had only recognized that I needed to be. This was probably my eighth all-time low, but it wasn't depressing. Instead, it hit me like the El train, senses heightened and overwhelmed.

I rushed to my car and breathed a sigh of relief once I closed and locked the door, protected by the bubble of glass and steel. I got the fuck to Patrick's place, less than two blocks away. He had it so dark in his apartment that it felt lonely. This was no way to do Christmas. I told him what just happened—needing someone to understand—but I think the significance was lost on him without the full context of my life since I'd left.

However, we did have one thing to talk about that he understood better than anyone else: how Kevin tried to burn both our lives to the ground. We had about an hour's drive, and I left no plot point unturned, including the sequel with Bella. Short of writing a book, that's about how long it took to explain the gist of what I went through.

We got back to my hometown. Patrick met my family. We hung out with Timmy. These two were meeting for the first time as they hailed from two completely different circles in my life. We got into a lengthy metaphysical discussion on the nature of God or "a higher power", as Tim described it. Timmy had recently come to an interesting view that I found intriguing.

"According to the theory of relativity, all matter is a form of energy. Therefore the universe itself is simply a network of energy. I believe the universe, altogether, is a single organism, composed of energy," Tim started with his explanation, "I believe that this organism is conscious on some level and that its consciousness runs through the human mind at the level of the collective unconscious as talked about by Carl Yung. Which, in my personal interpretation, is a frequency of thought shared by every human mind at a very deep subconscious level, and we are all very insignificant and minuscule parts of it."

"I love that you are down with Yung. I have a few ideas about the collective unconscious myself. As for yours—with human thoughts being energy," I said, "a higher form of that energy—a more evolved form of that energy—or at least something representing the sum of all those parts—could certainly exist," I added.

"Our brains are electrical machines," Tim said, "But this isn't something I hold to 'blind faith', as it were: it only makes sense insofar as we follow and accept these lines of logic, as supported by the evidence that suggests this view of the universe as a connected system of energy."

Patrick interjected with various attempts to keep these thoughts grounded and logical, but overall he just let Tim get through his thought process.

In fairness to proper representation of the dude, this isn't something Tim likely believes at the time of writing, at least with any significant earnestness.

'I don't know', I can imagine him saying 'All I know is everything is shit, and I hate it.'

Tim has since agreed that he'd definitely say the above sentence.

On Christmas, I got the gift card from my mom. The next day, I went to the local location of the electronic store and got my microphone. I now had everything I needed to get started. I just needed to find people to fill other roles like a guitarist and a keyboardist or synth guy. I'd cover vocals. It was too bad Tim didn't live closer, since he played guitar.

The lyrical content of this song and the next song thematically bleed into each other quite a bit. (Remake Myself and End of Fear respectively.) In this song I know that I need to make a change, and I've decided to make it, but no fix was in action yet, and I didn't know what it would even look like. All I had going for me was some fierce determination and the ability to do great things once backed into a corner.

END TO FEAR —
PART 1: THE FINAL CRESCENDO

ONCE I GOT BACK TO LOUISVILLE, I FOUND I'D MADE the trip to my hometown and back with a completely flat tire. I hadn't noticed, somehow. It must have been sheer will that kept the tire inflated, though I did get the tires replaced shortly after. (Used ones, of course.)

By now, I was keenly aware that my terrible luck must be a function of the year itself. With Christmas over, there was less than a week left in this shitty year. I knew as sure as the sky was blue that next year, I was owed a heavy karmic debt in my favor. Things would change, and I would change them. I could imagine Kevin rooting for me to fail, I could imagine Bella's dismissive snide comments, and it just motivated me more. On the other hand, I could imagine Trent rooting for me to succeed. But more than that, *I* wanted to succeed—for me.

I had a goal and it was simple: to make music. The desire had been simmering on a backburner now for years. I always seemed to have more pressing concerns given that most of my adult life so far was spent living paycheck to paycheck and working sixty-hour weeks just to get there. At this point, I was so beaten down that I didn't even care about surviving. Living paycheck to paycheck, my life was spent almost entirely on the goal of continuing to be able to live. I wanted something better to live for. Having fulfilled my goal of visiting home, the incredible weight of my sadness suddenly vanished. My run-in with Gemma didn't mean much now. I considered it songwriting fuel, and having that fuel gave me a renewed purpose.

After the Mysteria festival earlier in the year, I thought I might be able to get an EP's worth of material out of the interesting stuff that happened there. Now, however, it was starting to consciously dawn on me that I had a hell of a lot more experience to draw on than just that. I could write songs about this entire nightmare year if I wanted to. It could be the silver lining this year so desperately needed.

Ms. Fortune was working on some music of her own, though. Her final crescendo: a three-part symphony of some last-minute bad news designed to turn my world completely upside down for the third time this year.

Here's her first movement:

My remaining roommate, Trent's friend, was the nephew of the owner of the house we rented. That was how he and Trent initially got the deal to move in. His aunt was who I cut my rent checks to, though we'd never met.

"Just so you know, my aunt is thinking of selling the house," my roommate told me.

"Well, shit… It can take months to sell a house, maybe we still have time? Is she just *thinking* about it? Or is she selling it for sure?"

I was not looking forward to finding a new place to live on short notice for the third time this year.

"They actually have a buyer lined up, a friend of the family, I guess. They're already working on paperwork."

"Well fuck. So how long do we have?"

"About three weeks, apparently."

Well, shit. At least I had two jobs… well, three, technically… so rent might not be an issue—I just needed to find a place to live, and fast.

Ms. Fortune's second movement:

I breezed through the rest of the week at the electronics store.

"You know who you remind me of?" The security guy told me, "John Lennon. Just doing what you gotta do but without a care in the world."

It tracked that I must have had a different vibe. I don't look much like John Lennon, though... Maybe it was because my hair was becoming a bit long. Regardless, it felt apt because I was singularly focused on starting my music journey.

The shipping company manager actually asked me back to finish out the season. When it came time to figure out who they were keeping, he made a big show out of letting me know he wasn't going to keep me on, and I knew exactly why: I was fucking bad at this.

"*They're* fine," the manager said, gesturing broadly to everyone in my section except for me, "but *you* I need to talk to."

I knew exactly what was about to happen, but there was no better bridge to burn than keeping myself out of part-time manual labor. 'Fucks given' were at an all-time low. I walked out of that place like I won an award.

I let the electronic store know I now had full availability. The electronic store job was seasonal too, so I was hoping for a permanent role there. There was at least *some* opportunity there, unlike the shipping company. Even so, I now had one less line of income, meaning I'd really have to count every penny, now.

Ms. Fortune's third movement:

At the electronics store, they were also making permanent hiring decisions. When I inquired, this is what the store manager told me:

"We kept the process real simple. We just looked at who had the best availability and brought on those folks. You had limited availability and that's the only reason we didn't bring you on."

Ironically, my availability was open *now*, but they'd already decided by the time they knew that. I believed the manager's reasoning behind the decision, though, because my metrics at that job were very good. The irony here was palpable: I needed both those jobs to survive. I hated working at the shipping company but enjoyed the electronics store. And yet, having to work the job I hated tanked my chances of staying on at the job I liked.

Leaving the electronics store wasn't what I wanted, but I wasn't upset either. They helped get me through the last few months and helped me get the bare minimum I needed for music gear. They let me go home for Christmas. I could say none of these things about the shipping company. My last day was today, New Year's Eve. I could probably cover this last month of rent at the house. Other than that, I expected to be at the job-hunting grind right after the holiday.

In its final days, the nightmare year hit me with everything it had left. I needed a new place to live—*again*. I needed to find new work—*again*. When I dealt with that this year, I had a place but needed a job, or I had a job but needed a place. Now I needed *both*. I had a lot of work to do, and not much time to do it.

Despite my dire situation, I walked out of the electronics store on my last day optimistic and hungry for what was next. I was sure that I was finally due to happen upon some of the metaphorical lucky coins that spill out of Fortune's pockets—and I need them literally, too, if I had any chance of affording to live while searching for another job *and* a place to stay.

I hadn't even thought about what I was doing for New Year's Eve tonight. It was only hours away. That didn't bother me like Christmas did—I barely had time to think about it until now. New Year's Eve: the precipice of change. Whatever was coming next would be better. It would be exactly what the fuck I wanted. I was tired of settling for anything less.

If this is all there is
let's roll the dice
if this is all there is to life
it's not worth the price

END TO FEAR —
PART 2: NEW YEAR'S EVE

I'D JUST GOTTEN HOME FROM MY LAST DAY AT THE electronics store when I got a message from The Artist, who I hadn't seen since the weekend I moved to this town four months ago:

> "Hey man it's been a while I just wanted to let you know
> im having a little nye shindig tonight nothing big and
> youre welcome to come by sorry im bad with phones
> but id love to see ya"

Well, hell yeah; now I had plans. The bottle of bourbon I had lying around collecting dust—initially intended to curb my depression—could finally get some better use. I almost forgot that I had friends here. I *was* too busy working to hang out, but now I wasn't. The Artist still managed to have the same air of mystery as when I met him at the festival—where I had my DMT trip and saw some sort of metaphysical being who similarly sported a long beard and wore a top hat. Although not a metaphysical being, The Artist had revealed himself to be wise in his own way, and his unfamiliarity with modern technology reinforced his 'old soul' vibe.

The Artist had a whole different cast of characters at the party than those I met when I first moved to Louisville. Judy, who previously sold me out to my abuser and former friend Kevin at a land-speed record, was not at this party, so it felt safe.

I managed to make fast friends with almost everyone there. I'm usually not like that. I usually stick to my own circles, but at that moment I was in exactly the right mood and mindset to be making friends.

When the clock struck midnight, the couples kissed. Other folks did a little dance, and so did I. I still remember the moment: as the clock struck midnight, under the noise of celebration, I released the weight of my omens. I released my burdens back to Ms. Fortune. The relief was so tangible that I felt it in the room with me. That was a wrap on the nightmare year. That shit was *over*: not just because a calendar got thrown in the trash, but because I *fucking said so.*

The bridge back to my burdens could not be unburned. Ms. Fortune was now defeated, but in her death throes she still left me with an insurmountable task: I had to find new income and a new home—*again*. But not tonight. Tonight was my first night in Louisville since moving out of Bella's place that I got to do something just for me—not just to survive—but just for me.

The party guests made quick work of the bourbon I brought, so the general reminder of my potential downfall would now be absent from my windowsill. I never really had the temptation, but now I didn't even have the option.

I caught The Artist in his kitchen and struck up a conversation. He stood next to a makeshift charcuterie board along with some wine, cheese, and other less traditional fare.

"You know," I said to The Artist, "There's no better night than tonight to bust out the top hat."

I was thinking of the digs he often wore at Mysteria; that's how he still looked in my mind's eye.

"Yeah, true!" he said. Turning to a companion, he asked, "Do you mind fetching that for me? I haven't talked to this gentleman for quite a while." They agreed.

"You've got quite the collection of cheeses here," I remarked, "I couldn't find a knife to cut it all up, though."

"Don't you carry a knife?" The Artist asked.

"I used to. I lived in Chicago, so sometimes it felt like you had to, but years ago I lost one and never ended up replacing it."

"A knife is a *tool*," he countered, "Not a weapon. Everyone should have a knife. You never know when you'll need it. You know what… I think I've known you long enough, now…"

He reached into his pocket, fishing something out. He pulled his hand out of his pocket and a few coins spilled out onto the floor. I looked down; they weren't just any coins, but gold coins.

"Whoops…"

"I got you," I replied.

I knelt down to pick up the dropped coins as he politely thanked me. I was just as curious about them as I was just trying to help. They were a few of those Sacagawea embossed dollar coins that originally started circulating some years before.

"Huh, they still make these?" I asked, examining one of them.

"I suppose so; I got them for change from Highland Coffee," he replied. "…Oh, thank you."

I looked up: his companion had returned with his top hat. He was putting it on as he thanked them. Looking up at The Artist with his top hat on, I suddenly realized he once again looked like the unknown metaphysical being I had seen during my DMT experience at the festival—even my vantage point was now the same as it was during my vision—from the ground he seemed to tower over me.

The coins falling out of The Artist's pocket were reminiscent of the figure of Fortune, the theoretical being of good luck who had eluded me all year. I was familiar only with his counterpart, *Ms.* Fortune. As I held the gold coins and saw The Artist from this unusual angle, the dots connected all at once. Perhaps *that's* who I saw during my DMT experience: *Fortune.*

I got up and looked down at the coins in my hand as I returned them to The Artist.

"For a moment there, I thought maybe you were trying to give me these coins," I said.

As if these were the coins that would fall out of the pockets of Fortune himself, granting luck to those who would find them.

"No, no," he opened his hand to reveal a stainless-steel folding knife with a handle made of bone. It was small but well-made. "Take this as a gift from me. I've had it for many years and now I'm passing it on to you." He gave me a slight smile and took on a sort of ceremonial tone.

"Wow. Thank you," I said.

I'm a sucker for sentiment. Freely given gifts like those mean a lot to me and I accepted it with pride. This also signaled that I was now "in" with The Artist: we weren't just acquaintances, but friends.

"May it serve you well," he replied.

"I suppose this is a lot cooler than two or three bucks worth of coins," I said dryly.

He acknowledged the joke with a slight smile. The moment still felt poignant thanks to the connection I'd made to the theoretical being of Fortune. Just like at the festival, when I asked for The Artist's advice ("treat everything as worthwhile," he told me), the strange connection indicated I should take special consideration of my new friend's words in this moment.

"Well," he said, pausing as if something just occurred to him, "Change is good... but it can't be *given*. You gotta make the change on your own if it's really gonna stick."

That echoed my determination to wrestle my fate from Ms. Fortune's hands. In this poignant moment, that was reinforced tenfold. I had terrible luck through the last year, but now I was determined to make my own luck. Sure, I suppose luck can befall someone in the more random sense, but even better is creating your own destiny—not waiting for it to happen to you.

The Artist was merely the conduit for a realization I had to come to on my own. Fortune hadn't given me luck or coins, but a *tool*. Its value is in how I'd *use* it. I'm sure The Artist had no idea he inadvertently had that effect on me. He lived his own story, with his own teachers, and his own tribulations. But for me, that year, he was my accidental sage. Fortune's unintentional message served purely as a final piece of validation. I'd put together the puzzle of this realization through blood sweat and tears. Fortune offered me the final piece—I just had to put it together.

The Artist had a roommate, Andrea, who I was meeting for the first time. She dressed somewhat similar to my ex, Gemma, but without the accidental city-hipster twist. Andrea had a dash of '60s bohemian flair and absolutely none of the pretentiousness Gemma had. She was thin with long blonde dreads and a wide, warm, infectious smile. As the night wound down, we got to talking about shows we liked. She invited me to her room to watch one of her favorites. As the night wound down further, she invited me to sleep with her in her bed, with one caveat:

"*No funny business*," she said.

I agreed to the terms. I hadn't considered having any "funny business" with her at such short notice, though I suppose many other guys might have. Perhaps I exuded a particularly warm and trustworthy energy that night, because sharing a bed could've been a risky proposition with some guys. We fell asleep cuddling—half just because and half for warmth.

Andrea was the first woman I shared a bed with since Bella. It had only been a few months, I guess, but it was a *hell* of a lonely few months. This was nice: a warm welcome to the new year. My nightmare year had only been over for a few hours and already my luck was improving.

END TO FEAR —
PART 3: NEW FRIENDS

THE NEXT MORNING, I EXITED ANDREA'S ROOM, I wondering if anyone would see me and make any false assumptions. That could be awkward. There was no such opportunity, though: we were the first to wake. The house was occupied by me, Andrea, The Artist, and two of his friends: Jacob and Jack. I had barely known these folks for twelve hours, except for The Artist. I was perhaps medium hung over for the first time in years. Eventually, the others begin to wake.

"I think I'm going to go get some breakfast. Anyone want to come with?" I proposed.

Miraculously, the entire room agreed. Some didn't have money, and others offered to pay for them. Not everybody had a car, and I offered a ride. It was the first time I filled every seat in my car. From then on, I was in with that group. It immediately felt like I'd known these people for years, and they acted in kind. The Artist told me I should come around more, so I did.

It turns out one of the fastest ways I could make friends in Kentucky is to say aloud to a room: "I haven't been to a shooting range since I was like fourteen," at that point, the first and only time I'd been.

"Shit, I'll take you shooting," Jacob piped up.

We went the next day. We drove in his pickup truck, a vintage early '70s model Ford. It was so old it pre-dated tape decks. It didn't have paint, just a thin layer of oxidation. It showed every bit of its age: "...but it'll last forever if you keep up on maintenance," Jacob told me.

Jacob, it turned out, was a big fan of a band I liked that came up in the music scene in Chicago. He liked them enough that he had a tattoo of their logo, which is how I learned of his fandom.

Since the band started out locally in Chicago, they were more accessible than they'd be otherwise. As a result, I was nearly on a first-name basis with the singer. That was solidified when I ran into said singer at a Dandy Warhols show, which we both happened to be attending alone. We ended up hanging out for the whole show. So, instantly, Jacob and I had at least one interest in common, and I had a cool story about a singer from a band he loved.

Jacob had also recently separated from the same shipping company I just finished working for. He was in a different role, though: customer service. So, we also had something to *complain about* together—something to hate *and* something to love.

I should have been looking for jobs and apartments at this time, but I was really, *really* sick of struggling every moment just for basic survival. I had reached complete burnout, so I started doing fun things instead. My body and mind simply wouldn't let me stress myself out further.

I visited Andrea at the restaurant she worked at. I tried to hit all the other hotspots around town. I'd strike up conversations with strangers, which I rarely do. I talked to a guy at a great little burger joint about how we were both from Chicago. Small world.

The Artist, living up to his namesake, had art displayed at a local gallery, and our whole group attended the opening. The Artist's work was earthy and grounded. He often painted high contrast black and white portraits on sepia-colored backdrops of his alternative friends. The results were tribal yet dignified: they'd be right at home on a stylized stamp or dollar bill.

After we saw everything at the gallery, we continued to make the rounds in the neighborhood. Louisville had blocks and blocks of *nothing but art galleries*. I'd never seen anything like it. We ended up at a backyard gathering held by someone none of us knew—but we did now. We sat around a small bonfire and hung out into the night.

As I became a mainstay in the group, The Artist straight-up offered me a free tattoo. He worked at a tattoo shop of regional significance and would get booked up for months in advance, so I took him up on the offer. Much like his art, he tattooed primarily in black and white. I had a long list of ideas and picked one. I drew up my design and he applied it almost exactly as-is.

With Michael, Trent, and the folks at the sales job, we all came from different walks of life. With The Artist and his friends, however, I finally felt like I had a group in Louisville that was on the same weird artsy frequency as me. The cruel twist was that it was becoming increasingly unlikely that I'd find a way to stay in Louisville: even as my time with this group—and my new outlook—finally endeared me to this place.

If staying here could make sense, it had to be compatible with my new journey of making music. The Artist made music, actually. He played an off-the-beaten-path instrument: the mandolin. His personal hit song among his circle was a cover of a cult classic ditty where the chorus went "I hope they take food stamps in heaven." He had plenty of originals, too. Maybe I could make music with The Artist, I thought—who knows? The future was wide open. The sky was the limit.

I'll write a new script
Get on some new shit
I'll make a comeback
Like the hero in the last act

The song "End of Fear," which I'd later write about this time period, doesn't reference any real or tangible "fear," in the traditional sense. I just liked the title and got stuck on it. It felt good. The argument could be made that the fear was... mediocrity? Or maybe... being poor forever? It was definitely the end of something though—something I needed to escape.

END TO FEAR —
PART 4: THE NEW CAST OF CHARACTERS

HANGOUTS AT THE ARTIST'S HOUSE BECAME FREQUENT. Sometimes I'd crash there just to save the gas, knowing I'd be back the next day. Sometimes they'd stay up for hours working on projects—usually some type of painting—and having interesting conversations. One of these started with the thought: if society collapsed, how would people continue on? How would *this group* specifically continue on?

The Artist started things off. He was in his usual attire: A pageboy cap, a button-up shirt with a nice vest, and suspenders. As usual, he sported a long, well-kempt beard.

"Zombie apocalypse, meteor, global warming, whatever it ends up being. I wouldn't even be worried about it from a societal perspective. Things would get bad, sure, but we would continue to progress. All we would need to do is bring the community together and capitalize on each of our strengths."

"I'm recording now because this is too interesting," I interjected as I readied my phone's camera. (And thanks to that, the following is presented almost verbatim, with exceptions for brevity.) As soon as I hit record, Jack leaned into the camera with his tongue out, doing the metal hand sign.

The Artist continued: "I'm gonna combine, I'm going to use the full effort of what I have intellectually to create without the physical strain of full survivalist work. I'm going to pull together all the strengths of my friends and my community. Work smarter, not harder, as the saying goes."

At the same time, Jack tried to talk over The Artist: "Maybe we shouldn't record this. They're gonna think we're terrorists."

Jack had a permanently raspy voice and always sported a bandana that served as a headband.

"What? Why would—nevermind. Just don't worry about it, Jack. Don't fuckin' worry about it," The Artist assured him. "Just let me explain my *fuckin' thought.*"

"No, I'm serious. I'm worried about the new laws," Jack said.

"Jack, I'm not going to post this anywhere," I whispered, so as not to interrupt The Artist.

"I don't care," Jack interjected, missing the cue on my lowered volume, "It's on your *phone. It can be tapped.*" (That's not what tapping is, by the way.)

"*Just hold on, Jack,*" The Artist said, increasingly annoyed that he needed to interrupt himself.

I quietly laughed to myself at the absurdity of The Artist's intellectual musings constantly being punctured by Jack's paranoia.

The Artist continued: "I prefer working with solid steel. I just love the artistry of it. Jacob prefers other materials. We are a giant melting pot. We can work separately in our individual areas of expertise as leaders in those disciplines. Then, we can combine those efforts to improve our community—to improve our society."

"This really does bother me," Jack reiterated, his tone sounding genuinely concerned. "I don't *care* if he posts this somewhere or not, that can be *taken off his phone.*"

Clearly annoyed, The Artist simply continued, raising his voice further over Jack's. "*Ideas are always evolving* and combining to create the next phase of society: creating growth, technology, and creativity. Even if society collapsed, there's no stopping growth; no stopping *ideas*. We are living in the ultimate era of growth *right now*, thanks to the internet. It happened two hundred years ago—the Enlightenment period. It happened two hundred years before that—The Renaissance. We are in the middle of a growth period *right now…*"

"Ours is more badass," Jack commented for some reason.

The Artist began to respond, but Jack suddenly launched into a tirade, "We keep our shit to ourselves for a fucking *reason!* They can pull this off the internet and they can edit it to make it look like we're saying—" Jack assumed a pose and lowered his tone to indicate sarcasm: "'*Oh, we're going to bomb the United States government!*'"

I interjected with a laugh, "*If you're really worried about it then you shouldn't have said that because they can take that line out of context!*"

"Jack," The Artist responded, "don't be one of those folks that preaches 'We need to hide from everything.' Those types are *too stupid to realize* that they need to work with *what exists*, to make what exists *grow* into something better for *everyone.*"

"That's all I needed you to say," Jack responded, "There's no idea of trying to destroy anything or take away from what's in place now." He spoke to the camera to address the infamous 'they' that might be scrutinizing every word of this video and taking notes.

"Will you shut up for two fuckin' seconds!" As The Artist said this, he also put his arm around Jack and smiled. Even if they disagreed, even if Jack was being annoying, and even if he was becoming abrasive in response, The Artist still considered Jack a friend. "Just please let me get through my thought."

Jack leaned over and looked at my phone screen. "You know what, maybe it's okay. The way the lighting is, you can't really see any faces. We could always just paint over the mural on the wall and no one would know who the fuck we are. I'm okay with this now."

Lamps near the wall left everyone as mostly back-lit silhouettes but illuminated the wall perfectly. The mural Jack mentioned was at some point applied by The Artist directly to the living room wall. It was of a koi fish—a traditional tattoo visual that The Artist probably often applied to folks at the tattoo shop. It was expertly crafted in The Artist's unique style.

Jack was a cool guy. I respected him. However, I was starting to get some real Pinky and The Brain vibes from this conversation. Jack was not hearing what The Artist was saying. There was a completely different train of thought going on in Jack's head.

The Artist continued: "Listen—shut up, everybody—shut the fuck up. We all need leaders. There's a reason there are leaders and there are followers. I'm okay with this. I don't care if you're socialist, Democrat, or Republican—it's not a communist thing. It's not about politics; it's just about taking *what's there* and making it *better*."

"I'm not Timothy McVey!" Jack interjected randomly to no one, "He was a *dumbass*."

"Godammit, Jack," The Artist sighed, "for the love of God, or whatever deity you believe in, please stop talking and let me *finish my thought*. I have been very nice about this so far. Anyway, there's a reason that we all love living in Kentucky. We work together. We're a commonwealth—"

Jack suddenly leaned into the camera, "That's why all the candidates for president suck right now. Think about it; they're all *dropping out*—"

"*Hold on!*" The Artist interjected, "Don't interrupt! We take only what we need from the federal government—"

Jack intervened again "And we help everyone else—"

"Jack, *please*. I swear to god this is your last warning. Why can't I have a serious conversation without you being *stupid* in it?"

Jack got up and started pacing behind the couch, which stood in the middle of the room. "*Well, why can't I be stupid without you coming in and calling it serious?!*" Jack questioned back.

"This is *my* house and you know I can kick your ass," The Artist responded, "*Final warning...*" he turned back to the camera, "We take no more than we need from the federal government—"

"*Robin Hood!*" Jack exclaimed. That metaphor didn't *quite* apply there, though.

"Welp," The Artist said, "I gave you your chance—two, actually."

The Artist instantly leapt from his seat, over the couch, and tackled Jack to the ground. The Artist sort of had "grandpappy vibes"—he usually had a gentle wisdom about him, so it was humorous to see him so nimble. He put Jack into a hold and pinned him down. It was as if because this *was indeed* The Artist's house, it inherently made him the better fighter. They fought behind the couch, occasionally popping into view to deliver a dramatic move like one of those fights in an old-timey cartoon where the action takes place off-screen or in a dust cloud.

"Alright, alright, I'm sorry!" Jack conceded. Yet, The Artist continued the thrashing.

Finally, Jacob chimed in. Yeah, that's right, he was there the *whole time*, content to listen and observe. He spoke over the noise of the scuffle, with a slight slur and the enthusiasm of someone who'd been drinking: "Kentucky gave the world the tommy-gun, the Louisville-slugger, and bourbon. God bless Kentucky. God bless alcohol." (Indeed, parts of the tommy-gun were tested in Kentucky before being made standard by the military.)

"Yeah!" Jack agreed even as he was getting absolutely handled by The Artist. He relented again, "Okay, enough, please, I'll stop!"

"Yeah, okay," The Artist said, helping Jack to his feet. "You know I love you, but sometimes you just need to get some sense put in you."

"Yeah, I know. I'm sorry. I'm sorry."

"So anyway," The Artist said, instantly launching back into his monologue, "If everything went to shit, everything would get fucked up for a while, but we'd survive it all because we're badasses," he looked at Jack, acknowledging he was referencing his earlier comment. The Artist then looked at Jacob, "And we like to drink whiskey bourbon."

The room laughed with each comment.

"Listen, I want you to send me that video," Jack said, "Just to show some of my online friends around the world what Kentucky is *really* like."

"Daddy has been drinking," The Artist exclaimed, getting another laugh out of the room, "Cheers. Goodnight. God bless Kentucky. Thank god for bourbon."

That's where my recording ends. Even as they got rowdy, a certain amount of respect permeated every interaction. Jack only got handled after repeated violations of that respect, and after the incident, The Artist once again treated Jack as a gentleman. Maybe fighting was just a form of non-verbal communication in Kentucky. This might put some context to the bizarre fight I had with Lenny in the back of a minivan traveling at sixty miles per hour, actually.

The Artist talked about 'progress' and 'growing from what we have'—I could relate to that—or at least, I knew that pretty soon I'd have to if I was transforming my life for the better. Just like in the hypothetical post-apocalyptic scenario, things got fucked up, but I'd progress. Unlike that scenario, working together with others would only take me so far. For music, I was sure I'd have to work with other people. But the *change*—my *personal* transformation—only I could do that.

END TO FEAR —
PART 5: NEW CAST, CONTINUED

ANDREA, FOR WHATEVER REASON, WAS SHOWING ME HOW to do a ballet move one day: the classic balancing-on-one-leg move, with the other leg bent and arms above the head, pointed upward.

"It's way harder than it looks," she explained. "Go ahead, you try it."

I went to do it; fuck it, why not. I could technically do it, but it *was* harder than it looked as far as keeping the pose balanced and stable. I lifted my knee and the whole room suddenly heard a distinct *riiiiip*! …It was my pants.

"Godammit," I said flatly to the laughter of all in the room, "I wear these pants all the time! I guess I've never done that in them, though."

Andrea laughed, looked me in the eyes, and put a hand on my shoulder as if to indicate she was technically laughing *at* me, but still with love and respect.

"Get those pants off. I'll sew them up for you," the smile from her laughter still stretched across her face.

I sat there, somewhat defeated in my underwear. This kind of defeat felt really good compared to everything else I'd been through. Here I had friends who were correcting my misfortunes as soon as they occurred. Indeed, Andrea produced my pants with a new patch of wool that added some additional character to them.

I made good on my promise to send Jack the video of the conversation I recorded, which he was initially worried would be seized by the government in a conspiracy against… him, us, or whoever. I uploaded it to a fairly popular website used for large file sharing and sent him the link on Facebook.

The website was publicly searchable (although I made this one private). This made it a massive hub for media piracy for a few years. For a few years—yeah, you see where this is going—literally, *four days later* the website was shut down and seized—*by the government*—for unchecked media piracy.

Hopefully, Jack would never get around to clicking that link. If he did, he'd instantly see a splash page showing the site was seized by the FBI, with their massive logo front and center. He'd probably lose every bit of his shit, once again sure the government was singularly interested in taking the contents of that video out of context in a sinister plot against him specifically.

A couple of days later, Jack approached me outside The Artist's house as I walked up. As he approached, I worried he'd finally clicked on that link and gone down another paranoid spiral.

"Hey, man," he started.

Here it comes: the moment of truth. I didn't even respond. I held my breath a little, preparing myself for the coming tirade.

"I'd love to have a beer with you. Would you be into that?" He instead asked.

"Yeah, man. Just let me know," I almost felt like I owed the guy after that website got shut down.

"Well, I'd love to pick up some beer tonight and share some with you, but the *problem is*, I don't have any *money*."

Damn. Smooth sales pitch, Jack. I could see where this was going.

He continued: "So, would you be willing to spot me twenty bucks so I can pick up some beer?"

Jack cued up a deliberate pause. Obviously, this was just a sales pitch for free beer. Jack was in between jobs, though. I knew what that was like, because so was I. I also knew what it was like to be poor, another thing we had in common. Also, it was now clear he hadn't clicked on that link at all. I started to suspect he never would.

"You know what? Fuck it, sure. Let's go get some beer. I'm poor too, though, so consider this a one-time favor."

"Absolutely. Thank you. There's a corner store just up the block, let's go together," he suggested. "…Also, I won't be able to pay you back. I hope that's cool."

Generally, Jack *almost* had Lenny vibes, but I could tell Jack had a certain amount of humility and respect when he asked for something… nor was he randomly going to try to wrestle me.

"You good with PBR?" I asked. Seventy percent of beer sales…

"Hell yeah, dealer's choice."

Back at The Artist's place, I had one, maybe two. He had four, probably more.

It's all good. Still: fuckin' Jack, though.

END TO FEAR —
PART 6: HIGHLAND COFFEE

ON ANDREA'S ADVICE, I STARTED FREQUENTING THE LOCALLY famous coffee shop, Highland Coffee. I'd heard about it a lot. The coffee shop had excellent art on the walls by local artists. This town had a lot of artists and a lot of space for art. That could be perfect considering my newfound artistic goals. Although, I wasn't really sure what the music scene looked like here.

The coffee shop's clientele solidified how friendly of a town Louisville is. I could go there and shoot the shit with literally anybody else there for hours. This is even more peculiar when you know that I'm not the type of guy to strike up random conversations with strangers. With my newfound confidence, I was testing how far I could push myself outside of my own comfort zone. "Treat everything as worthwhile" as The Artist once said—people included.

Thanks to that, I met someone I will never forget. I started a long conversation with a random guy at the coffee shop. We got to talking about art and all the art galleries around town. I mentioned that even the art hung up in the coffee shop here was particularly cool, and I really dug it. He agreed. A woman in her mid-twenties turned from another table where she sat by herself and joined the conversation:

"Oh, thanks," she said, "That's my work."

I noticed her the moment she came in. She had a face that an artist would draw if asked to create a picture of someone beautiful—almost too pretty to be real. She dressed classy yet casual. Probably out of my league, I figured, and as my conversations with various other patrons went on, she hadn't said anything. She sat quietly sipping her coffee and writing in a notebook with a pink pen. She was the only silent voice on this side of the patio, indicating what I initially interpreted as a lack of interest—until now. As you probably guessed, the other guy I barely remember. But *her*—she's the one I'll never forget.

I replied: "Oh, holy shit. Which ones are yours?"

We got up, and she showed me. Her work was exactly the stuff I'd taken a shine to. She had the lion's share of the art featured there. What I loved about her work was its very ornate manually crafted patterns juxtaposed with a strong graffiti influence.

"My name is Lilianna, but people call me Killianna. Or Killy for short."

"I *love* that name. I'm Steven. I do not have a cool name, though."

"Steven is a cool name!" she assured me.

We kept talking from across our respective tables. She told me she was in the Air Force Reserves. You'd never have clocked that by looking at her, given her artsy nature and classy appearance. She told me she was half Asian and half Hispanic, which I thought was an intriguing mix of cultures. It turned out she knew The Artist too, at least in passing. Eventually, I joined her at her table. She said "rad" a lot. She seemed cool, so I was sure that the word "rad" must have come back into fashion without me knowing.

I shared some things about myself too, but I can't recall the exact words. I mentioned I was a pretty solid illustrator. I probably talked about film school. I told her in broad strokes some of what I had gone through in the last year. But those pitfalls were all just context for my next adventure: making music. Shit—if I was out here trying to impress people with my *intentions*, I'd better fucking get started...

It must have been her who suggested we hang out one-on-one because I'm not sure I'd have been so bold. I got her number, but she must have been the one to offer it up. I made no assumptions about what that meant, I just went with the flow. I was too busy soaking up life to over-think anything about that.

We hung out informally and talked about art; her art—my art. Unlike Gemma, she didn't think herself better for making art primarily in phys-ical mediums as opposed to digital. She did digital stuff, too. She got it. She wasn't trying to be pretentious or confine art into any particular box.

After our first hang out, she dropped me off at my car. I leaned over from the passenger seat to her driver's side to give her a sort of one-armed goodbye hug. When that hug landed, though, it somehow became a kiss. I surprised myself, because that wasn't my intent. It was like my brain had to sneak that kiss in. Without a missed beat, she kissed back.

When I ran into Gemma in Chicago—in that moment before I recog-nized her—I was sure *she* was out of my league. The irony, of course, is that I thought that about someone I just got out of a year-and-a-half relationship with and simply hadn't recognized yet. I thought that about Killianna, too, when she first turned around with a sly little glimmer in her eye to reveal herself as the featured artist at the coffee shop. But there we were: lips locked.

It seemed so seamless and casual. We saw each other every day after that. We never talked about what that kiss meant. We just started hanging out… and occasionally kissing.

END TO FEAR —
PART 7: ONE LAST NIGHT

THERE WAS A POPULAR SONG AT THE TIME THAT I connected to—rare for popular music—about driving—hitting the open road—freedom. That's exactly how I felt: free. I was finally unburdened and doing things I *wanted* to do, rather than what I had to do to survive. However, much like the song, it occurred to me that I might have to hit the road soon, too. I couldn't stay here. I'd love to, but I couldn't. I should have been sad about this; I had a bunch of great new friends and just hit it off with a rad chick (borrowing her vernacular). I wasn't sad, if only because I'd never felt more motivated in my life. I was singularly focused on my new goal.

I packed up all my stuff. I had no choice but to return to the shithole town of my youth. It turned out to be good that I had a station wagon after all. I'm not sure I could've fit everything otherwise, which is weird because I had a little less stuff than I left Chicago with, and everything had fit in smaller cars not just once, but twice. I guess I wasn't good at packing boxes *or* belongings.

I saw my friends from the sales job one last time. I had a chill time with Michael. Lenny on the other hand was having a sudden and dramatic coming-of-age moment.

Without even saying hi, he came up to me and said "She's pregnant, man..."

He had this faraway look in his eyes that told me that he knew playtime was over. He knew his entire world would change. He knew his priorities needed to change. He knew he needed to grow up fast and make sure he could provide for his future kid. Part of me had to wonder if she got pregnant from that time Lenny begged me to drive him—beer cans in pocket—to see her for twenty minutes. Just enough time to do the deed, perhaps.

I spent one last night at The Artist's house. I told the group it was my last night here. I told them this was "goodbye time". The night came and went. I wished I could stay. I'd miss this.

I talked to my friends in Chicago, Patrick and Dan. I individually told them I was heading back home and wanted to see them on my way through. They had unrelated beef with each other, but I asked them each if they'd be willing to bury the hatchet on their drama with each other to justify hanging out with me. They both agreed. I'd drive up and meet them the next night. I figured I'd hit the road a little before noon that day.

That day was now here. Killianna was hitting me up and had an idea for something we could do together that night. Whatever it was, she wanted it to be a surprise... but I was leaving *today*. She knew this; I was open about it. On the other hand... what's the rush? "Treat everything as worthwhile," after all. I knew I didn't strictly want to leave, so what's one more day?

When I finally got the nerve to call Patrick and Dan, it was already *way too late* for me to get up there by that night. I found myself on speakerphone with both of them. They were already at Dan's place, waiting for me to arrive.

"Listen, guys... I'm sorry to leave you hanging, but... is there any chance we could do this tomorrow night?"

I held my breath. If it were me I'd at least be annoyed. The silence hung in the air.

Dan interrupted the awkward pause:
"Awwwwwe shit! Is it because of a girl?"

"Umm, I can't believe you called it... but yes."

They egged me on, as guys do.

Patrick started now, "You dirty dog, you!"

I wasn't used to that. Call me old fashioned—idealistic—whatever it is—but the point for me was the connection, not the conquest.

"Well, I don't think it's like that," I said, with some discomfort in my voice.

"I'm just kidding, I'm just kidding. I get it. I get it," Patrick assured me. I guess that explained his choice of phrasing. I'm not sure anyone has used the term "dirty dog" in the past forty years.

Although I was sure Dan would soon high-five me into the ground, Patrick was more romantic at heart, more like myself. Not that Dan didn't have that in him, too.

Dan finally provided me with an answer, "You do what you gotta do. We are down for tomorrow."

I couldn't feel *too* bad about this: it would give them a chance to hang out, catch up, and otherwise reestablish their friendship. I suggested exactly that and they agreed. They were having a good time already, they said. I couldn't stand to see another close friendship fall apart; I'd just been through that. Even if my former friend Kevin was an asshole, it still sucked, and at this point, I was still very much processing it.

So, it was official: Killianna and I were on for one last night.

END TO FEAR —
PART 8: BREAKING IN

I WAS AT KILLY'S PLACE. IT WAS OFFICIALLY MY LAST NIGHT in Louisville.

"I wish I could stick around, I really do, but given I lost two jobs *and* my place all in the matter of a couple of weeks, I just don't see how that's gonna happen. Like, if it was just *one* of those—just a place or just a job—I'd give it a shot—but both? At once? That's a lot to overcome in a matter of days."

She knew, but it was worth repeating. She shouldn't feel like I abandoned her for anything less.

"I get it. That sucks."

"Speaking of change, I'm kinda sick of trying to pretend I'm not weird. I think I'm gonna grow my hair out again."

At this point, I kept my hair chin length or shorter—not quite long enough for it to be a statement. That choice now felt like a subconscious concession to how society expected most guys to look—which was already kinda bullshit, but no one was *actually* asking me to do anything; no one is that invested in someone else's hairstyle. My hair was a little longer now, close to shoulder length. I hadn't seen a barber the whole time I was in Louisville. I was too busy and too poor.

"You should put your hair up. Can I do it?" Killy asked me.

"Yeah, sure. We can even put chopsticks up in there if you want. Let's make it weird."

She lit up at the suggestion. "Oooh, yeah, rad! I think I have some you can use."

She found a fancy pair she had lying around. I had long hair some years before, so this situation reminded me that many ladies love playing hairdresser on guys with long hair. It always seemed to be a bonding experience. That's how I understood the context of this moment: it was a bonding experience. It might be our last. She helped me put my hair up, chopsticks and all. She smiled at me with a sly little glimmer in her eyes as she admired her work.

"This is rad. You should keep these," she said, referring to the chopsticks.

CUT TO:

EXT. DOWNTOWN LOUISVILLE – BUSINESS DISTRICT – NIGHT

Earlier, these streets bustled with suitcases and people wearing ties. Tonight, it was dead as hell. We arrived in my car, filled with every earthly possession I had. We approached a standard-looking office building. Some lobby lights were on, but otherwise, it looked closed for the night.

"There's an art show going on here tonight," she told me, "it's a paid entry... and sold out... but we're going to sneak in."

"I appreciate a good challenge; it'll probably be the easiest one I've had this past year."

The entrance to the show was through the elevator, so we took the stairs. The muffled sound of blaring music became clearer as we ascended. The fourth floor sounded like our destination. We came to a locked door. It had a lever handle with one of those locks like what you see on some bathroom doors. It didn't take a key, it just had a small round hole. You just have to poke it with something.

"Looks like this might be a dead end. Unless you have, like, maybe a pen on you?" I asked.

"You know, I didn't come prepared to sign autographs tonight..."

She turned to me, leaned in, looked up into my eyes, and gave me a kiss, putting one hand on the back of my head to pull me in. She pulled away after a moment and gave me a look.

"What is it?" I asked. She lifted up her hand. In it was one of the chopsticks from my hair. "Wait—why did you—Oh!"

She turned again and used the chopstick to poke open the lock on the door, then turned back and handed it to me again with the biggest grin on her face. The door exited to a currently unmanned coat check. This was perfect, it would look like we were already inside.

The event struck me as upper-class. It was a stark contrast to the homey art galleries I went to with The Artist. Painted nude models posed on pedestals wearing cartoonish farm animal masks—it was art, I suppose. There was a massive abstract chandelier hanging over the room. It was made from a bunch of different silver-colored odds and ends. A server passed out free drinks. A rapper performed on stage.

A videographer took short videos of some folks, posed up like it were a photograph. Killianna and I were among the few chosen. He gave us only one piece of direction:

"*Don't* smile."

I had that *on lock*.

The event was cool, but it was made even better by us sneaking in. We'd earned our entry in a way no one else there had.

"I went to something with a similar vibe to this in Chicago. It was a freelance video project for a hotel grand opening. I'd never get into something like that without being on the film crew." I mentioned.

We were surrounded by young business professionals and trendy trust fund folks who came to make appearances and network. We only came to crash the party. It wasn't my world. It wasn't Killy's either, but we made it inside anyway.

"Sometimes, if you wanna get somewhere, you gotta just break in."

"Literally and figuratively. I'm done with anything getting in the way of what I really want to do with my life," pausing for a moment, I recalled a situation from a few months previous, "I told you before about my friend Kevin who betrayed me this last summer... a few months before, he gave me this fortune he got from a fortune cookie. It said 'Good fortune will come to you in six months.' I marked the date. Even after we completely blew up, I looked forward to the day. A little superstitious, maybe, but you never know."

"Hmm. What happened that day? Something cool?" she asked.

"I thought that good luck would find me. It didn't. Not long after that, everything came crashing down *again*. I can't wait for some *fortune* to come true, because it's not *going to* come true."

"Well, make it come true," she advised.

"Exactly! I'm in a situation where I'm forced to succeed. It's my only option. Like, we had to basically break in to get in here tonight..."

"You're welcome, by the way," she interjected.

"Yeah, that was kinda all you. But what I mean is, that was the only way we'd get in. And I've decided I want to make music. Literally, fuck everything else, that's all I want to do. I'm making my *own* luck, and if I want something, I have to make it happen—or it won't."

"Yeah, rad. Do it—break in."

Everything I went through came together and made the pieces fit. Everything from struggles to loss, to loneliness, to new friends, and all the way down to a random fortune cookie, had to come together to finally bring me to my realization. Maybe Fortune was in the background the whole time. But I still had to assemble the pieces myself, or it would never have come together.

END TO FEAR —
PART 9: FINAL GOODBYE

RATHER THAN DRIVE ACROSS TOWN TO WHERE I TECHNICALLY still lived for my last night, I spent it at The Artist's house again, utilizing his open-door policy to friends. Once again, it saved me gas. When I walked in, of course, people were surprised to see me.

"Hey, I thought you left," Jack said, almost hurt, as if I had lied. "You said it was goodbye time."

"It was… but I ended up getting into some last-minute plans with a cool lady. This is it, though, for real this time. I promise."

It turns out these folks knew who Killianna was, too. It figures I'd get in with a popular and respected lady, only to have to leave it all behind. Small town, I guess.

The next morning I met up with Killy at Highland Coffee for one final goodbye. Today the mood was different. Even the weather knew it: the sky was completely overcast. We managed to put on some smiles for some final pictures together in front of her artwork, but… this was it. We'd probably never see each other again. In our final moment, she pressed up against me for one final kiss. My memory frames it like an out-of-body experience. I can see me and her standing in the parking lot, her pressed up against me, arms around my sides, looking directly into my eyes. A fog of forgotten details surrounds us. It's just me and her that I remember.

"I kinda wish you'd stay," she said, as wistfully as a cheesy romance scene in a TV show.

The last time I mused about a TV show scenario, it was an imagined situation where Gemma and I reunited when I happened to run into her in Chicago on my Christmas trip. That wasn't even three weeks ago. I'd changed so much since that it felt like that happened to a different person. Now, with Killy, it wasn't imagined. I *really was* living it—but it *still* didn't have a happy ending. The wistful mood wasn't thanks to a reunion, but because this was our final goodbye.

"Yeah, I know," I said regrettably. "If I could make it work, I would." I think I played it way cooler than I felt about it.

I am so inclined to leave it all behind
I'll leave you hanging with this kiss
(From Remake Myself)

That was the last I ever saw her. That was the last I ever saw of Louisville. Ms. Fortune managed to pull one last cruel trick on me. Her most clever yet: when the clock struck midnight on New Year's Eve, she knew my luck would change. She knew I'd have great times and meet great people. So, before she bowed out, she set up a situation to automatically take it all away.

END TO FEAR —
PART 10: WAIT, THERE ARE
OTHER TIMELINES

I PUT EVERY LAST CENT I HAD INTO MY GAS TANK. I knew from my Christmas trip that it took almost exactly one full tank to get home. No detours: it had to be a straight shot. As soon as I drove across the bridge from Louisville into Indiana, the magic of the town quickly faded. I put that new song I was into about the open road on constant repeat. There was no turning back—my gas tank wouldn't even allow it. I was past the point of no return, literally and figuratively.

To understand my exit from Louisville and how hard it was, you have to know exactly what I lost. I had a great group of friends: those who helped me when I was at rock bottom: Trent, Michael, and sure, even Lenny. I had a second group of great friends: fellow artists and creative thinkers who practiced radical inclusiveness with an open-door policy: The Artist and his group. I had the beginnings of what could have turned into a fulfilling relationship with Killy. Maybe it would've been my first healthy relationship in a while. Louisville was a fantastic town. That city has a soul. I was losing that, too. I could have had a rich social life there, but it simply couldn't be.

I wasn't just the town and the people I was losing. It was the *potential.* The potential of the fresh start I *thought* I was getting when I moved across the country to live with Kevin. If we take a sci-fi angle, we can theorize that other potential timelines exist where I stayed in Louisville, and my life ended up completely different.

There were probably a few dozen timelines where I stayed in Louisville and was just fucking homeless for a bit while desperately looking for a job. But, there was at least *one* timeline where I started another shitty job, but managed to barely eek things out and find a place to live.

In that timeline, I'd become best friends with The Artist. His whole group already felt like family. In that parallel universe, things would progress with Killy. Considering how seamlessly we got along, I'm sure we'd have made our relationship official. I'm confident we would've lasted long-term. Maybe we'd have collaborated on art shit. I bet that could've turned out pretty cool. We'd have gotten features in every gallery, I'm sure.

In that timeline, I'd eventually parlay my big-city creative skills into a respectable career in this smaller town, where my experience could go further. With a little persistence, I'd have gotten hired at a photography studio or someplace doing graphic design. Maybe The Artist and I did throw some songs together. I'm sure the results would've been nothing if not interesting.

Damn… I've had trouble getting through the process of writing some of the chapters of this book… but not like *this*. I was so hellbent on getting to the next phase of my life at that point that I couldn't process my feelings about leaving until writing them down now. I was too focused to consider all the possibilities I left behind. Certainly, though, I was at least somewhat consciously aware of that abandoned potential, but I was done focusing on the past.

END TO FEAR —
PART 11: STORY CIRCLE

Driving back home from Louisville offered plenty of time to reflect on the journey I'd been on all that year. There was an entire future I could've lived in Louisville. I was giving all that potential up—all for one dream. I was moving back home. Anywhere else I'd have to start the struggle for survival all over again. Living back home would be in no way glamorous—at least not for a while. But it was the only place that dream had any chance of taking off.

Before music, my main artistic passion was story writing. There's a fairly new framework for storytelling called a "Story Circle." It was invented by Dan Harmon, the creator of the TV show Community; the show that got me through some of these dark times. (And was taken off the air right before Christmas.)

It goes like this:
1. A character is in a zone of comfort...
2. but they want something,
3. so they enter an unfamiliar situation.
4. They adapt to the situation.
5. They get what they desire...
6. and pay a heavy price for it.
7. They then return to their familiar situation...
8. having changed. (Completing the circle)

My zone of comfort was Chicago, living with Gemma. I was beaten down by the recession and wanted a change in my life: a change of location and a clean slate. I entered an unfamiliar situation with Kevin. I got what I desired—not in that shitty hipster town, but more so in Louisville. I paid a heavy price for it, losing *fucking everything*: Gemma, my home—*three* times now—my best friend, my friend Trent, my sanity—nearly—and even the potential of a better home, social circles, and a relationship.

Now I was about to return to a familiar situation... having changed. The change was a change of passion. I might as well have called myself a musician right then, because in my mind, me making music was an inevitability. Nothing could stop me.

I'd come full circle: I began this year *leaving* a *long, bad* relationship that I didn't really want to separate from. I left Chicago: a city I had loved but recently came to *hate*. I felt *terrible* about the exit for months. Now... I was leaving behind the *potential* of a *great* relationship, exiting a town I hated for a bit but quickly came to *love* more than any other. This *should* be my ninth all-time low... but unlike when I left Chicago, I felt *great* about it. I was so determined to get exactly what I wanted out of life that I was completely reinvigorated.

I lived the story circle and paid a heavy price for the chance at my dream... so whatever came next, I thought, it better be worth everything I was giving up. It better be *fucking good*. If it wasn't, I'd *make it* good. I'd *make it* worth it. That last year threw curveball after curveball all the way through its final day. The whole past year I'd been subject to life and circumstance. I had hit reset on my entire life twice—now three times. In the next year, life and circumstances would be subject to *me*, I promised myself. I'd become my ideal self. The silver lining of my misfortune was that now it was songwriting fuel that would help me realize my music goals.

Nearing Chicago now, I remembered when I was here on Christmas Eve. It was only a few weeks ago. I was so homesick and lonely then that I cried at the mere sight of the skyline. I anticipated that same feeling to take me again because this time I was getting back what I lost, in a way— even if I would live a stone's throw away. I was returning to my place of comfort, *changed*—with a newfound love for Chicago. Sure, I wouldn't be *in* the city, but from back home, getting there was just a short drive. I expected my now permanent access to Chicago to be the catharsis to a year's worth of successive all-time lows.

However, in the couple of weeks since Christmas, my relationship with Louisville changed dramatically. I'd never fallen in love with a town so quickly and deeply. It was ironic I could only do that in my final weeks there. I was sure I'd miss it, but I was just as sure I was ready to love Chicago again. I was just as sure I'd feel those same feelings for Chicago again, just as I had driving up for Christmas.

I rounded the curve on the highway that would reveal the Chicago skyline. The anticipation alone was entirely its own feeling. I knew a wave of emotion was sure to hit me any second.

...The city revealed itself. Here it comes: a flood of emotion. It would all be worth it, to get back to the place that I had come to miss so dearly.

Any moment now.

Oh, there's the Sears Tower. That should do it.

No?

The train?

...*No?*

...Fuck.

END TO FEAR —
PART 12: GETTING WHAT I DESIRED

I MET UP WITH PATRICK AND DAN AS INITIALLY PLANNED. We had a good time. Dan was on his way out of the city as I was on my way back in. He got a great job in San Francisco, so this was a final hurrah for us. I had my suitcase, and he had his. We stayed up. I crashed on the couch. My car, full with all my earthly belongings, managed to survive the night in Chicago without a break-in, which would've been pretty devastating. Last year, I wouldn't have been so lucky.

After that, it was time to complete the trip back home. Home-home, north of the city—not Chicago. I was no fan of living there, but at least I had friends. At least I could take my time figuring out my next moves.

After some introspection, I decided to make my transformation about more than just music. I didn't want to find myself in a terrible position like I was in this past year ever again. This also meant elevating my career—but that would come later. For now, I was *singularly devoted* to artistic endeavors.

I hung out with Tim again and asked him if he'd want to try getting some music done together. I pretended to ask offhandedly, but really it was my main intention that day. He instantly said yes. Years later, I realized it was no less than a miracle that this whole project worked out long-term with the *first guy* I asked to join.

Tim had music writing and playing chops but had never recorded a single thing in his life. I was willing to learn that. I opened up my computer— the one Kevin previously tried to steal out from under me almost a year ago, now. Little did I know then, it would become the centerpiece of my music-making journey. The album that these events inspired wouldn't exist without it. Perhaps I wouldn't even be writing this.

I opened a piece of music production software for the first time with real intent, having no idea what to expect. I didn't even know what the interface would look like. Huh—it kinda looked like all the video editing software I learned in college—just timelines and effects. I could figure that out. I quickly picked up the basics.

I tried to get other people involved. I always intended on getting someone versed in electronic and synth music to balance out the guitar provided by Timmy. The first person I invited agreed and would hang out with me and Tim… but would do nothing but sit there and talk about: 'What Would Nine Inch Nails Do?' Meanwhile, Tim and I sat there putting songs together and actually *making music* in between the white noise of his never-ending tangents. Another synth guy initially agreed but then backed out as soon as he realized what a time investment it would be.

Those synth folks not working out was the best thing to happen to my music chops since deciding to get started: If no one else could do it, I'd *fucking do it myself.* I fairly quickly learned some rudimentary music theory, music recording, and how to create software synth patches. Within a month we had the bones of two or three songs. Mastering these skills would take much longer, but I was willing to put in the time.

I missed Louisville. I still missed my ex Gemma in Chicago, too. What I gained from my departure was more than worth it, but maybe—just maybe—Gemma and I could pick up where we left off. I had no idea how I'd even begin to try and open that door, though. The sadness of my longing was palpable. However, these early days of making music with Timmy are still among some of the best memories of my life. It feels great to even write about.

When I thought about the hard times I endured in my last days in Chicago, that hipster town, and Louisville, I always appreciated them in the context of what I got out of it: the ability to make music, and having some real, gut-wrenching shit to write about. Every song started with the intent to write something about some bullshit or another I had endured over the past year. The pain and heartache became a necessary muse for my impending creations. Every time I think about it, I land on the same conclusion: if I could do that whole year over again...

Hold on, my phone was vibrating—

—Holy shit...

Gemma... was calling me?

EPILOGUE —
PART 1: TO BE CONTINUED

I'M NOT SURE HOW BOOKS ARE SUPPOSED TO TREAT EPILOGUES, but in this case, I'm counting it as part of the story. We're in epilogue territory now because we are entering into events not represented on the Perseverance album.

The year after the nightmare year was both completely fulfilling and completely insane. I got into my new grind—not the retail grind or the putting boxes in a shipping container grind—the *music* grind. I completely transformed my priorities, outlook, and goals in life.

I was doing great, but everyone around me was crumbling to dust. That, too, could fill a book. Maybe I'll write that. An album about the post-nightmare year is also in the works. Tim and I were so prolific that year and into the next that we developed bones for one album and a whole bunch of nuggets for a second, based on my next interesting year: the year I started making music.

I was awesome now, and people could tell. But I had *one thing* that still secretly made my heart sink. *One thing* that could tank my newfound confidence with just a thought. One big, ominous hanging fucking thread from the last year that I couldn't ignore. *One thing* that loomed over me like a dark cloud. Until I dealt with that, I was really only 70% there on my transformation. This story wouldn't be complete unless I address that last loose end.

This final struggle would be purely internal, I thought at the time. But, no... as it turned out, I'd deal with it in the *one way* I thought I couldn't: head on.

EPILOGUE —
PART 2: THE ONE LESSON I
HADN'T LEARNED

FOR ALL MY BETTERMENT SINCE THE NIGHTMARE YEAR, for all my motivation, confidence, skills, and even gravitas—one big heartache still hung over my head. It was the conflict I started the nightmare year with and the conflict that made a cameo near the end, too. I was definitely still dealing with it emotionally. Of course, I'm talking about my ex in Chicago, Gemma.

In any other case, ten months would've been plenty of time to get over Gemma and move on, but those moving-on attempts had all fallen flat: the relationship with Bella turned out to be an emotional hit-and-run for her. With Killianna, we never really had the chance to get off the ground—what we had wasn't official or defined—it didn't even have enough time for that. The roots of emotion had not taken hold like they did with Gemma.

Truthfully, even with everything that happened, I kind of wished Gemma and I could get back together. Yeah, she was abusive, and to be fair I didn't even fully realize that until I wrote it all down here—but you know what? With this all written out, I finally understand why that was so easy to overlook at that moment; since we were together, I'd gone through a whole hell of a lot more than what she had put me through.

After starting my life over three fucking times in the span of a year, nearly being homeless twice, being betrayed by people I trusted—*twice*—and in *the same way*—after losing a friend to suicide—after having to abandon all this potential I had going for me in Louisville—yeah, being punched in the eye didn't sound so bad. It was a fucking *vacation* compared to everything else.

The last I saw Gemma, in an unplanned encounter, she looked me straight in the eyes and then just fucking walked away without a word. That was probably the coldest shit anyone had ever done to me at that point, and it came at a time when I was already at my most vulnerable. Nothing else could so clearly indicate just how fucking little I meant to her.

So, color me absolutely fucking shocked when my phone vibrated one cozy evening at home—I looked at the call screen and saw her name: Gemm. Yes, reader, we've finally caught back up to our cliffhanger: the woman I couldn't quite get over all year was calling me *right now*. Was this a pocket-dial? Did I have anyone else with her name in my phone? No... I stared at it for way too long. It almost went to my voicemail—almost. I picked it up. Perhaps I'd hear nothing more than her phone shuffling around in her pocket.

"Hello?" The caution in my voice was audible, but Gemm was unaware of any such subtleties.

The word 'hello' often ends in a question mark, but this time it genuinely *was* a question. Was there someone on the other end? Was I being called intentionally?

"Hey, dude." A standard greeting for her, even when we were together.

"What's going on?" I asked, nearly confused, fishing for a reason for the call.

"Are you free the next couple of days?" she asked.

Okay... now *that* I did not expect to hear. I was now in danger of becoming filled with a hope that I wasn't sure was safe to feel. After everything I'd been through, any sense of optimism wasn't getting in without a full-body search.

"I... *suppose* I am. Why do you ask?" I responded. Was this real life?

"I just got out of a bad relationship," she explained, "We got into a fight. He hit me—I hit him. I got a black eye. It's over now."

At that moment, the irony did not even occur to me: a black eye is what ultimately prompted me to want to leave her. Now, another one was the reason she wanted to reconnect. One thing was ultimately certain: the irony would not occur to *her*, and probably never would. I was sure she was too stubborn to change—too dense to see the connection.

"What happened?" I asked.

"It's... I don't even have the energy to talk about it, she replied. "Could you just come over and just hang out with me for a few days? I need someone here, someone *familiar*, just to help me get through the next few days."

That sounded nearly identical to my reasoning for wanting to call her when I was lonely in Louisville. Maybe I was her "constant," too, after all. There was part of me that just wanted to help and a part of me that hoped this might snowball into us getting back together. It was late when she called, but I couldn't sleep on this. That this was even happening triggered an adrenaline rush.

If we had any chance of getting back together, I knew this was it. I borrowed some money for gas and left that same night.

EPILOGUE —
PART 3: PLAYING HOUSE

GEMMA BUZZED ME INTO THE BUILDING, AND I CAME up and knocked on the door. There she was: black eye and all. The same eye as when she did it to me. We even stood in the same spot where she gave me mine a year earlier.

It was surreal to be in that apartment again. I thought I walked out of it for the last time last year in an avalanche of tears. The bookshelves I left behind were still there. Gemma practically begged me to let her have them. I left a bunch of posters hung up of various design projects I'd done—those were all gone. She couldn't exactly start a new relationship with monuments to her ex hung up on every wall, I suppose. My old desk was still there. It used to live in the bedroom, now it was in the living room and had sloppy stripes of different colored paint on the side.

"I miss that desk. "Do you use it much?" I asked.

"Occasionally, yeah. It's my art desk, now," she said.

"What's the paint for?" I asked.

"I was testing some colors while working on a painting. It was just as good a spot as any."

"Do you have any more finished paintings?" I asked. "I'd love to see them."

"Not really, honestly," she admitted. "I started some stuff but I didn't like how they turned out."

If her other relationship had an analog in another painting, it made sense nothing ever came of that one either.

ma asked, nearly gasping.arly gasping.asping.asping.

"Did you ever finish that painting with the dead bird in the grass?" I asked. "You spent our entire relationship working on that thing. There was at least one iteration of it I really liked."

"Nah, I painted over it. I think I might turn it into something else."

The painting really *did* die along with our relationship.

"I loved that concept," I told her. "You should make it again."

"Maybe I will," she responded hesitantly. "I should," she added, more determined.

Foreshadowing, or nah?

She continued, "How about you? What have you been up to?"

"Well, that's a loaded question. A fucking *lot* has happened."

I told her the whole story in broad strokes. She stopped me for a second when I got to the part about Bella. Not even the bad stuff, just the *mention* of her.

"You were in another relationship?!" Gemma asked, nearly gasping.

"Yeah. Why is that surprising? I mean, so were you. It's not strange."

"No, no, it's not," she responded, with some trepidation. "I'm just... surprised, is all."

"Well, yeah... I never had too much trouble with that, you know. But then she turned around and did the same shit Kevin did." I explained the broad strokes of the situation with Bella, too.

"I'm sorry to hear that, dude," she consoled at the end of my explanation.

I talked about Trent, though I might not have gotten into the rest. At the time, I was still processing everything.

"Also, I've started making music these last few months," I told her.

"Oh, that's cool."

"Yeah, I have maybe two songs most of the way done and others in the process."

In turn, she told me about her recent relationship. I didn't particularly want the details, but I still listened. The guy had a peculiar job. He hand-made eyeglass frames and sold them online. Gemma would get fixated on the most innocuous and random shit and then lose interest after some months. Just as she had found lost eyeglasses on the ground interesting (harkening back to her box of found trinkets that helped us bond on the night we met), she probably found *making* eyeglasses interesting as well—at least for a bit. I was utterly perplexed by the idea of that as a job. I didn't understand how anyone had disposable cash to buy hand-made eyeglasses in this economy, but I guess rich hipsters were still doing well.

"You know, when we were together we only had *one picture* we ever took together, since you hated getting your picture taken," I recalled. "Do you still have that? Just for the history of it?"

"Actually, no. The computer it's on is broken. I tried *everything* to fix it, but *trust me*, it's gone."

Foreshadowing or nah?

I appreciate the sentimentality of photos, so I found it *really* annoying that she hated being in them. Because of that, I could barely even prove we had even been together.

"That last day we had together…" I started, "that goodbye? That was something else, huh?"

I wasn't sure where I was going with this. I'd become pretty unfiltered since the nightmare year.

"Yeah," she replied, with a hint of sadness, "I cried for *hours* that day."

"I definitely did some crying too," I admitted somberly.

For a moment, we sat in silence with that thought.

Then I broke it: "Hey, I just remembered, didn't I see you on the street on Christmas Eve?"

It must have marked a lot of growth that I so casually asked about this when only two months before that very same incident was absolutely devastating to me. It said something about the gravity of *her* situation—why she asked me there—that I'd forgotten about it until now. That less than 1% chance encounter was probably the only reason she thought I might be back in town. I might not be there with her at this moment otherwise.

"Yeah! I remember that," she said. "You coulda said 'Hi', you know."

Yeah, no. There was no fucking way I could've played it cool as lovesick as I was in that moment—but *now*? After my transformation? I was cool all day.

"I mean—don't put that on me, you could've said 'Hi' too," I said dismissively.

"Yeah… I suppose so…" she conceded with a touch of sadness in her voice and looked away.

Before long, we decided to go to sleep. It was already late when I arrived, after all.

"Do you have any blankets or pillows for this couch?" I asked.

"Oh, you can sleep in the bed with me."

That surprised me. I couldn't be sure what that meant, really. I didn't make any assumptions. She had just been through a lot and had the shiner to prove it. It was best to let her set the pace of whatever this was.

"Just one thing," she asked, "can you sleep on the wall side? I don't want to get all squished against the wall."

I agreed. All the bedroom furniture was re-arranged. She was the type of person who would sometimes move everything around just for a change of pace. The bed used to be in the center of the room but was now pushed into a corner. I used to live here, but now it didn't look like home.

We got into bed.

"Can you cuddle me?" she asked.

I did. She didn't make any moves beyond that. With all my music creation binges, it was earlier than I usually went to bed. I laid there thinking about how surreal it was to be in this bed again—not just in it, but with Gemma, cuddling. It was actually my bed—or *used* to be. When we moved in, we got rid of hers but kept mine. Her breathing slowed. She was asleep. I was shoved most of the way into the wall and could barely move. After a bit longer, I was asleep as well.

An alarm on my phone went off at 5 AM. That's when you had to start paying for street parking ever since some faceless foreign corporation bought up the parking rights for Chicago streets not long before. 5 AM was way too fucking early, though. I'll just risk it, I thought. Who's really patrolling parking that early?

Chicago, that's who. I woke up to the ticket, of course.

EPILOGUE —
PART 4: HIGH TIME FOR A CHANGE

"How are you feeling?" I asked Gemma the next day, "Like, emotionally."

"Oh, I'm fine. Fuck that guy. I'm not going to be upset about it. Like I said, I just needed some company, really."

We did some fairly normal stuff over the next couple of days: a movie, some thrifting. Throughout, she occasionally threw out some mixed signals, though they happened at a level of subtlety that I knew she was incapable of, so I figured none of them were intentional. There were moments where I wished I knew what this was, others where I conceded this trip was happening purely to help her heal emotionally, and others where it didn't matter—we were just hanging out.

One of these days she asked me a fateful question, almost in jest:

"Do you want to get high with me?" Gemma joked with a bit of a laugh.

As I indicated earlier, going into the nightmare year, I had never done any type of drug. Gemma knew this full well—many people did. She expected a no. This was a policy I held even knowing full well that marijuana had long since been proven to be largely harmless for most people.

However, this question came when I was actively burning the bridges back to everything I used to be. Not having done any drug was—for some fucking reason—a point of pride that I held onto up until the Mysteria festival. Even after that, I decided—somewhat arbitrarily—to still abstain from smoking weed if only to keep up my personal tradition. If I decided to join Gemm for a smoke, then I'd break myself of this arbitrary point of pride and force myself to find better ways to be interesting.

Besides, what kind of bullshit is it to define myself—even in part—by something I *haven't* done? I started asking myself why I *shouldn't* do things, rather than why I *should*. Pay attention to people who frequently ask why they *should* do something because those people hardly do anything at all. "Treat everything as worthwhile," as The Artist said. (Take that as a *general* rule and less in the context of Gemma's question. *Plenty* of drugs out there have *very good reasons* not to do them. Even for weed, a "good reason" for me may not apply to someone else.)

I thought about it for a day, and the above is the philosophy I settled on. So I did it. It felt right to break that personal edict with her, as she was the first person I had a long relationship with who smoked with any regularity. DMT was more or less hallucinogenic. Mushrooms had made me hyperactive and super engaged. This was different from either of those. It made me feel content and kinda cozy. It was kind of a go-with-the-flow vibe. "Everything is just kinda good and fine right now", I thought. Maybe it was just the stuff that she got, but that was the feeling.

"Holy shit... I understand the context of our *entire* relationship now," I told Gemma, clearly telegraphing that this was a reality-altering epiphany, "You were *just... high*."

I got the laugh from Gemma that my joke warranted, but I was simultaneously also sort of serious. I suddenly understood what parts of her personality were her sober traits and what traits I could attribute to her being almost perpetually high. It's not like I didn't know if and when she was high when we were together, but I had no context for what that meant, and now I knew firsthand *exactly* what it meant. It became clear that we were more compatible when she was perpetually high.

Sober, this woman was a hell of a lot more ornery. And then, if drunk, well, you know the story... I never had a problem with her getting high, but I do think that the merits and compatibility of a relationship should probably align with someone's sober personality above anything else. This realization was almost depressing. But then again, I was having exactly what she was having: I was high, so it was just... kinda fine.

EPILOGUE —
PART 5: A REMINDER OF WHAT I LOST

"CAN WE GO ON A CAR RIDE?" GEMMA ASKED ONE DAY, "It's been forever since I've been in a car."

I agreed to her request. It seemed like she thought I was 20% cooler for having a car, as if we were both in high school again. It might seem odd to some, but you don't really need a car in Chicago. I'd never owned one before Louisville, and I went months and sometimes even a year or two without driving someone's car in Chicago.

I wore sunglasses because I always do. Gemma wore sunglasses at my request: "I don't want people thinking I gave you that black eye," I said.

I had to do the same after *she* hit *me*, which was an irony that finally began to dawn on me, but I kept that to myself.

The drive was quiet up to a point, except for music playing at a volume that didn't inhibit conversation. Even with the play order set to random— wouldn't you fucking know it—one of the songs I'd been working on comes on. Timmy and I were working on song concepts roughly in the order of the events they were based on, so the first song we assembled was an early version of Sunshine.

The significance of this moment, of course, is that this song was *about* Gemma. I could avoid any internal awkwardness and simply skip the song, but this type of discomfort can often offer growth, so I let it play. I sat in my car with the ex-girlfriend I thought I'd never see again with a song playing that I wrote about *her*. I wrote the song from the perspective of experiencing those feelings as they happened. My conflicting feelings from that time are reflected in the lyrics:

Is it the perfect fit?
Or am I sick of it?

That same conflict existed now during this reunion. Clearly, when I wrote these lyrics, probably less than a month prior, I was well aware there was a version of events supporting my awareness that this had not been a good relationship. Then, at other times, it was clear that I missed her terribly.

I wasn't going to tell Gemma this song was about her. That can go one of two ways and neither was good. Maybe she'd go over the moon about it and think it's so great that someone wrote a song about her that she'd overlook her current feelings about us and our former relationship, whatever they were. It could give her a rosy-tinted view that would soon be liable to wear off.

The other way it could go is that it could make me look clingy and attached. Which of the two ways that went all depended on how she felt about me at that exact moment. Did she have lingering romantic feelings, as I did? Was our time together now fostering a new fondness? I had no idea, so I wasn't going to tell her the song was about her.

What I *could* do was tell her that this was one of my songs. I knew Gemma: I knew she wouldn't figure out this song was about her in a million years.

"People say I sound a lot like this singer," I said—hopefully cleverly—finally breaking a long silence.

No response from her. She was zoned out, looking out the window.

"...because it *is* me," I continued after a pause, trying to get her attention one last time.

"Huh? Oh, what was that?" she said, breaking out of her trance, "Sorry, I guess maybe I'm not in the right mindset to listen to sad music."

Wow. I expected nothing, and somehow I still overestimated her. She had no idea what I just said. She didn't even hear that this was one of my songs. And I get it: she had been through a lot in the few days since her other relationship self-destructed. But it reminded me that I always took an interest in her work while she never cared to take an interest in mine—or anyone else's, for that matter.

Or, maybe—*maybe*—she had absorbed every word of the song, applied it to her most recent relationship, and got in her own head about it. I suppose the lyrics were generalized enough. She was probably thinking about the circumstances of the relationship she had just exited. She wasn't particularly intellectual and almost entirely intuitive. She didn't internalize and analyze herself with much regularity. Perhaps this was a rare moment where she was, and I had inadvertently snapped her out of it.

After another few minutes of silence, Gemma came in with: "You know, you're only supposed to drive in the right-hand lane."

"Uhh, I'm pretty sure that's only on the highway. That doesn't make any sense on a city street."

"No, dude, it's true. That's what my dad taught me."

That was a peculiar line of reasoning to me. She hadn't heard from her dad in five years. She didn't even have a current phone number for him. He knew how to reach out to her but just *didn't*. Yet, she could still consistently hold the guy in high regard. That was not a bear I wanted to poke right now, though.

"Look at all these people driving in the left lane. Are they all wrong?"

If her answer was yes, then I could at least respect her consistency, even if she was wrong.

"Not necessarily."

"Then why is it wrong when *I'm* doing it?"

"Because you're not passing, dude."

I wasn't going to entertain this any further for now.

A few minutes later she asked if I wouldn't mind letting her drive—she missed driving. I agreed, so we pulled over and switched seats. Within minutes, she was doing *all the same shit* that was wrong when *I* did it.

"Okay, hold on, you're driving in the left lane, didn't you say that's wrong?"

"No, not the way I'm doing it."

"...How are you doing it exactly?"

She paused for a moment, considering her response. "I'm a *very good* driver. I know what I'm talking about."

Oh, okay. My bad.

Clearly, we had hit that intellectual wall that was so easy to hit with her, so I dropped it. For context, this wasn't a fight for us. When we were together, conversations like this would happen and never come up again. It was all coming back to me: this was classic Gemma. She was the first relationship I had ever been in where I was not only incredibly certain that I was the smarter half of us, but also the first where I had to actively make up that gap.

It might be pertinent here to mention Gemma is from Florida. Maybe you could tell. Listen, at the time of writing, well after the nightmare year, I've been to about half the states in the U.S.—*including* Texas—and Florida drivers are the worst—bar none, hands down—if you disagree, you are incorrect. While in Florida, I once saw three near-accidents, all unrelated to each other, within two minutes, at the *same intersection*.

Gemma had a brazen lack of regard for logical consistency, a bizarre and twisted version of driver's etiquette, and a complete lack of even the most basic social niceties. These traits were not the result of her hailing from another planet, where its inhabitants have only recently infiltrated Earth to study humans in close proximity. No, she wasn't still getting the hang of human cultural norms as an outsider. She's just from Florida.

I was happy to help Gemma through a difficult time and I was consciously aware that this trip was appropriately more about her than about me. However, this served as a sobering reminder of what being with her was really like. Absence makes the heart grow fonder, but it can also make you forget the bad times. Now, I suddenly remembered.

More importantly, though, there was no way this stubborn-ass lady had any concept of—or respect for—the journey I'd been through or the evolution I'd made. To her, I was probably still that same old guy from before the nightmare year. Other people could see the new fire in me, but I was sure she never could. Worse still, if she couldn't see it, would that inhibit all the progress I made?

I straight-up didn't need this shit.

I was done settling in life and that meant I shouldn't settle for her. That was a milestone revelation. It took a complete transformation to realize how backward it would be if I went through *all that shit* just to end up *right back where I started*. If I was going to evolve, any potential relationship I'd get into should be compatible with that. I had a taste of that with Killianna. If I could find that with her, I was sure I could find it with someone new, too.

The biggest thing that gave me pause was this: I stopped everything to come down here and make sure she was okay. But would she have done that for me if our roles were reversed? I was 100% sure she wouldn't. In fact, she had done *the very same thing* to me that caused her to ask me to come down here to start with—having given me a black-eye all those months ago. That didn't mean I should regret coming down here—I did the right thing—but it did mean that any continued exploration of a relationship reboot was probably a bad idea.

After about four days, I headed back home. I wasn't bitter or sad. I almost didn't even think about it. My own silence spoke volumes. That was my *real* story circle: gaining perspective on that fucked up relationship. If I really wanted to get back into that relationship, that was the time, that was the opportunity—but I kind of just... didn't try. And I'm glad I didn't.

I used to think the 'big bad' in my life that year was Kevin. After all, his efforts to hurt me had forethought and malice. Bella was just damaged, and I was only an unintended casualty. But Gemma was chaos incarnate; she thrived on conflict. Her chaos wasn't targeted like Kevin's was. Everyone got her wrath—she was a true chaotic neutral. She was in the background of the nightmare year the whole time. Any notion of wanting her back was regression. She was the main villain that year, not anyone else. With this realization, my transformation was complete—but I still had a lot of work ahead of me.

EPILOGUE —
PART 6: BURY THE PAST

A FOG OBSCURED ANYTHING BEYOND A HUNDRED FEET. The sun was so guarded by clouds that there were no shadows that day. We had lots of days like that in Chicago. I was near a tree—the only notable landmark I could see in these conditions. The tree was beginning to sprout leaves but wasn't quite there yet—from a glance, it looked barren, but life would soon find it.

I had a shovel and began to dig. It must have been my grandpa's shovel. Everything he had left to my family was from an era before modern stainless steel, so it was dark brown with a fine layer of oxidation and had a worn, but sturdy, dark wood handle. It had seen its fair share of use. I zoned out as I began to dig. Dig, dig, dig.

"That's not for me, is it?" a familiar voice asked me.

I hadn't heard anyone approach, but I was probably too engrossed in my task to notice. I looked up, it was Bella. I was damn sure I had seen the last of her. She was hundreds of miles from home. Why did she just... show up?

"What are you doing here? How did you even *know* I was here?" I asked.

"I asked my question first." she countered.

Ah, the usual Bella mind games.

"Okay... is *what* for you?" I asked.

"The hole you're digging. Is it a grave?"

"What are you implying?" I asked. I knew the answer, but I sure as hell wasn't going to be the one to say it. "It's not like I expected to see you any time soon," I reasoned.

"You said you didn't hate me, remember? So this can't be for me."

"Well, this isn't for you. And honestly? I lied when I said that: I *did* hate you... Maybe I still do, honestly. But you got me out of a terrible situation. Now that it's all said and done, I'm going to call that a wash, so I have no ill will toward you. Now... What are you *doing* here?"

"Well, I guess we have mutual friends now, so I'm in town. Maybe I'll see you."

As she said it, she turned and walked away, disappearing into the fog. What friends? Weird.

She had a valid question though: why *was* I digging this hole? The action did not have any forethought. I was just kind of *there*, digging a hole. It could be a symbolic thing: I was burying my old self in a lot of ways. I could call this a symbolic funeral. This could be a creative therapy session, like what I did at Mysteria with The Redhead. I could bury a symbolic token of my former self.

"Here lies Steven ...the old Steven," I said aloud to no one in particular. I almost said my full name, but when I started to say it, it felt wrong. I was more alive than ever. It was only my *old self* that I was saying goodbye to.

Just then, another figure approached through the fog.

"Did you really think I wouldn't find you?"

I still couldn't see the origin of it through the fog, but I recognized the voice. It couldn't be him, though... but in another moment, I had my confirmation: my former friend Kevin parted the fog and hurried towards me.

"Good thing you dug that grave, I'm going to need that," he seethed at me as he approached faster and faster.

I expected him to stew in the anger of his own mangled reality and make occasional threats—but to be organized enough to track down Bella and—I guess—actually manage to succeed at manipulating her into helping him fuck with me, and then plan a trip? I was honestly surprised he pulled it off.

This realization happened all within a fraction of a second: in the moment, he was still quickly closing in on me in a blur of anger. He wasn't coming in for a hug, I was sure of that. I didn't see if he had any type of weapon on him, but he was obviously coming at me aggressively.

I didn't have enough time to think about how to respond. All I had was this shovel, so I hit him with it, right in the head. He went down immediately. The adrenaline hit me so hard that before I could even realize what I was doing, I had hit him maybe three more times, each time in the head.

My adrenaline slowed. Only then did I realize what I'd done. He wasn't moving. I guess it *was* good I dug that grave. And I guess he *was* going to need it, just not how he thought. I could put him in it… or I could call the authorities and tell them what happened. Hopefully, this would qualify as self-defense, I hoped.

I took out my phone, hands shaking, and managed to dial the nine. Fuck. *No, it wouldn't qualify as self-defense…* I mean it was, but I suddenly realized how this looked: was I really about to invite the authorities into this situation, let them walk up and see me with a *shovel*, having *dug a grave*, and have them *actually* believe me that this was *self-defense*? There was just *no fucking way*. I had no options here. Using my foot, I haphazardly rolled Kevin's limp body into the grave.

My phone was still in hand. It buzzed. I looked at the screen.

It was a text from Gemma: "I should have mentioned this a couple days ago but Kevin might be trying to do something to fuck with you."

Thanks for the warning.

Only then did the panic truly set in. Only then did I finally wake up.

Wake up, Steven. I was in my bed. It was a fucking dream. The adrenaline was real. It always feels real until the moment you realize it was a dream. I sat up, just me, in the quiet of the night. No graves. No murders.

Being angry at Kevin was well justified, but did the dream mean I wanted to murder him? I don't think so. I think it's a mistake to over-interpret dreams—it's just random neurons firing, connecting often unrelated dots in your brain. My grandpa's shovel? That was just the archetypal shovel of my childhood. If you say "shovel," that's the one I think of.

Perhaps that dream manifested from the fear that Kevin could someday come at me, and I might have to defend myself. I don't know why I dreamed about digging a grave. I could say it was symbolic of me burying my former self, sure, but it also could've been random. The tree that was beginning to sprout? Renewal, I guess. But just because it fits the metaphor doesn't necessarily make it profound.

My former friend was on my mind. I was well aware he'd try to crowbar his way back into my life to try and fuck it up. There was no deeper meaning there, it was just something that occupied some space in my brain. Kevin attacking me? It's the most obvious metaphor the subconscious mind could come up with. He spent a lot of time trying to harm me, so the shoe fits. I fought back—the obvious, logical response. It just as well could've been random neurons firing off bits of information currently occupying my thoughts and connecting the dots in ways my brain deemed logical.

Did I still have a lot to work through internally about this? If we insist that the dream represented a genuine feeling, then sure. Even if that's true, that's what the music was for. It was and still is cathartic. This book kinda is, too.

EPILOGUE —
PART 7: HAVING CHANGED

I SPENT THE ENTIRE NEXT YEAR WORKING ON ALMOST nothing but creative endeavors. I landed on the band name "Shards of Grey," serving as a metaphor that translates to "pieces of me." I wrote lyrics so literal and personal that I'd have a moment of pause before I performed or released them, wondering if I really wanted to put those feelings out there for anyone. I worked on some of my writing projects with Alex (In fact, I got more writing done that year than the previous five years combined).

I donated plasma for spare cash—my only form of "income," if you could call it that—earning less than a hundred dollars a week... and I fucking loved it. Everything I did was exactly what I wanted to do. Nobody got the time of day from me unless I was better for being around them, because my time was too valuable. I had too much work to do. I put anywhere from two to twelve hours a day into working on music or some other creative project. That habit stuck uninterrupted for years.

I was unflappable before the nightmare year, but now I had emotional resilience like Superman has strength. I didn't even know that about myself until people commented on it. I no longer hid anything about myself out of shame. I no longer kept secrets about how I felt about anything. I no longer told white lies. I had no filter. (Which, by the way, *only works* if you're *not* an asshole.) I had taken so many L's that previous year—no one envied that—but surviving it and making myself better seemed to endear people to me.

Tim came and left a few times as he dealt with his own year of bullshit. Regardless, he took up the mantle of one of my best friends, replacing my former best friend Kevin just when the spot opened up and I needed it. It actually helped my development as a musician having to plow forward without Tim at some points. I cobbled together enough music theory—almost exclusively from Tim at first—that after about nine months, I wrote my first song entirely on my own, from start to finish. Lyrics, of course, but this time also music, bass, and rhythm—everything.

The first song I wrote solo was Mysteria. When I play my music for people, they still often say it is their favorite. I wrote another one and a half songs before Tim could combine forces with me again. Other than lyrics, there are a few tracks Tim flat-out wrote, too, more or less—even if they all got filtered through my particular production style. To this day, it's clear we complement each other musically.

EPILOGUE —
PART 8: VH1'S WHERE ARE THEY NOW

SOME YEARS LATER, THE REDHEAD KIND OF SELF-DESTRUCTED from a mental health standpoint. Our creative little pseudo-therapy session could only go so far. Her own paranoia fueled her decision not to take prescribed medications that would have treated that paranoia.

The Rapper is doing well and moved to a better town. His fanbase there is growing. He and I still talk about music-making, occasionally. The Creep is still a pretty entertaining guy. Once when I was in his town some years later (he actually lived about an hour outside of the hipster town), I hung out with him for an evening. He was still full of ideas and creativity. I'm still great friends with Patrick and Lola. In fact, Patrick and I are better friends now than we were back in college—is that because of the nightmare year? In a way, yeah.

Bella? Thanks for the save, genuinely, but let's stay strangers. She has not reached out in any way, and I don't plan to either. I can at least listen to the song she ruined for me now that enough time has passed, but honestly, it's still not the same as before. Gemma? I hope we never see each other again, but still, I wish her well and hope whoever she's ended up with has half the patience I did.

My boss from the hipster town moved on to a more traditional pyramid scheme, selling organic soaps or some shit. My "old boss"—the one in Chicago who owed me thousands—kept paying my phone bill for another few years until the value of it paid me back (minus what I owed for the camera that Kevin stole). The last I saw him, a few years later, he was relying on unpaid internships rather than employees he can't afford—still shitty, but at least it was honest.

The guy who stiffed me on my freelance work in Chicago, who called himself "the worst of the worst" drug addicts, became a drug crisis intervention counselor, I found out. That probably means he's clean. It also means he's helping other people get out of the same position he put himself in. I could sympathize with that. Maybe there's an inspirational story in there that he tells to the folks he helps get back on their feet. That motherfucker still owes me 700 dollars, though.

Michael is still around. Of all the people in this book, he's the one overall that I think I should catch up with. Trent, I know from his Facebook page, is still remembered fondly all these years later by many. Phil, the saintly man who lent the household a car in that shitty hipster town, I never really kept in touch with; I guess I was too busy dealing with all the new shit coming my way. I wish I had though, because he'd get a Christmas card every year.

I fell out of touch with Jack, Jacob, and Lenny. I wish them all the best. To my knowledge, there have yet to be any government conspiracies against Jack. Andrea has a family and kids now. Highland Coffee unfortunately no longer exists, to the bane of many locals, but you can still get their coffee to make at home.

The Artist is still kicking; he remains an intriguing fellow with an interesting life. Both Killianna and The Artist let me use some of their work for the cover of a demo EP that Shards of Grey put out. (Those songs were later refined for the album.) I asked them to contribute because they were an essential part of my story that year. The cover itself was a collage of a bunch of pictures and art representative of that year. (For credit where it's due, some of the images on that are pictures I've taken. Timmy has some art on there. Some photos were provided by my friend Lara who passed away a couple of years before I wrote this book. She is remembered fondly by many. She was considered an amazing photographer, with accolades and awards to prove it. Lastly, one or two images are just public domain stuff—significantly less interesting, but worth mentioning for clarity.)

My friend Alex (who may or may not have ridden a roller-skating horse earlier in this book) recently started making music, too. I feel partly responsible since music creation takes up such a large part of my brain. I think that rubbed off on him. He's pretty fresh, but he's stuck to it, and I think he may get some great results; he's surrounded himself with other musicians who are more seasoned and can really help bring his ideas to completion. He's itching to get me and Timmy involved, and I'm sure that will happen.

I haven't been to a Mysteria-like festival since that year. Part of me would like to go to something like that again, and another part feels like I don't really need that anymore. I have stopped personifying Chicago—it is inanimate and therefore cannot disappoint me. I still haven't been back to Louisville. I still miss it, but it too is just a location: the people and circumstances there gave it its magic. I have since learned that I can be happy almost anywhere.

I got into a relationship the year after the nightmare year. It was probably the first healthy long-term relationship I had. At the least, it served to show me that healthy relationships do exist, and these days there's no way I could see myself settling for any relationship that's less than functional. I now have a son, and I take parenting him very seriously. He is very fuzzy, has four legs, and occasionally demands belly rubs. He is treated far, *far* better, and gets way more attention than my former friend Kevin could muster with his dog.

EPILOGUE —
PART 9: SOMEHOW, KEVIN RETURNED

KEVIN OCCASIONALLY POPPED BACK UP IN MY MESSAGES to try and fuck with me and my life. That went on for many, *many* years. He'd pop up through several different accounts. It was some real long-term stalker shit. There is a long paper trail of harassment. I had a lot of rent-free space in his brain. Inversely, I initiated contact with him exactly zero times.

He briefly tried harassing my then-partner as well, trying to give her a vague, twisted elevator-pitch version of the events that transpired between us where he cast himself as the hero and me as the villain. His version was very vague and ambiguous, because the truth would've been far too damning for him. The only problem with that approach is that she already knew all the details. *Everyone* knew the story in at least some detail. I was an open book. I had nothing to be ashamed of. I slogged through the shit, made it out a better person, and even more, people respected me for it.

After a few years, he switched from antagonizing me to trying to be friends again. Much like with Patrick, Kevin never offered any apologies. He remained still so deluded that he acted as if I had wronged *him*, and *he* was forgiving *me*. He acted as if I'd just welcome him back because he's so fucking cool that my life was incomplete without him.

Since I put it together that he was a textbook narcissist, it makes sense that in his mind he's always the hero, always the victim—even when he's actively fucking over me, Patrick, Lola, Valerie, Claire, Kat, etc.—even as he continued to harass people for years after the fact. I don't think he's capable of meaningful change. I saw him regret the consequences, but not his actions. I only ever saw him repeat the same cycles with a different flavor each time. I thought I was above that treatment, but I found out the hard way that no one is.

What little hints I've heard about him since indicate a continued pattern of moving to a new place, fucking over a bunch of people, and then getting bored and moving on or getting run out of town. That tracks with narcissism too: when he runs out of a validation supply in one location, he moves on to a new place to suck all the validation out of there.

As of writing, I haven't heard from him in a few years, and I think he might actually be done. Even in hindsight, the world is worse with him in it, and he has no redeeming qualities. There's no way for me to make peace with that. He's genuinely a bad person—a true chaotic evil. Sometimes a person is just terrible, and the only silver lining is the character you built by dealing with them.

EPILOGUE —
PART X: COMPLETING THE CIRCLE

I SERIOUSLY UNDERESTIMATED HOW LONG IT WOULD take to complete a full, professional-sounding album from the ground up. Writing lyrics and doing vocal takes didn't account for even 5% of the work I put in. I did about half the music writing. That took maybe 20%. I did the mixing and mastering all myself—that's the vast majority of the work. I figured out the technical stuff on my own from the ground up, graduating with honors from the school of YouTube. Some of the time the album took accounts for the learning curve, but most of it is just perfectionism. My album took so long to make that I mixed and mastered three projects by other musicians before my album even came out.

I didn't fully appreciate what it would take to upgrade my career, or how long that would take, but I fucking did it. I have things now that I never dared to dream of. A lifetime of being poor conditioned me to keep my dreams low and grounded. I have since put myself in a position where it is much less likely I will ever have to deal with something like the nightmare year again. If the shit with Kevin or Bella happened today, I could nope out on day zero and get a hotel at any second. I couldn't do that when I was starting from the bottom. I was shocked I pulled enough together to get a shitty car in the nightmare year. Now I own actual property.

When I told people what happened in the nightmare year, I could give them a five-minute bullet point version, a twenty-minute summary version, or a one-hour version with some details. Even the one-hour version never truly communicated everything I went through—all the weekly and sometimes daily twists and turns. The album is pretty long—over an hour—and there's not enough time to include all the details there, either. It was always going to take a book.

I didn't make the album for anyone else except for me. It's just me, putting my feelings out there and releasing them into the universe. It doesn't matter how good it is, I'll be lucky if even ten people listen to it. I'll be lucky if four people even read this book... but it doesn't matter. I did what I set out to do when I made that album, and even when it's frustrating, I really enjoy making music. Unlike the album, this book is for *you*. It is a tool for those who seek to truly understand what I went through that year. For those that made it this far, thank you. If only four people read this, I'm sure it will be the right four people. If you're the fifth, let me know.

With all the shit I went through, it's natural to wonder: what would I do differently, if I could go back and warn myself? Sometimes I think about that. I could've stopped that car accident and avoided almost all of this. Then I could've separated from Kevin slowly and without drama. Theoretically—maybe, and I really mean '*maybe*'—I still could've ended up in Louisville and hopefully have had at least *some* of the good times I had there. I *definitely* doubt, however, that I would've mustered up the willpower to learn music from the ground up and stick with it for years. I doubt I would've had the drive and confidence to upgrade my career. I doubt I'd have the experience to realize how I deserve to be treated in a relationship—and in a friendship.

So, when I think about the nightmare year, I'm forced to conclude that I wouldn't change a goddamn thing. Everything I gained in my life after that—my music, fuckin' Timmy, my voice, my career, and even my pup—are all things I got because of how I responded to that year. The past cannot be undone. I will forever be better because of that year.

Even if I lost *everything I had* right now, I've still had it and enjoyed it for years now. I got the good karma that was owed to me tenfold. Better still, no one can take away the perseverance that I gained. When times get tough *now*, well, they are never as tough as they were *that* year, which means that whatever life could throw at me, I could take it—and believe me, it has, and I fucking did.

FADE TO BLACK

THE MOST EXPENSIVE SALAD EVER

OH, MAN. WHAT A RIDE THAT YEAR WAS... Of course, everyone loves a good long, long story before their recipe, but now it's time for the *good stuff*. This is the real meat of the story. (No pun intended because this *is* a salad after all!) Now, to get to what we all came here for: my legendary salad recipe! If you normally hate salads but want to eat healthy anyway, this salad is for you. It kind of skirts that salad-y-ness of most salads without completely defeating the purpose by just throwing a bunch of fuckin' bacon in there or some shit.

Prep time:
- A year of your goddamn life

Ingredients:

- Spinach
- Olive oil
- Sliced jalapenos
- Your roommate's '89 Buick LeSabre

Optional add-ins:

- Maybe some sliced olives? Idk
- A not-so-secret belief that a malevolent, sentient force is solely devoted to fucking with you, specifically

I'm racking my brain here, and honestly, those were really the ingredients. It wasn't anything fancy, like... at all. I usually paired it with a pickle and/ or a pickled carrot because I was really into pickling stuff at the time. It also didn't have traditional dressing because—let's be honest—all salads are terrible and live or die on the quality of the dressing they utilize. However, oftentimes the dressing can be the least healthy part, which also defeats the purpose of a salad. That is where the jalapenos come in, and it's also why I skip the traditional forms of leafy greens like iceberg or romaine lettuce, because that's the part that's terrible.

Preparation:

Prepare to go to the grocery store. Then, take your roommate's 89 Buick LeSabre to the nearest cliff, quarry, or sufficiently high bridge and just drive that motherfucker right off it, because if it's going to be considered totaled and he is going to come at you *that fucking hard*, you might as well have that thing go out like a boss. Then, buy the supplies tomorrow.

Honestly just throw a bunch of spinach in a small plasticware container with about ten-ish sliced jalapeño pieces, throw some olive oil in there as dressing, close it up, and shake. Was that really all it was? Honestly, I think so, yeah.

Then, eat the salad in a bulk discount store that also sells hot cafe food for so cheap it'd be more economical just to buy lunch there, but you can't because you have zero cash on hand and can only buy food from the grocery store and only with food stamps. Spend the next year getting caught up in more and more elaborate scenarios designed to test your emotional resilience. Let simmer for several months, then decide to be a badass from then on.

ABOUT THE AUTHOR

Steven Grey is a musician, writer, and artist hailing primarily from Chicago, where he lives with his very good dog, Koda. He graduated as a film major and has worked with noteworthy writers and directors throughout the industry. Steven is the lead singer, primary creative force, and sole lyricist behind the band Shards of Grey, which led to his becoming a producer for several other musical acts. Blending these two art forms, his first album with Shards of Grey and his first book are tandem concepts that tell the same story through the lens of different mediums.

visit
shardsofgrey.com
for more info & links

Socials:
facebook.com/ShardsOfGrey
instagram.com/shardsofgrey

Music:
shardsofgrey.com/s/spotify
shardsofgrey.bandcamp.com
Also available on all other major digital platforms

MORE ROADSIDE PRESS TITLES

By Plane, Train or Coincidence
Michele McDannold

Prying
Jack Micheline, Charles Bukowski
and Catfish McDaris

Wolf Whistles Behind the Dumpster
Dan Provost

*Busking Blues: Recollections of a
Chicago Street Musician
and Squatter*
Westley Heine

Unknowable Things
Kerry Trautman

How to Play House
Heather Dorn

Kiss the Heathens
Ryan Quinn Flanagan

St. James Infirmary
Steven Meloan

Street Corner Spirits
Westley Heine

*A Room Above a
Convenience Store*
William Taylor Jr.

Resurrection Song
George Wallace

*Nothing and Too Much
to Talk About*
Nancy Patrice Davenport

*Bar Guide for the
Seriously Deranged*
Alan Catlin

Born on Good Friday
Nathan Graziano

Under Normal Conditions
Karl Koweski

The Dead and the Desperate
Dan Denton

Clown Gravy
Misti Rainwater-Lites

Walking Away
Michael D. Grover

All in a Pretty Little Row
Dan Provost

*These Are the People in
Your Neighbourhood*
Jordan Trethewey

*They Said I Wasn't
College Material*
Scot Young

Radio Water
Francine Witte

And Blackberries Grew Wild
Susan Mickelberry

Licorice Heart
Miles Budimir

Disposable Darlings
Todd Cirillo

Full Moon Midnight
Belinda Subraman

Innocent Postcards
John Pietaro

Cistern Latitudes
James Duncan

*Another Saturday Night
in Jukebox Hell*
Alan Catlin

MORE ROADSIDE PRESS TITLES

www.ingramcontent.com/pod-product-compliance
Lightning Source LLC
Chambersburg PA
CBHW020654110726
47901CB00001B/188

* 9 7 9 8 9 9 9 2 5 0 0 9 8 1 *